FIGHTING
for you

RIPPLE EFFECT
BOOK TWO

ALISE MONROE

Book Cover by Melissa Doughty, @mel_d.designs

Formatting by Brittany Uller at The Author Experience

Chapter Headers, Scene Break, Artwork, and Maps by Anastasia Campo

RED Logo by Hannah Pendleton

ISBN:

979-8-9919008-2-9 (Paperback)

979-8-9919008-3-6 (Ebook)

1st edition 2025

Authors' Note

The Ripple Effect series takes place in a fictional lakefront town called Indigo Hill, SC. This book contains mature content and is intended for an 18+ audience. Your mental health matters. If any of the following content warnings trigger you, please read with caution, and always put yourself and your mental health first.

Alcoholism
Emotional and mental abuse/trauma
Undiagnosed mental illness (depression and anxiety)
Depictions of smoking
Violence
Medical scenarios depicting blood
Stalking
Parent death
Funeral
Gun violence
Explicit language
Explicit sex scenes

Playlist

WHISKEY WHISKEY	Graham Barham
Streetlight	Sam Barber
Wanna Be Loved	The Red Clay Strays
Death Wish Love (From Twisters: The Album)	Benson Boone
Sorry	Buckcherry
Sweet Dreams	Koe Wetzel
Love Me Less	MAX & Quinn XCII
MISTAKE	NF
HAPPY	NF
If You Love Her	Forest Blakk
strangers again	Matt Hansen
sun to me	MGK
Lonely Road	MGK & Jelly Roll
Darkerside	David Kushner
Fall Into Me	Forest Blakk
Change Your Mind	Alex Warren
I'm the Sinner	Jared Benjamin
S.O.B.	Sam Barber
Project (Acoustic)	Chase McDaniel
Wondering Why	The Red Clay Strays

Playlist

You Should've Seen the Other Guy	Nathaniel Rateliff
Let It Happen	Gracie Abrams
Diet Pepsi	Addison Rae
SOMEONE TO YOU	Matt Hansen
Million Eyes	Sam Barber
Bad Choices	Kode
Let You Down	Zach Bryan
Holding On	Bailey Zimmerman
I Can Fix Him (No Really I Can)	Taylor Swift
i'll be damned	gavn!
Black Friday	Tom Odell
God Needs The Devil	Jonah Kagen
Sweet Love	Myles Smith
Ordinary	Alex Warren
broken	Jonah Kagen

Dedication

For anyone who feels like they aren't worthy or deserving of love, you are. Don't let anyone tell you otherwise. Regardless of your mistakes, your flaws, or what the voice inside your head tells you, you are worthy.

You are enough.

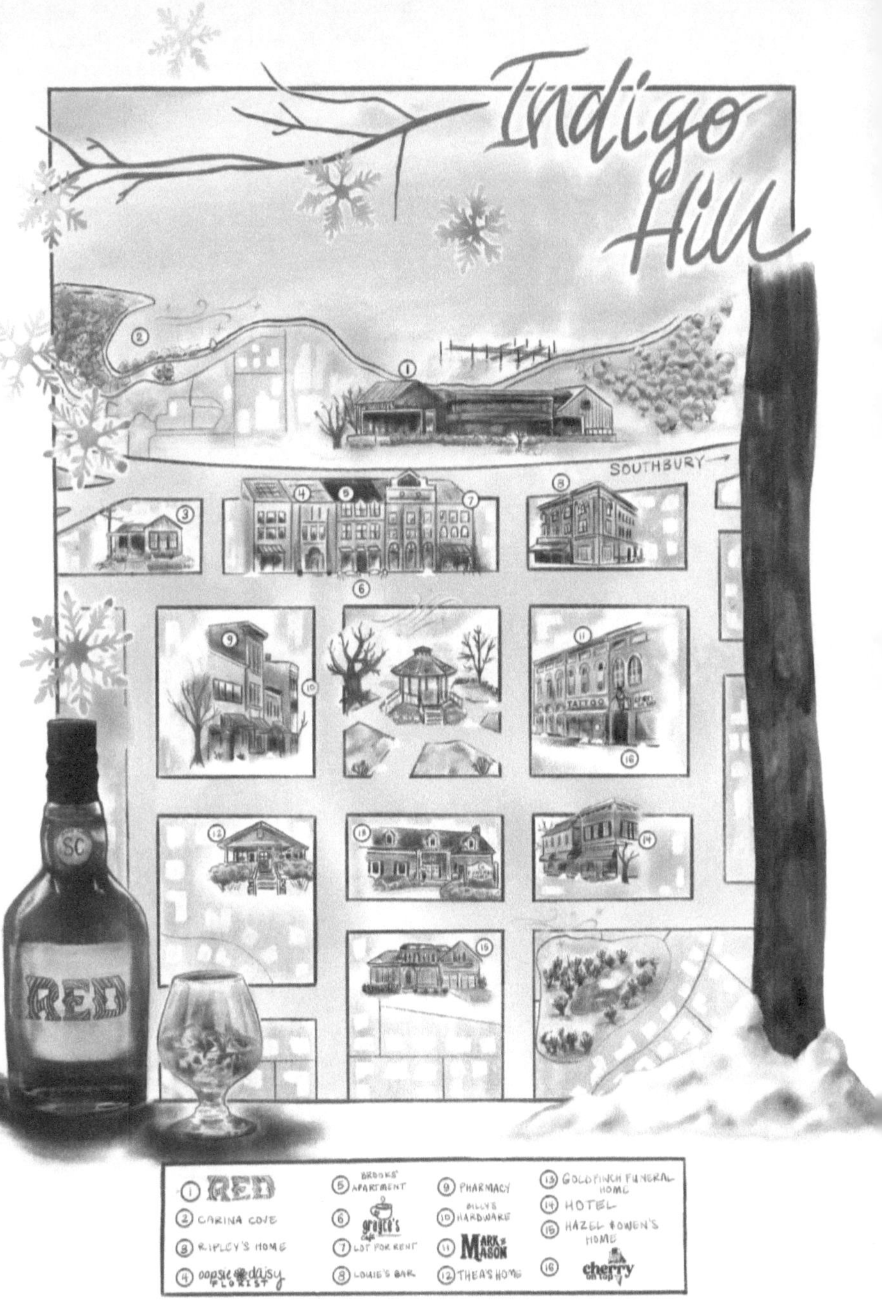

Indigo Hill
SOUTHBURY
TATTOO
RED
1 RED
2 CARINA COVE
3 RIPLEY'S HOME
4 oopsie daisy FLORIST
5 BROOKS' APARTMENT
6 grayce's cafe
7 LOT FOR RENT
8 LOUIE'S BAR
9 PHARMACY
10 BILLY'S HARDWARE
11 MARK & MASON
12 THEA'S HOME
13 GOLDFINCH FUNERAL HOME
14 HOTEL
15 HAZEL & OWEN'S HOME
16 cherry on top

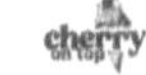

Southbury
SOUTHBURY DRIVE-IN THIS WAY
POP CORN
1 JAMES ELSHER'S OFFICE
2 BAR
3 LEROY'S CORNER STORE
4 SAINT STEPHEN'S
5 MARGOT'S HOUSE
6 SOUTHBURY DRIVE-IN
7 THE PIT
8 KEATON'S HOUSE

Prologue

11 Months Ago

Staring at a live human heart will never get old.

The image of it is burned into my brain after spending the last five hours watching over the doctor's shoulder as he gently maneuvered the organ this way and that to fix the ventricular septal defect. The adrenaline is still flowing an hour after the patient was moved to the CICU, and the next shift nurse relieved me so I can go home and get some rest.

I head to the nurses' station to check over the rest of my patients' charts before I leave for the day, making sure nothing has been missed since I was tied up in the operating room.

"Hi, Margot," Sam says with a smile. "You got in on the Mathers' VSD repair?"

"Yes," I say gleefully. "But I'm exhausted now. Going to go home and immediately crash before I have to be back here early tomorrow."

"Ah, yes. Those can be brutal. Before you go, though, Blackstone would like you to stop by his office to review post-op notes."

"Thanks, see you tomorrow?"

"You bet!"

I turn to the elevators and press the up button.

I gently knock on Dr. Julian Blackstone's office and hear a muffled "come in" from the other side. Stepping inside, I find him sitting behind his desk, going through charts, making notes.

"Margot. Close the door, and have a seat," he says with a welcoming smile. Though only in his late-thirties, Dr. Blackstone is a renowned heart surgeon whose work has put our relatively small hospital on the map. Patients come from all over the country to consult with him and hopefully, end up in his care. He's earned numerous prestigious awards and recognition for his work, every single one of them well-deserved.

As in-demand and vital as he is, Dr. Blackstone is just as kind. He mentors all of the personnel on his team, from the resident surgeons at his side to the nurses he handpicks to be in his OR. He is constantly nurturing their strengths and making sure everyone is working at their best. I've been lucky enough to be placed on his service at his request for the last four months, which is unheard of for someone who graduated from nursing school eighteen months ago.

Julian stands from his chair and steps around his desk, stopping just in front of where I sit. With his lab coat hanging on the back of his chair, he is left in a pale blue button down and black slacks. He leans back on his desk and loosely crosses his arms over his chest, exuding his usual commanding confidence.

"That was remarkable today, wasn't it?" he asks.

"It really was," I say dreamily. "I still can't believe this is my job. Thank you again for this opportunity. I know there are other nurses with much more experience you could have in there with you. I'm so grateful you took a chance on me. I hope I'm living up to your expectations."

"There's no need to thank me. You've earned this spot. You're..." He looks down at me, his eyes running over my face and then lower, making me heat with slight discomfort at his perusal. "Sensational." Clearing his throat before continuing, "Intuitive. You have a good sense for what I need in the OR."

"Thank you," I say quietly, shifting in my seat. "Was there something you needed to see me for?"

"I just wanted to debrief after today's marathon surgery. Check in on how you feel about the program. Make sure you're... satisfied." Something in his tone makes me uneasy.

Our relationship has never been anything but professional, and I would never cross that line. I've heard about Julian, just whispers here and there that he has his favorites. Some joke he only chooses attractive young women for his department. I never gave it much thought, until now.

This conversation is leaning toward uncomfortable, so I look for a way out.

"Yes, I'm very happy here and so thankful for the opportunity. I hope I can continue to impress you," I say. "But I really must get going if there isn't anything else." I stand, but he doesn't move to give me space to step away, and I find myself hedged in between the chair and his body.

"You are definitely impressive," he murmurs, his hand rising and finding the ends of my curls. He twirls the strands between his fingers, our eyes tracking the movement. His face is one of awe, hunger. I'm frozen in place, unsure how to extricate myself without touching him.

"Dr. Blackstone," I say, instilling as much confidence as I can muster. "Wh-what's happening right now?"

"Julian, please." His eyes shift to my face.

"Julian," I say, my voice betraying my rising panic.

"Oh, I like the sound of my name falling from your mouth," he whispers, leaning in even closer. My fight or flight finally kicks in, and I use my shoulder to gently check him back and step away from him. I move toward the door putting some distance between us.

"I'm sorry, but I think you must have gotten the wrong idea," I say quickly as I turn around when I reach the door. "I'm here strictly in a professional manner."

"Ah, yes. Certainly. I'm sorry for being so forward," he replies in his default easy tone. His eyes don't match his words though. He looks slighted and maybe even a little angry.

"I really am sorry if I gave any sort of impression..." My words trail off as he gives me his back and returns to his desk. I'm dismissed. "I'll see you tomorrow morning."

At that, he looks up and smiles robotically. "Have a good night."

I exit his office, my mind whirling with what just happened. Sure, Dr. Blackstone—Julian—is an attractive man, with his dark hair and eyes, and I admire his skill as a surgeon, but I have never had any romantic interest in him. I'm trying to recall a time I may have led him to think any differently, but nothing comes to mind. I shake my head to clear the thoughts.

"Margot." I turn to the sound of my name and see Sam hustling down the hall.

"I'm just on my way out. What's up?" I want to go home. I want to shower and wash away the interaction with Dr. Blackstone, get my head together so I can face him again tomorrow.

"I think you dropped these. I found them on the floor in the lounge." He holds out my keys.

"Oh, thank you. I didn't realize I dropped them…" I trail off. I could have sworn I had them clipped to my purse earlier today.

Sam shrugs and hands the keys over before turning and quickly disappearing down the hall. I stare after him for a moment, keys tucked in tight against my chest. What happened in Blackstone's office has me on edge.

I snap myself out of it and head for the hospital exit. As an attempt to shake the unease and confusion from my interaction with Julian, I stop by my favorite Italian restaurant for a comfort bowl of alfredo and a chat with the elderly couple who own it.

I've been visiting them at least twice a month since I moved to Charleston for nursing school, my first time living away from home, away from my brother and dad. Not only do they make the best homemade pasta, they're also easy to talk to, always regaling me with stories of their children and many grandchildren.

They also love each other in a way that's palpable from afar and have given me a standard to strive for in my own relationships. Gino looks at Maria like she's his reason for living, and watching their unwavering affection over the years has made me yearn for the same for myself.

With my tummy full and my spirits lifted, I walk the three blocks to my apartment building. Two flights of stairs and I'm at my front door. My *unlocked* front door. Sighing, I internally scold myself for forgetting to lock up after myself again. What's that make now? Three times? Four?

My brother would kick my butt if he knew how lax I've been with remembering to lock up when I leave. Growing up in a small town on a secluded property, I rarely thought about locking the front door, but since moving, I get the security reminder talk from him at least once a month.

Not to mention, the long back-to-back shifts have been getting to me. Running out the door at six after getting in at eleven the night before leaves me forgetful.

Pushing the door open, I step inside and go through my bedtime routine. I'm asleep as soon as my head hits the pillow.

Chapter One

C rack. My teeth clank together as the hit reverberates through my body. I'm off my game tonight. I wish I could laugh and make a joke about it. *First time for everything* and all, but honestly, I think if I take one more hit to the head, I might be down for good.

As the thought runs through my slower-than-normal-processing brain, Colton's fist comes flying in my direction again. *Fucking hell.* I duck, just barely dodging it. Way too late for comfort.

He's taunting me. I see his lips moving, but my ears are ringing, and I can't hear him for shit. He's fucking loving this. He's been waiting for the day he'd get to beat my ass. Again.

Well, you're fucking welcome for the opportunity, asshole.

For a split second—after squeezing my eyes shut for a moment to refocus them—my ears stop ringing, and I hear the crowd throughout The Pit going wild.

The make-shift fighting ring is set up in a field in the middle of nowhere. There's no seating in an attempt to keep it as inconspicuous as possible, so the spectators line the edges of the ring, which is just dead grass at this point. They surround us, making it hard to distinguish which direction the booing or cheers come from.

Fighting is the only thing that's ever helped me channel my emotions. Which is why I started in the first place. The second everything around me becomes too much, and I feel like my emotions might drown me, I seek refuge in someone's fists. I know it doesn't make sense to others, but it always made sense to me. I redirect the pain and trick my brain into letting go of the other shit in my head.

Being in The Pit, and even in the bar fights I'd get in before Hayes brought me into the fold last year, is the only place I've ever felt any semblance of control. I could never stop the disappointing looks or the way I seemed to always react poorly to situations with my parents. But I can control the way my body moves in a fight. I can make it do whatever I want—cause pain or duck away from it. Especially during the fights in The Pit, I have a clear goal in mind, I know what I'm after, and I know I have the ability to succeed. In those moments, everything else disappears, and the world isn't sitting on my shoulders like concrete blocks.

Sweat drips into my eyes, blurring my vision and stinging. I shake my head to clear some of it from my face, but now I feel the blood seeping from the wound Margot patched up on my cheek. I should have known it would reopen. My thoughts shift to how mad she'll be.

In my mind, I see her small, freckle-covered face screwing up in annoyance when she has to deal with me again. I hear her ridiculing me for being so reckless and jeopardizing her careful bandage job. The singsong lilt to her voice sounds nice even when it's telling me how much of a disappointment I am.

Shaking the thought out of my head to refocus, I take a few steps back, transferring my weight from one foot to the other, fists ready to go in front of my face despite the spinning all around me.

"What's wrong, Brooksy boy? You ready to call it quits?"

Brooksy boy.

Fuck. Him.

No one gets to call me that. Not anymore.

I'm charging him before I even realize what I'm doing.

My fist flies toward his face but not before he uppercuts me, and everything goes black.

"Brooks. Wake up," Hayes Mason's voice floods through my brain as I come to. He's tapping my cheek with his big, rough hand.

I immediately wince at the burning pain under my chin as I give him a grunt in reply.

I try to open my eyes but slam them shut again as the lights around The Pit burn my fucking retinas.

"Can you stand? They gotta... uh, clean up some before the next fight."

The hesitation in his voice makes me wonder how much of the dampness I'm feeling underneath me is my blood and not just sweat. I nod in response, not yet trusting my words to come out coherently. At least the ringing seems to be gone, and the noise of the crowd has died down.

Hayes grabs my hand then shuffles beside me from the sound of it.

"Alright, count of three. One, two—" His words cut off as he tugs me up from the ground.

"Fuuuuuck you, that was not three," I complain as he throws my arm over his shoulder. A shooting pain radiates across my rib cage, and my opposite hand flies to my abdomen, another moan escaping me.

"Yeah, I was tired of waiting," Hayes says, but there's a hint of amusement in his voice.

I'm not sure what he finds so fucking funny. I just had my first ever loss in The Pit–all I am is pissed.

I raise my hand enough to give him my middle finger which only makes him huff an actual laugh. My one win of the night.

Now that I'm standing, he leads me out of the ring. The crowd is a rowdy combination of boos and cheers as we walk through them.

"You wanna crash with me, or do you want me to take you home?" Hayes asks as he basically drags me toward his parked truck.

"Fuck you. I'll drive myself home on my bike."

"Not happening. You can barely walk, Brooks."

"I'll be fine."

He doesn't respond. Once I'm able to open one of my eyes enough to see the blurry image of the field in front of us, I see why.

He isn't listening, he's taking me to his truck regardless of what I say.

With the bed of his truck a few steps in front of us, he finally says, "You have two options. My place or your place—courtesy of me driving you there. Pick your poison."

I decide at this moment I both love and hate Hayes. I know he means well, and I'd do the same for him, but fuck—I don't like depending on anyone other than me, myself, and I. And that's saying something since I do a shit job even for myself most of the time.

"Can my bike at least come with us?" I ask, knowing he has the ramp to put it in the bed of his truck.

He grunts in response, helping me into the cab, and slams the passenger door shut. I'm left to sit there with my thoughts and the pain riddling my body, neither of which are good company.

I can't believe I got my ass handed to me in front of a huge crowd of people who came out tonight thinking I'd win. I probably lost some of the regulars hundreds of dollars. Who knows if they'll bet on me again considering how epic the loss was.

I try to peel open my other eye that's still burning, but the air from the AC hits it as soon as I do, making me wince. Taking a deep breath, I listen as Hayes loads my bike into the bed of the truck. In the silence, I remember what set me off right before the hit that did me in, and I'm pissed all over again.

Brooksy Boy.

Before I can spiral too much, Hayes opens the driver's side door and gets in. He's so big, it makes the truck look smaller than it is.

As he puts his hand on the gear shift, he looks over at me and asks, "You good?"

"No," I grumble, still attempting to stifle my simmering anger.

"Everyone loses every once in a while, it's not as big of a deal as you're making it."

I huff in response, not wanting to discuss it further.

He shakes his head, puts the car in drive, and takes off for Indigo Hill.

I pull my arm over my face as the sun assaults me. When the side of my hand touches my battered cheek, my eyes jolt open in pain. Last night comes rushing back: the wound on my cheek reopening, the black eye I'm sure I'm sporting, and the throbbing in my jaw where Colton landed an uppercut on me.

As much as I'd like to go to back to sleep, I need some painkillers before it's possible, and I'm wide awake now.

I reach over to grab my phone from beside me in the bed when I see it's already noon, meaning my 9 a.m. alarm did jack shit for me this morning.

"Fuck!"

My plan had been to wake up early and see if Thea needed help setting up for tonight, but she'll be done by now. She's more than used to me being unreliable, but I'm trying to change that. I don't want to keep letting everyone down all the time.

Every year we have a family dinner the night before Thanksgiving at Ripple Effect Distillery and Restaurant—or RED as most of us call it—then host our annual Thanksgiving lunch for the town the next day. This is the first year without my parents. It's the first one Thea has to plan on her own.

RED used to be a rundown diner, aptly named Indigo Hill Diner. My parents had renovated and rebranded the establishment with Thea's help, finally relieving themselves of the mountain of debt the place had accrued over the years. Along the way, I think Thea realized running RED was her dream job, but I don't think she ever expected to have to run it without them. She definitely never expected to have to co-own it with my dumbass younger brother.

I look at the time on my phone again, silently cursing myself for sleeping as late as I did. Thankfully, I hadn't told her I wanted to come by and help, so it's not like she knew I'd ghosted her. Again. But *I* know.

I'm just as fucking done with myself as I'm sure everyone else is. I can't stop though. I can't seem to do one thing right, so I keep doubling down on doing everything wrong.

Pulling myself out of bed, I try to stretch, but my abdomen is too sore to do much. I immediately notice the new bruises marring my ribs, hating myself again for allowing Colton to win last night.

I make my way toward the bathroom, bypassing the mirror because I know I won't like what I see. I feel the tattered pieces of more than just my soul today.

As I reach into the shower to turn it on, I decide I won't let the day go to waste. Despite looking like I got run over by a truck, I'll go see Hayes at his tattoo shop. I'll put myself out there for once and see if it goes anywhere.

The reddish pink color of the water puddling near my feet as I wash the grime off my body makes me itch for a paintbrush. It's the first time in a long while, and I blame my delusional idea of working at Mark of Mason for even letting my mind go there.

I've tried really hard not to get my hopes up about much of anything anymore but especially when it comes to anything creative. I can't remember the last time I sketched or considered painting. I did some branding work for a few businesses in town after creating RED's logo, but no one aside from Thea knows it was me.

She begged me to let her tell everyone and start offering my services to more people, but I didn't see the point. I only took on the other businesses because they hounded Thea for the name of who she hired. Once she brought it to my attention and asked if I'd be open to her giving them my name, I told her I wasn't interested in going full out, but I'd communicate via email if it would get her off my back.

Even graphic design had sparked the tiniest flame in me again. I suddenly had the urge to *create* rather than destroy. I know better than to let myself want it though. It isn't practical. I just can't help it. So this idea to talk to Hayes is… a long shot at best, I know that. I'd been willing to give my life to Ripple Effect Distillery and Restaurant like my parents had, despite never really wanting it. But now they're gone, and I wasn't named the new owner, so I'm a free man.

A free man with a stupid dream and almost no hope of it coming true.

"You want to apprentice? Here?" Hayes asks, the confused tone in his voice apparent. The only interest he's seen from me in regards to tattoos before this is watching as he works on the many pieces he's given me over the years. I've never told him he's living my dream.

"Is it so hard to believe?"

He stops tattooing Archer for a moment to look up at me. The answer is clear on his face.

"Yes, I want to apprentice here," I repeat to make myself clear.

"Why?" he asks as his attention focuses back on Archer's arm. I can't tell if talking to him while he's working is making this better or worse. He's hard to read on a good day.

"I just think I'd be good at it." The words feel like ash on my tongue. Saying out loud I think I'd be good at something is so foreign I almost take it back immediately.

"Right. Well, I don't have an open chair."

The letdown is subtle because I can't tell if it's the real reason or just a convenience. Either way, I let it roll off my shoulders and swallow down the burn of rejection.

I'd told myself the whole way over this would happen, but I'd also let myself have the smallest bit of hope that maybe, just maybe, I was wrong. And that's the problem with hope, it always convinces me of shit that isn't true. It twists my logical thoughts into whimsical dreams that aren't real or possible. That's why I haven't fucked with hope in too many years to count.

"I knew it was a long shot. Can you keep me in mind in case anything changes?" I ask, trying to keep the disappointment from my voice.

"Yeah, of course."

"Thanks, I appreciate it."

I turn to walk away, but he speaks up again, eyes still on his canvas, "You look like shit."

The laugh that comes out of me seems to surprise him as I say, "Thanks. See ya, man."

I walk past the counter and wave at Kori, who's manning the receptionist desk, before opening the door to Mark of Mason, leaving the remnants of my dream behind me. The moment the door shuts, I pull a pack of cigarettes and a lighter from my pocket, in desperate need of a nicotine fix.

The first pull of the smoke into my lungs calms my nerves. I hold it in as long as I can before exhaling and letting go of the sinking feeling in my chest. As I start walking down the sidewalk of the town square, I see a curly haired brunette come around the corner. She's looking down at her phone, not paying attention.

When she gets a few steps away from me, I speak up, "Hey, Doc."

She jumps a bit then puts her hand to her heart like I caused it to leap out of her chest.

"Didn't take you for a jumpy one."

"You caught me by surprise," she retorts, and I realize I was slightly off with the memory of her voice last night. The way I replayed it in my head was a tad too high. I blame the bourbon. I won't forget its perfect pitch next time I need a distraction and she comes to mind.

"Clearly. Sorry about that," I say with as much sincerity as I can conjure. I can't say I'm sorry I'm running into her though. I haven't been able to get this pocket-sized woman out of my head since I formally met her. Her lilac-cherry smell is more intoxicating than the nicotine I'm inhaling. I pull the cigarette back to my mouth, taking another long draw.

"You look terrible..." she says as her eyes finally meet mine. She takes longer than necessary roaming over my visible wounds. Her nose scrunches, bringing my gaze to her freckle covered face, there's almost no patch of skin where one doesn't exist. Staring at her is like being entranced by a car crash you can't look away from. It's intoxicating, addicting. As I exhale the smoke, I make sure to turn my face and the toxic fumes away from her.

"So, I've heard." I don't mean for it to come out clipped, but I can't help the tinge of annoyance in my voice after having it brought up a second time in a matter of minutes.

"Your umm... your cheek reopened, and your chin is black and blue. Do you—"

"Oh, no," I cut her off. "It'll be fine. Besides, I hear scars are sexy," I say, trying to play it off to remove the look on her face and so she doesn't feel the need to rush me to the hospital.

"Oh? And who told you that?" A bit of a smirk crosses her face, and a stupid sliver of hope creeps back into my heart.

"I was hoping *you'd* think that."

The shameless flirting makes her laugh to the point of snorting. "Sorry," she laughs again. "Sorry, I just... does that usually work?"

Confused, I scratch my head with my free hand, my cigarette almost forgotten at this point. "Does what usually work?"

Her laughter calms down enough for her to reply, "The whole bad boy routine and look." She waggles her finger up and down my body to make her point crystal clear. "I'm assuming you think that's also sexy?"

Well fuck.

"I have a bad boy routine?" I ask, genuinely curious. I definitely wouldn't call myself that, but clearly, she thinks otherwise.

"You get into... altercations. You drive a motorcycle. You smoke. You have tattoos."

I scoff. "Tattoos make me a bad boy?"

A blush covers her cheeks, and I lose any sense of the annoyance I was feeling.

"Sometimes."

"And you... don't like that? So, I shouldn't ask for your number and if you're free Friday night?"

The blush deepens before she answers, "Oh, no. Please don't. I am not your type."

My brows furrow, pulling at the tender wound on my cheek. "How do you know what my type is?"

She looks down at her watch, the blush still spreading down her neck. "I umm... I have to go. But please, get your cheek checked out. It looks like it could be getting infected."

Before I can say much else, she's walking past me, and for the first time—maybe ever—I realize I just got turned down by a woman.

My helmet balances on the handlebars of my motorcycle, gently swaying back and forth as I shove the keys into my pocket. Based on the number of cars in the parking lot, it seems like the lunch rush has probably died down. I'm here to get my check so I can cash it before the banks close, but I figured I'd see if Thea still needs help with anything for tonight.

Ripple Effect Distillery and Restaurant has two sections to it. The restaurant has a full bar and panoramic lake views; the distillery and tasting room are where the bourbon is made and stored. They're separated by a walkway and swinging doors on each side, and both sides have their own entrances. I do a little bit of everything here, but I usually spend the most time working at the distillery. So I opt to use this entrance, especially considering my current state. I have no desire to hear anyone else's commentary on how I look. Aside from Thea. I know she'll berate me, but that's okay. I expect it. And if anyone's allowed to, it's her.

I push through the door into the empty rackhouse, passing by the barrels I spent most of this past Saturday reorganizing. I'll be happy once we start the tours in the tasting room again. We postponed the last few due to my parents' deaths, and then with Thanksgiving tomorrow, we pushed the schedule to next week.

Ripley and I usually run them together and have created a good bit of banter the visitors enjoy. I'll admit, it's cool as fuck to see people going insane over the bourbon Ripley creates.

Our house bourbon, appropriately named RED, is becoming one of the most sought after small-batch bourbons on the market. We've got people traveling from all over to come see the facility and do a tasting with us. They love the deep vanilla notes and crisp cherry finish.

I've never seen a tasting where every single person doesn't rave about it by the end. It's so smooth we've converted more than one non-bourbon drinker.

As I walk behind the bar to grab my check from the safe, I pour myself a finger pour of the spirit then throw it back, setting my glass in the sink for later. Once I've opened the safe and secured my check in my wallet, I make my way toward the restaurant side of RED.

The moment the door connecting the two sides swings open, I hear Thea's voice filtering through the hallway.

"—I don't know, Travis. Maybe he'll show up. Maybe he won't. I've stopped depending on him for even the smallest of things. I asked him to bring up the new bottles of RED the other day, and even that didn't get done."

My mood instantly sours again. I've spent all day dealing with letdown after letdown. Even coming here to help, I've already fucked up.

I don't go any farther, turning around to leave instead. As I stomp back through the distillery, I throw a chair to its side as I walk past, doing anything to expel the anger roiling in my chest.

As I slam my helmet on my head, I decide if everyone else has already given up on me, what's the point in trying? I've got a whole check's worth of money I can spend drowning my sorrows.

I rev the engine on my bike and exit the parking lot, some bar a couple of towns away the only thing in my future.

Chapter Two

"I'll be back here around noon, and we can head to RED together," I say as I finish folding the blanket I collected off the wheelchair Lydia uses and place it on her dresser.

"Thank you for everything today. Have a good night," Lydia says with a smile, turning back to the soap opera playing on the TV mounted in the corner of her room.

I dim the lights and step out of her suite. Lydia Ashford is one of my favorite patients here at Saint Stephen's Assisted Living. She's kind and has a sharp sense of humor. We've gotten close over the last six months I've worked here since moving back to Southbury. Taking care of her hardly feels like work at all. The time I spend with her flies by with us gossiping about the other patients on her floor—Susan from a few rooms down who's constantly losing her dentures and Georgie who faked dementia symptoms when he got caught with not one, not two, but *three* girlfriends. Weeks of testing resulted in the doctors declaring he is nothing but a horny old man.

Lydia is one of the youngest patients at the facility by a few decades, but her MS symptoms progressed past a point her daughter, Thea, could handle a few years ago, and she ended up moving here. I've gotten to know both of them well and consider them to be the first friends I've made since coming back. Thea often invites me out with her boyfriend to check out the local bar, and maybe one day I'll take her up on it.

With my shift over, I step into the nurses' lounge and collect my jacket and purse from my locker before wishing a good evening to a few of the other staff members milling about.

I make a mental note to bring in a few more pairs of back-up scrubs tomorrow before Lydia and I head over to RED for a Thanksgiving Day lunch in honor of Hazel and Owen Grant, Brooks' parents. Apparently the lunch is something they do every year, and anyone in town who doesn't have a place to go or some-one to celebrate with is welcome. The event—hosted by Thea and the Grant brothers this year—will serve as a memorial of sorts.

It's dark when I step outside, the air is crisp now with it near-ing the end of November. Thoughts of the memorial lead me to recount my run-in with Brooks from earlier today. That man has trouble written all over him. In my short time here, I've heard whispers about him around town. About how he gets into fights constantly, all the women he's been seen with.

He checks off all the boxes for a stereotypical bad boy: tattooed all over, loud motorcycle, killer smile. That last one had me sec-ond-guessing saying no to his invitation today. Between the smile and piercing blue eyes, it's no wonder he has women throwing themselves at him—women who would probably know what to do if they got him alone. I'm not looking to be another notch in his belt, and I'm sure he's not looking for a twenty-three year old virgin he'd have to walk through everything past a blowjob.

Still, the thought of seeing him tomorrow has my tummy clenching and my heart rate picking up.

I smile to myself as I round my car. Opening the door, the back of my neck prickles. My eyes dart around the lot, but I don't see anyone in any of the cars. The sense of being watched never really leaves me, I'm constantly on edge, but something feels more off than usual.

I'm being paranoid. Shaking my head to clear the feeling, I get in my car and start the engine. With another deep breath, I pull out of the spot and onto the road. Grocery store and one more stop before I can head home.

"Hi," I whisper as I gently pull the half empty plastic bottle of whiskey from his hand. He's passed out on the recliner, TV playing sports recaps at a low volume throwing shadows over his gaunt face. His mouth is open, and he's snoring gently. I can't remember the last time he was awake when I visited.

I look around the rundown living room and sigh. I pick up a couple of empty bottles scattered around his chair and the takeout containers that appear to have been sitting on the coffee table for a few days already. Carrying everything over to the kitchen, I see it's not in any better condition. Dirty dishes overflow from the sink and line the counters. The stench from the trash assaults me from across the room.

I flip open the top on the trash bin, and my shoulders drop. The pamphlets I left last time along with the calendar of meetings taking place in the basement of the local church sit on top, covered in oil stains and cigarette butts. I guess he's still not ready. I drop the food containers I collected and turn to the rest of the kitchen.

I spend the next forty-five minutes tidying up and then throw a load of laundry in the wash. The dishes take me longer than usual because the dishwasher refuses to work, so I clean and dry everything by hand. Once all the dishes are put away, I wipe down the counters and toss all the old and questionable food from the fridge. I restock the freezer with the frozen-ready meals he likes and sneak in some fruits and vegetables into the crisper drawer. I don't expect he'll eat them, but at least he has the option.

I drop and sort through the pile of mail I picked up at the end of his half-mile long driveway, tossing the junk and separating the bills and royalty checks. He was a songwriter and got lucky with a few big hits back in the 90s. The songs still get played on oldies stations and in nationwide commercial campaigns for paper towels and a major office supply chain. He routinely gets two to three checks a month, making just enough to keep the lights on and the bottom-shelf liquor plentiful.

The bathroom down the hall is in much better shape than the kitchen. *Thank God.* Using a single-use scrubber wand, I scour the toilet and make a mental note to bring some body wash next time I come by.

Once the laundry machine signals the end of the cycle, I swap the clothes into the dryer. After emptying the trash and recycling bags, I place them by the front door to take to the outside bins.

Looking around the space, I can't believe how decades of neglect have turned what used to be a cozy family home into a purgatory for the man at the center of it—just waiting for the day he can reunite with his late wife. At least that's the story I tell myself, it's more romantic than drinking himself to death as a shut-in on his eighty-acre property.

I watch as he breathes steadily. His chest moving up and down under his flannel shirt. Looking at my phone, I see it's after midnight already. Draping a threadbare blanket over him, I whisper, "See you later, Daddy. Happy Thanksgiving."

Then I grab the trash bags I left by the door and close it behind me.

CHAPTER THREE

I'd spent my whole day at some shithole-in-the-wall bar two towns over. I'd even lost track of time, almost missing our night before Thanksgiving family dinner. But as I rushed out of the bar and onto my motorcycle, pulling out my phone, I realized none of them had texted me to find out if I was still coming.

None of them expected me to show up.

The closer I got to Indigo Hill, the madder I became. So by the time I walked into RED and saw them all having a grand fucking time, not at all fazed by my absence, I let my fury out. Specifically, on Cary. I decided to throw a grenade into his shitstorm and watch it detonate in his face.

Cary saw it coming, and the moment I said, "Oh, he didn't tell you? He and Thea go way back. High school sweethearts and all that," you could practically see the fumes coming out of his ears. He tried to turn it around on me, but I only dug his grave deeper by outing him for the other secret he'd been keeping. And I won't lie, even now after the air has cleared from the explosion I set loose, I still feel pretty smug about the whole thing.

I am well aware—despite what everyone thinks—about the shit going down in this town. I just don't parade around shouting everyone's business like most. From the second Cary came back into town, I knew it would all implode. I knew what he was hiding. He thought living in Seattle and shunning our family meant none of us would keep up with him, but I had. I'd read every article. The second I found out about Carina Cove opening, I was on their website looking at photos. I kept up with my little brother even when he didn't care to keep up with me.

And we'd talked—if you could call it that. It wasn't much, but we had our every-other-month phone call. I stuck to it. I kept up with him. I asked questions. So I knew all the dirty secrets he was keeping close to his chest when he arrived in Indigo Hill. I watched him fall for Thea all over again, knowing he has someone else in Seattle.

And maybe it made me an asshole to light the proverbial match and then sit back and watch it all go up in flames for him, but he made his bed. Now he needs to face his fuck-ups and figure out how to move on. I'd tell him that if he wasn't so pissed he isn't speaking to me currently.

Once both women left, Cary had unloaded on me.

"You just couldn't fucking help yourself, could you?" he'd spat.

"Me? *You're* the one who chose to fuck around and find out, don't blame me for your bullshit." I was seething listening to him berate me like I was the one who started the whole mess, but all I'd given him was an eye roll.

"I was handling it."

"Oh, right, like you 'handled' being with two women at once? Fuck off, Cary. You fucked up. For once, just own it."

He'd gotten up from his chair, shoving it back so hard it made a scratching noise against the floor. "Fuck. You," he'd thrown in my direction before heading toward the bar.

Now, he's drinking his problems away. Ripley and I are the only ones left at the table. I'm surprised neither of them ran after Thea, but I wasn't about to ask why. Ripley's been happily munching on all of the small plates, watching the exchange.

"Well," Ripley starts as he brings his glass to his lips, "That was an epic dumpster fire."

I laugh it off without responding. Then he promptly says, "I'll be right back, gotta piss," and gets up from his seat beside me. I give him an up-nod in response as I signal Tiffany over for another drink. My gaze flits around the now empty table, one filled with my closest friends and family just thirty-minutes ago. I'm sure they'll all blame me for what happened.

I'm just finishing my bite of some sort of crab-stuffed pastry puff when my eyes catch on Ripley's phone as it lights up on the table with a new incoming message. I look over at it, expecting the message to be from Thea, maybe an update on how she's doing. It is definitely not from Thea, and the text itself exposes another secret from within our circle.

11/27 9:57 p.m.

West: Couldn't find someone else to stretch that pretty asshole? **wink emoji**

My eyebrows shoot to my hairline, and I can't even pretend to hide the smug look on my face. Before Ripley and Thea started "dating," I'd wondered if he was gay. Then they started with their date nights, and I figured I'd read the situation wrong. I never said anything because it wasn't my business, and I don't care one way or the other. He may not think so, but I consider Ripley one of my closest friends. It's clear now from the text and the drama between Cary and Thea what all of this was. The realization wipes the look right off my face.

The only reason to pretend to be dating a woman when you bat for the other team is if you don't feel comfortable telling people your truth. I hate that for him. I hate that this town made someone I care about feel like they can't be themselves. I hate even more that he doesn't feel safe with me. Although, why should he? I've given him no reason to.

I watch as he makes his way back to the table, immediately picking up his phone like he was waiting for a message to come through. His cheeks turn red as he reads the screen, and I try my best not to laugh.

"I didn't peg you for a bottom," the words slip from my lips without much thought. Not that I have much of a filter to begin with.

"Wh—what?" Ripley stutters the word, the shock rippling through him.

"A guy named West was asking about your pretty—"

"Oh my God, shut up!" he says, an octave higher than usual and cutting me off. His eyes are huge. His cheeks are even darker now, and he holds his phone to his chest.

"Hey, I don't care," I say as I put my hands up and shrug. "Not sure I blame you for keeping it hush hush. Just wish I'd been a better friend so you felt like you could confide in me. I'm sorry for that."

"You don't... care? Really?" His shaggy dark hair falls over cautious eyes.

"Why would I?"

It's clear he's surprised by my lack of reaction. I guess he assumed everyone would judge him. And honestly, I get it. I have my own secrets I keep for fear of people's reactions. It's entirely different, but I get it. Small town, small minds.

"I don't know... I just—I guess I thought you'd see me differently." He shifts in his seat, adjusting his glasses, clearly uncomfortable, which is unusual for him. I'm not sure I've ever seen Ripley uncomfortable. He's the guy who revels in the midst of awkward situations, delighting in the tension. I guess it's different when he's the one in the spotlight.

"Nah, you play," I lower my voice and cup my hands around my mouth, "hide the salami with whoever's dick you want, I don't give a fuck."

The tension seeps out of his shoulders, and he guffaws. It makes me wonder just how long he's been holding this shit in. His laughter tapers off, but I'm not one to sit in the awkwardness, so I only let the silence go on for about ten more seconds before I'm fucking with him again.

"So... is his dick bigger than yours? Have you compared?"

He slaps me on the arm, but at least he's laughing again. "Brooks..."

"What? It's a valid question. I'd be comparing if I were fucking a dude. It's okay if you're smaller. Someone has to be, right?" I pick my drink back up, bringing it to my mouth as I wait for him to answer.

"I'm not having this conversation with you, man."

"Oof, so you *are* the smaller one," I say as I pat his shoulder. "It's okay, we can't all be blessed."

He pushes my hand off of him, still laughing just a bit. "Fuck off."

I take a moment, allowing the laughter to wind down between us. "But for real, if you ever need someone to talk to, I'm around."

Ripley turns to meet my eyes. "You're serious?"

I nod as I say, "Dead." The expression on his face screams shock which pisses me off. "Don't look so surprised, shit." I turn away from him, feeling slighted by his reaction.

"Sorry, man. I just wasn't expecting that from you."

I lift my drink to my lips once more before saying, "Yeah, I get that a lot." I put the beer back down on the table and stand. I want to be pissed about it. I want to yell and scream they're all judging me for how I deal with shit, but they never seem to judge anyone else. I don't say any of that though. I don't say anything at all because what's the point? They've all made up their minds. They decided I wasn't worth their time or effort anymore. Worst part is, I don't even blame them. I blame me. I just thought maybe me showing Ripley he could trust me with this would change something. But it didn't. Being surprised or hurt by it is my own bullshit.

"You're leaving?"

"Yep. See ya."

He reaches over, placing a hand on my arm to stop me. "Hey, I didn't mean anything by it, Brooks."

"It's cool, dude, I got shit to do. I won't tell anyone. You have my word... not that anyone thinks it means much." I pull my arm away as his mouth opens with a retort, but I leave before he has an opportunity to say anything more.

Chapter Four

My eyes blink open to the bright December morning. I forgot to close my blackout shades again. It's my day off, and though I'd love to sleep in, I have so many chores to get done and errands to run today.

Sitting up, I stretch my arms over my head and roll out my neck. Mentally, I'm compiling my to-dos for the day: laundry, trip to the grocery store, stopping by Dad's again, and baking cupcakes for the residents at Saint Stephen's for their monthly bingo night are the top priorities. If I can squeeze in an hour of self-care before bed—typically consisting of a face mask and a glass of sweet tea—I'll consider myself lucky.

Goosebumps pepper my skin as soon as I peel back the covers and place my feet on the floor. I guess it's time to turn on the heat. I consider grabbing a sweatshirt to throw on over the oversized shirt and sleep shorts I'm wearing but decide I'll just hop in the shower to warm up.

As soon as I step into the bathroom, I know something is wrong—mainly because the floor is wet, and it's not just damp but flooded.

"What in the world…" I say to myself.

I flick on the light and find the entire floor of the bathroom covered in water. I look first to the bath, then the toilet, and lastly the sink. Nothing seems to be running.

Bending down, I open the cabinet under the sink and see it's wet inside as well.

I know very little about plumbing, but from what I can tell, the water appears to be coming from the back of the cabinet where the hose bit connects with the wall thing—yes, those are the technical terms.

I reach in and grasp the knob above the connection where the water is leaking, reciting "righty-tighty, lefty-loosey" in my head. A small spark of hope lights within me as it turns easily but is quickly extinguished as the knob breaks from the mechanism and comes away in my hand.

"Oh no, no, no!" I hold it closer to my face and see it's rusted and heavily corroded—there's not a chance I can reattach it. Thankfully, it doesn't look like the leak is any worse, just a constant trickle, continuing to spread.

I rush back into the bedroom, tracking wet footprints behind me. Grabbing my phone, I hit my brother's name on my Favorites list, the line connects after just two rings.

"Booger," his deep, gruff voice answers.

I cringe. I hate his nickname for me, and he knows it. "Please, stop calling me that," I beg even though I know it's a lost cause. "I need your help. My sink is leaking, and the bathroom is flooding."

"Did you try turning it off?"

"Yes! The knob thingy broke; I can't turn it off."

There's a huff on the line followed by a beat of silence. "Put a bucket under it. I'll get someone out there."

"You can't come?" I try to hide the slight panic in my voice, uncomfortable with the idea of strangers being in my space.

"My whole day's booked, and with the new shop opening up in town, I can't start canceling on people," he replies. "Look, I have to make some calls. Someone will be out there today."

"Thanks. Still on for lunch tomorrow?" I ask. I miss him. Moving back to my hometown means I live and work twenty minutes from my brother, but somehow I still rarely see him. He works nonstop in his tattoo studio one town over.

Recent rumors of a new shop opening up in Indigo Hill became hard to dispute when the "Opening Soon" sign appeared last week on an empty storefront just across the town square from his space. Though he has a devoted client list, I know competition—especially so close—is causing him stress.

"Sure thing, see ya." The call ends, and I'm left staring at the blank screen in my hands.

"Guess I'm not showering just yet," I say to myself. Throwing my unruly curls into a bun on top of my head, I grab a mop bucket and a bunch of towels from the hall closet.

After setting up the bucket in the cabinet, I mop up the floor using the towels. The whole time, my mind wanders to all the chores I had planned. Unfortunately, going to visit my dad will have to be pushed to tomorrow since I have to wait for a plumber now.

Thirty minutes after I hang up with my brother, there's a loud knock at the front door. I had just enough time to toss the wet towels into the washing machine and throw on an oversized sweater and my favorite pair of cable-knit thigh-high stockings—my usual look when I'm lounging at home.

I look through the peephole, but the sun glare makes it impossible to make out the man standing on the other side. It takes a few moments for me to unlock the door since I installed the chain lock and two extra deadbolts shortly after moving in. I suck in a deep breath before swinging the door open. I miss the days when I used to be excited for visitors.

Once my eyes focus on the man standing on my front stoop, I'm immediately confused. I look around behind him and then take in his six-foot-something frame, buzz cut, nose ring, and the sharp blue eyes staring at me—correction, his eyes are roaming up and down my body, snagging on my legs. Despite having most of my skin covered by the large sweater and fluffy thigh-highs, I feel naked in front of him, and my cheeks flame from his perusal.

"You've got to be fucking kidding me," Brooks mumbles under his breath before letting out a small groan I don't think I was supposed to hear. He shifts on his feet and runs his hand down his face. As if the movement flipped a switch in him, his face transforms into his usual smug look, a devilish smirk now in place. "You going to invite me in?"

"What are you doing here?" Genuine concern flits through me for a split second. "Are you stalking me?"

"Uhh, no," he draws out, eyebrows furrowing. "This is your place? Hayes gave me this address and told me to come fix a leak."

My worry eases hearing my brother sent him, but it does raise a lot of questions. "How do you know Hayes?"

"How do *you* know Hayes?" he volleys back.

"He's my brother," I say.

"What?" He looks taken aback. "He told me his sister lives in Charleston."

"I used to," I say, shifting my eyes from his. "I had to move back seven months ago. Why are you here?"

"I heard you're wet," he says and then chuckles when my face flames again, and my eyes widen. "I'm here to fix a leak?"

I take a deep breath and will—in vain—my blush to fade. I weigh my options, but seeing as he's my best bet at getting the sink fixed today, I stand back and make room for him to enter. Brooks steps inside, and I'm hit with a whiff of bergamot and leather. I don't know how he does it, but it smells sweet and dangerous at the same time.

His head swivels around as he takes in my home. He seems too big for the space, I feel his presence everywhere. His eyes are on me as I turn to close and lock the door, and when I turn back around, our eyes meet.

"Paranoid much?" he teases, eyeing the many locks.

"Just... security-conscious."

He hums and continues looking around the small space. I haven't gotten a chance to paint yet, so all the walls are a muted gray. I've added splashes of color with the vibrant paintings I've collected over the years. There's no underlying theme to the art, I chose pieces that spoke to me at different moments in my life. The set of six paintings of brightly colored fish and coral hanging in the entryway brought me peace when I was studying for finals in my last year of nursing school. Coming across the large abstract one titled "Lucky Penny" that hangs above my couch in the living room felt fortuitous when I was waiting to hear if I got into my top choice nursing program.

I shuffle around behind him, watching as he catalogs my space. As my discomfort rises, I redirect him to the issue at hand, "Follow me, it's upstairs." I step around him and climb the stairs, somewhere around the third step from the top, I realize Brooks is about fifteen seconds from stepping into my bedroom. The thought of him there—a space I've invited no man but my brother into, and that was only to help me move in my bed—sends a jolt down my spine, half anxiousness, half anticipation.

By the time we broach the bedroom, the anxiousness wins, and I usher him straight to the bathroom.

"So, I don't know what happened. I woke up and found water all over the floor, and then when I tried to turn it off underneath, the knob just... came off," I say and show him the rusted piece of metal I left on the counter as proof.

Brooks looks from me to the knob and back. His lips quirk like he's fighting back a smile, but then he steels himself and drops down to stick his head into the cabinet. He feels around at the pipes and utters a few "hmmms" before popping back up.

He steps closer and looks at me from under his gorgeous, full lashes. "Want to show me your downstairs?" he murmurs.

I rear back from him and squeak out, "Excuse me?"

The smile he gives me is sinful. "Your basement." He cocks his head with a glint in his eyes. "What did you think I meant?"

I swallow thickly and avoid his gaze as my face burns. "Uhh… nothing. Follow me." I lead him back downstairs and around the corner to the door going to the basement. I open it and switch on the light before motioning him to go ahead. Brooks is about halfway down the stairs when he realizes I'm not following him.

Turning around, he says, "You coming?"

I shift around on my feet and play with the doorknob as I continue to lean on the door. "No, I—I don't like basements…" I feel silly and juvenile saying it out loud, but I've never liked basements. Maybe it's growing up in South Carolina where most homes don't have them, or maybe basements are just inherently creepy, I'm not sure.

He looks at me a moment longer, eyes roaming up and down the length of me again. Then with a narrowing of his eyes and a click of his tongue, he says, "You stay up there, Doc. Would hate to see anything dirty up those cute stockings." Then, with a wink he turns and takes the rest of the stairs down before disappearing past where I can see him.

His words and the heat in his gaze as he eyed me up and down stay at the forefront of my mind, making something in my belly coil. I think I like the way he looks at me.

I'm still turning over his words when his boots thud up the stairs, and he's suddenly next to me.

"I've turned off the water to the house," he says looking down at me. I feel every inch of our height difference in this moment, and I'm caught on the masculinity of his face in the morning light: the angular nose, deep set eyes, and day-old scruff. It takes a few moments of me staring at him for his words to land.

"What do you mean? I have to shower, do laundry. How am I supposed to get anything done with no running water?" I say, trying not to get too upset because I know it won't help the situation.

"Well, you're always welcome to come shower at my place." He smiles wickedly. "But I hope you know, I'm very serious about the environment, we'd have to hop in together. You know, for water conservation," he says.

I give him my best attempt at a dead stare. "I think I'll just go in to work and use one there. Thanks for the generous offer though, Killer." Recalling the nickname I gave him the night I patched him up, it's hard to keep a straight face. His lame flirting is sweet in its own way, and it's making my belly swoop in an unfamiliar but exhilarating manner.

He smiles and nods then continues, "Well, it looks like you need a new shutoff valve and cold supply line."

"Oh, okay. Will those be hard to find? How long do we have to keep the water off?" I ask, dreading his answer. My mind is already conjuring ways to get my scrubs washed for the next few weeks—maybe I can go stay with Hayes for a while. Though I remember how well that went when I first came back, before I bought this place, and think better of it. His studio apartment above the tattoo shop is barely big enough to fit him. We were at each other's throats for those few months.

Brooks' light, flirty tone from before is gone, serious now as he says, "It's unlikely the small hardware store in town will have it, I'll have to order it and hope it gets here quickly." He pauses while his words sink in. "Why don't you give me your number, and I'll text you when I have it so I can come back and install it for you?"

I bite my lip and nod, holding out my hand for his phone. I program my name and number in. "Thanks for doing this. I know it's out of your way. I appreciate it," I say as we head to the front door.

"Anything for you, Doc," he says and climbs on his motorcycle before it rumbles to life under him. He lights a cigarette, places it in his mouth, and with one last glance in my direction, he's moving down my driveway.

I grab the front of my sweater and air it out. The temperature feels like it's rocketed up twenty degrees all of a sudden, or maybe it's just the memory of his dark blue eyes undressing me.

"Oh, fudge nugget," I grumble as I remember the laundry I had running before Brooks got here, and it acts as a bucket of ice water to my overheated thoughts. I trudge up the stairs, praying it finished before the water shut off.

Chapter Five

I lied. And I'd like to say I feel bad about white-lying my way into getting Margot's number, but I don't. I saw an opportunity, and I'm taking it. It's obvious she wants nothing to do with me, so I needed the in. Any hardware store—even our mom-and-pop shop in town—should have shutoff valves and cold supply lines. Lucky for me, she has zero clue about plumbing and didn't question me.

What are the fucking chances Hayes' sister is the same girl I haven't been able to get out of my head for weeks? I was aware he has a sister. Everyone is. He's made sure to let everyone he knows she's off-limits. I didn't know her name though. He calls her "Booger" or some shit, which only makes me laugh now that I know who she is. I guess I always assumed she was a teenager.

But fuck me, I can't have the hots for Hayes' sister. She's probably barely old enough to drink. Plus, he'll murder me. Not in the funny-ha-ha-I'll-kill-you sense, he will actually gut me alive. I've seen what he can do in The Pit, and I don't want to be on the receiving end of his wrath. I've been trying to focus on that fact, keep it in the forefront of my brain, but every time I try to push her out, the vision of Margot in those fucking thigh-highs is front and center again. *Fuck me.* I feel like such a creep.

I slam the gear into first right in front of Billy's Hardware and turn off the bike. As I push through the glass door, the bell above it dings.

I don't see Billy, but I hear him down an aisle yelling, "Welcome in. If ya need somethin', holler."

The parts are so common, I don't even need to ask Billy if he carries them or where to find them. As I pass by the aisle he's in, I say back, "Nah, I know where it is. You having a good day, Billy?"

At the sound of my voice, Billy stops stocking the items in his hands and turns to me. "Brooks, my boy. It's been a little bit since you stopped in, thought I maybe scared you off with all the crazy stories I jabber on about."

A low chuckle falls from my lips, Billy's stories aren't crazy, but he does talk a-fucking-lot. He's lived a tough life—fought in Afghanistan, lost his wife to cancer, and almost lost his store a couple years back.

"Takes a lot more than some war stories to scare me off, Billy-Bob."

I start to walk away when he says, "Brooks, wait."

Taking a step back, I peer into the aisle he's standing in. "What's up?"

He looks down at the ground, fidgets a bit, then eventually clears his throat. "I umm... I never told you how sorry I am about your folks. It's real sad what happened, and I just want you to know I'm... well, I'm here if you need to talk."

You'd think it was his parents who'd just died less than a month ago. I give him a nod of appreciation before saying, "Thanks, Billy. I'll keep it in mind." We both know I won't be taking him up on it, but it was nice of him to offer. I walk away without being stopped this time, and I'm in the plumbing section grabbing what I need within seconds.

As I walk back toward the front of the store, I yell, "Yo, Billy, I'm ready to check out."

After a minute or so of him shuffling down the aisle and setting down everything he's carrying, he comes to the register.

"Uh-oh, you got a broken sink?" he asks as he scans the shutoff valve.

"Fixing a friend's actually. Small problem, big mess, if you know what I mean," I say laughing a little to myself as I think back on the flooded bathroom and the way she looked terrified to go into the basement.

He shakes his head in understanding. I hand him the cash to cover the parts, knowing it's more than the total he's yet to tell me. Grabbing the bag, I turn to walk away as he's still counting the bills.

I'm almost to the door when he yells, "Damnit, son, you and I both know this shit don't cost fifty dollars!"

The bell above the door goes off again as I exit the store. "Sorry, Billy. Didn't catch that! I gotta go, see ya next time!"

"Hello?" even on the phone, she sounds so suspicious.

"I'm back. Wanna let me in?" There's a bit of shuffling on her end like she jumped up from wherever she was sitting.

"Back? Why? You said the parts would have to be ordered," she huffs.

"Guess I got lucky."

I know she doesn't believe any of my shit. I'm not attempting to be all that believable though honestly.

"Right..." I can practically hear the eye roll in her voice, it makes me laugh under my breath. "And why are you calling me? Why didn't you just knock like a normal person?"

I scoff. "Knock? So you can accuse me of stalking you again? Nah, I'm not showing up unannounced ever again if that's how I'll be greeted."

She makes a "hmph" noise like I'm the one in the wrong here.

"You gonna let me in? I'm freezing my balls off out here."

A giggle echoes through the phone, and my heart just about stops at the sound. It's something I want to hear again and again—every damn day of my life.

"It's only forty degrees, Brooks, don't be a baby." *Fuck, I like the sound of my name on her lips.*

I'm standing at the door now, hardware store bag in hand, perfectly content with the temperature. I just needed an excuse to make her come to the door quicker.

"I like it when you call me—"

She opens the door, cutting off my statement. I raise the bag between us, shoving my phone in my pocket as she ushers me back into her house. Being in her home is overwhelming, it's like an overdose of Margot, the space drowns me in the lilac-cherry scent of her.

The door clicks shut behind me, and all her locks snap into place. Security-conscious is what she claimed when I asked about it. My gut tells me it's something else, but she clearly isn't willing to share more. I start toward the bathroom when I hear the pitter-patter of her feet behind me, attempting to catch up. I turn to look back just as she appears at my side.

"Calm down, Freckles, I don't need directions to your bedroom, I remember," I tease, giving her a devilish smirk.

The flush in her cheeks is instant, causing the freckles on her face to stand out even more. I love how easy it is to rile her up. Taking advantage of her shocked silence, I continue into her room and toward the bathroom. I make it right past her bed, almost to the door before she says, "Freckles?"

Sitting the bag on the counter, I turn toward her and say, "Yeah," with a gesture to her face.

"No, I get why. But I thought I was 'Doc?'" she questions, sounding genuinely upset at the nickname switch.

"You were. But then you reminded me on more than one occasion you're a nurse, not a doctor. And I like Freckles better." I shrug, not willing to give her more on the topic.

She stands there, not saying anything. I expected some kind of retort. I wasn't going to give her anything else but expected it regardless. She's still wearing the oversized sweater and those goddamn thigh-highs. I take the moment to look her up and down, finally landing on her face and watching her cheeks pinken again.

"This will take me about an hour, then I'll be out of your hair."

She shakes her head and leaves the bathroom without another word. I start to wonder if I upset her somehow, then I remember I shouldn't care. She's just a girl, a *young* girl. Whether or not she likes me or finds me charming shouldn't be something I care about.

An hour and seven minutes later, I'm done. I just need to go back into the basement, turn the water back on, and hope I didn't fuck it up. The second I exit her bedroom, the smell of whatever Margot's cooking hits my nose. My mouth waters as I realize I didn't actually eat lunch today thanks to the random handyman job Hayes sent me on. As I make my way down the stairs, I hear soft music playing.

When I walk into the kitchen, her back is toward me, standing at the stove.

"Hey, I—" She nearly jumps out of her skin, a yelp following. "Whoa, it's just me, Margot," I say to calm her down. My hands are up in front of me, attempting to reassure her I'm not trying to spook her.

"Sorry!" she says, her hand to her chest covering her heart. "I just didn't hear you coming up behind me," she explains.

"Oh, yeah, light on my feet, I guess," I scramble to ease her embarrassment. "I just gotta go turn the water back on…" I point toward the basement before heading that way.

Once I'm back in the bathroom, I test my handiwork. No more leak. I clean up the mess and make my way to the kitchen where Margot is still fiddling at the stove. Jokingly, I exaggerate my steps so she's sure to hear me and not pull a knife on me.

She spins around, less terrified this time and rolls her eyes at my dramatics. "I had to make sure I didn't scare the living shit out of you again."

She doesn't say anything, but she bites her lip, a contemplative look on her face.

"Right, well… everything is fixed. I should go." I put the trash from the repair into the trashcan in the kitchen, readying myself to leave when she finally speaks again.

"Please don't make me regret this, but… would you want to stay for dinner?"

My eyes meet hers, shock written all over my face, I'm sure. It takes me half a second to think of a clever response, "You asking me out on a date, Freckles?"

Her nose scrunches as she says, "No."

I can't help but laugh. "Ouch, you're really bruising my ego here, woman." I won't tell her this, but at least one of us knows it would be a bad idea.

"I'm sorry, I didn't mean it like that! I just… it's just dinner. Yes or no? As a thank you," she tacks on.

I let the silence sink in between us for a moment, hoping it'll make her sweat a bit before saying, "Sure. Just dinner."

She nods her head in agreement and turns around to serve said dinner. Over her shoulder, she says, "Go ahead and sit down, I'll bring you a plate. What would you like to drink?"

"Normally, I'd say a beer but—"

"But what...?" she asks, her brows furrowed, looking over at me.

"Oh, I—uh, I just figured it's probably hard to get alcohol with a brother like Hayes," I answer sheepishly, desperately trying to tread carefully.

"Why would I—" she starts before her eyes go wide. "Wait. How old do you think I am?"

A nervous chuckle slips from my lips before I say, "Oh, I know better than to answer that question. I just assumed early twenties..." I let my words trail off, not sure if she's going to see it as a compliment or an insult.

"Uh huh, but you also assumed too young to drink legally?"

I don't say a word. I know a trap when I see one.

"I'm old enough to buy my own liquor, I just choose not to."

"Got it, not a drinker. I'll keep it in mind," I say as I chuckle to myself. Ruffling her feathers is way too entertaining.

She rolls her eyes at my response, then turns her attention back to the fridge. "I have sweet tea or... uh, well, water." She's peering inside like another option will suddenly appear if she stares long enough. All I can focus on is how the bottom of her ass cheeks peek out from her sleep shorts with her bent over like that. I take a moment to readjust myself as another part of me takes notice.

"Sweet tea is fine." The table is small, with only three chairs instead of the traditional four. Just another quirk I find fascinating about Margot Mason.

Seconds later, she's setting my plate and glass of sweet tea down in front of me. The pan-seared chicken and asparagus looks fucking delicious. I grab the glass to take a drink before I dig in but immediately spit it back out. She sits across from me, wide-eyed like she has no idea why.

"That," I point to the glass in front of me, "is not sweet tea. That's pure sugar water, Freckles. And it's fucking disgusting."

She folds her arms over her chest, staring me down like I've pissed her off. "I... might enjoy it a tad sweeter than most—"

"A tad?" I question.

"Okay, a good bit. Whatever!" She's getting all mad and huffy again which makes me smirk. "What?" she demands.

"Nothing. You're just cute when you're mad."

She grumbles. "I'm not mad, I'm offended."

I shrug. "Semantics." I bring the first bite of the chicken to my mouth, an audible moan leaving my lips as the flavors burst on my tongue. This woman could give Cary a goddamn run for his money. "Fuck, that's good."

Just like that, the blush returns, and a small smile quirks her lips. "Thanks," she says shyly.

We eat in silence for a few minutes, only the sound of Billie Eilish's "Ocean Eyes Remix" in the background surrounding us, before she points to her head where my scar is and says, "What happened there?"

I take another bite, trying to decide if I should make some shit up or tell her the truth.

"You want the truth or what I tell everyone?" I'm staring at my food but feel her gaze burning into me.

"Obviously the truth. Not sure why you'd offer it if you've lied to everyone else."

It seems like every time I speak, I give this woman another reason to think I'm a shit person. And I am. I can try and fool her with charm, but at the end of the day, I'm exactly who she thinks I am.

"I'm two years older than Cary. So for a couple years, we were in middle school together. He was kind of a scrawny kid, believe it or not. And kids are fucking mean." I pause to shove another bite in my mouth, catching her eyes laser-focused on me.

"Long story short, he got picked on some, and one day I decided I was tired of it. I'd caught fucking Colton Riley talking some shit at the bus stop. He was a big kid—maybe bigger than me at the time and much bigger than Cary—and I'd seen him roughing my brother up a few times. I grabbed him by the back of the shirt and dragged him behind some trees. I got *maybe* one good punch to his arm before he hit me so hard I was seeing fucking stars. I tripped on a tree root and stumbled backwards into a low branch—hard. He laughed and walked away. I missed the bus. And I wasn't about to tell people what actually happened, so I said I fell off my skateboard.

"It bled a good bit. Our neighbor called my parents. My mom was hysterical, and my dad was pissed he had to close the diner for the day to deal with my bullshit. My dad and I were never very close, but I'd pushed his limit that day." A huff of a laugh escapes me at the memory. He'd said I was being a chickenshit about a little blood. It was a lot of blood. The doctor told my mom I'd gotten lucky I didn't end up with a concussion too. But fifteen stitches later, I was left with a three inch scar on the right side of my head, just above my temple.

Right as I'm about to take another bite, Margot says, "And then what?"

I give her a confused look. "What do you mean?"

She puts her fork down, the clink of the silverware hitting the edge of the plate echoes through the room. She almost seems... mad?

"I mean what happened to the Colton kid? Did he get in trouble? And if you lied about it, did you at least tell Cary you tried to stop him from being bullied? Did you ever tell your parents you were just protecting your brother?" Her voice is slightly higher pitched than usual. She seems genuinely concerned about an event that happened twenty years ago.

"No, I never told any of them. It wasn't worth it. And as for Colton, he's still local and still a pain in my ass." My tone is serious. I'm not trying to paint myself as a knight in shining fucking armor. The story sounds like I'm trying to win points with her, convince her I'm the kind of person who sticks up for someone in trouble. I'm not. And I wouldn't have told her the story had she not asked.

"But—"

I cut her off, "Margot, it doesn't matter. It happened, it's over. I've got a sexy scar from it." I give her a smirk, attempting to play the whole thing off. "Let's drop it."

The rest of our dinner is mostly silent. I can tell she's still mad, but I'm not willing to do anything about it. When I'm finished eating, I take my plate to the sink, rinse it off, and dry off my hands.

"Thanks for dinner. It was delicious. I should get going."

She sets her plate on the counter, biting her damn lip, and shuffling her feet on the floor which only draws my attention back to the thigh-highs. "Oh, okay. Yeah. Umm... thank you again for fixing my sink. I really appreciate it."

Grabbing my keys from the counter, I give her a two-finger salute and walk toward the door. It takes me a second to disengage all the locks, and I'm reminded of how anxious she seemed when I brought them up.

By the time I've got them all unlocked, she's right behind me, ready to lock them all back the second I leave. I'm not sure why, but it brings me some comfort knowing she'll be safely locked away in her house.

I don't say goodbye as I open the door, and she closes it immediately without another word.

CHAPTER SIX

I'm hit with the sound of a tattoo gun buzzing and nineties grunge music as soon as I open the door to Mark of Mason.

Hayes has done a great job creating a space with a gritty yet sophisticated aesthetic. The lounge area in the front has a large black leather sofa pushed against a dark forest green wall, strewn with photos of his pencil drawings and some of the more impressive tattoos he's done. The whole space is one large portfolio for his art.

Industrial-style lighting illuminates the dark wooden reception desk, currently being manned by a stunning woman in her late twenties with purple streaked hair, a silver hoop through her eyebrow, and countless earrings adorning the shells of both ears. She's reading one of those celebrity gossip magazines I often see by the check-out counter at the grocery store, the front headline speculating if some A-list actress is pregnant or not.

The desk separates the front of the shop from the work stations in the back. One is occupied by a tattoo artist I've seen here before, currently in the middle of placing a stencil on a woman's ankle. At another, Hayes is focused and in the zone working on someone. He texted me earlier this morning and canceled our lunch, saying he had to take on a last minute client. I knew if I didn't bring him something to eat, he'd probably skip the meal altogether, so I'm here with a sandwich and a very large iced coffee.

I don't have the opportunity to visit the shop often, so I'm not familiar with all of the people Hayes has working for him. The woman—who I assume is the receptionist—finally looks up and locks bored amethyst eyes on me.

"How can I help you?" she says in between chews of her gum.

"Hi," I say and smile at her lukewarm welcome. "I'm here to bring Hayes some lunch." I hold up the coffee and Grayce's Cafe bag. Her eyebrows shoot up, and I'm suddenly realizing she must assume I'm a girl Hayes is seeing. "I'm Margot, his sister."

She looks me up and down, and her demeanor immediately changes as a smile breaks across her face. "Oh my God. You're actually real. Hayes has talked about his 'Booger,' but I was half-convinced he was lying to us about how wholesome you are. But aren't you just a button?"

I shift from foot to foot, confused about what he could have said to these people to make them talk to me like I'm a child. I know my cheeks are flaming, but I'm not sure if it's because I'm embarrassed or slightly annoyed with Hayes.

Thankfully, it seems the woman catches on to my discomfort because she continues, "I'm just kidding. The man barely speaks, just keeps telling us all to keep our hands off you. I'm Kori, by the way. Go on back, he's just working on Archer."

At least that's a name I recognize. Archer has worked with Hayes for about a year now, though I haven't had the opportunity to meet him yet.

I step around the desk and make my way over to where Hayes' hulking form is bent over, tattooing Archer's forearm. It looks like he's doing some continuation of previous work to shade parts on a full sleeve. He catches me coming from the corner of his eye and stops the tattoo gun before looking up and gracing me with a small smile.

"Hey," I say and then turn to the man in the chair. "Hi, I'm Margot."

"Hey, Margot," the blond says without the usual South Carolinian accent I'm used to. "That's a pretty name. Can't say I've seen you around here before." Dimples. The man has dimples. And yet again, my cheeks are blushing, giving away every thought in my head.

My eyes swing to my brother as he grumbles out, "You really want to start flirting with my sister when I've got you under the needle?" Archer's dimples disappear quickly as his flirty smile falls away.

"Ah, shit. I'll shut up now," he says, and Kori cackles from her stoop at the desk.

"He was just being nice, Hayes," I say indignantly. "You can't keep scaring people away from me. I'll never make any friends." Hayes goes back to his work, the sound of the tattoo gun buzzing back to life.

"Trust me, Booger, Archer's not trying to be your friend," he says with a glare at the man in front of us. "You said Thea wants to hang out. Go be her friend." His tone is flat, and annoyance flares in my chest at his dismissal. Sometimes I feel like Hayes still sees me as a child he needs to take care of.

But then I consider his suggestion. "Hmm, maybe. It seems like she has a lot going on right now. I think Cary went back to Seattle, and she's not in a good place."

Archer looks up and asks, "Thea's the one who works over at RED?" I'm surprised he knows her, but then I remember there's little to no privacy in a town this small. No one can keep a secret in Indigo Hill. Thank goodness I live in Southbury.

"Yeah." I sigh. "Cary's parents left the restaurant to both of them, and it's been a difficult transition. There's some history there."

"Some present too," the lady in the next chair pipes up, her eyes wide and sparkling with conspiracy. "I hate to gossip, especially when I don't have all of the facts, just what I've heard in passing."

"So, then shut it, Tiffany," my brother snaps in his deep rumble as he sits back and wipes at the spot he was working on before hunching over again. "No need to start rumors. You know how this town is."

I change the subject away from Thea, knowing I wouldn't want anyone speaking about me like this. "Why did you send Brooks to my house yesterday?" Not that I'm complaining. I had a nice time with him. The shameless flirting, the slight vulnerability—seeing a new side to him yesterday makes me think people write him off too soon. He clearly has a soft spot for his brother, despite what he wants people to think. I have a feeling his devil-may-care attitude is all one big act, and something about the look in his eyes last night makes me want to find a way for him to drop it.

"Why? What happened?" His tattoo gun shuts off as his gaze snaps to mine.

"Nothing happened," I say, trying to calm his overprotective side. "He fixed my sink. But you could have warned me."

"Warned you about what? How do you know Brooks?"

"Through Thea, actually. She asked me to... help him once. Does he work for you or something?" Hayes looks around, avoiding my eyes, but he catches Kori's gaze, and they seem to have an unspoken conversation. *What isn't he telling me?*

"Yeah, he's my... handyman," he finally says, the last word almost coming out as a question. Then, his attention is back on Archer's arm.

"Your handyman? I thought he... okay, whatever," I say, shaking my head, not believing him but also knowing I won't get any more from him. "Have you gone to see Dad recently? I'm worried about him."

Hayes scoffs. "You've been worried about him for twenty years. He's fine, I saw him last week."

"Last week? Hayes, you know he needs our help. Every time I go over there, the place looks worse and worse. What if something happened to him? He wouldn't even be able to call for help since he never charges his cell."

Hayes shuts off the tattoo gun and places it on his work station. "Archer, go take a break. Five minutes." He quickly covers his forearm with saran wrap and secures it with medical tape. Archer shuffles off the table and steps into the break room in the back of the shop. Hayes covers his station with saran wrap and removes his gloves.

"Can we not do this here? I don't need the people who work for me knowing my business."

"We could have talked about it over lunch, but you canceled on me. Again," I singsong, teasing him. He opens his mouth to argue, but I continue, "And I get it, you're busy and worried about the other shop."

"I'm not worried."

"Okay, sure. You're not worried. You're just working fourteen hours a day, seven days a week because you love it so much." He grumbles something under his breath in response, but I can't quite make it out. "I'm here because I miss you. And if this is the only way I get to see my favorite brother, then it's what I have to do."

"Favorite, huh?"

I smile sweetly at him. "Favorite. Only. Same difference," I tease him, but he knows how much I love him. Hayes is my everything. He's been the best brother to me my entire life. But he's also been a friend when I needed it, a father when my own couldn't handle the responsibility, and—quite unfortunately for both of us—a health ed teacher for a few very awkward conversations when I was in middle and high school.

When our mom died, I was only two, and my dad slowly shut down and checked out. Hayes was the one to step up. I don't remember the early years, but I can't imagine it was easy for him to be the most responsible person in the house at fourteen years old.

He also helped me get back on my feet when I came back from Charleston with no notice. He'd known I was having a hard time at work, but I didn't give him a heads up when I showed up on his doorstep. He took me in without a second thought.

I've only ever known him as my rock, my protector. He's never been anything but dependable and stalwart in any situation. He's always my first call when things aren't going right. At least with most things.

The door to the shop opens, and a man beelines for the front desk to check in with Kori. Hayes stiffens and straightens at the sight. My time with him is up.

"I guess I'll let you get back to it," I say, winding my arms around his torso. Hayes' arms engulf me in a bear hug.

"Love you, Booger," he says loud enough for only me to hear.

"Love you," I say as I pull back. Then I add more forcefully with a playful glare, "Go see Dad." Hayes grumbles in response, and I make my way to the front of the shop. I pass by the man who walked in, lounging on the sofa.

"Caine," Hayes calls from the back, and the man stands up. I smile at him and note the prominent red and black scorpion tattoo on the front of his neck.

I spend the ride to work wondering just how much a tattoo like that—or any—hurts and if I could find the courage to get one someday.

"What's got that brow so furrowed, Margot?" Lydia's voice pulls me out of my head and back into her room at Saint Stephen's. I don't know how long I've been lost in thought as I've folded and refolded her extra blankets. Shaking my head, I bring myself back to the present.

"Sorry," I say with a sheepish smile. "I'm up in my head today. Just the meds and I'm done here. Do you need anything else before I head out?"

I log the medication, dosage, and time on the tablet before turning to her and holding it out.

"Yes," she replies, taking the small plastic cup containing her pills from me. "Sit and talk to me. Clearly, you have something brewing up there." She motions toward her head with a chuckle. I hesitate for a second, not sure what to tell her. I don't even know where my head is. Remembering how warm and thoughtful she's been when I've come to her with my issues in the past has me sitting down in the chair next to hers, both situated next to the window overlooking the gardens in the back of the building. I stare out into the crisp day for a moment, the trees swaying slightly in the breeze, sun bright.

"I'm thinking of doing something a little... reckless," I breathe out finally, my eyes still peering outside.

"Reckless, hm?" she hums thoughtfully. After popping the pills into her mouth, she takes a sip of water from the glass sitting on the table next to her. "Well, I've done my fair share of reckless things in life, and let me tell you—they're always the most fun." I turn my head and find her smiling fondly at me. "Want to tell me about him?"

I huff out a laugh, and my cheeks heat. "Am I that obvious?"

"I've watched Thea fall in love before, I know what smitten looks like."

"I'm not smitten," I rush out. "Just... interested."

"Okay, *interested* then," she says, humoring me. "So, why are you hesitating?"

I look down at my hands as I play with the ends of the drawstrings on my scrub pants. I bite my lip, unsure how much to tell her.

"He might not be the best choice. And people won't understand." I look up at her and add, "They'll definitely talk."

Her eyes narrow on me as she cautiously says, "It's not Cary, is it?"

I bark out a laugh. "Oh my God, no! It's actually the other Grant brother who keeps running through my head."

"Oh, whew, we were about to have a very different conversation," she says, her eyebrows rising as realization hits. "So, Brooks, huh?"

"Yeah..." I draw out with a slow nod. "He feels dangerous in a way but not unsafe. Does that make sense? I think there's a good heart underneath all of that... baggage. Am I crazy for wanting to pursue him?"

"I've seen that boy grow up, and he's had a hard time of it, some of it because of his family, some of it his own doing. Unfortunately, he was the emotional punching bag for his father when he was still alive, I'm not sure why, but it wasn't fair to him," Lydia replies, her tone somber.

We're quiet for a moment as I let her words sink in.

"But that motorcycle," she says, her eyes sparking and her lips quirking. "If I were thirty years younger, I'd let him take me for a ride."

"Lydia!" My eyes widen at her insinuation, and I tap her forearm with a laugh. "You're just as bad as Georgie."

"I may be sick and old, but I'm still a woman with eyes," she says. "You *know* that man knows what he's doing."

My cheeks heat again, and I'm back to fiddling with the drawstrings. "Yeah, that's also a concern for me. I'm not exactly what you'd call experienced." My chest tightens with my confession, and I look up to gauge her reaction, but all I find is warmth and understanding.

"You said he has a good heart and makes you feel safe, trust your instincts. Go at your pace and remember 'no' is a full sentence," she says, then tacks on, "And if he does anything untoward, I know people who can rough him up."

We both laugh, and the tension in my chest eases. "Thanks, I'll keep it in mind."

Chapter Seven

The smell of coffee invades my senses as I rummage through my kitchen drawers looking for my spare lighter. The rent on this place is great, but the drawback is living above a damn cafe constantly brewing coffee from five in the morning to two in the afternoon. I've always hated the smell of it. Growing up at my parents' diner is probably the reason why.

Luckily, I've been spending most of my time at my parents' house renovating so I can sell it. Which is where I'm heading as soon as I find my fucking lighter. Just as I pull the next drawer open, my phone vibrates in my pocket.

12/5 10:42 a.m.

Hayes: FYI, I told Margot you're my handy-man when she asked how we know each other.

12/5 10:43 a.m.

Me: You're fucking kidding me.

Delivered

12/5 10:45 a.m.

Hayes: No? What was I supposed to say?

12/5 10:45 a.m.

Me: Literally anything else, dude.

Delivered

12/5 10:48 a.m.

Hayes: Why does it matter? Just play along if she mentions it.

12/5 10:48 a.m.

Me: I hate you.

Delivered

Great. As if I didn't already feel like a loser, now Margot has verification I am. Fucking handyman. Out of all the things he could come up with, of course he went with that. So it looks like I did a fucking house job for her by fixing her sink.

I shake my head at the thought, hating that I even care. My spare lighter is nowhere to be found, and I really need a nicotine fix. The drawer slams shut as I fling it closed, rattling everything inside. I'll have to stop at the gas station on my way to Elsher's office.

He called me yesterday while I was at Margot's. I hate talking on the phone, so I wouldn't have answered anyway, but I had it on silent and never saw the call come through. When I got home,

I finally saw the notification. He'd left a voicemail telling me the papers for the house were ready for me to sign. I knew it was coming, but it didn't make it any easier to hear.

Initially, I'd been pissed my parents left their house to me in their will; I'd expected to get RED. I thought putting all the time and effort into the place would show them I could handle it, but it didn't. Instead, I got a house in need of a fuckton of work before I can even consider selling it. *Figures.*

James Elsher—the executor of their will—is an attorney in Southbury, about thirty minutes west of Indigo Hill. It's also the town Margot lives in, not that it matters. It's chilly out today, so I grab a jacket before leaving my apartment.

The moment the door shuts, I hear soft music playing from Grayce's Cafe just below me. The woman is nice enough, but her taste in music is shit. She doesn't know me very well, aside from the blend of common knowledge floating around town and the rumors whispered every time I enter a room. She has no idea I designed her branding a few years ago, and she never will. Unless Thea decides to spill, none of them will ever know.

I'm proud of the work I did, it was a good temporary distraction, but it isn't my passion. I want to tattoo, I just need to land an opportunity at a shop. Maybe I'll finally leave this shithole town once I sell my parents' house and move to a city with more studios.

Putting my helmet on, I swing my leg over my bike and bring it to life. The engine revs, and a group passing by on the sidewalk looks over. I throw a wink to the women, along with my signature smirk, as their eyes finally meet mine after scanning me from head to toe. One of them waves, making me chuckle to myself. Margot had me thinking I'd lost my charm, but clearly, I've still got it.

"Just sign right here, son," Mr. Elsher says as he points to the line. His desk is just as messy as it was the last time I was here a little over two weeks ago. I'm no professional, by any means, but I wonder how he conducts any kind of work. He's constantly looking for things buried under stacks of paper. The guy makes me look put-together.

"You need anything else from me?" I ask, placing the pen back in the holder on his desk.

"No, this was all, but..." he starts as he shuffles through a stack next to him. "I did forget—ah-ha! Here it is. I forgot to give this to y'all when you were here." He's holding out a manila folder, my parents' names written on the corner.

"Right. Thanks," I say as I take it from him, shoving my copy of the deed I just signed into it. "I'll see myself out then."

I go to turn around when he stops me. "Hugh—"

I cut him off, "Brooks. No one calls me Hugh."

"My apologies, Brooks. I just want to extend my condolences once more about your parents. I heard the man responsible for the accident was charged with a DUI and prison time. I'm glad y'all are getting some justice after this tragedy."

The appropriate response would be to say "thank you" or agree with him about the drunk who ran a red light and caused my life to upend in an instant. Instead, I just stare at him. I'm not sure what to say, it all feels too complicated. My relationship with my parents wasn't rainbows and fucking butterflies. They consistently let me know how much of a disappointment I am. I stayed. I was here. And yet, I was the son who was told how much of a letdown he'd become. It was all bullshit. I'd been willing to give up everything for their stupid fucking restaurant while Carrington was off in Seattle pretending none of us existed.

And yeah, I am bent out of shape about their deaths. I can't remember the last thing I said to my mother, and that shit haunts me. We'd been so close when I was a kid. It wasn't until she sided with my father about my "unrealistic aspirations" that things changed. Then I watched as she let the same thing happen with Cary. And I understood why. She didn't want to be on the receiving end of Owen Grant's temper. He'd never been physically abusive, but he could be a mean son of a bitch—not to mention as close-minded as they come.

Ironically, the only soft spot he seemed to have was for Thea. It was some kind of unspoken agreement that none of us told her what he'd thought of her years ago before she and Cary left for Seattle. When she came back to care for her mom, Lydia, he'd somehow turned over a new leaf. I never understood it, and quite frankly, I never asked. A part of me wondered if he thought being nice to Thea would make Cary come back. Joke's on him since he only came back when they died, only to leave again.

Still not knowing what to say, I nod, turn around, and walk out. The last thing I want to discuss is my parents' death and the man responsible for it. What I want and need is a drink and a smoke.

Lucky for me, Southbury has just the kind of hole-in-the-wall bar I need. It's the same place Cary and I came after the reading of the will. I'm sitting in the same booth, thinking back on the conversation we had that day. He'd been so dense, thinking he understood why I was upset about our parents leaving RED to him and Thea.

It felt good to take him down a peg or two, remind him how his move to Seattle affected all of us. And it felt good to witness him realize how selfish he'd been as a kid who never saw anything past his own issues, wants, and needs. I can't say it wasn't amusing to watch him finally realize we had two very different upbringings in real time. Cary got away with everything as a kid, while I was punished and lectured for every move I made. I never knew why, and I never had the balls to ask before my parents' untimely death.

I pull my glass to my lips just as I hear a voice that instantly makes my blood boil. Colton is with John and Trevor—or Tweedle Dipshit and Tweedle Dumbass, as I call them—at his side, sliding up to the bar and already hitting on the bartender.

Not ten seconds later, Tweedle Dumbass turns around and sees me. He wastes no time whispering into Colton's ear like a fucking schoolgirl. I'm already having a shit day. The last thing I need is to deal with these assholes.

"Save it," I say from my booth the moment Colton turns around.

"I was just going to ask if losing to me meant you quit. Haven't seen you at The Pit since that night. Didn't take you for such a chickenshit."

My eyes roll. I hate this dude. "Just been busy, Colton. Some of us have lives." That's a lie. I don't exactly have a life, but I'm not about to tell him I've been too busy nursing a bruised ego to ask for another fight.

"Sure, sure. Working at your dead parents' restaurant as what... a busboy?"

"Your uppercuts are better than your insults." He thinks pointing out my dead parents will get a reaction out of me, takes a lot more than stating the obvious.

"Whatever you say, *Brooksy Boy*."

I instantly see red again. I'm pissed he knows the nickname gets to me. I'm even more pissed he knows why. I slowly get up, walking toward him without saying a word. Once I'm in his face, I lean in farther so we're chest to chest, and my mouth is right beside his ear as I say, "Call me that one more fucking time, and I'll put you six-feet-under right next to my parents." I punctuate my threat by quickly grabbing his head and slamming it onto the bartop. "I fucking dare you, Colton."

Tweedle Dipshit jumps up, spilling his beer. "Dude, what the fuck?" he screams as blood seeps from the corner of Colton's lip. He wastes no time, and before I know what's happening, he headbutts me while mumbling something about me being outnumbered.

"You'll pay for that one, Grant," Colton says. My vision is slightly blurry now, thanks to his crony. Colton spits blood onto the bar, a smirk playing on his lips like he can't wait for his retribution as if Dipshit didn't just take care of it for him.

"Sure thing, Riley," I mutter, shooting him a middle finger. I'm about to turn around and leave when I hear someone clear their throat from behind me, and the mirror on the barback tells me I'm fucked.

"I'm gonna need you to come with me, son," says the deputy I didn't realize was in the bar with us.

"Fuck me," I mumble to myself as I turn to face him.

"Let's go."

"Any chance you'd believe it was self-defense?" I try to joke, hoping it'll charm him into letting me go and pretending he didn't see anything.

"You can plead your case when we book you," he replies, unfazed. Taking a deep breath, I pull my hands behind me before he has to ask. The handcuffs squeeze my wrists as he clasps them then shoves me toward the exit of the bar.

On the fourth ring, Ripley finally answers, "Hello?"

"Hey—"

"Brooks? Where are you calling from?"

I run a hand down my face, dreading what I have to say. "Jail." I don't elaborate. I knew the second I said the word, he'd start in with a million questions, so I didn't see the point.

"Excuse me? Did you just—holy fuck. Thea is going to kill you! Jail? Again? What did you do this time?"

When he finally takes a breath, I interrupt, "Can we just... keep it between us, maybe? The shithead decided not to press charges, so I just need someone to come pick me up. My bike isn't here."

"Oh. Uh, shit. Yeah. Give me like... ten minutes, and I'll leave here."

"Thanks, man. I'm in Southbury, not Indigo."

"Got it. Okay. Be there soon. I expect the full story when I pick your sorry ass up."

"Yup," is all I say in response before I'm hanging up.

Chapter Eight

I shift my car into park and look out at the dilapidated house in front of me. In the dim light of the moon overhead combined with my headlights, I can see one of the shutters on the second story is hanging askew, there are a few roof shingles missing, and the front porch steps are crumbling. I heave a sigh. I've asked Hayes repeatedly to get someone out here to fix the structural issues at least; the last thing we need is for the steps to collapse under someone.

Maybe I can ask Brooks to come take a look. I'm surprised Hayes hasn't already, since Brooks is his handyman.

But then I reconsider—it would lead to questions I'm not sure I would want Brooks to know the answers to. He'd see my dad, how he lives, how he's let everything go.

I'd have to explain how my brother raised me, making my lunches for school, signing permission slips, and driving me to and from dance classes. All the while my dad drank himself unconscious in between crying bouts and telling me I look just like our mom.

But maybe Brooks would understand. From what Lydia said, he had a difficult relationship with his own father. Mine wasn't mean while I was growing up, mostly he just wasn't there. Physically, he was parked in front of the TV with a bottle in hand, but a big part of him died alongside my mom, at least that's what I've been told. Besides the short moments of sobriety he managed over the years—which were few and far between—this is the version of him I grew up with.

Things were different before I came back. Hayes and I lived here before I went to college, and my brother took a more active role in caretaking for our father. He wanted my sole focus to be on school and being a normal teenager.

Once I moved out to Charleston, Hayes moved out on his own too and only checked in periodically with Dad. I guess he was done raising a kid, he didn't feel like raising his father also. I didn't realize all he did for him until I came back and assumed the responsibility myself.

I make a mental note to talk to Hayes about the condition of the house again as I step out of my car and up the precarious steps. As soon as I open the door and the stench of stale alcohol hits my nostrils, my phone rings.

Hayes.

"Hello?" I answer.

"Margot," he says. *Not the usual "Booger" I'm used to, this must be serious.* "Where are you?"

"I'm at Dad's," I reply. "Everything okay?"

He grunts, and someone else speaks in the background on his end, but I can't make out what they're saying. "Fuck," Hayes mutters. "I need you."

"What's going on?"

"I need you to come to The Pit—I mean, the clearing that backs up to woods off the Pineville Road dead end." Something in his voice tells me not to ask any more questions.

"I'll be there in a few," I say, already closing the door behind me.

There's only background noise on his end, then he clips out, "Bring your bag," and the line goes dead.

My bag. The emergency bag I keep in my car in case I need to staunch bleeding or bandage a wound or administer naloxone. My stomach bottoms out, but I keep moving, getting behind the wheel of my car and peeling out of my dad's long gravel driveway, hooking a left toward Pineville Road.

Hayes has never asked me for help before, not like this at least. Potential scenarios run through my head, each one more dire than the last, but what I'm most confused about is the location—'The Pit' as he called it. The clearing he referred to is set about three hundred feet back from the dead-end road, past a cluster of woods. It's technically located on the back end of Dad's property, right around where it abuts the nature preserve. There's nothing there. The closest neighbor is miles down the road in the opposite direction. What could he possibly be doing there, and why did I hear so many voices in the background?

As soon as I turn off my car, the thumping of bass reverberates throughout the small space, coming from somewhere beyond the trees in front of me. I parked on the grass off Pineville Road where it hits a dead end that backs up to the woods at the edge of Dad's land. There are a few other cars scattered around the entrance to an off-road path about the width of one car. Time and what appears to be regular use by cars have worn tracks into the grass and dirt.

I open the car door, and the music gets louder. Not seeing anyone around, I grab my emergency bag from the trunk and head to the makeshift road, using my phone as a flashlight. About fifty yards in, I'm blinded by a bright light in my face.

"Shit, sorry, Margot," a familiar voice says, coming closer. The flashlight lowers, and in the dim illumination of both of our lights, I make out Kori approaching. "C'mon, it's just up ahead."

She turns and quickly makes her way back from where she came. I walk a little faster to catch up to her. "What's going on, Kori? Where's Hayes?"

She throws a look over her shoulder, a blend of guilt and sadness, but doesn't say anything. I follow her, the music continuing to get louder. There's light ahead pouring out from between the trees.

When we finally step into the clearing, the bass vibrates my chest cavity as I look around at the mass of people milling about. Some are standing around, laughing and drinking in small groups, some are sitting on the tailgates of their pickups smoking. Off to the left appears to be a dancefloor of sorts with a DJ on an elevated platform.

The whole area is lit up by tall floodlights, the majority of which are aimed on a leveled center area where the grass is almost non-existent, just trampled dirt. The space is about twenty feet by twenty feet, and I can't take my eyes off of it, mainly because they catch on the small pools of blood slowly seeping into the ground in the middle of the brightly lit area.

Kori moves me quickly through the throngs of people around the perimeter of the cleared space to a trailer hitched to a large truck that's just outside the reach of the lights. A generator rumbles next to the trailer with wires leading out in all directions.

"He's just in there," Kori says, motioning with her head to the trailer door. I heave out a sigh and turn the knob to open the door to whatever my brother has gotten himself into now.

"Booger, thank fuck," he says, relief and worry evident on his face. The door bangs shut behind me, and as soon as I take in the rest of the interior, adrenaline begins to course through me, and my heart speeds up.

Hayes is standing at the edge of a small table, his hands cradling the head of a young shirtless man who's lying on the surface, his legs dangling. The man—boy, really—groans, and I take in his state. His face is covered in bruises and cuts dripping blood onto the table beneath him. One of his shoulders looks dislocated, and he keeps trying to reach for it.

"Shhh, don't move, Max. You're going to be okay," Hayes murmurs and looks up at me. "Margot's going to take care of you." Hayes' usually composed, stoic face is etched with concern. There have only been a handful of times I've seen Hayes be anything other than calm, controlled. He can usually assess a situation and immediately take charge of resolving any issues. Seeing this boy hurt has him unravelling.

I move closer to get a better look at his condition. "Hi, Max. I'm Margot. Is it okay if I take a look?" I ask, my eyes running down from the cuts on his face to the deformed shoulder to the bruising on his ribs, all the way down to his sneaker-covered feet. I catalogue the injuries I can see, all consistent with a physical assault.

Max groans and slightly nods. I look up to Hayes. "What happened?"

"He was in a fight."

I look at him incredulously. "Yeah, I got that. What happened?" I refocus on Max as I use some hand sanitizer and put on examination gloves. I gently feel around his ribs, and he winces. I then move to his shoulder and lastly, his face. A few of the cuts might need a stitch or two, but nothing appears to be broken. Reducing the dislocated shoulder is the priority.

"He took a couple of big hits and went down hard right onto his shoulder," Hayes explains. "It took him a while to come to."

"He probably has a concussion. And his shoulder is dislocated. He needs to go to the hospital," I say.

"No, no hospital. Just set it, and fix up his face," Hayes insists.

"Hayes. Wh—what is going on here?" I ask.

"Just fix him, Margot!" he snaps, and I flinch. I rarely see his anger, and it causes a pit in my stomach to open up. I push the anxiety away and focus on Max.

"Okay, Max. We're going to reduce your shoulder first. I'm going to go slow, and I'm sorry in advance if it hurts," I say gently as I place one hand on his upper arm near the elbow and grip his wrist with the other, positioning his elbow at a ninety degree angle. "Try to relax your arm as much as possible, and take a few deep breaths." I hold steady as his chest moves up and down in long pulls, and his arm grows more lax in my hands.

Slowly, I rotate the arm toward myself, keeping the elbow tucked into his body. His face screws up in pain, and I pause my movement, giving him a minute to breathe and for his muscles to relax. I start moving slowly again, and once his forearm is rotated almost ninety degrees from his body, I see the shoulder joint slot into place, and Max groans.

After gently placing his arm across his chest, I dig through my bag for a sling. Hayes helps me raise Max's torso off the table, and I slide it behind his back and secure his arm in place.

"It needs to be iced regularly for the next few days, and he needs to take ibuprofen to help with the swelling," I say to my brother since I expect him to take responsibility for the boy.

I then pull out my wound care kit and set up the supplies next to Max.

"Any chance you have warm water here? I need to clean up his face," I say, looking around the small trailer.

Hayes stands and opens the door. "Kori," he says to her. She must have been standing right outside, waiting for us. "Bring me a few bottles of water." Hayes comes back to us, and we sit and wait for Kori.

A few minutes pass, and then the door opens, Kori walks in carrying an armful of bottled water. "How's the kid?" she asks, eyeing Max from afar. Another young face sporting a bruised eye pops in through the door to get a look but quickly rushes out following a glare from my brother.

Hayes grunts in dismissal and turns to me. "It's not warm. Will it do?" I nod to him and grab some packets of gauze, wetting them with one of the bottles and gently wiping at Max's face to clear off the blood and dirt.

Thankfully, the cuts don't seem as bad as I first thought once the grime is gone. I can apply liquid bandage to most, the others are shallow enough I'll be able to place Steri-Strips.

Applying the bandages to Max's face reminds me of the last time I had to fix someone up after a fight. *Brooks.* Did he get his injuries in a fight like this too? What is happening here? Who is Max to my brother? Hundreds of questions swirl through my brain as I work.

I check him over for a concussion and recommend he sees a doctor, avoids screens, and rests. I clean up all of the dirty gauze and used supplies then dispose of everything, including my gloves, in the trash in the corner of the trailer.

After giving Max instructions on how to keep everything clean and what to look for if the wounds get infected, I give him a couple ibuprofen, and Hayes helps him out of the trailer and into the back of the truck. He makes sure he's comfortable and closes the door, allowing Max to rest.

I stand at the trailer and look out over the crowd, still partying—not a care in the world, like a kid wasn't just beaten.

As soon as Hayes steps up to me, I round on him. "What in the world is happening here, Hayes? Who are all of these people?

What happened to Max?" My voice rises with each word, my calm nurse demeanor forgotten.

"Calm down, Booger," he says, in his usual gruff way. "Max is a good kid. He just lost tonight." He winces as though he didn't mean to say that.

"Tonight? How long has this been going on? How often does he fight?" I ask.

"It's fine, Margot. He's fine, you made sure of that," he replies.

"I made sur—Are you kidding me? You can't justify a young kid fighting and getting hurt like that just because I'm here. What would have happened if you couldn't reach me? And what is this anyway?" I say, looking around, *really* taking in my surroundings. "Is this some sort of fight club?"

"No," he says, but his voice gives him away. After a moment, he sighs and resignedly adds, "They do it for the cash. I help them train, and they get a part of the winnings. A lot of these kids don't have anything else. Shitty families and all that. Max and his brother are living with a junkie uncle, and this is how he earns enough to feed the two of them."

I'm appalled and heartbroken for Max. "I... How, Hayes? How could you have gotten mixed up with this?"

"Would you rather he be fighting in the streets, with no over-sight, no one to help him? Or worse yet, dealing?" His expression is hard with conviction, but his eyes plead for me to understand. And I do—partly. My brother has always had a big heart. He's a caretaker and a problem solver. This feels misguided though.

Loud music fills the air of the clearing while I'm quiet for a long moment, trying to process everything I've learned. I feel like

I don't know my brother at all right now. "I... have no words, Hayes," I finally say. "I need to get out of here and try to wrap my head around you running an illegal fighting ring out of Dad's backyard."

"You're making a bigger deal out of this than it deserves," he says quietly. "Sorry for snapping at you before. And thank you. For what you did for him. He really is a good kid. " My heart softens at his tone, genuine and maybe even a little contrite.

I wrap my arm around his back in a side hug. "He's important, huh?"

"I just want to help," Hayes says.

"I know. I'll call you tomorrow to check on him. Please bring him to the hospital if his head doesn't seem right."

"I will, I promise," he says and pulls me in for a real hug. "I love you."

"I love you too, big brother," I murmur into his massive shoulder.

CHAPTER NINE

I spent a whole two hours in lockup yesterday before Colton decided going up against me wasn't worth it. If he'd pressed charges, I would have gotten Hayes to dig up some shit on him, but thankfully, he came to his senses. Would "he pissed me off" have held up in court? Probably not, but Colton isn't squeaky clean. I would have been fine, I'm just glad I don't have to deal with it.

Would have been nice to not have to deal with Rip's smug face when he picked me up, but it was better than calling Thea or Cary. I didn't tell him everything, just that Colton said some shit and I retaliated.

Once I got my phone back, I saw the multiple texts I'd missed.

12/8 4:47 p.m.

Thea: Hey… I just wanted to check in. I haven't heard from you in days now…

12/8 5:01 p.m.

Freckles: Hey! Happy to report the sink is still working. Thank you again!

12/8 5:36 p.m.

Freckles: Hayes was right, you are the best handyman in town haha.

I haven't been back to RED since the night before Thanksgiving when Cary's life blew up—over a week now. Maybe closer to ten days? Shit, I don't even know what day it is. I'm sure they're all pissed at me for missing Thanksgiving lunch.

The last thing I wanted to do was be at a sad as fuck memorial for my parents, which is what they'd turned it into. I get it—my mom loved Thanksgiving. But I just... I couldn't do it.

Thea made sure to inform me Cary flew back to Seattle the next day. I have no idea what's going on between the two of them, and quite frankly, I don't care. All I'm concerned about is finishing these renovations so I can sell this place, getting an apprenticeship somewhere, and beating Colton's ass again.

I'm back at Billy's but for myself this time. I figured starting in the kitchen would be easiest, since I have some experience after doing some upgrades to Thea's house a couple years back. Granted it was simpler than this, just some painting and a new countertop for her island. The pictures I found online all look fancy as fuck. They've got new, shiny sinks with weird-ass faucets and modern hardware for the cabinets and drawers. Currently, the Grant house is sporting the bright gold round knobs from the 80s. Not going to lie, I didn't think I'd need to change them until I saw photos of some other flipped houses.

Turns out, the fancy shit is what sells homes. I just hope Billy carries something meeting those standards. As I walk past the register at the front, I holler over, "Hey, Billy-Bob, not working too hard, I hope." He chuckles and shakes his head.

Just as I'm about to pass by the plumbing aisle, my eyes catch on a mess of brown curls. The familiar strands cascade over Margot's shoulders, and my gaze traces the lines of her body, clinging to her curves. A smile threatens to take over my face, so I do my best at reeling it back.

"What's got you thinking so hard, Freckles?" I ask as I saunter toward her. She doesn't jump this time, which brings me more joy than it should.

"Oh, Brooks! Hi. What're you doing here?" she asks with a smile, lighting up the dreary world around her. But before I can answer, she starts up again, her good humor dropping with each word. "Oh my goodness, your face!"

Shit.

I forgot about the massive bruise on my forehead where Colton's lacky headbutted me like a fucking child to get me back for slamming Colt's face into the counter of the bar.

"Margot, chill." Her eyes narrow. "I'm fine. Bruises fade, you know that." She sets her lips in a tight line. I think back on what I said and come to the conclusion it was probably the word "chill" that caused the scowl.

Noted, won't be using it again.

"What happened?" she asks as she runs concerned eyes down the rest of my body, probably looking for other injuries.

"I'm fine, promise. You should see the other guy though," I say with a smirk, hoping it'll get me off the hook.

"Okay, Killer. I think we established last time I fixed you up, this isn't a good look for you. Did you get these," motioning to the bruises on my face, "at The Pit? Are you part of Hayes'—" she cuts herself off as Billy turns down the aisle, already talking to me from the other end.

"Brooks, my boy, I hate to interrupt, but I've just gotten a shipment of toilets in, and James called out today. Is there any way you can help me move them to the back?"

I start to walk backward but point to Margot and say, "Don't go anywhere, I'll help you find what you're looking for."

Margot gives me an incredulous look then says, "Do you work here too?"

I chuckle as I spin toward Billy to follow him to the back of the hardware store. Once we're out of earshot, Billy turns around and says, "She's pretty."

Yeah, she fucking is, I think, but without missing a beat, I reply, "She's Hayes' sister."

He nods his head in understanding as he says, "Oh…"

Moving the toilets for Billy went fairly quickly and saved me from a conversation I'm not ready to have with Margot. The start of it sounded like she knows about Hayes' side gig, but as far as I know, he's kept everyone not involved in the dark about it. And knowing him, he'd want to keep her out of the shady parts of his life, keep her protected.

She's in the same aisle I left her in, scrolling through her phone. "Sorry about that. So, what're we fixing today?"

She lifts her gaze, a hint of a smile playing on her lips as she makes eye contact with me. "Toilet issues, funny enough. It won't stop running, and I figured I'd try to fix this one myself."

"Uh huh, how's that going?" I ask, trying not to sound too flirty.

"Don't make fun! I just need to find the flapper-thingy. I plan on watching a video on how to replace it so I don't have to bug anyone." Her cheeks flame a pretty pink shade, making the freckles covering her face pop even more.

"Don't forget to cut the water off before you start," I remind her, knowing the conclusion she'll jump to.

"I have to go down to the basement to fix this?" Her eyes widen, fear shining through.

"Nah, there's a knob shutoff behind the toilet, don't worry," I tease.

She looks back to the shelves in front of us, scanning the items for what she needs.

"Pro tip, it's easier to find things when you're in the right aisle." The look on her face is priceless. She's spent the last however many minutes looking at sink plumbing.

She brings her hands to her face, covering it as she mumbles, "Why did I think I could do this?"

I grab one of her hands, pulling it away and lacing my fingers through hers to pull her down the aisle. "Come on, Freckles, this way." I try not to think about how perfectly her hand fits in mine or how it warms a part of me I didn't know was frozen over. It's not that I mind affection or human touch, I just don't get it very often—unless it's preceded by a few beers and a not-so-discreet look in a dimly lit bar. Definitely not in this way.

Her hand is small in mine, soft and warm. My own calloused palm engulfs it fully, my tattooed knuckles acting like a protective shell. It serves as just another reminder of how different we are, how precious and innocent she is and how hardened and jaded I've become.

Even without Hayes' constant warnings for everyone to stay away from his sister, I know I need to steer clear. I can't taint her with my uselessness.

But her sweetness is also drawing me in. The idea of corrupting her innocence just to hear the sounds she'd make, see the way the green in her eyes darken with desire, feel what her small hands would do to my body is too tempting.

I need to get my thoughts back on track.

Once I've led her to the next aisle over, I abruptly pull my hand from hers as if it burned me. I reach for the part she needs with that same hand, knowing damn well I didn't have to let go of hers to grab it. I had to pull away before I allowed my delusions to run wild, before I crossed a line.

I clear my throat, ridding myself of the inappropriate thoughts about her hand and how good it would feel somewhere else on my body.

"This is what you need. It's an easy fix, and I have full confidence you can do it by yourself, but if you need help, let me know," I say as I hold the flapper out to her.

She takes it from me, looking down at it like the whole contraption is perplexing. "Thank you."

Shoving my hands in my pockets, I nod my head and say, "Yeah, you're welcome, I'll uhh—"

"Hold on. Do you actually work here?" she asks, her head whipping in my direction.

"Oh, I... No." I run my hand over my buzzed hair, feeling slightly embarrassed for some reason. "I'm renovating my parents' house. Or well... I'm trying to. Turns out, people like modern hardware for cabinets and drawers. So I'm here to see what Billy has in stock, but I'm realizing I might not be cut out for the design part of reno."

A spark of something—excitement maybe—shines bright in her eyes. "Let's go look," she says as she starts to walk toward the end of the aisle where the knobs and handles are on display before I can respond. I follow close behind, a little bewildered and very enchanted by her enthusiasm for something as stupid as cabinet hardware, but more than willing to let her help me since I don't have a clue what to choose. "What about that one?" she asks, pointing to a matte black round knob.

"Is that what you would pick?" I ask, partially because I didn't expect her to pick plain black and partially because I'm curious which one catches her eye.

"Oh, no. If it were my house, I'd probably pick..." she trails off, scanning the display for her ideal cabinetry hardware. "That one," she says more excitedly, pointing to a much more detailed option.

"'Classic oil rubbed bronze,'" I read aloud from the sticker. "Why that one?"

She shifts on her feet a little before answering, "Well, it's still classic but more modern looking than your usual gold or silver, and it has a rustic look to it. It'll go well with whatever paint color you choose."

I reach up to grab a few. "Sold."

Her head whips to me. "What?"

Grabbing a few more, I count them as I pull them down to make sure I have enough for the whole kitchen. "What do you mean 'what?' I'm getting them, you convinced me."

For whatever reason, this seems to make her uncomfortable. I try to use humor to break the tension, "Hey, the future owner of the house will thank you. I probably would have gotten pissed off at all the options, said 'fuck it,' and just kept the old ones." I shrug my shoulders, hopefully letting her know it's not a big deal.

"Probably," she says with a small laugh.

"Anyway, I should go," I say as I point over my shoulder, as if she doesn't know where the exit is.

"Right, me too. I need to fix the toilet and finish some other things around the house."

We walk toward the front in silence, all the while I steal quick glances at her profile. Billy sees us just as I'm setting the ten knobs on the counter. I got two extra just in case. Margot is standing behind me, so I reach back for the flapper in her hand and place it next to my things.

"Brooks—"

"Oh, there's no sense in trying to reason with him about it, you might as well save your breath, sweetie," Billy says, cutting her off before she can complain.

I throw a smirk over my shoulder at her, which only seems to annoy her more. Billy gives me the total, and I pull some bills out of my wallet. He hands me the two bags, and I hand Margot hers.

"Consider it payment for helping me out with this," I say, lifting the bag slightly.

"You helped me first," she argues back.

I laugh and shrug, walking backward toward the door. "See ya, Billy-Bob!" I yell across the store. He raises his hand in a wave but doesn't say anything back. Then a little quieter, I say, "Bye, Freckles." I shoot her a wink, mainly because I love her reaction. And she does not disappoint—the stunning red I already love stains her cheeks, and her mouth falls open just a bit. She's still standing there with the same dazed look on her face when I turn and exit the store.

My bike is sitting in a parking spot right in front of the door. I sling the plastic bag over the handle while I grab my helmet. I'm swinging my leg over to straddle my bike when the bell above the door dings as Margot pushes it open. I rev my engine and back out of the parking spot, never pulling my gaze from hers until I'm racing away.

The whole way back to my parents', all I can think about is how bad of an idea it would be to get involved with Margot Mason.

Every time I see her, I have to resist the magnetic pull to her, the way my body instinctively reacts when she's around. She's too innocent and too off-limits for me to go there. I just about have myself convinced I'm only resisting because she's Hayes' sister, and I'm not trying to get my ass kicked. But deep down... I know I'd take everything perfect about her and ruin it like I ruin everything else.

As I pull into the driveway, my phone vibrates in my pocket.

12/9 3:24 p.m.

Freckles: Thank you again. Let me know when I can repay you. Maybe I can cook you dinner again? **blushing smiley emoji**

12/9 3:25 p.m.

Me: **thumbs up emoji**

Read 3:25 p.m.

I put my phone on *do not disturb,* so I don't see if she immediately replies and shove it back into my pocket. I can't go down this road, no matter how much I want to.

CHAPTER TEN

My empty notification screen glares back at me. I navigate to my text thread with Brooks. His last text—a thumbs emoji of all things—sits there on the left of the screen. Accompanied by four messages from me.

Four messages.

In a row.

With no response.

A tiny groan escapes me as I rest my forehead on the cool table, trying to tamp down the embarrassment. This is one of those moments where if I had a best friend, they'd be saying, "He's just not that into you."

I keep my head down as the nurses' lounge door swings open, and Jan and Aubrey stroll in, too absorbed in their conversation to notice me. They flit around the kitchenette, opening drawers and cabinets. The distinct sound of the coffee maker gurgling to life.

"Did you see Old Man Matthews' nephew? What a snack!" says Aubrey.

"Oh yeah, haven't seen him here before, but I hope he visits more often," replies Jan.

"That's probably not likely since the poor old man is pretty much comatose."

"A girl can dream," Jan says on a sigh. "Are you up for drinks this weekend?"

"Oooh, maybe, maybe." There's a pause, and Aubrey adds with a chuckle, "Colton not calling you back?"

"Colt and I aren't exclusive. I can—Oh, hi, Margot. I'm sorry, I didn't see you there," says Jan. "You heading out soon?"

I pick my head up and give the women a smile. "Yeah, in about an hour or so—I'm going to do a final round, make sure everyone is settling in for the night."

They both nod and smile warmly, but then continue their conversation, making plans to meet at a local bar this Saturday. I look down at my phone again and try not to think too hard about how the invitation isn't extended to me.

"What's going on, girlie? Still spinning your wheels with Brooks?" Lydia's voice pulls me back from my thoughts. I look down at the plant I'm overwatering and quickly move to the next one. Her words finally register, and my eyes quickly shift to the open suite door through which I can see other residents and nurses milling about in the hallway.

"Keep your voice down," I say, turning around to face her as she sits in her wheelchair by the window but casting my eyes down to the floor. "And no. Well, yes—he's confusing me. He keeps flirting with me... a lot. But then I put myself out there with him yesterday, and he's been ignoring me ever since. Maybe I read the whole thing wrong."

I look up and see she's looking right back at me, her mouth set in a grim line. "That boy needs to get his head out of his ass," she finally says.

"Lydia!" I say with a chuckle.

"Oh, please. He never knows what's good for him," Lydia huffs out. "But if it's not him putting that look on your face, what's going on?"

I sigh heavily, weighing if it's even worth mentioning. It makes me feel immature and young to bring it up. What kind of grown adult person gets their feelings hurt by not being invited out? It's not like my coworkers are my friends. "It's silly. Jan and Aubrey were in the lounge making plans to go out this weekend, and they didn't invite me along. I'm not particularly close with them, but it would be nice to make some friends here." I swallow down the lump forming in my throat and force out, "Like I said, silly."

"It's not silly if it hurts your feelings," she mutters gently, motioning for me to come sit next to her by the window. I place the watering can down on her dresser and make my way over.

"Really, it's fine," I say as I take a seat. "I think between Brooks ignoring me and now this, I'm just a little in my feelings. I've been here for over six months already, and making friends has been tough with my work schedule."

Lydia nods at me, her face warm and accepting. She doesn't make me feel immature or invalidated, always listening to my problems. Sometimes I wonder who takes care of whom here.

I know if I went to Hayes with this, he'd tell me to forget about those women and just keep focusing on my job. He'd do it in a way that makes me feel like a child again, most likely telling me to stop whining. It takes a lot of energy from me to not revert to my fifteen-year-old self around him when he treats me as such.

"Why don't you reach out to Thea?" she asks. "She's told me she's invited you out with her and Ripley a few times. I know she can ramble sometimes, and Ripley's a bit of a smartass, but they're fun to be around, and they mean well."

"You don't think I'd be imposing? They seem so in love. I wouldn't want to be a third wheel," I say, looking down at my hands.

Lydia chuckles. "I don't think you have anything to worry about. If they invited you out, they want you there."

Thea and Ripley have always been very nice when I run into them here at Saint Stephen's. They pull me into conversations, making me feel like I've known them forever, not just in passing while I'm at work.

I smile at the thought of what a night out with them would consist of. Ripley's a bit of a loose canon, so I know I'd be in for some fun. "I'll think about it. Thanks," I say, finding I feel better and appreciating Lydia for helping me get out of my head. Again. "Do you need anything else? Jan will be with you for the evening."

"Hmmm, I'll be sure to keep her running around," she says conspiratorially.

"Be nice! I'll see you tomorrow," I say with a laugh, getting up from the chair and moving across the room to put the watering can away before I head out for the night.

I check on a few other residents before making my way back to the nurses' lounge. Stepping over to the kitchenette, I rinse out my water bottle and notice a few dirty dishes left in the sink. I set my phone on the counter next to me while I wash the plates and glasses, "10,000 Emerald Pools" by BØRNS starts playing quietly.

Once the dishware is resting in the drying rack, I go over to the locker room just off the lounge to grab my jacket and purse. I pause when I see a red gift bag sitting in front of my locker. There's white and red tissue paper sticking out of the top of the bag. As I get closer, I notice a gift tag attached to it. Reaching out, I turn it over and read "Margot" printed on it.

Confused, I pull the tissue paper out of the bag and lift a square wrapped in the same tissue paper. The sound of the paper ripping under my fingers echoes throughout the empty locker room. I look around as though I expect the person who left the gift for me to pop out of the showers around the corner.

Once all the paper is removed, I realize the square is actually a canvas, about ten inches by ten inches in size.

"Oh," I whisper to myself as I take in the painting. It's a surreal depiction of an anatomical heart, blood red set on a bright yellow-orange background with black, purple, and blue veins running all over it. My heart races at the sight. The piece is gorgeous, and goosebumps rise up my arms in reaction to it.

"Oh! Look at that," says Jan from the doorway, startling me. "Looks like you got your Secret Santa present early, lucky girl! I usually end up getting something thoughtless and last minute right before I leave for the holiday." She steps closer and looks at the painting. "Hmm, pretty," she adds, then seems to lose interest and goes over to her locker to grab whatever she came in here for.

"Uhh, yeah, it's very… thoughtful." I look back down at the heart. It is pretty. But the more I look at it, the more it makes me feel uneasy. Something about the brush strokes makes it seem a little eerie; despite the bright colors, it looks sinister. Then I peer into the gift bag to see if maybe there's a card but see none. I look at the painting again. "Are we supposed to find out who our Secret Santa is?"

"Sometimes. There are some people who take it very seriously, and they never tell," Jan says, and I can hear the eye roll in her tone.

I turn the painting over, and tucked into the corner of the frame is a paper with details of the piece. My mouth instantly dries, and my stomach plummets as I read it over and over.

MISS ME?
Artist: Craig Stevenson
Acrylic on Canvas
2021

Chapter Eleven

Did I spend the last two days since seeing Margot in the hardware store drinking and smoking nonstop? Maybe. I don't have it in me to feel shitty about it. The girl has infiltrated my brain in a way no other person has. In a way I didn't even know was possible. And it would be fine, if she weren't Hayes' sister. But she is.

But God, if she weren't? I'd let myself have her. Trick her into thinking I'm a decent guy, let her think she could change me or whatever bullshit women think when they see my tattoos, motorcycle, and surly attitude. I'd charm her into my bed, show her a good time for a night, and not feel a shred of guilt as I leave before she wakes up the next morning. But the second I found out her last name is Mason, any thought of being my normal asshole self to her went to shit.

At least that's what I've been telling myself. It's all about Hayes and her relation to him. Underneath it all—buried so deep I can barely even sense it's there at all—I know it's more than that. I have to stay away because she's pure, good, sweet, kind—all of the things I'm not. She's the kind of person who would donate a kidney to a stranger without much thought just because they're in need. She lights up a room when she walks in, causing every pair of eyes to look her way. She's beautiful in more than just physical attributes, it's her soul that's so captivating.

I'm a shitty person who's done shitty things, but even I can't stand the thought of damaging a soul as pure as hers. When I walk into a room, I suck the energy out of it, people leave to avoid the onslaught they see coming. My soul is too blackened and toxic for someone like her.

I'm on my fourth beer of the night, right around the point of starting to feel the effects, the point where the constant buzz of doubt quiets. I can almost push all thoughts of Margot's unopened texts to the back of my mind. The little red circle indicating how many unread messages I have waiting for me never bothered me before. I could ignore it for days, weeks even. But knowing one—or more by now—is from her makes the stupid little number feel as though it's taunting me.

I left my phone in the bedroom, knowing if it's too close, I might get brave as the night goes on. I still could. It's only in the other room, but in the moment when I made the decision, it gave me some hope I could avoid the temptation if it wasn't right next to me.

"What the fuck is wrong with me?" I ask myself out loud, running a hand down my face and letting my head fall back on the couch. I'm staring at the ceiling when there's a knock on the door. I ignore it, it's probably the same kid from earlier trying to sell shit.

Grabbing my beer from the coffee table, I bring it to my lips just as there's another knock, more forceful this time. "Fuck this,"

I mumble as I push off the couch, pissed I have to tell this punk to fuck off for the second time.

I stomp over to the door, flinging it open, prepared to scare the kid shitless when I see Thea standing there instead. My face instantly softens. I haven't seen her since the night before Thanksgiving. I was too drunk to care about how broken she looked that night. Cary had been the reason, but I'd thrown gasoline on an already out of control fire. I'd used her as a way to get back at my brother, and I hadn't felt the gravity of what I put her through until now.

"It's just me. Jesus," she says as she pushes through me and into the house.

I run a hand over my buzzed hair. "Sorry, Thea. Some guy pushing solar shit came by earlier, and I just assumed it was him again."

"No worries." She brushes me off, peering around the room, judgment seeping out of her. "So, this is what you've been doing?"

Of course she sees some beer bottles scattered around and assumes this is all I've done in the almost two weeks since she's seen me. For a second there, I was happy to see her. Happy to maybe talk to her like we did the last time she was here, right before everything got even more fucked than it already was. But it always comes back to everyone assuming the worst of me.

Everyone but Margot. I push the thought away as quickly as I can.

Letting out a huff in response, I walk over to the couch and pull a pack of cigarettes from my hoodie pocket. "Did you come here to lecture me, Thea?" I ask, grabbing a smoke from the pack and bringing it to my lips as I reach for my lighter on the table in front of me.

The sound of her purse hitting the counter echoes through the room before she answers. "Would that help? Because you missed the memorial. You've got Margot asking questions. You didn't even say goodbye to Cary before he left. And now I find you... surrounded by beer bottles with more bruises on your face than the last time I saw you."

Her response halts my movement, the cigarette hanging from my lips, Zippo aimed and ready. I pull the lighter back and put the cig on the couch beside me. "Margot is asking questions about me? Why?" I ask, knowing there was probably something else she said I should have latched on to, but the second Margot's name left her lips, I didn't hear anything else. She walks into the living room, sitting down on the couch across from me.

She makes a face like she wants to roll her eyes, but she's holding back. "Oh, I don't know, maybe because she had to bandage up wounds you refuse to talk about, and then you apparently neglected to answer her texts? She said she was trying to check on you and make sure your face was healing okay."

Right. She is a nurse after all, of course she's just concerned with how I'm healing. I pick the smoke back up, bring it back to my lips, and finally light it. I shake my head, internally scolding myself for thinking it could be any more than that. I should have opened the text instead of torturing myself for days thinking it was more.

"You know your mom hated that you smoke, and now you're doing it in her house?" Thea says, her voice laced with incredulity.

I make sure to take a nice, deep inhale of the toxic fumes before exhaling them in a ring of smoke. "Not like she can stop me now that she's dead." I know it's a shitty thing to say. And based on the look on Thea's face, I hit the nerve I was aiming for. None of them realize I don't need their looks of disappointment, I feel it enough without seeing it on their faces.

"Cool. Good talk, Brooks," she says as she stands up, clearly done with my shit. "Listen, either tell us what's going on with you, or figure out how to get your shit together on your own. You're like a fucking bomb ready to go off, and I can't deal with another explosion in my life." She walks out of the living room toward the kitchen.

I don't have anything to say in response. I just sit there, slowly inhaling and exhaling the smoke of the cigarette, watching as it burns down to the filter, imagining it's the bomb she mentioned and how much longer I might have before it explodes. I wish I could ease her worries, tell her I'm fine, and everything will be okay, but the one thing I'm not is a liar. I won't sit here and lie to her face when I know damn well the other shoe is soon to drop. I've felt it for weeks. It's kept me on edge. Cary may be gone for now, but he opened old wounds by coming back—and not just for Thea.

"What are these?" Thea asks, pulling me from my thoughts. I think back for a second and remember I put the papers from Elsher on the counter.

"I don't know. A bunch of shit Elsher gave to me when I signed whatever bullshit got me the golden key to this humble abode," I say, taking another puff, doing my best effort to blow smoke rings and make it look like I'm anything but falling apart at the seams.

"Brooks..."

"What?" I ask, slightly annoyed she's going through my things like she owns the place.

"There are letters here," she says, but her voice is emotionless, void of the lilt I usually love to hear. The one I spent years waiting to come back after she all but broke in front of my eyes.

"What?" *Letters? What letters?* Within a second, I'm off the couch, pulling the cigarette from my lips, and walking toward her to see what she's holding. Sure enough, there are two letters in her hand. One is addressed to me, and one is addressed to Cary and Thea. Together. Not separate. Not that I have the capacity to think about that part right now. "What the... I swear, Thea, I didn't know these were here. I fucking swear."

She doesn't say anything, she just stares at the envelope with her and Cary's names on it. I wait for her to say something, but when she doesn't, I decide I need to see what's inside the envelope more than I need my next breath.

I snatch the one with my name on it from her hands and head for the room I've been staying in for the last two days, slamming the door behind me. I snub the smoke out in the ashtray on the bedside table, my eyes never leaving my name written in my mother's cursive lettering.

I turn the envelope over, feeling the weight of it in my hands, focusing on the texture of the material. I don't know what to expect from her last words to me. If it's her telling me how disappointed she is from the grave, I'm not sure I'll survive. The thought makes me wonder if I should even open it.

Somewhere in the distance, I hear the front door close. I know Thea probably needs someone right now—I just can't be that person. Not with this grenade resting in my hands.

I'm not sure how long it's been when I finally decide to grab my dad's pocket knife from the bedside table, slicing open the seal. I pull a single sheet of paper from the envelope, slowly—like it might attack me. It's folded in half, but I can already see the ink that's bled through the page.

As I unfold the paper, my heart clamors in my chest. I'm not sure I'm ready to face whatever's on the other side of this, but the second I see my nickname written at the top—the name only she was allowed to call me—I realize I couldn't stop even if I wanted to.

My Brooksy Boy,

If you're reading this, it means your father and I are no longer with you. I hope this letter finds its way to your hands in your later years of life, but I know that isn't a guarantee, and I could be gone tomorrow.

Your father and I weren't the best at parenting you, but I hope you know it was never your fault. You always had big emotions, and although it was never a bad thing, we didn't always know how to handle them in the way you needed us to.

You, my Brooksy Boy, were the light of my life. You made me a mama, and I loved watching you grow up and seeing your eyes light up when you found a new kind of art that spoke to your heart.

I also hated watching your light die. It especially broke my heart because I know it was our doing. You don't know how much I hope you've found your inspiration again.

We didn't leave you the restaurant, and I hope you aren't upset by it. I need you to chase your dreams, baby boy. Those dreams aren't here in Indigo Hill. I know you saw the hurt your brother leaving caused us, and I think it's why you chose to stay close. But this town is too small for your talent, my love. We should have told you sooner.

We were so proud to see your work hanging on the front of the family business. And if you think we didn't notice more of your work popping up around town, you're mistaken. It brought us such joy to see you with a passion again, even if you didn't trust us enough to share it with us.

So, we didn't leave you the restaurant because I don't want you to feel like you have to stay. I don't want that burden on you any longer.

We left you the house so you could choose to sell it to fund your dreams or keep it as a refuge. The choice is entirely yours, though I do hope you choose to leave it all behind.

I love you with all my heart,
—Mom

I read the letter over and over, fumbling with my dad's old pocket knife while tears fall down my cheeks and onto the page, cascading onto the paper like tiny explosions of relief. I had no idea what to expect from her last message to me, but... it wasn't this. I *never* expected this. I read it once more, just to be sure I understand. Just to feel close to her for another moment. For the first time since they both passed, I allow myself to feel grief. Grief I watched Thea and the rest of the town go through for weeks now.

I didn't let myself feel it, I didn't feel worthy of feeling it. I thought they were probably relieved they didn't have to deal with me anymore, like maybe their deaths were actually burdens being lifted from their shoulders, from their souls. The burden of me.

I had myself convinced my parents didn't love me. I thought my childhood was a labyrinth of twisted feelings and dead dreams. I didn't even think they saw me or knew I was suffering. I'd spent so much time cursing myself for caring about people who I didn't think cared about me. But they did. It hits me like a tidal wave that they not only cared about me, but they loved me.

And they knew. Despite me trying my best to keep my work under wraps, somehow they'd found out. Maybe Thea told them. Even if she did, knowing it meant something to my parents has mended a piece of me I never knew how to fix. I choke myself up rereading the words *"We were so proud to see your work hanging in front of the family business."*

The realization of it all hits me like a ton of bricks. I can't keep back my sobs as I lay down on the bed, placing my hands over my face to try and stop the tsunami of tears. I never knew how much I needed to hear these things. A part of me is so *fucking* mad they didn't tell me when they were alive, and the other part of me is upset they aren't here for me to hug them and tell them how much I love them too.

And the house... knowing they left it to me on purpose so I could sell it to chase my dreams only pushes me even more over the edge. Everything about this moment brings so much clarity to the surface. Cary may have been blind to the things going on around him during our childhood, things I held against him into adulthood, but maybe I was blind too. Maybe I'd held my parents to an unattainable standard and then held it against them when they didn't meet it.

I reach for my phone on the bedside table, clicking on the messages app, ignoring all the unread texts as I scroll through for Cary's name.

12/11 9:42 p.m.

Me: I'm sorry.

Delivered

I know it isn't enough, but it's all I can give right now. I just hope it isn't too late to make amends with him. I don't want to make the same mistakes as my parents and rely on a letter to explain what I couldn't say all along.

I decide I'm done being the pathetic letdown I've been ever since Cary moved to Seattle and I told myself my dreams were dead. They aren't. They don't have to be. If Hayes doesn't have a chair for me, I'll look somewhere else, some other town. The thought gives me more determination than I've ever had before. So before I go to bed, I write out a list of everything I need to do to get the house ready to sell.

I promise myself I'll finally do something that makes me happy because maybe, after all, I *do* deserve it.

Chapter Twelve

"What are we drinking?" Thea says a little too loudly with a big smile aimed at me. Her eyes are glossy and cheeks pink, apparently she and Ripley started drinking before I called her an hour ago.

I'm grateful she didn't give me much notice for when to meet up because I'm sure I would have cancelled if I had more time to second-guess. I changed my outfit three times before I left my house, and my hands were clammy in the back of the rideshare the whole way here.

I'm not entirely sure why I called her. Maybe Lydia and Hayes finally got through to me. Or maybe, if I'm going to be honest with myself, the painting has left me rattled, and I don't want to be alone right now. Taking Thea and Ripley up on their standing offer to go out seems like a great way to get my mind off of it.

By the time I met up with them outside of Louie's, I had convinced myself I'd stay for one drink and make a polite excuse to leave. But within five minutes of being in their company, I'm finding myself relaxing; their constant chatter helping me escape my own head.

"Maybe some water, babe?" says Ripley over the sounds of the Thursday night crowd. She gives him a bemused look. "Ha! Kidding. I'll grab some shots," he says and then adds as his eyes snag on something behind me, "Let's grab the booth in the corner."

Thea doesn't hesitate as she snatches my hand and leads me through the small group of dancers in the middle of the bar to a recently vacated booth. We settle on opposite sides, pushing glasses and empty plates from the previous occupants to the end of the table to be picked up by a busboy.

"So, Margot," Thea says with more enthusiasm than I've ever heard from her. "I'm so happy you called! I've been trying to get you out with us for months."

"I know, it's been tough with my schedule, but I'm glad this worked out. I'm sorry if I'm crashing a date," I say, suddenly hit with a wave of discomfort for having inserted myself in their night out.

Thea laughs like I've made a joke. "Don't worry about it. I'm sure Ripley's glad to get a break from listening to my incessant Cary talk."

"Things not going well at RED? Your mom mentioned he went back to Seattle." I can't even imagine what she's going through. From what I heard, she had a close relationship with Brooks and Cary's parents, and their death has been difficult, but now having to navigate working with your ex while grieving seems like an impossible situation.

She sighs dramatically like only someone after a few drinks can. "Yes, he left. And now he's stopped texting me. He was texting me, you know? I sent him this letter his mom left for us, and he didn't respond. And he stopped texting me. What do you think that means? It has to mean something." She's rambling in true Thea fashion, and I open my mouth to respond, just waiting for a moment where I can interject to cut her off.

As soon as she pauses for a breath, I say, "A letter?"

"Yeah, Brooks had them," she says with an eye roll. Clearly there's a story there. "He's just been sitting on them, can you believe that? Cary's mom left us letters with her will, and he just left them in a folder on his counter for God knows how long."

"Brooks got a letter too?" I ask, to which Thea nods, and then her attention is on her phone as she's texting. She looks up toward the bar with a mischievous look. When her phone pings, she giggles and types out a response. I turn to the bar and see Ripley's also on his phone, a big smile on his face, as he waits for the bartender to pour our drinks.

Brooks got a letter from his mother. I want to ask when and if this has anything to do with him ignoring me, but I know this is not a time for that conversation with a tipsy Thea. My heart breaks a little for him. From what little he told me about his relationship with his parents, it was complicated. For his sake, I hope whatever the letter says brings him some comfort or, in the very least, some closure.

I look down at my phone sitting on the table, tempted to send him another text. Thankfully, I'm saved from myself when Ripley plants a tray of shots on the center of the table.

"Here we go, ladies," he says. "The rules of Redneck Wrecked are very simple." He smirks, his eyes jumping from me to Thea and back again. "There are no rules, and we're all losers at the end of the night with a killer hangover tomorrow, but we'll have fun, that's a guarantee."

He squishes himself in on Thea's side of the booth and slings an arm around her. Thea melts into him, already reaching for one of the shot glasses. Ripley quickly slaps her hand away playfully. "Okay, tonight's rules..." he trails off as he looks around, and a devious look crosses his face as his eyes catch on something across the room. "We'll have the usual: if Shelley gets hit on, Thea has to take a shot. If Bob plays that stupid cowboy song, I'll drink. If—"

"If Ripley gets hit on by anyone over the age of forty-five, we all drink!" says Thea and devolves into a fit of giggles. "Those cougars want you baaaad, *babe*," she adds after coming up for air. "Don't think I didn't notice Mrs. Davis talking you up at the bar."

"Ew, she's practically my grandmother. And happily married. Pretty sure she changed my diaper a time or two," Ripley says and rolls his eyes, but I do notice a few appreciative gazes turned in his direction.

I've never really paid much attention to his looks, since he's very much taken with Thea, but Ripley is attractive. Mossy green eyes, shaggy dark hair that looks almost black in the right lighting. He's got that sweet southern charm but with some biting wit, I can see how people are drawn to him. And although he's usually laid back, with a bit of a worldly rockstar vibe to him, I know from both Thea and Lydia he's serious when it comes to crafting his whiskey.

"What I was going to say before I was so rudely interrupted," he throws a playful, sideways glare toward Thea, "is when—not if—Tiffany hits on someone other than her boyfriend, Margie here drinks," he says, his usual smirk in place.

"Oh, umm... it's Margot, actually. Not Margie," I say, feeling awkward at having to correct him.

They both chuckle. "Oh, I know... *Margie.* I bestow nicknames to all the best people in town," he says with another wink. "It's a badge of honor really." The explanation has a small smile pulling at my lips. I've never had many friends and certainly never any who liked me enough to give me a nickname—unless you count Brooks. Only Hayes has ever done that, and that nickname is less than desirable.

"Ripley," Thea says, sounding sober all of a sudden. "I actually want her to *want* to hang out with us again. And we'll be taking her to the hospital with alcohol poisoning in an hour with that rule." They stare at each other with serious expressions for a long moment, and I'm a bit lost since I'm not familiar with Tiffany. Then they both burst out laughing and turn to me.

"Okay, okay, okay, no need to scare the poor girl. You're right, she'll never come out with us again. Don't worry, her current boyfriend is surprisingly good at reining her in, you'll probably be okay," says Ripley, placing a shot glass in front of me.

Though I wasn't totally comfortable with coming out tonight, I'm deciding to just lean into it. Thea and Ripley make me feel like I've known them forever, giving me a glimpse into the small town they've known their whole lives. "So, what are we drinking?" I ask Ripley.

He purses his lips and looks almost contrite for a second.

"Ripley," Thea scolds.

"Margot needs to get the full Redneck Wrecked experience, and you know tequila is the only way to do that."

"Fine, but I'm holding you responsible for anything that happens tonight," says Thea right before she downs a shot.

"Don't worry, baby girl. I got you," he coos. "You'll be coming home with me tonight." He kisses her cheek and takes a shot of his own, making a face at the burn. "All right, nurse lady. Bottoms up!"

I can't help but smile at their back-and-forth as I lift the glass to my mouth. "I hope you guys know I almost never drink, but here goes nothing." I hold their eyes as I pour the contents of the shot glass down my throat, the liquid burning all the way down. A few minutes later, a warmth floods my system, and some of my worries ease.

The music in the space suddenly changes to "Save a Horse (Ride a Cowboy)" by Big and Rich, and everyone in the bar cheers. Everyone but one guy who slaps a palm on the jukebox.

Thea and Ripley burst out laughing. "He must have forgotten his glasses again and picked the wrong song," Ripley explains. "Bob plays 'Should've Been a Cowboy' by Toby Keith at least three times a night here."

"That doesn't count, does it?" asks Thea.

"Margie, what do you think?" he asks me.

I look between them, Thea's face clearly asking for clemency and Ripley's is hoping for chaos. The alcohol in my veins makes me brave, and I say, "A cowboy song is a cowboy song. Drink!" Ripley laughs delightedly with me, and Thea takes her shot.

"Okay, don't look now, but there is a very tatted, very badass looking dude who keeps looking over here. Looking at you, Margie," Ripley says much too loudly for the conspiratorial tone he's trying to use. I stiffen, my mind immediately assuming he's talking about Brooks.

We've been hanging out and playing Redneck Wrecked for a while now, all three of us getting drunker as the night wears on. Ripley kept adding more silly rules as we kept drinking, and I've lost count of the shots I've taken. Thankfully, the bartender noticed how quickly we were putting them back and sent over some food and glasses of water for the table.

I whip my head in the direction he's looking. I can't help the small pang of disappointment when I see Archer standing by the bar. He shoots me a megawatt smile and gives me a nod in hello. I turn back to face Thea and Ripley and look down into my water.

"What's that face? He's cute!" says Thea with a slight slur.

"Ah, nothing. I just thought you meant someone else," I reply. "That's Archer."

"Ooo, Archer," both she and Ripley sing-song, sounding an awful lot like preteen schoolgirls.

"Oh, he's coming—he's coming over!" Thea whisper-shouts before turning to greet Archer, "Well, hello there." Ripley elbows her, and they fall into a fit of giggles together.

I roll my eyes at them, and the room swims a little before I focus and look up at the smiling blond standing next to our table.

"Hi, Booger," he greets, causing the Chaos Couple—as I so aptly named them at some point in the night, though I can't recall the exact reason why now—to cackle even louder.

"Hi, Archer," I say with a smile. "What brings you here?" *Oh my God, am I flirting? Do I want to be flirting with him?*

Archer looks around the table and clears his throat as his eyes land on Thea, who is still giggling into Ripley's shoulder. "Uh, I'm here with my sister. She just moved to town, I'm showing her around." He hooks a thumb behind him in the direction of the bar. I look to where he's pointing and can make out a stunning woman with fire engine colored hair and a punk-goth vibe. She has tattoos running up and down both arms, her hair is tied up with a bandana, and her make up is making me jealous. I need to know how she does that thing with the eyeliner. I realize Archer's speaking again, so I bring my attention back to him.

"...with her kid. I plan on bringing her to RED soon too. I'm sorry to hear Cary left." He directs the last bit to Thea, whose happy smile slowly falls. Every time he's mentioned, it's more and more obvious I'm missing a lot of details. I feel terrible for Ripley though. It seems like no one is ever concerned about his feelings; they talk about it right in front of him.

Thea gives him a small smile but doesn't say anything else.

"I better get back to Calla before she tricks Shelley into falling in love with her," Archer says with a laugh. I can't tell if he's joking or serious, and my alcohol-induced mind is no help. Before I can even respond or say goodbye, he's walking away, and I realize I must have missed the rest of what he said.

I look over to Thea, melancholy still painting her face, and I'm shocked again by how open she's being about her feelings for an ex with Ripley sitting right here. Without another word, she gets up from the table and strides out to the dance floor.

"Sometimes you just have to let a girl dance her heartbreak away."

"Heartbreak? But I thought..." And suddenly the shift in Thea's mood makes sense. *Cary left.* Though I don't know the details there, I know she's been sad since. I distantly recall my trip to Hayes' studio and someone mentioning *present history.* I can't imagine what Ripley's going through watching her right now. "Oh... I'm so sorry, Ripley."

He looks at me, his eyes slightly narrowing as if he's really taking me in. His lips quirk in a small smile. "You, my dear Margot, look like a good egg," he says right before he takes another shot. "And because you look like a good egg, I think I can tell you Thea's heartbreak only hurts me in the same way it hurts you. Watching someone else go through whatever," he waves his hand loosely in the direction of the dancefloor, "that is, is tough for anyone—but especially a *friend.*"

His words take a moment to sink in. "But I thought..." I trail off, not really sure where my thought was going.

"You thought I was in love with a spunky little blonde who unfortunately happens to be in love with someone else?" I nod, and he continues, "Sadly for me, I am." He downs another shot and stands up but continues to look at me. "What's most unfortunate is *he's* 3,000 miles away."

I imagine my eyes are as wide as saucers as the truth of what he's telling me settles around us. "Oh."

Ripley smirks again. "Close that mouth, you'll give the men staring at you the wrong impression." I slam my lips closed and look around, my cheeks heating. He slides a full shot glass in my direction, some of the tequila spilling over the side. "Bottoms up, buttercup."

And then he's gone. Swallowed up by the bodies on the dance floor, popping up next to Thea a moment later, stepping in and not missing a beat in the song as they move together.

My alcohol soaked brain can barely wrap itself around what I just learned. I'm feeling grateful to Ripley for trusting me with his truth, but at the same time, I feel like I have to reframe everything I know about him and Thea from the last six months.

Unable to really process it, I whisper, "Fuck it," and down the shot before heading out on the dance floor to find the first two people I can truly call friends in Indigo Hill.

"Answer, answer, answer," I whisper as the phone rings, the sound making my head pound to the tune of regret. I shouldn't have drank as much as I did.

I don't know what time it is at this point, but we closed down the bar, dancing and singing to everything from Dolly Parton to Chappell Roan. As soon as we stepped outside, I remember there are no rideshares available in a town so small at this time of night. Leaning on the side of the building so I don't topple over, I call my brother to pick me up.

I'm so cold. It's one of the rare freezing December nights in South Carolina, and I didn't bring a jacket. As the sweat dries on my body, my dress clings to my skin, not offering me much warmth.

Ripley props Thea up nearby. They're planning on walking to Ripley's house as soon as I secure a ride. Ripley offered for me to stay over as well, and if I can't get ahold of Hayes, I may not have a choice but to take him up on it.

Hayes' voicemail picks up, and I hit end. My hands shake from the cold, and my body sways from the alcohol in my system as I press on his name again.

Four rings later, a gruff "what" rumbles in my ear.

"Hi," I mumble out, trying my darndest to downplay my intoxication. "I... I need you. I need a ride."

"Are you drunk?" he growls, but I can barely hear him over my own chattering teeth. "Where are you?"

"Louie's," I say, knowing I'm going to get an earful from my brother, despite being old enough to drink.

"Don't move." And the call ends. Great, he's annoyed. I try to make out the time on my phone, but I'm seeing double. I close one eye and squint, but that only makes me lose my balance, so I give up and wrap my arms around myself.

"Margie, you good?" Ripley asks.

I nod. Leaning my back against the building, I close my eyes and wait.

CHAPTER THIRTEEN

Twenty-eight hours and thirty-six minutes. That's how long it's been since I opened the letter from my mother that—once again—turned my world on its axis. Despite making myself promises, I'd woken up this morning pissed off at the world.

I was pissed at Elsher for not giving us the letters after the funeral. Pissed at Cary for leaving—again. Pissed at Thea for being her annoying self and badgering me about how I'm doing, despite needing *someone*. Pissed at Ripley for not being there when I needed him, even though there'd be no way for him to know. I was even pissed at Margot for being such a bright light that all I wanted to do was run to her so maybe she could chase away the darkness inside of me.

I'd texted Hayes this morning and had him book me for back-to-back fights for tonight. I'm up against Landon, and I don't see it being a challenge. Maybe he'll surprise me, but from what I've seen, he's got a killer right hook, but it's his only move so we all know how to avoid it.

Normally, I'd hang out at The Pit leading up to my fight, but I didn't feel like socializing or putting on a mask. When I was twelve, my mom convinced my dad to put a punching bag in their garage because they thought it would help with my "anger issues," so I've been beating the shit out of it for the last hour to warm up.

I'm unwrapping my hands, about to go change so I can head over to The Pit when my phone starts ringing inside the house. It's on the fourth ring by the time I get to it, and I don't even look down to see who it is before pressing the accept call button. I bring the phone up to my ear, making my way to the fridge for a water bottle.

"What?" This close to a fight, I automatically assume it's Hayes since I'm usually there by now.

"Hi." The sound of her voice stops me in my tracks, I can hear her holding back a giggle. "I... I need you. I need a ride." I'd expect her words to excite me not cause my anger to boil back to the surface.

She needs me. Those are three words I never thought I'd hear her say to me. They're words you say to someone you feel safe with, and I'm not that person. For her or anyone.

Unless...

"Are you drunk? Where are you?" I grit out, doing everything in my power to keep my voice even.

"Louie's," she replies. I'm already on the move, not bothering to change out of my sweat-soaked shirt. I grab my keys off the counter, heading for the door without another thought.

"Don't move," I tell her, ending the call.

I quickly shoot off a text to Hayes.

12/12 11:36 p.m.

Me: Something came up, won't make it.

Delivered

It's not the first time I've bailed on a fight. It is the first time I've let Hayes know. And the first time it's for a woman, not that I'll ever tell him. But Margot and her safety are more important than a stack of cash and a boost to my ego. I swing my leg over the seat of my motorcycle, slamming my helmet on my head at the same time.

I let the wind calm my anger the closer I get to Louie's. I should be happy she's calling me when she's in need. But hearing her drunk when I know she doesn't drink struck a nerve in me. I should think it's great she's expanding her horizons, but it's not like her, she's made it abundantly clear.

By the time I'm pulling up to Louie's, I'm convinced I've caused this. I've made it seem like smoking and drinking aren't a big deal. I poked fun at her by telling her she didn't look old enough to drink. Maybe this is her trying to prove some point to me, and now I'll be to blame for anything that happens to her because of it.

Fuck, is she alone?

Pulling my helmet off, I look around the area for her. Louie's closes early this time of year since it's off-season, so she won't be inside anymore.

Suddenly, a familiar laugh rings out, it's not Margot though. It's Thea. My focus shifts across the street, where I see not only Thea, but Ripley and Margot. They're all sitting at one of the small tables in front of Grayce's Cafe. Thank fuck Thea and Ripley had the sense to stay with her. I see Margot shivering from here. It's close to freezing tonight, and the temperature is only going to continue to drop.

I hang my helmet on the bike before I stomp in their direction. Thea sees me first and starts to sing-song my name. Drunk Thea is fun, I'll admit, but not right now. Right now, I'm more concerned about the woman in front of me whose freckle-covered face haunts my dreams.

"Margot, let's go." My words are clipped.

Thea pouts out her lip. "Oop, Brooks looks mad; he must be the fun police tonight. Ripley, we better gooooo," she says, stumbling a bit as she pulls Ripley up from his seat.

Margot's striking light green eyes find me in the dark, she looks me up and down before saying, "You're not Hayes."

My face scrunches in confusion. "Uh... no, I'm not. And thank fuck for that."

She tilts her head. "No, I mean I called Hayes." It clicks then that she *thinks* she called Hayes, not me. This whole time, she thought Hayes was the one coming to her rescue.

"Right. Well, sorry, Freckles, you got me instead. Seems to be a running trend."

Ripley and I lock eyes as he says to Margot, "Margie, you good?"

The asshole is so drunk, he can't even remember the woman's name.

Margot looks to me then back to Ripley. "Yeah."

Without missing a beat, Ripley shoots back at me, "Brooks, behave."

I scoff. "Me? Fuck off, Ripley. Go get some water into Thea. *Margie* and I will be just fine." Sometimes I wonder why I like the dude. He shakes his head in amusement as he holds up a loose peace sign and pulls Thea into his grasp. I watch as they stumble down the street toward Ripley's house. "Let's go, Margot. Where'd you park?" I ask her, already turning for the parking lot.

I hear her stumble a bit, and the chair screeches against the concrete as she pulls herself from the seat. "Oh. I... umm... I don't know."

Turning around to face her again, I say, "What do you mean you don't know?" It's then I realize what she's wearing—or rather, what she's not wearing. "Margot, the fuck are you wearing?" She's dressed in a sweater dress and ankle boots. Her legs are bare from mid-thigh down to her shoes. I slink out of my jacket, my own rage keeping me warm enough, and drape it over her shoulders.

Her teeth chatter as she answers, "I don't remem—remember what s-street I parked it on—" She guffaws in the middle of her sentence and continues laughing for a long moment. When she finally gets a hold of herself, she says in between giggles, "I t-took a rideshare."

She ignores my other question which is honestly the smartest decision she's made all night. I imagine all the guys inside Louie's who must have been drooling over her, and my simmering anger ratchets up to just below boiling over.

"It's fine, we can just—damnit! No, we can't go to my place. I'll have to take you to my parents'. It's closer than your house."

Hayes called me yesterday morning asking if Max and his brother could stay in my apartment. Apparently, things had gotten worse at their uncle's. I agreed since I'm staying at my parents' house while I'm renovating. But it means taking Margot upstairs isn't happening.

Margot is so drunk, she's barely listening to me, only furthering my resolve on how to handle the situation. I grab her hand, pulling her toward my bike across the street.

"Where—" she pauses to hiccup, "are we going?"

I look both ways before crossing the road, not that there's much traffic at this time of night, still pulling her behind me. "To my bike."

She hiccups again before saying, "Your... motor... bike–cy-cle?" Confusion laces her tone, but I just keep walking. This girl needs a bed.

"Yes." I walk her down the sidewalk to the curb where I'm parked, immediately grabbing the helmet. "Do you have a hair tie?"

The question makes her giggle as she nods her head and pulls a scrunchie from her purse to hand to me.

"Turn around."

She laughs again, then says, "Yes, sir." Her face scrunches in faux seriousness as she turns around. The words just about bring me to my goddamn knees, but I try not to focus on them as I gather her hair in my hands and wrap the hair tie around her mess of curls.

I spin her back around then grab the helmet from the handle of my bike. "I'm going to put this on you, okay?"

She nods her head, another hiccup escaping her lips. I only have one helmet since I wasn't expecting a riding partner tonight, so I opt for her to have it. She's the one worth saving if there was ever a choice.

"Here's how this is going to go. I'm going to get on the bike like normal, but I want you to sit in front, facing me, instead of behind me. Then I want you to wrap your legs around me so they aren't in the way," I tell her, not sure if she's fully comprehending my words. I'll kick Ripley's ass for this.

"Wh-why?"

"Because with you drunk, it'll be safer this way."

She slowly nods again. If I'm being honest, none of this is safe, but I don't know what else to do.

Without giving it more thought, I throw my leg over the seat and scoot back so there's room for her. I wave my hand to signal for her to get on. Hesitantly—and with more grace than I would think her drunk body could muster—she swings her leg over the seat. I watch as her dress lifts some, exposing a glimpse of her light blue underwear, but once again, I push those thoughts away. Getting hard right now would really complicate things.

I take two deep breaths before instructing her again, "Wrap your legs aroudnd me, Margot. Then I'll need your arms around my neck too."

She does as I say, laying her head in the crook of my shoulder so the helmet is out of my way. The only reason this is working is because of how short she is.

My body is on fire with her proximity. Her small frame wrapped around me, and I'm sparking with awareness at each touch point.

"What now?" she mumbles through the helmet.

I turn the key in the ignition, the bike rumbling to life as I say, "Just hold on tight, baby."

I never thought this would be the way I'd feel Margot wrapped around me for the first time. She held on so tight, I could barely breathe. Her safety is my top priority though. By the time we arrive at my parents' house, she's still not ready to let go.

"Margot, we're here. You can let go now."

She shakes her head no, so I pull her back, unlatching the chin strap and sliding the helmet off. Her cheeks are flushed a pretty pink, and her eyes are hazy, their light green hue is lit up by the motion sensored lights on each side of the garage.

I tip her chin up, making sure she's looking me right in the eyes when I say, "Hey, you're okay, yeah? I wouldn't let anything happen to you."

Without ever looking away, she replies, "I know, I just don't want to let go. You smell so nice."

I swear my heart cracks in my chest at her words. I'm not sure how I'll survive the night.

Without another word, I lift her into my arms, one hand cradling her gorgeous ass, the other fumbling with the keys to find the right one. With her legs still wrapped around my waist, I walk us to the door.

Once we're inside, I set her down to peel my jacket off of her and hang her purse by the door. "Let me get you some water—"

She grabs my hand, stopping me. Her face is all scrunched up like the idea of water right now disgusts her. "Can we just—can we go lie down?"

I can't focus on anything else when her skin is touching mine. All I manage is a nod as I lead her to my room. She said 'we,' but I'm fully aware she's drunk and definitely didn't mean it in the way my mind is taking it. Even if she did, I'd never entertain the idea while she's intoxicated. I'm an asshole, but I'm not a predator.

Pushing through the door, her hand still encased in mine, I cringe thinking about how the sheets aren't exactly clean. Hopefully, she'll be so hungover tomorrow, she won't care.

"Make yourself comfortable," I say as I grab one of the pillows. "I'm going to sleep on the couch, but let me know if you need anything."

And then she's hugging me, squeezing so tightly I'm wondering how she's suddenly so strong. "Please don't leave me," her muffled words come out as a plea.

Instinctually, my arms wrap around her, holding her as if I'm scared she'll disappear if I don't. "You're drunk, Freckles. I—Goddamn, I can't sleep in the same bed as you."

She pulls away but only enough to peer up at me. Tears line her eyes, waiting to fall.

What the fuck is this girl doing to me?

"Please," she starts, the first tear rolling down her cheek. "I don't want to be alone." Her hiccups are back, and I can't handle the tears. I realize I'd do anything to never see her cry again. I also realize saying no to her might be impossible.

"Yeah... okay..."

A smile lights up her face as she pulls away from me. Her hands shoot down to the bottom of her dress and out of nowhere, she's pulling it up her body.

I slam a hand over my eyes, giving her some semblance of privacy. "Fucking hell, Margot, what are you doing?" I cry out, trying to contain my shock while internally repeating, *'don't look, don't look, don't look.'*

"I just—I need—" She lets out an annoyed and muffled sounding grumble, forcing me to peek through my fingers. She's sitting on the edge of the bed with her dress stuck over her head and her flawless body on display.

I let out a sigh as I remove my hand from my eyes. The freckles covering her face cascade down her body as well. I don't know what it is about them, but I'm *obsessed*. I want to count every individual one, trace them all, see if I can make some kind of picture by connecting the dots. She's a fucking work of art. The tone of her skin reminds me of honey. Her bra is light blue and matches the lacy scrap of fabric she thinks passes as underwear. But the color against her skin is a mindfuck, only adding to her perfection.

I never thought this would be something I'd have to deal with tonight. "Here, let me help." With minimal effort, I pull the dress off of her and release her from the self-made sweater prison. She giggles again, falling back on the bed. The makeshift ponytail I put her hair in must be uncomfortable because she reaches back, pulls at the scrunchie, and throws it in my direction.

As it bounces off my head, a laugh falls from my lips at the ridiculousness of the whole situation, which only makes her laugh more. She's grabbing her stomach, she's laughing so much. Her boots hit the floor with a thud as she flings them off as well.

I shake my head, huffing out another laugh before I lay her dress over the chair in the corner and head to my dresser to get her a shirt. I pull out the biggest one I can find, hoping it'll go all the way down to her knees.

As I walk back over, I shove the shoes out of the way and stand in front of her. "Sit up, we gotta put this on you." She holds out her hand, and I grab it to pull her up into a sitting position. As I slip the shirt over her head, her laughter tapers off. I gently tug her hair out of the T-shirt, my fingers feeling the delicate skin of her neck, and our eyes lock. She pushes up onto her knees and wraps her arms around my neck. "Margot..." I start, but I'm rendered speechless as she stares into my eyes.

She's pure radiance. I can't find a single thing wrong with her. She's completely flawless. I never knew perfection existed until I met her, and I'm constantly terrified I'll ruin it.

"You're not as scary as you try to make yourself out to be, but you are scary beautiful," she says, her heavy-lidded gaze locked on mine. Her eyes intent with the truth—she honestly believes what she said.

I open my mouth to argue, tell her she's wrong, and the best thing she can do for herself is stay away from me. But before I can, her lips are sealed on mine.

She's kissing me.

We're kissing.

And for a moment, I get lost in it. Lost in the softness of her lips, her sweet cherry-lilac scent, the warmth of her torso pressing into me. My hand tangles in her curls as I deepen the kiss, and the tiniest moan escapes her. I—*fuck*!

Pushing her away gently, she whines and whimpers at the broken connection. "Margot, I—we can't. Please. Just... lie down, can you do that for me?"

She casts her eyes down, and her lip pushes out in a pout, rejection written all over her, but I know it's the right call. She nods her head as she slinks back onto the bed. I pull the covers down so she can climb underneath them. Once she's settled, I pull the covers back up and lay on top of them. I'm only staying until she's asleep, then I'll go into the living room. She'll be pissed tomorrow if I stay.

Knowing I'd never touch her while she's drunk but also knowing how tempting it is when she's throwing herself at me, I put my hands behind my head and stare at the ceiling. It's got to be close to one in the morning by now, but I left my phone on the dresser, so I can't be sure.

Not five minutes later, Margot is already asleep. I take a deep breath, not sure how I survived the last hour. Trying to make as little noise as possible, I slide out of bed and grab my phone, knowing I'll need to send off some texts before I go to sleep. Just as I'm about to walk out of the room, my eyes land on her boots. Moving them to beside the chair where her dress hangs, I turn to leave again. I take one more glance at the woman occupying my bed and my mind. I don't let myself linger though.

Walking into the kitchen, I grab some ibuprofen and water, intent on leaving it on the bedside for when she wakes up. I know going back into the room is risky, but I push the thought aside.

She's kicked the covers off, leaving her legs exposed, and the shirt I put her in rides up her stomach. I close my eyes, burning the vision of her almost naked in my bed into my brain, before placing the medicine and water on the table, grabbing my pillow, and quickly leaving again.

How the fuck am I going to explain this tomorrow? She thinks she called Hayes. She had no intention of seeing me tonight, let alone sleeping in my bed.

I throw the pillow on the couch and sit down, bringing my head into my hands. I never saw this coming. Shit, I never saw *her* coming. But this situation isn't one I know how to handle.

I pull out my phone and scroll through my contacts, landing on Hayes's name. I'm about to call him and tell him what's going on, but then I remember Margot is a grown-ass woman and doesn't need me tattling on her. Instead, I start a group chat with Ripley and Thea.

12/13 1:12 a.m.

Me: Next time you invite her out, maybe don't get her plastered. You're both ass-holes.

Delivered

I send it off knowing they won't see it until morning when they wake up hungover and regretting their decisions from the night before. I lay down on the couch, closing my eyes, and hoping Margot won't wake up with the same regret.

I've never truly felt addiction before. I smoke, sure, but I feel like I could quit if I wanted to. But her? Kissing her? Feeling the way our bodies lined up so perfectly? I can see it becoming my new addiction—and one I won't ever want to quit.

Chapter Fourteen

My brain feels too big for my head, my eyes are like sandpaper under my eyelids, and my mouth tastes like a dumpster. As I wake more, the pressure in my head turns to a pulsing pain behind my eyes, and nausea roils in my stomach.

I'm never drinking with Thea and Ripley again.

Last night is a blur of loud music, fried food, and tequila. *So much tequila.* I remember laughing, real belly-aching laughter, and dancing with Thea and Ripley. Was Archer there too?

I roll to my side, trying to find a more comfortable position, and take a few deep breaths hoping my stomach will settle. Then I freeze, and my eyes spring open. A comforting bergamot smell I recognize surrounds me, but I can't place it. It's mixed with an undertone of cigarette smoke, making my stomach squeeze. The room is large and unfamiliar. My eyes scan the window and bedside table, snagging on my phone lying next to a glass of water and a bottle of ibuprofen.

Please let me be alone in this bed. Please let me be alone in this bed.

My heart pounds in my chest, I can almost feel it in my throat, and it makes the throbbing in my head even worse.

As slowly and gently as possible, I turn my head to look around. With a quick glance behind me, I'm greeted by nothing but more rumpled bedding. Letting out a relieved breath, I push myself to a seated position and take in the rest of the room. The furniture and wallpaper are dated—a style that looks like it belongs back in 1992—but in good condition. Unfortunately, nothing in the space is giving me any hint as to where I am.

I reach for my phone to check the time, but it's dead. *Of course.*

I'm just going to assume I ended up crashing at Ripley's or Thea's. They wouldn't have let me go home with someone in my state, right?

My dress from last night hangs neatly on a chair in the corner, my shoes on the floor next to it. I look down and see I'm in an oversized grey RED T-shirt and—thankfully—the panties and bra I wore out last night are on underneath.

Other than my head, the next body part screaming for attention is my bladder. Squeezing my thighs together, I slowly climb from the bed and go to the only door in the room. I'm thankful to find the large T-shirt falls to mid-thigh, covering me just enough. With one hand on the door handle and the other cradling my dead phone, I listen for any sounds on the other side for a few moments, and when I don't hear anything, I push through into a dim hallway.

Several closed doors line the length of the space, but I spot a partially open one leading to a bathroom. As I tiptoe toward it, I keep my ears pricked for any noises from other parts of the house, but it's silent. The walls in the hallway are a drab yellow, punctuated by numerous nail holes and discolored square and rectangular outlines indicating dozens of pictures hung here at one point.

I sigh in relief after plopping myself on the toilet and massage my temples, willing the headache to ease. Unfortunately, the action does almost nothing. *I'm never drinking again.*

While washing my hands, I catch a glimpse of my reflection in the mirror and groan. My hair looks like a rat's nest, curls frizzy and limp. The makeup I painstakingly applied last night is smeared, mascara and eyeliner smudged under my eyes making me look about as good as I feel.

I splash some cold water on my face and use a tissue to clean up the best I can. Looking back at the mirror, instead of looking half-dead, I appear like I haven't slept in a week, so... an improvement?

Men's toiletries litter the bathroom, all-in-one shampoo-conditioner-body wash in the shower, a stick of Dove for Men deodorant and a straight razor next to the sink. We must have gone back to Ripley's. I recall Thea saying he lives close enough to walk to the bar. Relief surges through me at the thought I'm not in some stranger's home.

I open the mirrored medicine cabinet, hoping to find confirmation I'm at Ripley's house. No luck—just some topical pain relief cream and floss.

Okay, I'll just go downstairs and either find a charger and call Hayes to come get me, or I'll find Thea or Ripley, and they can help me get back home or at least to Hayes' shop. I wish I could tell what time it is.

A couple more deep breaths and I won't empty my stomach on the hallway floor. I quietly step out and creep down the stairs right outside the bathroom door. The stairs spill out into an empty entryway and dining room.

The space isn't exactly how I'd imagine Ripley living. Everything is dated—the furniture, rugs, even the curtains look like they were hung by a middle-aged woman, not a twenty-something man living on his own. Maybe he inherited the place from his parents? I don't know much about his family—from what I've heard, he grew up in Indigo Hill, but his parents aren't in the area anymore.

Suddenly, there's rustling from the couch. I can't see what's making the noise because the couch faces away from the stairs, so I creep closer.

Long, elegant fingers twitch. The muscular, tattooed arm they're attached to covers most of the face of their owner, who quietly snores. A long body drapes over the sofa, feet and calves hanging over the end. He's shirtless, miles of muscles and dark tattoos on display interrupted by bruises and scrapes in various states of healing. A blanket covers his lower half.

There are a few empty beer bottles strewn on the coffee table along with an overflowing ashtray. The pang in my chest of how similar this scene is to what I find at my dad's house on a weekly basis is eclipsed by the shock of seeing Brooks splayed out. My hand comes up to my mouth, barely keeping my gasp inside.

Why is Brooks here? Please, please, please don't let this be his house. What happened last night?

I slowly back out of the living room, right up the stairs where I hurry into the bedroom I slept in. I reach for the dress I wore last night, and I'm about to switch it out for the T-shirt I'm wearing but get a whiff of last night on the material: day-old liquor, smoke, and sweat from dancing.

Realizing I can't wear it outside, I rummage through the dresser and luckily find a pair of mens' basketball shorts a few sizes too big. I try not to think about the fact the clothes belong to Brooks. I roll up the top of the shorts and stick my feet into my ankle booties. I look and feel ridiculous, but I just need to get out of here.

I'm not entirely sure where I am, but Indigo Hill is pretty small, I should be able to find my way to the center of town and to Hayes' shop. My stomach roils at having to explain my state to my brother—and it has nothing to do with my hangover.

As silently as possible, I sneak back downstairs. Holding my breath and with my shoulders tucked up under my ears, I try to make as little noise as possible. I'm just a few feet from the front door when I hear a deep, raspy voice say, "You could at least have breakfast with me as a thank you for last night."

I empty my lungs, and my body deflates at being caught. When I turn around, Brooks is sitting up on the sofa, lazy grin spread across his face and eyes still sleepy.

"I'm sorry, I didn't want to wake you," I say feebly. There's a long pause as we take each other in. His cerulean eyes rake up and down my body, something akin to satisfaction reflected in his expression when he sees I'm wearing his clothes. I immediately heat from my head to my toes, my cheeks especially. "This is your house? How did we get here?" I ask, trying to deflect from my discomfort at his scrutiny.

He says something as he stands and stretches his long limbs. I'm distracted from his answer by the plain black T he's now wearing riding up and giving me a good look at his toned abs. My eyes graze lower and catch a bulge in the briefs he must have slept in. A very prominent bulge.

It's the morning, and he's a man. It's very common.

Somehow I can't tear my eyes away—at least not until he clears his throat, at which point I meet his amused gaze, and my body heats even further, this time in embarrassment.

"My eyes are up here, baby," he says with a chuckle. His morning voice causing a shiver to cascade all the way down my spine. I barely suppress a tremble.

The endearment triggers a flash of last night in the back of my mind: the feeling of his warm body, holding me close, vibrations from his motorcycle underneath me. It's quickly swallowed up by the grey cloud of nothing that is my drunken memories.

"How do you like your eggs?" Brooks asks as he adjusts himself and walks over to the adjoining kitchen.

I follow him, feeling rude for trying to sneak away, and plant myself on one of the stools at the breakfast bar.

"I'm not picky," I say, and then add, "Do you have a charger? My phone's dead." My words are stunted. I'm embarrassed by my state this morning and by what I may have said yesterday. I've never been drunk before, I don't know how I act when intoxicated. I've never woken up in a man's house before after a night of... well, I'm not really sure of what.

Did he change me out of my dress? I'm too mortified to ask.

The shame of not remembering what could have possibly happened claws up my throat, and I stammer out, "I—I'm sorry. If I did—or said—anything last night." My hands come up to cover my face. "I don't drink usually. It was a first for me, and I'm sorry if I embarrassed myself."

Brooks pauses his perusal of the fridge and looks over. His face is blank, but his eyes take in every inch of me. After a brief moment, he steps over to me and invades my space. His arms cage me in against the counter. The warmth of his body doing nothing to cool my overheated skin. "You have nothing to be embarrassed about, Freckles," he murmurs, eyes hooded and locked on mine. "I'm just lucky my mama taught me to be a gentleman."

He steps away with his lips quirked in that way that makes my brain stutter, and I'm left reeling with what his words could possibly mean.

"The charger's right there," he says, indicating with his chin, before he turns back to the fridge and pulls out an armful of ingredients.

I charge my phone while Brooks cooks, my gaze straying to the way his clothes hug his body, his sure movements. He hasn't bothered putting on anything over his briefs, and the moment feels strangely domestic, like something we've been doing forever.

As my phone finally powers on and I see it's close to ten, Brooks drops a plate of scrambled eggs, toast, and bacon in front of me. It's nothing fancy, but the smells promise protein and grease—a welcome scent to my hungover tummy.

I dig right in, and he joins me on the nearby stool. We eat in silence for a bit, and then I ask, "So this is your parents' house? The one you're going to fix up?"

"Yeah," Brooks says around a mouthful of eggs and then adds after swallowing, "I figure if I can update it enough, I can sell it for a decent price."

I nod. "Definitely. Imagine if you opened up the window here," I say pointing to what's now a tiny over-the-sink window. "You'd be able to see the whole backyard and get so much more light. And these cabinets should definitely be white. Oh, or sage!" I get so lost in the dream of renovating the small but cozy kitchen, I don't even notice Brooks has stopped eating and is listening intently. "And the island should really be facing the other direction. Imagine how much more usable it would be if it was turned..." I trail off as I catch sight of the look on his face.

"I like your ideas," he says in his deep rumble. "Maybe... maybe I can take you out to dinner and you could tell me more?" His eyes are vulnerable and his expression open.

My stomach bottoms out. I can't tell if it's the instant nerves from Brooks asking me out or the alcohol still gripping my stomach, but I feel ill. I want to say yes, but all of my insecurities from last night and this morning make me feel raw. I'm curious about him, but I think he'd lose interest in me quickly.

"I... don't think that's a good idea," I finally say, and his gaze narrows at me in question. "I'm not sure I'm the right girl for that... for you. I'm not what you're looking for. I'm... not like that."

There's a silent pause that lasts for a beat. Two. Three. Our eyes are still locked, and I can't look away, despite the adrenaline in my veins.

And then Brooks breaks the quiet as he cocks his head and says, "Not like that, huh? Not like *what* exactly?"

I scramble for the right way to tell him how we're not a good fit. I have no experience in... home renovation, let alone much else. My mouth starts forming around the words explaining how his reputation paints him as someone I wouldn't know how to handle, how my inexperience would be of no interest to him, but I'm saved by my ringing phone.

Hayes.

"Hey, Hayes," I say into the phone, my eyes locking with Brooks' and hoping he knows enough to keep quiet. I'm not ready to explain what I'm doing with Brooks to my brother.

"Margot," he snaps, and for a split second I think he knows where I am. Panic fills me, like I'm about to be scolded. "You need to get over to Dad's. I tried to go over there today, but he started spewing his bullshit, and I can't deal with him."

I let out a relieved breath. "Uh, yeah. I'll head over there. Is he okay?"

"Honestly, I don't even care anymore. I have too much shit going on to have to babysit his sorry ass." Hayes' voice is elevated, and I'm not sure if Brooks can hear what he's saying, but his face is slowly morphing into a silent rage—eyebrows slanted, molars clenching so tight the muscles feather at his jaw. I instinctively place my hand on his forearm to placate him.

"Okay, I'll go over there. I'll call you later," I say quickly and hang up before Hayes says anything more.

Brooks and I are still caught in our stare off for a few seconds when his eyes slide to my hand on his arm. I didn't realize I started stroking the soft skin there with my thumb. I pull it back and say, "I, uh, I need to go."

"Does he always talk to you like that?" His voice is strained, like he's holding back.

"Not usually," I reply in almost a whisper. "He really only raises his voice after... after seeing our dad. That's where I have to go. They don't get along and had a fight, so I have to go check on him." That seems to do the trick, and he visibly relaxes.

"Come on. I'll take you." He gets up and takes our plates to the sink.

"Oh, you don't have to. I'll get a rideshare. He's all the way out in Southbury," I say.

He scoffs and heads out of the kitchen, shaking his head.

"If you think I'm letting you get in a car with a stranger, you're sorely mistaken," he throws out over his shoulder as he steps over to his makeshift bed. He produces jeans from somewhere next to the couch and slips them on while making his way to the door. Stepping into his boots, he grabs a leather jacket from a coat closet and then turns to me, holding out a woman's parka and my purse.

I still haven't moved from my stool, having lost all train of thought as I watched him move around the space. His expectant look snaps me out of my daze, and I hurry over.

He must see the question on my face when I look at the parka because he says, "It's my mom's."

To my surprise, Brooks holds out the jacket for me and helps me into it, then gently turns me around and zips it, his hands lingering right below my face. With his eyes on mine, I feel the faintest brush of his thumb across my bottom lip. It's so quick and light, I'm not entirely sure I didn't imagine it.

"What did you mean by 'not like that?'" he murmurs, his piercing blue eyes boring into me.

I take a breath and a step back, averting my eyes as I do. "I'm not looking for... a hookup. I'm not that girl. I know you like to have fun, and there's nothing wrong with that. I'm just... not that. I'm looking for something more serious. Permanent."

His lips thin as his head nods like he agrees with me, but I see the flash of hurt in his eyes. For a moment, it looks like he's biting the inside of his cheek to hold back saying more. Then he's turning away and out the door with a clipped, "Let's go."

By the time I've closed the door and taken the few steps off the porch, Brooks is straddling his motorcycle, holding out a black helmet toward me.

"We're going on this?" I say, hoping my voice doesn't betray my nerves. "Wait, is this what we rode back here last night? How?"

His smirk is back as he answers, "We got... creative. Trust me, you loved wrapping yourself around me."

I roll my eyes and take the helmet, securing the strap under my chin. He chuckles and pulls the second helmet off the handle bars and slips it over his head.

"Climb on," he says.

I hesitate, but then throw a leg over the bike behind him, trying to keep some space between our bodies. I flounder looking around for where to put my feet when he grabs my ankle and places it on a peg and then does the same with the other foot.

"You're going to need to hold on to me, Freckles." Thankful he can't see my cheeks flush under the helmet, I gently place my hands on his sides. He grips each one and tugs it farther forward so I'm tucked in tight behind him, my body plastered to his.

The motorcycle rumbles to life underneath us. The sound sends a spark of excitement through me, concentrating low in my belly. Then with practiced ease, Brooks raises the kickstand, and we're off. I squeeze my arms tighter around his torso, holding on, but trusting Brooks to keep me safe.

CHAPTER FIFTEEN

Having Margot's arms wrapped around me again felt just as good as last night, making me feel less empty than I have in ages. A part of me wanted to think her being sober this time meant she was squeezing me so tightly because she wanted to. The more rational side reminded me of the conversation we'd had right before she got the call from Hayes, squashing the thought altogether. It's the motorcycle; her punishing grip was from fear and nothing else.

I spent the ride thinking way too hard about the way Hayes spoke to her. I'm still fuming over it. Not that it matters. I'm not her protector. I'm not her *anything*. She made it perfectly clear. She wants a relationship. A boyfriend. Probably a husband and babies. All things we both know I can't give her. I'm not that kind of guy. I'm not sure why I keep trying to convince either of us otherwise.

I'm familiar with Southbury, so when she told me where her dad's house is, I knew the area well enough to get us mostly there. We pull onto the main street on the outskirts of town, and she directs me to the next turn. As I drive down the dirt road, I realize we're on the other side of the property that houses The Pit. I've never been on this side of the lot, but it's familiar enough from the treeline on the edge of the property.

The recognition brings me back to the moment at the hardware store when she mentioned The Pit. I never gave her an answer, and I never asked how she knew about it. I certainly didn't bring it up to Hayes out of fear of him asking why I'd been around his sister long enough for her to even ask about it. But seeing how close we are as we pull up to her childhood home, I'm not sure how she wasn't aware of the fighting ring in her dad's backyard.

I cut the ignition in front of a run down farmhouse, push the kickstand down with my foot, and unhook my helmet. The second Margot's hold slips away from me, the emptiness creeps back in. An emptiness I never registered until she came into my life. It's making me question everything. But her words echo back to me, *"I'm looking for something more serious. Permanent."*

It shouldn't bother me. Knowing she doesn't think I'm capable of being serious or permanent should have cut the cord between us. *I* don't even think I'm capable of being serious or permanent, so why do I care if she agrees?

She clears her throat, snapping me out of my thoughts. "You can just... you can stay out here."

My brows crease as I let my eyes linger on hers. "Ouch, not even gonna invite me in, Freckles?" I tease, hoping it'll change her mind. Going inside means getting another glimpse into her life, it means feeding the obsession. Regardless of what she thinks, and regardless of what I can offer her, I'm too fucking addicted to be a bystander when it comes to her.

"Oh, no, you can," she says, sounding guilty for even suggesting I stay outside.

I place my helmet on one handlebar and hers on the other. The only sound filling the air as we walk toward the dilapidated house is the crunching of the gravel beneath our feet. The closer we get, the worse it looks. There are shutters hanging off the windows. The porch steps look like they're ready to crumble the moment any weight is placed on them. Shingles are missing all over the roof. The list goes on.

As we get to the steps, she turns to look at me, and shame is written all over her face even before her desperate words leave her lips. "The place is a wreck. I know. Please... well, please don't judge me for the way it looks. I do as much as I can. And I know—"

I cut her off by placing my hands on her shoulders. "Baby, hey, I'm not judging you, okay? I don't have any right to judge anyone—but especially not you." I pull her toward me, placing a kiss on the top of her head. Everything in me screams to shield her from all the bad things in her life. Including myself.

I hate seeing her so scattered like this. I don't know the deal with her dad, but it's clear she isn't comfortable with people seeing this part of her life. If I were a better man, I'd get on my bike and drive away, let her handle this on her own and respect her wishes to do so. But I'm selfish and yearning for any morsels I can get from her.

I pull back, but my hand skates down her arm, linking our fingers together. She has a dazed look on her face like she isn't sure what's happening. That makes two of us.

"Come on," I say as I lead her toward the stairs. "Watch your step, this doesn't look very sturdy." I test one of the boards with my foot, quickly deciding it's not trustworthy at all. Before she can say no, I pull her to the side, grab her by the hips, and lift her up to the porch, bypassing the death trap entirely. The shock on her face is adorable, making me huff out a laugh. "What?" I ask as I step up and over the rotted boards.

She looks up at me, her five-foot-one stature laughable next to my six-foot-one. "You, umm, you just didn't have to do that."

I shake my head as I say, "I know," leaving it at that. "Should we knock?" I ask, changing the subject.

"Oh, uhh, no. I have a key." She opens her purse, digging out a keychain with an array of keys on it. She fiddles with it before finding the correct one then inserting it into the lock. As the door opens, she peeks into the house like she's not sure what she may find. "Dad?" she asks as she pushes the door all the way open and walks inside.

I follow behind her, immediately noting the smell of stale beer wafting through the home. As the room comes into view, I notice the beer cans on the end tables, even a couple on the couch. A pizza box sits half open on the coffee table, and Jeopardy silently plays on the muted TV. Margot looks over her shoulder to face me, her cheeks are a rosy pink. I could blame it on the cold, but I know it's from embarrassment.

I meant what I said, I'm not going to judge her. Did she grow up this way? Seeing the house makes me question a lot of things about Margot Mason. Things I never thought to ask about. Where's her mom? Does she have a good relationship with her father? He clearly drinks, is that why she never did? How many times does she come over here to "check on him?" And why does he need to be checked on? Why is Hayes not helping with any of this?

I don't ask any of the questions out loud, I just watch as she hastily picks up the trash from the living room. Once she's got a good handful of it thrown in the garbage bin in the corner of the room, she walks down the hallway saying, "Dad?" a few times before a grunting noise filters through the house. She rushes toward the sound, and I follow closely behind her.

As we round the entry to the bedroom, we see him on the floor covered in his own vomit. My hand covers my mouth to block the stench; I guess the smell was more than stale beer.

"Oh, my goodness, Dad!" she cries as she drops to the floor to assess him. I'm right beside her, trying not to breathe through my nose. She touches his forehead, checks his pulse, and peels his eyes open. The action jolts him. He shoots up so quickly, Margot barely has time to move out of his way. I pull her back to my chest and notice the tears running down her cheeks.

"Margot?" he croaks, his voice raspy and dull.

"I'm here, Daddy." She pushes away from me, wrapping her arm around him to pull him up. I don't waste any time going to help her. Unlike Hayes, I won't just stand by and let her handle it all on her own.

We're able to get him standing, though most of his weight is on me.

"We need to—" she makes a grunting noise as she shifts his arm around her neck just a bit, "get him to the bathroom." She points her chin toward the door on the other side of the room.

It takes a few minutes, but we finally get him through the door of the bathroom. Thankfully, there's a standing shower. Fighting with the ledge of the bathtub would have been a nightmare. I reach out my hand to pull the shower door open, hefting him up just a bit.

We lower him to the shower floor, the hope of him standing non-existent. As I straighten up, I turn to find Margot with her arms wrapped around herself, tears still streaming down her cheeks.

"I'll clean him up so you don't have to see this. Why don't you take care of the mess in his room?" I ask knowing no one should see their father in this condition but especially not a daughter. He'll need to be undressed, showered, clothed. I don't know how she's handled this alone in the past.

She nods her head, more tears welling in her eyes as she stutters, "Th-thank you."

The door clicks shut behind her, and I turn to look back at the man who made her cry. I realize I have zero sympathy for this guy, whose name I don't even know. He's putting her through hell. Hayes is yelling at her. I'm starting to look like the fucking good guy in her life, and that's not only backwards but not the life she deserves.

I walk toward the shower, reaching for the lever to turn on the water as I say, "You're not going to enjoy this, Mr. Mason. But I am." Maybe it makes me an asshole, but dousing the man in cold-ass water sounds appealing after seeing the heartache he's caused Margot.

After a few solid minutes of rinsing Mr. Mason down, I finally peel off his clothes so I can clean him off the rest of the way. The cold water does the trick in sobering him up enough to almost bathe himself. I do what I can but leave him to handle his junk on his own.

I reach into the shower to turn off the water at the same moment it seems to register to him a stranger washed his vomit off of him. The towel I'm holding out hangs between us for a beat longer than necessary. Embarrassment heats his cheeks as he takes the towel from my grasp and asks, "Who are you? And why are you with my daughter?" His words are slurred, and he sways where he stands, but he seems coherent.

Despite the man being found covered in the contents of his stomach, he has the balls to look me up and down like he's judging me. I know nothing about him, but I've seen enough to know he's a shit father and has no room to pass judgment on me.

"My name is Brooks, and I'm a friend of Margot's. I'm here with your daughter because I want to be." The words sound matter-of-fact because they are. I've told a lot of lies in my life, but this isn't one of them. He keeps his gaze locked with mine, probably waiting for me to say more, but there's nothing more to add.

Finally, he nods his head in what I hope is understanding before he stumbles out of the shower. I catch his arm and drape it over me to help him into the bedroom.

As I push through the door, I mentally prepare myself for the rancid smell to perforate my senses again, but it never comes. Margot has cleaned it up, making it seem like the incident never happened. It makes me wonder how many times she's had to do this. Not just cleaning him up from soiling himself in some way but cleaning up messes that aren't hers. Making problems disappear for others so they don't have to worry about the aftermath.

I heft him onto the bed, hoping his towel doesn't slip, I've seen enough of the man to last me a lifetime. He runs his hand through his hair then meets my eyes again.

I'm not sure what he's about to say, but I cut him off before he has a chance. "Listen, Mr. M—"

"Keaton. You can call me Keaton."

"Right, Keaton. I don't know you—"

He immediately goes rigid, cutting me off again, "You're damn right you don't."

I let my anger simmer to the surface but hold back from unleashing on him for Margot's sake. "But I do know Margot," I seethe. "And she deserves better than this."

I watch as his affronted attitude morphs into one of understanding. "I see."

Shaking my head, I say, "You don't. But I do. I see what she's been dealing with on her own. I see what she's been put through with you. She deserves more."

Turning from him, I walk to the dresser in the corner, pulling open drawers to find clean clothes. I grab a T-shirt, a pair of briefs, and a pair of pajama pants before throwing them in his direction. He just barely catches them.

As I turn the doorknob to leave his room, he clears his throat, stopping me in my tracks.

"Thank you."

I don't turn around. I don't say anything else. I just pull the door open and walk out of the room. As I walk through the house, I take my time to really look around before going to find Margot. Since the moment I met her, I had an idea of her home life and upbringing in my head. I'd painted her as a girl who grew up loved, nurtured, spoiled even. I'd built her up as the complete opposite of me. She had a career, a loving sibling—despite how overprotective the dude is—everything I thought made her who she is.

But as I look at the peeling paint on the walls—walls that raised the girl I can't get out of my head—I realize I'd been wrong all along. I saw Margot as the rounded corners to my jagged edges. Two pieces that could never fit. I thought she was perfect in every way and being around me would taint her soul. Turns out, she grew up with those same jagged edges, and deep down, maybe she has some of her own.

Our home life was still different. Alcohol was never a problem in our house. But seeing this side of her makes me wonder if she feels unworthy too. Maybe she feels like no one else truly sees her the same way I do.

Margot's in the kitchen washing the overflowing sink of dishes. Looking around the room, I see she's picked up all the beer cans, old food, and trash. I'm not sure how long I spent cleaning Keaton up, but it didn't feel long enough for her to do a deep clean.

Attempting not to scare her, I clear my throat, but it backfires as she yelps, just about jumping out of her skin. "Oh, my goodness, you scared the bejesus out of me!"

Her adorable lack of swearing makes me chuckle. Normally, I'd tease her for it. But none of this feels normal, and it doesn't feel like the time for teasing. It's out of character for me to even acknowledge someone else's feelings, but I try not to look too hard at it right now. "Sorry, Freckles. Believe it or not, that was my attempt to *not* scare you."

I can still see the dried tear tracks on her cheeks, and I hate it. I hate seeing her cry. It's quite possibly my least favorite thing in the world. And for a man who hates most things, that's saying a lot.

"I believe you," she says. It's such a simple thing to say, but it rattles something deep in my soul. I don't say anything more though, I walk over to her and wrap my arms around her. She leans her back into my chest, letting me support her weight, and we stand like this for a minute or two. Then I pull away and begin drying the dishes she's washing. After a few moments, she opens her mouth like she's going to say something but thinks better of it.

So we work in silence. Her washing dishes, me drying them, neither of us bringing up the shift in the air between us. I'm not sure I ever will because having any hope crushed when it comes to her might do more damage than The Pit ever could.

CHAPTER SIXTEEN

Brooks and I exchanged only a few words as we finished tidying up Dad's house. I can't remember the last time I've been so embarrassed. There's something about Brooks seeing this side of my life that makes me feel overly exposed.

I'm not usually self conscious about my dad. He's been this way pretty much my entire life. He has an illness, and he can't help his addiction. It didn't feel like Brooks was judging me, but for some reason what he thinks and how he sees me matters. He seems to hold me in high regard, and I don't want to disappoint him. I'd hate for him to treat me differently now after seeing how I grew up.

The way Brooks jumped in and helped clean up my dad has given me pause. It's not something I asked for and certainly not what I expected him to do. He doesn't come off as the overly caring type, but I'm starting to think he doesn't let many people see the real him, hiding behind an abrasive attitude and cocky smile.

I appreciated what he did more than I could articulate in the moment. I've had to clean my dad up multiple times, and it never gets easier. I'm thankful Brooks was there to lighten the load today.

The ride back to my house was quiet. I held on to him tightly, and he covered my hands with his large palm, running his thumb across the back of my wrist the entire way.

The small touches calmed my entire system, and I was left with a sense of loss when I had to extract myself from the back of the bike.

He waited until I had my door open and with a quick, "See you around, Freckles," he took off, his bike kicking up gravel in my driveway.

Having showered the minute I got inside, I'm finally feeling less hungover. I have all of my supplies out to meal prep for the next few days since I'll be working without another day off for a while when my phone dings with a text message. And then dings again. And again. I look over at the screen and see I've been added to a group chat with Thea and Ripley.

12/13 2:04 p.m.

> **Thea**: Margot! Are you alive?

12/13 2:04 p.m.

> **Ripley**: OMG, please no. It's too early.

12/13 2:05 p.m.

> **Thea**: It's 2 p.m. Stop pretending to sleep and get out here already so we can go get some coffee. Margot, join us!

12/13 2:05 p.m.

Ripley: NO, devil woman. Let me rot.

12/13 2:05 p.m.

Ripley: But if you're going, I'll take my usual.
angel emoji

Ripley named the conversation "Pour Decisions".

12/13 2:06 p.m.

Ripley: Margie! Are you alive? Did Brooks take care of you?

12/13 2:06 p.m.

Ripley: Oh shit, no, I hope he didn't "take care of you" take care of you.

12/13 2:07 p.m.

Thea: I will kill him.

12/13 2:08 p.m.

Me: Hi! I'm fine, guys. Had a rough morning, but I'm fine. Finally feeling better. Y'all go too hard for me.

Read 2:08 p.m.

12/13 2:08 p.m.

Ripley: Ugh, we go too hard for ourselves. No. More. Tequila.

12/13 2:09 p.m.

Thea: It was your idea!

12/13 2:09 p.m.

Ripley: Stop listening to me. I'm full of bad ideas.

12/13 2:09 p.m.

Ripley: Speaking of bad ideas… Margie, why did you call Brooks last night?

12/13 2:10 p.m.

Me: **peeking emoji** I meant to call Hayes but must have clicked Brooks' name instead.

Read 2:10 p.m.

12/13 2:10 p.m.

Ripley: Likely story.

I smile at my phone. Thea and Ripley are fun. They're genuine and accepted me into their fold no questions asked. And after what I learned about both of them, I feel like I can call them friends. The thought fills my chest with a warmth I'm not used to. This feeling of connection is what I've been searching for since I moved back.

I debate if I should share the events of this morning. They might have insight into Brooks. They've both known him a lot longer than I have. Perhaps they can help answer some of my questions. Such as why does nothing I've heard about him match up to the man I've come to know?

With a deep breath and feeling empowered by the natural trust I feel for Thea and Ripley, I type out my next message.

12/13 2:11 p.m.

Me: Can you guys tell me more about Brooks?

Read 2:11 p.m.

12/13 2:11 p.m.

Ripley: **monocle emoji**

12/13 2:12 p.m.

Thea: What do you want to know?

12/13 2:12 p.m.

Ripley: Thea grew up with him. She can give you all the dirt.

12/13 2:13 p.m.

Me: I know what people say about him around Indigo Hill. How much of it is true?

Read 2:13 p.m.

There's a long pause before the next message pops up.

12/13 2:15 p.m.

Thea: Brooks is… complicated. A lot of what people say about him is true. But I think a lot is also exaggerated or at least superficial. People have made a lot of assumptions, and he hasn't denied them, mostly because I don't think he cares enough to.

12/13 2:15 p.m.

Ripley: Are you… interested, Margie?

12/13 2:16 p.m.

Me: I'm… intrigued. I can't seem to match up the Brooks I've gotten to know with his reputation. Am I crazy for being open to spending some time with him?

Read 2:16 p.m.

12/13 2:17 p.m.

Ripley: I don't know about Thea, but I'm a BIG fan of Brooks. Yeah, he has his moments where he'll actively try to burn every relationship he has to the ground, but I think it's part of his charm. There's always that thirty seconds when he first enters a room and you're trying to figure out if he chose violence that morning. It's pretty exhilarating.

12/13 2:18 p.m.

Thea: I don't think that sounds as appealing as you think, babe.

12/13 2:18 p.m.

Ripley: In all seriousness, he's always had my back. He might have his own set of rules he lives by, but the man gives his all to whatever he cares about.

12/13 2:19 p.m.

Thea: Despite my annoyance with him 99.9 % of the time, I agree with Rip. Brooks isn't as hard as he wants people to think, and he'll never say it, but he genuinely cares. When he can get out of his own way, he's a good man to have in your corner.

My whole body warms with confirmation of what I think I've known all along about the man in question. It's comforting to see he has people who know enough about him to love him despite his sharp edges.

12/13 2:20 p.m.

Me: Thanks.

Read 2:21 p.m.

12/13 2:22 p.m.

Ripley: I will say this, a lot of the rumors about him may not be true, but some definitely are. Take it from both Thea and me and our (unfortunate) eye-witness experience: Wrap. It. Up.

My cheeks heat at Ripley's insinuation. I put my phone down and go back to prepping veggies for my lunches for the next few days.

Spending time with Brooks is one thing, getting intimate is a whole other beast. Thinking back to when he asked me out, I'm feeling a slight pang of regret at how quickly I dismissed him. Should I open myself up to going on a date with him?

He's been nothing but sweet to me since the moment I met him. He's undeniably hot; it's not even subjective—just fact. How would he react if things escalated and I told him I'm a virgin? I'm getting ahead of myself. We are so far from anything like that.

The other major issue is my brother. More than once he's insinuated I need to stay away from Brooks, even though he's the one who sent him to my house to fix my pipes. But they're friends. Surely he's aware of what Brooks is really like, right?

The more I think about it, the harder it is to come up with reasons I shouldn't take Brooks up on his dinner offer. If he's even still interested after I turned him down and everything he learned about my family today.

CHAPTER SEVENTEEN

I've spent the last hour trying to find the balls to bring Margot up to Ripley. I know he'll be chill about it—or as chill as Ripley is capable of being. He tends to get excited about things prematurely. When I told him I wanted to help in the distillery years ago, he was so stoked he put together a five-year growth plan with the two of us at the helm and presented it to me with crazy eyes and a creepy ass smile. I almost took the offer back because of it.

I'm embarrassed I even have to ask for his advice. I've seen dates on TV. I know what the concept is. My issue is Margot. I don't think she's the type of girl who wants to go to dinner and a movie. Plus, that sounds boring as fuck.

I also hope she says yes this time. If she doesn't, there won't be a fourth. I may be slightly obsessed with her, but I won't humiliate myself. Being turned down twice has already bruised my ego, but I can't deny the pull I have toward her or the moment we shared at her dad's house.

She's more than *just a girl* though. I see that now. I feel it in my bones, my soul. The desolate yet beautiful look on her face after we dealt with her dad is ingrained in my brain. So much so, I picked up my sketchbook for the first time in years last night just so I could get it out. I haven't drawn in over a decade at this point, the most I've done is graphic art, which isn't the same. Using my hands to make something as beautiful as Margot is its own artform.

When I finished the drawing, it felt like a piece of my shattered heart found its place again. I've suppressed that part of myself for so long. I've wanted it back, needed it back even, but it felt impossible. Over the last fifteen years, I've put my shit aside to be what I thought my parents wanted me to be. Now they're gone, and after reading my mom's letter, I've started to wonder why I ever let their view of me interfere with my passions. I shouldn't have let their laughter deter me when I told them I wanted to become a tattoo artist. I should have let it fuel me.

I'm walking around the distillery, shifting barrels and doing whatever else Ripley needs me to do to get ready for our tasting in thirty minutes with the sketch in my back pocket like a fucking stalker. Clearing my throat, I get his attention from behind the bar where he's restocking before patrons get here. "Hey, uh... after the tastings, can we talk a bit?"

His brows crease as he meets my eyes. "Shit, you aren't quitting on us too, are you?" The despair from the possibility of me saying yes to his question is written all over his face.

I jolt back in confusion. "What? No. Who's quitting?"

"Travis. He put in his notice, and Thea's scrambling to find someone to replace him," he answers.

"Oh shit," I say. "I just have something I want to ask you—talk to you about. It's not a big deal." I'm making it sound like a big fucking deal.

"Right. Well, if you're not quitting, does it have anything to do with Margot?"

How the fuck?

I'm fairly certain my face does a thing the moment he says Margot's name, giving me away. I push past it though, ignoring the knot forming in my stomach at the possibility I'm being too obvious. "After the tastings, Ripley."

I head out into the restaurant side of RED, beelining my way to the back patio for a smoke.

This patio has always been one of my favorite spots here. It overlooks Indigo Lake, but even inside, you get a view. The whole backside of the restaurant has floor to ceiling windows, so even if you're not lucky enough to get outdoor seating, you still get a killer atmospheric vibe from it.

I spend the next half hour out here chain smoking and hiding from Ripley so he doesn't corner and pester the shit out of me for information. Asking for his advice before the tasting will only throw me off my game.

The RED tasting room is filled with people, some on the stools around the bar, others looking at the bottles we have for sale. We had a sold out afternoon with three of these back to back; we're on our final one of the day now. Some of the customers we've seen today are regulars, and a couple are from out of town. We don't typically get many tourists in the winter months, but Ripley and Thea are putting us on the map, and it's happening more often.

"What do you think, Rip? Should we share the recipe secret? They seem trustworthy." The regulars know the skit, but they're all champs about it and let us get through it without interruption. Honestly, our whole spiel is corny as fuck, but people still laugh and have a great time.

"Nah, you know I like to keep it close to the chest," he scoffs, being overdramatic like usual.

I roll my eyes back at him. "And they call you the 'fun' one."

"Hey!" he says defensively as he throws a towel at me. "I'm the most fun, and you know it!" He looks to the crowd around us. "Right, guys? I'm fun?"

They all chuckle, some pick up their glasses to avoid the awkwardness. A man at the end of the bar yells, "You'd be more fun if you told us!" He's not someone I recognize, so he must be from out of town. They all laugh at Ripley's pouting face.

Like fuck would we ever tell anyone the secret recipe. It would only fast track us back to being nobodies in this small town. Even hints would be too much of a risk.

In the last few weeks, since we were closed, Ripley has opened a new barrel. It's a new recipe he's had aging for years now with a caramel and chocolate undertone. This crowd doesn't know it yet, but they're about to get a taste of it.

The last two tastings raved about it. As usual, I watched Ripley preen from the attention and compliments. Not going to lie, it made me wonder if the guy has a praise kink. Which immediately made me wonder what kind of kinks Margot may have. Which then led to me excusing myself to walk off the half-chub before the next tasting started.

Once the group has calmed down from the laughter, Ripley reaches down to pull the decanter from below the bar. "Well, since I'm no fun, I guess no one wants to try our new batch, huh?" They all perk up, rumbling about how they were wrong, and they *definitely* want to try it. Ripley replies with a mumbled, "Uh huh," before uncorking the bottle.

"He thrives off of praise, y'all. If you compliment him, he tends to be a more generous pour." Ripley snickers at me. "Don't even pretend like it's not true."

"Yeah, yeah. Whatever. Anyway, this is one I've been working on for the last few years. It's got a nice caramel-butterscotch finish with a chocolate undertone. It's not as good as RED, but I think it has some potential."

He's already pouring the samples into the patrons' glasses, watching them intently as they swirl the bourbon and smell the aroma. I swear to God, the moment he hears someone make an "ooo" noise, his chest puffs up with pride. The sight makes me chuckle under my breath. I've seen it all day, and it never gets old.

Not surprisingly, they all love it. The chatter and compliments start pouring in, and I laugh from the corner as I start cleaning the used glasses. From behind me, I can hear Ripley giving refills. I peek over my shoulder to confirm then shout, "I told y'all compliments are his weakness."

Ripley answers some questions about the new batch, like when will it be available for purchase, when will we carry it in the restaurant, is it limited or a permanent release, all questions we haven't even decided on yet from what I've been told. Then he asks the crowd if they have any other questions before they pack up and leave.

An older lady, an out-of-towner, asks, "Where did the name Ripple Effect come from?"

I jump in before Ripley can answer because it's one of my favorite questions. "Partially from this guy right here," I say as I grab his shoulders from behind. "And partially from the vision he and Thea had for this place." I move closer to the bar to recount the story of Ripple Effect Distillery and Restaurant. "The locals know this, but most from out of town don't. This place used to be a hole-in-the-wall diner. We had the checkered floors and everything. It was called Indigo Hill Diner and owned by my late parents."

I let that sink in for a moment before continuing. I may have had a complicated relationship with them, but speaking about them is still difficult. The lady's face drops as she realizes what I said. "Then Thea, an angel of a woman, came back into our lives and revitalized the place. She proposed we give it one last hurrah and turn it into something bigger. By some miracle, my parents listened. Then Ripley came back into town itching to break into the distillery business. The two of them were masterminds. They brought the plans to my parents, who loved their ideas, and somehow convinced the bank to give us a shot.

"When it came time to name it, Ripley said, 'What about Ripple Effect?' We all laughed thinking he just wanted to name it after himself. But he got real serious—he never does that, by the way." I look over to Ripley who shrugs. "He said, 'A ripple effect means change, and that's what this is. A change for us all. Thea came back causing a ripple effect for all of us, so it feels right.'" I keep my gaze locked on his as I recount this part of the story. It was so insightful for someone who communicates primarily through sarcasm.

"That's beautiful," the lady who posed the question responds. The rest of the group mumbles the same, all raising a glass to Ripley and Ripple Effect as a whole.

The second the tasting is over and I've locked up after the last customer, Ripley turns to me. "Talk." His eyebrows are raised like he's been counting down the minutes to get to this conversation.

I shake my head, barely holding in a laugh at how excited he seems. "I'm not so sure I want to anymore," I tease.

"Oh, fuck off. What's up?"

I throw the towel I've been using to dry glasses over my shoulder before walking to a stool to sit down. "Give me some of the new shit first," I say, pointing my chin toward the almost empty decanter.

Ripley gives me a decent pour, grabs himself a glass, and empties the rest into it. As I take a sip, savoring the new flavor profile he's created, he walks around to sit next to me.

"So you, uhh," I start, already feeling embarrassed, "you know women, right?"

His face screws up with confusion. "Uh, a few, yeah…"

"No, I mean like… what do they like?" He stares at me, blinks a few times, like no one is fucking home inside that head of his. I run my hand over my buzzed hair, trying to find the right words to get my point across. "Like… what do they like to do?"

He finally comes back to life and says, "…This isn't a sex thing, right? Because one, I think you get laid way more than I do. And two, you know I'm gay, right? You weren't *so* drunk at that dumpster fire of a dinner you forgot… Please say you didn't forget."

I huff out a laugh. Ripley is probably the only one who could make me laugh right now. Maybe Margot too. "I remember. And this isn't a 'sex thing.' I just need advice on dating. But I don't feel comfortable asking anyone else. And I figure, no matter what team you bat for, you've got to know more than I do."

He weighs my response, his head bobbing back and forth for a moment. "You're probably right. And I'm happy you feel comfortable coming to me. Can I just ask… does this have to do with our very pretty, very sweet curly-haired nurse?"

I shoot him a look in response, feeling like I don't need words to get my answer across. And I have to tell myself he isn't into her, he's just being Ripley. The possessiveness I feel for a moment takes me by surprise though. I've never been a jealous guy—mainly because I've never cared enough about someone to feel jealous.

"Got it. Okay. Well, first off, she's a fucking catch so you've at least finally found some good taste."

I flip him off, the hidden insult about my previous "taste" obvious.

"Can we not?" I ask, and he just laughs.

"Listen, Brooks, women just want your time and attention. It's really that simple. What you do isn't as important, but it can certainly help. I'd stay away from the tired dinner and a movie idea though. No woman wants to sit in a quiet movie theater for most of your date; they like to chat, get to know you."

Nodding my head, I say, "Right. Okay. So, not dinner and a movie. Got it. Any... other ideas?"

"You gotta find something that *looks* like you put a ton of effort in but still isn't so flashy it's unbelievable you came up with it on your own. Flashy isn't your style anyway."

I take a deep breath, blowing it out to relieve the stress building up in my chest. "You're making this too difficult. Maybe I just shouldn't. I'll fuck it up anyway."

He laughs, which only pisses me off. "You're making it harder than it needs to be. Just pick something with the right blend of activity and hanging out. You want her to be comfortable. Oh, and food. There should always be food. Specifically cheese. Girls are animals when they get hangry and not in the fun way."

I'm already feeling the pressure. Ripley must notice because he pats me on the back as he adds, "Look, I can't do all the heavy lifting. This is your girl, so it's got to be your date. She'll know someone else planned it if it doesn't seem like a 'you' idea. But I'm confident you'll figure it out."

Glad one of us is, I think to myself.

Before turning to leave, Ripley adds, "Just uhh... maybe don't bring her here to cap off your night? I don't need to walk in on another one of your umm... dalliances." I snicker at his back as he walks off laughing to himself. He clearly has more confidence in me than I do.

Chapter Eighteen

The bell above the door of Mark of Mason rings as I push it open, grabbing Kori's attention from the desk. She's reading some magazine straight out of the 2000s. When she sees it's me, she gives me a chin nod then goes back to looking through her trashy tabloids.

I decided if I'm going to ask Margot out on a date—officially this time—I need to talk to Hayes. I'm fully aware he might kill me for this, but I want to do right by my friendship with him. Maybe he'll make me fight him in The Pit. He seems like the type of guy who would want a fair fight no matter how pissed off he is.

Within seconds of entering the building, I hear Margot's voice.

Fuck. What is she doing here? I wonder if she's talking to Hayes about their dad. Maybe she's asking for help so she doesn't have to handle it herself or rely on me.

As I round the corner, she comes into view. I remember a second too late, as her eyes meet mine, I have her dress from the other night—washed and neatly folded—tucked under my arm. I'd planned on explaining myself and what happened in great detail to Hayes before handing it over to him to return to Margot. Well, maybe not *great* detail. I'd leave out the part where she kissed me. And the part about her being half-naked.

But she's here. At Mark of Mason. Her eyes shifting back and forth between me and the dress I'm holding. Before I have time to say anything, Hayes' phone is ringing, and he's getting up from where he was sitting. "I'll be back," he says to everyone in the room, giving me a chin nod as he passes.

The second he's out of view, Margot grabs my arm and pulls me into the break room. "Fuck—ow!" I grumble as her nails dig into my arm. For such a small thing, she's surprisingly strong. She closes the door behind us, immediately crossing her arms over her chest with a pissed off look on her face. "For a nurse, I'd think hurting your patients is against your code of conduct."

Her face scrunches up a bit as she whisper-shouts, "Okay, first off, you aren't my patient. Secondly, you deserved that! Why did you bring *that* here?" She indicates to the dress I'm now holding in front of me like a shield. "Are you trying to get yourself murdered?"

Watching her green eyes spark and her lips thin in annoyance is turning me on, which might be a problem.

"Stop it," she whisper-shouts again.

"Stop what?" I whisper back. "And why are we whispering? You ashamed of me, Freckles?"

Her face instantly blushes, and my cock stirs to life even more.

Fuck.

"I—what? No? Why would I be ashamed of you? And I meant stop *looking* at me like that."

I sling the dress over my shoulder then slowly walk toward her. For every step I take, she retreats with one of her own. After just a few, she's pressed against the door, allowing me to cage her in. "Like what, Margot?" My heart is racing, I'm pumped up on adrenaline from being this close to her. She opens her mouth to speak, but nothing comes out. Her pupils dilate as her eyes stay locked on my mouth. "Come on, baby. How am I looking at you?"

I put my arm above her on the door, leaning in so our mouths are only inches apart now. "Like... like you want to kiss me."

I let out a soft chuckle. "I really fucking do."

She leans in the tiniest bit like she just might do it, putting us both out of our torture. Then her eyes shoot up to mine, and she pushes me off of her, only making me laugh more. "Why are you here with my dress, Brooks?" she says as she steps away from the wall, and her shoulders move with the deep breath she inhales.

I toss the dress in question over to her. "I was going to give it to Hayes to return it to you."

Her eyes widen in shock. "You—what? You were going to just hand Hayes my dress? You realize he would assume the worst, right?" She's back to whisper-shouting now that we aren't right in each other's faces.

"The worst? What's that, Margot? What would be the absolute worst he could assume from me handing him your dress?"

Her cheeks redden even further. She's once again opening her mouth to speak then closing it. This happens a couple times before she looks off to the side and says, "He'd think we slept together."

I scoff. "No, not slept together. He'd think we *fucked*," I correct her. She may have meant the same thing, but the words were wrong. And it's true. If I'd handed it over with zero context, he would think that. I'd planned on giving him a very thorough explanation, but messing with Margot is more fun. "I'll make you a deal."

Her eyes shoot back up to me. "A deal?" I nod my head. "Okay…"

I walk toward her again, but this time, she doesn't retreat. She stands her ground, allowing me into her personal space. "Go on a date with me. Give me a chance to prove I'm not the guy you and everyone else thinks I am, and I won't walk out of this room and hand Hayes your dress."

The smile blooming on her face is the last thing I expected. "You're blackmailing me into going out with you?"

My tongue darts out to wet my lips, and her eyes follow the trail. "I am. But I should warn you, this is the last time I'm going to ask you out. Not sure if you realize this, but you've turned me down twice now."

Her hand shoots up to her mouth, covering the delicate laugh escaping her lips as she nods her head. "I'm very aware."

I try not to let the words bring me down as I wait to see if she'll say more.

"Fine," she says with resignation in her voice. I'm not sure if I should be happy or concerned with how easily she agreed.

"Fine?"

"Mhm, fine."

I don't waste any more time questioning it. "I'll pick you up on Friday then."

I go to turn around when Margot says, "Wait, on the motor-cycle? And what time?"

Looking over my shoulder, I say, "Nope. In my dad's truck. And five—sharp. Be ready." Then I walk out the door like I wasn't just locked in a room with the girl of my fucking dreams, black-mailing her into a date like a goddamn creep.

It's a few minutes before Margot walks out of the breakroom, her features schooled like she has nothing to hide. I don't miss the smirk on Kori's face as she watches Margot walk out and into the main area. She finds me from across the room, her eyebrows raising in question. I turn my back to her and put my hand behind me, middle finger glaring in her direction. She laughs from her stool but says nothing.

I'm fairly certain Kori is cool, but I guess I'll find out after this. If Hayes shows up on my doorstep in a fit of rage, I'll know who ratted me out.

Speaking of, Hayes walks back in looking more pissed off than usual, putting all my plans to talk to him on the back burner for another day. His huge frame and ragey energy steal all the space in the shop.

The similarities between him and Margot when they're mad are painfully obvious now: the same scrunched brows, the way their light green eyes darken, even their stance is similar with their arms crossed over their chests in the same exact way. They're so different—both physically and in temperament—unless you're familiar with their mannerisms, it's hard to see the resemblance.

Margot is short, has pale skin, void of any ink, and soft features. Hayes is tall, massive, covered in tattoos, and all hard edges. If I didn't know they're siblings, I'd never guess it by just seeing them in the same room.

Margot tenses at the sight of Hayes. Her reaction puts me on alert. I've never seen Hayes be violent, and I think he's a good dude, but between hearing how he spoke to Margot the other day and now this, I'm on high alert. She rushes over to him, and I can't hear what she asks.

"Goth-Barbie gets to fucking stay," he seethes. I'd forgotten about his petition to the city about having two tattoo shops within a certain square radius. He'd told them it shouldn't be allowed considering how small the town is, and he was here first. We'd been waiting for the last week to hear back.

"What? How?" Kori says as she walks toward us.

"There's no ordinance saying two similar businesses can't be in the same town square. And apparently, Otis doesn't own that strip, so he has no control over it. He said if it were up to him, he wouldn't have leased it to her regardless of how long it'd sat empty."

That was the other problem someone had pointed out when he'd first brought up the "issue." The storefront in question has been empty for close to four years now. It used to be a vacuum store or some shit, but not surprisingly, it didn't do well in this era, so they closed up. Not sure Otis is telling him the truth though. An empty space is a money pit, I'm sure he would have leased it to anyone willing to sign. He probably just didn't want to be on Hayes' bad side, and honestly, I can respect that.

Everyone in the room nods their head in agreement, despite us all knowing it's a load of shit.

"So it's... a woman tattoo artist?" Margot asks, her voice much smaller than usual. Probably in an attempt not to piss him off more. We'd all get our heads bitten off for asking something like that, but I'm hoping he's kinder to her. I'm self-aware enough to know if I had no skin in the game with Margot, I wouldn't question anything Hayes did in regard to her. I've heard enough about "Booger" to know he loves her.

"Un-fucking-fortunately," he replies as he runs his hand down his face.

I look out the window, hoping to catch a glimpse of the woman who has Hayes more worked up than I've ever seen him. There's a ladder in front of the space like they're getting ready to install the sign. I see a bright redheaded woman in overalls carrying a box toward the front door and a kid trailing behind her.

"Do we know her actual name?" Margot asks.

"Calla," Archer pipes up. Hayes shoots him a death glare before turning to Margot and softening his face, almost like he forgot it was Margot he was talking to and not someone else. "I don't know. And I don't care. None of you should," he says as he stomps off toward the back.

I look over at Archer who now has his eyes trained on his iPad mocking up a custom for someone, he looks about as awkward as

I feel watching this all unfold. He keeps his head down, eyes fixed to the screen.

As the door to Hayes' office slams shut, rattling the walls, Kori lets out a big sigh and says, "Well, this should be a blast."

Chapter Nineteen

I'm annoyed. I'm annoyed as I change my outfit for the fourth time. I'm annoyed as I redo the cat eye makeup I learned on a YouTube tutorial for the third time. I was annoyed in the shower when, after a heated ten-minute internal debate—so many cons, one very big pro—I shaved my legs... along with everything else.

I'm annoyed at the butterflies in my stomach. I'm annoyed that I'm nervous and excited and giddy about this date and have been since the second I agreed to it three days ago. I should know better. It's incredibly likely I'm setting myself up for disappointment.

I shouldn't be looking so hard into how much trouble Brooks has gone through to ask me out. The more I think about it, the harder it is to convince myself it means nothing though. From what I've heard about him, he doesn't date in the conventional sense. And I'm not a casual dater. I really don't want to be one of those "I can fix him, no, really I can" girls.

I'm trying to protect my heart, keeping it from getting entrenched in Brooks, but it's hard to fight the pull to him when I think back on the man he's given me glimpses of. I'm mostly annoyed because I know it's a lost battle, and I'm already smitten.

I'm applying some lip gloss as a final touch to my face when there's a loud knock on the front door downstairs. After a last look in the mirror to fluff my curls and shaking out my clammy hands to rid myself of some of the nerves, I make my way down. Unlocking the door is more of a challenge than usual since my fingers don't seem to want to work properly.

Swinging the door open, the first thing I notice is the way Brooks is biting on his bottom lip. Coupled with the tension around his eyes, I realize I'm not the only one who's nervous about tonight. Somehow that eases some of my anxiety.

"Hi," I say, and it comes out much more breathy than I intended.

"Hey, Freckles."

The nickname makes the giddy nerves surge again. My eyes trail down to his black slacks and button-down, a RED logo peeking out from behind his open leather jacket.

"Are you just coming from work?"

"Uhh, no." Brooks' face reddens, and he brings his arm up to rub at the back of his neck. He won't meet my eyes. I tilt my head in question. Is this what Brooks looks like when he's embarrassed? This might be my favorite version of him yet.

"I was hoping you wouldn't notice," he mumbles and then sighs, shoulders slumping. "I don't have 'date' clothes. I realized about twenty minutes before I had to leave, so this is the best I could do."

He looks up at me, and the sweet, sheepish look destroys any reservations I have about tonight.

I burst out laughing, mostly as a way to expel the last of my nerves. Brooks' face turns even pinker. "I'm so sorry," I say, still giggling. "I'm not laughing at you. That's just the cutest thing I've ever heard." I reach over and grab my coat from the hook and step outside. "Let's go, Killer."

I lock up, and we make our way down the couple of steps. Brooks gently places a hand on my lower back as he leads me to an older model truck. As I reach for the handle, he places his hand on the door, preventing me from opening it.

"Let me," Brooks says but doesn't immediately open the door. I turn to him to see what he's waiting for and find him looking at me. My eyebrows raise in question, and he seems to snap out of whatever trance he was in. His other hand comes up, and his fingers gently play with one of my curls as he says, "You are *scary* beautiful."

And just like that I forget how to think or breathe. A hazy memory flickers to life in the back of my brain. Kissing. Kissing Brooks. My hands running over his chest and shoulders as he pulls me impossibly close.

Oh my God, I kissed Brooks.

Just as quickly as the memory flashes, it disappears. I'm hit with a pang of sorrow. Sorrow for forgetting. Sorrow for all the missing details I didn't get a chance to lock away in my hippocampus, like the way his lips taste, the sounds he makes, the exact temperature of his skin under my fingertips. All the details I would recall daily and inspect and reinspect because I just know kissing Brooks is life-altering.

I'm never drinking with Thea and Ripley again.

By the time I tune back in, Brooks has let go of my hair, and the car door is open. I climb in and buckle up. Disappointment claws at me. I ruined our first kiss. It's stupid, juvenile, but the idea of the first kiss is something I hold dear. It makes me feel too young, too inexperienced, but I can't help it.

Brooks must notice my pouting after he gets in on the driver's side and asks, "Everything okay?"

Keeping my eyes forward, I say, "I kissed you."

"Yeah, you did." His words are gentle, and I feel his eyes on me, but I can't make myself look at him.

"I'm sorry. That's... that's not how it should have gone." I look down at my hands and chew on my lip.

There's a long pause. Long enough for me to wonder if he heard me, so I glance over and find him smirking. He turns himself forward and starts the truck. "Don't worry, baby. We'll have plenty of do-overs."

I have no idea where he's taking me. The Red Clay Strays play quietly in the cabin of the truck when I ask for the second time, "Where are we going?"

"You'll see." I'm getting really sick of those two words.

We've filled the drive with idle chit-chat about work and the crazy things my patients get up to when they think no one is watching. We caught Georgie in the bed of another patient again yesterday. While it's not against the rules, fraternizing between the residents of Saint Stephen's is discouraged. And I'm getting tired of hosting condom use demonstrations to a crowd of people who could be my grandparents, many of whom—sadly—don't even know where they are.

Brooks finally slows and turns off onto a side road, which we follow for a few minutes before it ends at the opening of a large open gravel lot with a sign for 'Southbury Drive-In' at the entrance.

The realization of where we are and what we're doing brings a huge smile to my face, a smile I couldn't fight if I wanted to.

"Oh my God, I've never been to a drive-in before!" I say, my face plastered to the window, looking at all the other people and cars, the concession stand, and trying to find a sign showing what movie will be playing. I'm familiar with the local drive-in, but it only opened about a year ago, and I haven't had a chance to go yet.

Brooks drives up to one of the high-school-aged kids directing traffic and rolls down the window.

"Reed, what's up?" he says.

"Hey, Brooks. We got your spot set up. Just go left here and around, you'll see it."

"Thanks, man." He bumps fists with the kid, and then we're moving down the lane. As soon as we round the corner, Brooks heads toward a spot set away from other cars marked off by LED tea lights set in the gravel. He backs into the spot so the bed of the truck faces the huge screen at one end of the lot.

Looking out the back window, we have a perfect, unobstructed view of the screen. Our spot has also been isolated by parking cones preventing other cars from parking immediately next to us. It feels like we're the only ones here, even though I know there are dozens of other cars parked nearby.

"You have an in with the high school crowd?" I ask.

"I had to call in a few favors," he says with that sexy teasing tone I've come to crave.

"You didn't have to go through all this trouble."

His face suddenly rearranges into something too serious for the moment. "I probably should have done more. I'm just not good at this."

I don't have a response. This is already way more than anyone has ever done for me for a date. I'm used to the tired dinner and a movie, with the meal taking place in a stuffy, too-fancy restaurant where the food is great but the atmosphere suffocating, followed by whatever rom-com is currently out.

I'm saved from answering by another young person at the window.

"Hi, Brooks! Where do you want these?" the girl says as she holds up an insulated cooler along with a tray stacked with what looks like a variety from the concession stand we passed at the entrance of the drive-in.

"I'll grab those, thanks," he says and then turns to me. "Ready?" I can only nod before he's out the door, grabbing the offerings from the girl's hands. I follow his lead and hop out of the truck, meeting him at the back, just as he's struggling to put down the tailgate one-handed, the cooler on the ground and the tray balanced in his other hand. I grab it from him, and he drops the tailgate, revealing the truck bed, which is housing a pile of what looks like quilts and pillows. At least that's what I think it is, it's hard to see in the dim light of the theater lot.

"Ah, shit. It's all fucked up. Give me a second." I can't help but smile as he hoists himself up into the truck bed with ease and shifts everything around, fluffing pillows and straightening out blankets. Once he's done, he shifts over and reveals a cozy set up, complete with a dimming camping lantern and an old school boombox.

"This is…" I trail off, losing my words as I look upon his expectant face.

His face drops. "You hate it." He hops off the truck bed and looks like he might walk away, but I grab his arm before he can.

"Wait, stop. I was going to say this is amazing. I'm blown away by all of this." The smile that breaks out on his face could make a girl forget her own name.

"Yeah?"

"Yeah," I say with a small nod.

Brooks takes the tray from my hands, placing it in the truck bed. Then his hands are at my hips, and he's lifting me up just enough for my butt to land on the tailgate. My hands end up on his shoulders from the surprise. Neither of us moves to separate.

Brooks steps in closer, my jean-clad knees widening to accommodate his torso. His large hand comes up to cup my face and neck, and his eyes shift between mine. Though my gaze is locked on his, I can see his breathing speed up, the rising and falling of his chest growing shallower. My pulse races, something I'm sure he can feel under his fingertips.

Just as he's leaning in for the first of the many do-over kisses he's promised, a few people pass by and one of them calls out, "Yo, Brooks! That you? Happy birthday, man!" The others holler a few more greetings before they move on.

"It's your birthday?" I cry, shocked it's the first time I'm hearing about it. "How old are you?"

Brooks shrugs, dripping with nothing but nonchalance. "I'm thirty-three, but it's not a big deal." He steps back and out of my hold, picking up the cooler. "Scoot back, get comfortable."

"No, wait. It is a big deal. It's your *birthday*! We should be celebrating," I say as I do what he asked.

He chuckles as he hops up. "You want to help me celebrate? What do you have in mind?" His insinuation is clear, and my face heats.

Thankfully, the screen lights up, signaling the movie will be starting soon.

I scoot back, giving Brooks room to move around the bed as he closes the tailgate, opens the cooler, and starts pulling out... cheese? Blocks and wedges and mini wheels of different types of cheese.

A little perplexed by the sheer amount of dairy being removed from the cooler, I busy myself with turning on the boombox and tuning it to the radio station listed on the movie screen. I know I've found the right station when I hear a recording welcoming us to the Southbury Drive-In.

Refocusing on the man in front of me, I'm now acutely aware that, with the tailgate closed, we are shielded from the other patrons at the drive-in. If it weren't for the voices drifting over to us, I'd think we were alone.

Brooks meets my gaze and gives me a small smile while motioning to the spread of fried concession food and mountain of cheese and crackers in front of us.

I can't help but tease him a bit when I say, "What if I told you I'm lactose intolerant?"

As soon as the last word leaves my lips, Brooks' face pales, which is shocking to see since our space is lit up by only a small camping lantern on the lowest setting.

I can't hold back the giggle from bursting out of me. "I'm not, I just couldn't help teasing since you've brought the entire cheese section from Leroy's Corner Store."

Brooks rolls his eyes and tosses a cracker at me. "Ripley told me girls like cheese, okay?" That turns my giggle into a full-on cackle, punctuated by a really attractive snort. At that, Brooks starts laughing too, and we're lost to it still when the radio broadcast announces previews are starting.

We shift around, settling with our backs against the cab of the truck cushioned by the many pillows Brooks brought. He drapes a blanket over our laps, which is just enough to insulate us from the chill in the air. We start to pick at the food with Brooks cutting a few slices of each of the dozen or so cheeses.

He reaches into the cooler and pulls out a couple of cans.

"I've got beer, cider, or seltzer." I'm still chewing, so I motion toward the seltzer, and Brooks opens it for me before opening the beer for himself.

"So what's the movie we're seeing?" I ask when my mouth is no longer full, eyes on the preview on the screen.

"*Serendipity.*"

My head snaps in his direction. Brooks is watching the preview too, his face illuminated by screen. His gaze shifts to me. "What? That's okay, right?"

"Yeah... it's perfect," I say. What I don't say is it's one of my favorite movies, one I watch every year around the holidays because I believe it's the most underrated Christmas movie. And John Cusack does things to me; there's something about the guyliner.

"You like the actor, right? I saw you have a bunch of his movies," says Brooks as if he's reading my mind while popping a fry into his mouth, washing it down with a swig of beer.

The opening credits of the movie start, the soundtrack playing softly from the radio next to us, but I'm only half-paying attention as John Cusack and Kate Beckinsale flirt and fight over a pair of gloves.

I don't know why Brooks noticing such a small detail about me is overwhelming, but my chest feels tight. I turn away from him and blink to clear my eyes. He's been in my house two whole times. I grew up watching this movie, and I would comfortably bet all the money in my savings account Hayes would have no idea what it is, let alone an actor featured in it.

Brooks is nothing like what I had built up in my head, and it's difficult for me to reorganize what I thought I knew about him into what's true and what is so wildly, wildly false. He's sweet, attentive, and a little awkward when he's nervous. Yes, he has his hard edges and abrasive side, but it's just the tip of the iceberg of what he brings to the table. I don't know why he hides behind this persona—if I had to venture a guess, I'd say self-preservation—but the urge to continue to peel back his layers is overwhelming.

I want to know what his passions are. I want to see all the ways he helps the people around him, because he does. And usually without any expectation of reciprocation. The way he handled my father is a prime example. He graciously took charge that day, lifting the burden off my shoulders. He didn't have to do that. He doesn't know my dad, he barely knows me. But I want to know him. I want to know everything there is to know.

And I think I want to start with learning just how soft his lips are and how his calloused hands feel running over my body. The thought of Brooks' hands on me lights a fire deep in my belly, and I have to shift my legs in a fruitless effort to ease the ache between them. I've never had such a visceral reaction to just the thought of a man touching me. But there's something about Brooks that calls to me, makes me trust him implicitly—both with my body and my heart. Am I getting ahead of myself? Probably. Should I be thinking of doing what I'm about to do? Probably not. But as the lust haze only seems to get heavier, I can't think of a single reason why.

We're sitting close—shoulders, thighs, knees touching. My body burns at each point of contact, and I can't keep still. A twenty-foot Jeremy Piven quips at John Cusack's character on the screen, but I'm barely following along.

"You okay?" Brooks whispers. "Cold? Want me to grab another blanket?" He doesn't wait for me to answer before reaching around to search in the dark. But I'm not cold. If anything, I'm burning up.

The anticipation from earlier in the day is back, and it mingles with the low level arousal I've been doused in ever since I realized we've already kissed.

Before I can talk myself out of it, I throw the blanket off my lap, grab Brooks' shoulder, and swing my leg over his thighs.

Then I freeze.

Oh my God, I'm straddling Brooks. I had this idea of throwing myself on top of him and just going at it, but now that I'm here, looking into his deep blue gaze, which is probably mirroring my own surprise at the position we're suddenly in, I'm at a loss.

What do I do with my hands?

I've never been the one to initiate intimacy. I'm not inexperienced—having experienced everything but penetrative sex—but the handful of men I've been with always took charge and led the way. And I would willingly follow up until a certain point, and then I'd set limits. Thankfully, aside from one guy who got frustrated and left shortly after, they all respected my boundaries. None of them felt right for taking the final step, and the relationships fizzled out before I ever got comfortable enough.

With Brooks—despite feeling like a fish out of water for the position I've put myself in—it feels right in every possible way. His initial shock morphs into heated amusement as his lips turn up in that smirk I want to lick off his face.

"Whatcha doin', Freckles?" he murmurs as his hands slip under my jacket and shirt, lightly holding onto my hips, fingertips caressing the skin there.

"Shut up and kiss me," I whisper as I grasp his face and slam my mouth to his.

And then we're kissing and kissing and kissing. I'm lost to it while at the same time cataloguing each movement of his hands as they run up and down my back, the way his tongue moves across mine, the feel of his stubble under my palms. I know now I'll be revisiting this moment often when I'm alone in bed.

I kiss down his chin and neck, and he turns and extends it, giving me more access. His eyes are closed, and he groans out a quiet, "Goddamn," when I reach an extra sensitive spot right behind his ear.

I move back to his lips, officially addicted to the taste of him. He gently nips at my bottom lip before nudging me away a few inches. When I finally open my eyes, I'm met with swollen pink lips and glazed blue irises radiating nothing but want. The same want is confirmed by the way his cock has hardened in his pants underneath me.

My mouth practically waters at the idea of what he looks like under the layers. Seeing him half naked the other morning left very little to the imagination. It's the last little bit of mystery spurring me on.

I know people can probably see up over the walls of the truck bed, but I don't care. With my eyes locked on his, I gather my hair and tie it up in a messy bun at the top of my head. I then slowly unbutton his shirt, running my hands over his pecs and abs. His muscles contract under my fingertips, maybe from my touch, maybe from the chill.

I can't make out all of his tattoos, but they seem to be a mishmosh of styles and placement with no real theme tying them together—I recognize my brother's work in many of them. I want to know everything about them. When he got them, what they mean, but right now is not the time. Right now, I need to taste more of him.

As John Cusack boards a plane back to New York on the screen, I kiss Brooks' lips, then his neck, then I move to his chest. I give into my intrusive thoughts a little and run my teeth across his skin, and he hisses in response. "Damn it, woman."

I chuckle and keep moving lower, licking at the divots between his abs. When I reach his pants, I look up. I'm now spread out on my belly beside his legs. He dips his head, and it's all the permission I need. I make quick work of his belt and fly.

Reaching in, my fingers find velvety soft skin and trimmed hair. *Commando.* I look up, eyebrows raised, and Brooks gives me an impish smile and a small shoulder shrug. Somehow it doesn't surprise me.

Getting back to the task at hand—no pun intended—I wrap my palm around his length, his very girthy, very generous length. It's hard as steel and hot as coals under my touch. I maneuver his cock out of his pants and pause to take it in. Even in the dim light it's intimidating: standing up tall, the tip glistening, an attractive curve leaning it toward his body.

I pump my fist over the length of it, seeing more pre-cum bead at the head. My mouth waters at the sight, and I give in and wrap my lips around the tip, swirling my tongue to collect the salty evidence of what I'm doing to him. My eyes flutter closed at his taste: salty, slightly bitter, but not unpleasant. The flavor mixes with the scent of his musk and whatever cologne he wears, overwhelming my senses. It's intoxicating.

"Yes, fuck. Yes. Please. Please keep going," he rasps out. *I like the begging.*

I take him further into my mouth, gliding up and down a few times. I chance a glance up and see he's fighting to stay quiet, one hand fisted at his mouth. It's at this moment a chorus of "awwws" sound around us at something in the movie, and I'm reminded we're in public. I've been so lost in my lust for this gorgeous man, I've completely forgotten where we are.

Somehow it only stokes the arousal coursing through me, the ache between my legs intensifying. I shift trying to find some friction, some relief, but my soaked panties offer none of either.

My own desire compels me to continue. I've always loved giving head. It's an empowering, heady feeling to know I can bring a man to his knees by getting down on mine. Especially a man like Brooks, who looks like he could break me in half if he wanted to.

I bob faster, knowing our time is running out with only a couple more scenes left in the movie. Next time, I plan to draw this out, really push him to the edge, but there's no time for that now. I use my hand in tandem with my mouth, and I still can't cover his full length. Brooks quietly groans, still stifling his sounds, but his breathing has picked up, so I know he must be getting close.

I hollow out my cheeks on the upstroke, and after a few pulls, Brooks' entire body tenses under my hands, he might even stop breathing. He taps my shoulder, signalling what's about to happen, but I keep going. With a quiet but obscene grunt, he empties into my mouth. I greedily swallow down everything he offers, keeping his softening cock in my mouth as he comes down, just watching all the various expressions play out on his face before he finally opens his eyes, and they find me.

He looks sated and maybe a little bewildered. I pull back and use the back of my hand to wipe at my mouth and chin, cleaning up the last of the evidence of what just happened. Brooks tucks himself away, buckling his belt and quickly doing up his shirt before he pulls me back on top of him.

"What the fuck was that?" he whispers before plunging his tongue into my mouth. We kiss for a few minutes, when I feel him hardening under me again. I grind down on his lap, so turned on I could cry.

He slowly kisses down my neck, gently sucking on a few spots, spots I know will bloom with his marks by tomorrow morning. I'm not sure how I'll explain it at work or to Hayes, but that's a problem for future me.

"Do you want to come home with me?" he murmurs, his lips still brushing against my skin.

My answering "yes" is more breath than sound.

Chapter Twenty

Somehow we managed to extract ourselves from each other, unceremoniously throw the cheese back in the cooler, roll the blankets into a heap, and exit the drive-in all before the end-credits appeared on the screen.

We're both quiet on the ride back. I'm still reeling from what I did now that the lust fog has cleared a little. Anyone could have looked over and seen us. I'm thankful Brooks had the forethought to close the tailgate. Along with how dark everything was, I'm confident no one got a free show, even though the thought seems to reignite the same desire from before. I wasn't aware I had an exhibitionist side to me, but here we are.

Brooks keeps sneaking glances at me, like he's making sure I'm still here. Like I'd be anywhere else. He's pulled my hand into his lap, playing with my fingers, and I'm tempted to play with him again, but I reel it back. I'm not sure what's gotten into me, but now that I've had a taste of him, I don't want to stop touching him.

All these thoughts have me squirming in my seat and silently begging him to drive faster. I'm imagining all the ways I'd like to touch him, how he'd touch me. I wonder if he's talkative when he doesn't have to keep quiet.

But my daydreaming comes to a screeching halt when I get to a certain point. A certain slightly important point we haven't discussed. I'm pretty sure I know where tonight is leading, and... I'm okay with it. There's nothing in me screaming *stop* like it did with the other men I've been with. Instead, all I hear is *more, more, more.*

It should worry me. I barely know him; it's our first date for Pete's sake. But I feel secure, safe. I've seen a hidden side of Brooks, and it makes me feel like he'll take care of me at my most vulnerable. Resolving myself to tell him about the big step I'm excited to take with him, I open my mouth, but the words die on my tongue as the phone he tossed onto the bench seat between us buzzes and lights up, drawing my eyes.

12/20 9:37 p.m.

Cary: Happy Birthday, bro! I'm back in town. Can we get a beer this weekend?

Brooks frowns at it, and his brow furrows. He lets go of my hand and turns the phone face down before clasping my fingers again.

"So are you going to tell me why you know a bunch of high schoolers?" I ask to break the silence and weird tension that's settled around us.

Brooks clears his throat. "They come around to The Pit some-times," he finally says. "They're friends with this kid Max, who's pretty good. Or he will be good after Hayes—uh…" he trails off, looking for the right words to finish telling me how the kid will be great in a fighting ring after my brother is done coaching him. "He's got potential," he finally finishes. He must see the concern on my face as he quickly adds, "It's not as bad as it sounds, the rules are different for the younger crowd." The Pit is not a topic he ever brings up, and it's something I've been dying to dive into with him, but right now is not the time.

After a few moments, Brooks squeezes my hand, and I catch his eyes. His smile is sweet, causing a warmth to sprout in my chest, and my returning smile is involuntary. How does he do that? Just as I'm about to climb into my head and get stuck thinking about Hayes and whatever he has going on with The Pit, Brooks gives me one smile, and all I can think of is him.

"So, why didn't you tell me it was your birthday?" I ask.

"I don't celebrate it," he replies, eyes back on the road. "It's really not a big deal."

"Well, I feel bad. I wish I had known; I would have gotten you a gift." I can't imagine not celebrating my birthday. Ever since I can remember, Hayes would make such a big fuss every year. He'd pull me from school, and we'd spend the day doing something fun like going to the movies for a whole-day marathon or taking me to Charleston for a shopping spree and a fancy dinner. I'm of the strong mindset a birthday must be celebrated to the fullest.

"Trust me. This is already the best birthday I've had in a long time." His smile flashes quickly, and heat rushes to my face at the reminder of what I just did. All I can think, though, is how I can't wait to make it even better.

We're quiet for the rest of the short trip to his house. With each mile the butterflies in my stomach intensify. I'm nervous, but it's that about-to-jump-out-of-an-airplane nervousness, where you're on the precipice of doing something scary and exciting, but the excitement is winning out.

When he parks, he softly says, "Wait here," and jumps out of the truck. My door opens just a few seconds later, and he takes my hand to help me out. He holds my palm clasped in his the whole way to his front door. Those butterflies multiply.

Once we're inside, he slips my jacket off my shoulders and hangs it beside his in the coat closet, and I slip off my shoes. Then he steps into me and brushes the curls off of my face. The heat from his body seeps into me, and my eyes flutter closed in anticipation of his lips on mine.

But the kiss never comes. Instead, he asks, "Can I get you a drink?" I blink my eyes open, and he's smirking down at me. Oh, he knows exactly what he's doing.

"Sure, what are my options?" I try to keep the irritation out of my voice, reminding myself we have all night. I feel like an addict looking for her next hit. The overwhelming lust I felt at the drive-in still simmering below the surface.

Just as quickly as he invaded my space, he's gone. I follow him like a lost puppy to the kitchen.

"I've got water, obviously. Beer... I can probably find some wine. Sweet tea?" he says, eyeing the contents of the fridge.

"Sweet tea sounds great, thanks," I say, and he pulls out a glass pitcher. He pours the amber liquid into two glasses and hands one to me. I take a sip and hum when the sugary drink hits my tastebuds. I look over to Brooks, who's taking his own sip, but his face twists in a grimace, and he puts the glass back on the counter, pushing it away slightly.

"You don't like..." I trail off at the realization. "Brooks?"

"Hmm?"

"Did you make this just for me?" I ask, a smile slowly stretching across my face.

"I mean... I know you don't drink much, so..." He shuffles around a bit, clearly uncomfortable with where the conversation has led.

I step over to him, close enough to crowd him, and place my glass next to his on the counter. Putting my hands on his chest, I run them up to his shoulders just as his come up to my hips, tugging me closer still. With our eyes locked, I push up onto my tiptoes and press my lips to his. It's soft at first, sweet, tentative, but then a dam bursts, and we wrap ourselves around each other.

Surprising myself, I use my tongue to seek out access to his. He greedily opens, one hand sliding up to cup my head.

We kiss right there in his kitchen for a long time—hours, days, a year. At this point, I'd be happy to spend the rest of my life just like this, pressed against his hard body, his hands running through my hair, tugging deliciously at the roots every once in a while.

I eventually come up for air as he kisses down my neck. But there's no air to be found. I'm panting and burning up with desire from the inside. I feel like I might combust at any second.

"Take me to bed." The words tumble out of my mouth before I even make the conscious decision to say them, but I find I mean them wholeheartedly. I can't think of anything I want more in this moment than all the dirty, sweet things I know he can do to my body.

Brooks pulls back, and his pupils are blown wide. He gives me one more lingering kiss and says, "Lead the way."

Hand in hand, we make our way up the stairs, back to the room I woke up in a few days ago. After flipping the switch, the room is bathed in a dim light from the lone lamp on a desk in the corner. Everything looks the same as when I last saw it, except the bed is neatly made. The image of Brooks getting his house ready in case I agreed to come back with him makes me smile, and those darn butterflies take flight again.

I feel his warmth behind me as he leans down and kisses the side of my neck. It's tender, unhurried, and goosebumps erupt down my arms. I turn in his hold and remove my shirt, dropping it to the floor. His eyes bounce down to my blush pink bra.

Running a finger along the strap on my shoulder, he hooks it under and slides it down.

"I love these so much," Brooks says as he skims the pads of his fingers across the many freckles on my clavicle, down my chest, all the way to my nipple, gently circling it through the lacy fabric. "I've been thinking about them since the first day we met. Wondering if they're everywhere."

"They are," I whisper, mainly because I can't get my voice to work properly.

He hums and glides a hand to my back, unclasping my bra in one quick move. It joins my shirt on the floor.

"Fuck, you're so pretty," he says as he unbuttons his own shirt. His eyes don't stray from me, and they're filled with lust and wonder, like he can't believe this is really happening.

My skin is buzzing, and I feel like I'm vibrating with the desire I feel for this man. He's awoken something in me, and as much as I love the slow approach he's taking, the sheer need within me wins out, and I launch myself at him. Brooks lets out a surprised grunt and scrambles to catch me as I wrap my legs around his hips and practically maul him.

He chuckles into my mouth and steps over to the bed, where he lays me down, covering my body with his but still holding up most of his weight on his arms. Our tongues tangle, and I finally have a chance to skim my hands down his strong, smooth back. I touch as much as I can, memorizing each lean muscle and divot.

Brooks grinds his hips into my spread thighs and groans. My jeans prevent me from finding any real friction from the movement, and I groan too, but it's more in frustration than pleasure. Brooks smiles against my lips and pulls up to his knees as he says, "Need something, Freckles?" His smile is smug as I nod quickly. "Tell me."

"Ju-just... touch me. Anywhere. Everywhere." My tone is pleading and on the verge of desperate as my hands fist the comforter.

"I got you, baby." He deftly undoes my jeans and slides them down my legs, leaving me in just my soaked panties. His eyes drink in all of me, shifting from one part of my body to the other, like he can't decide where to look.

His fingers then come up to grip the sides of my lacy underwear and slowly—ever so slowly—he slips them down my thighs, knees, calves, and finally off over my feet.

He grabs my left foot, gently kissing the arch, before moving to my ankle and planting a soft kiss there too. "I—I'm clean," he murmurs against my calf, his breath skittering against my skin, making it pebble.

I hum in question, lost to the sight of his torturous progress up my body. His hands follow his lips, his nails scraping. The mix of sensations has all of my nerves firing. I know I must be dripping onto his covers by this point.

"I test regularly. I'm clean," he repeats, still inching up, at my knee now.

"Oh, yes. Me too," I gasp out as he reaches a particularly sensitive spot on the inside of my thigh. "I-I have an IUD." Somewhere in the back of my mind I know what this conversation means, and a quick self check-in confirms I want this. I want it all with him.

He finally reaches the apex of my thighs and settles his broad shoulders between them.

"Your pussy is so fucking wet for me. Have you been like this all night?" he asks as he gazes upon it reverently. Without warning, he licks straight from my opening to my clit, and the shock of it zings all the way to my toes. "God, you taste so fucking good."

I'm lost to the sensation of his tongue and lips kissing, sucking, and flicking at my clit. It takes no time at all for my orgasm to surge up, and I'm so close to the cusp, I close my eyes in anticipation.

Then everything stops, and I cry out as I look down to see what happened.

"Look at me, Freckles." I shudder at the command, the ache in my lower belly almost unbearable. The intense eye contact unsettles me but is somehow still a huge turn on. I guess I really do like being watched.

He goes back to giving my pussy the attention it needs, and in no time, I'm again ready to come, right there on the edge. My eyes slip shut.

And again, Brooks stops moving. I cry out with the loss and blink back tears of frustration. Looking back down at the infuriating man between my legs, I find his devilish smirk in place.

"Ugh, okay. I'm looking at you. Please. *Please* let me come," I beg, one hand trying to find purchase in his short—almost nonexistent—hair to bring him back to where I need him most.

"You never have to beg with me, baby. Just keep your eyes on me." He takes pity on me and licks at me with the flat of his tongue, eyes still boring into mine. He increases the pressure as my muscles tense and speeds up when my breaths turn into pants.

Finally, *finally*, I combust. My abs clench, thighs lock around Brooks' head, and I shudder as wave after wave of my orgasm washes over me. He continues to lap at me, guiding me through the intense pleasure. Somehow our eyes stayed locked throughout, pure lust pouring out of his blue gaze.

With one last kiss to my sensitive clit, he crawls up my body, laving sensitive areas with his tongue on the way. He reaches my mouth and dives in, letting me taste myself and feel his hard cock on my hip, still clad in his pants.

I reach down and fumble with the belt and zipper before he kicks them off. His heavy cock lands low on my belly, leaking from the tip like it didn't have a release just an hour ago. Brooks grinds against me and groans.

His eyes, though hard to see in this light, are glassy with need. There's a question in them, to which I nod my consent. *Yes* and *I want this* and *please be gentle* float through my head, but the words die on my tongue as Brooks notches himself at my entrance and slowly pushes in.

I tense at the invasion, the stretch. He's huge and probably not the best choice for my first time. The toys I have at home don't compare to the size of the monster between his legs.

I pull Brooks closer and bury my head into his shoulder so he doesn't see the tears pricking my eyes. I don't think he's even all the way in, but I have to bite my lip to keep a whimper from escaping.

He must sense my discomfort because he pushes back to look at me and pulls out slightly. I wrap my legs around him to keep him from going too far.

"Keep going, please," I whisper. *Can he tell I'm a virgin?*

"Hey, hey, what's going on?" His brow is furrowed in concern, eyes soft and searching. Brooks nudges my face up to him with his large palm. "Are you okay?"

"It's ju—it's just a lot." His concern morphs into understanding, and he kisses me softly, shifting slightly until I feel his hand at my clit. With slow, even circles with the pad of his thumb, my body relaxes, sparks of pleasure rippling from the point of contact.

Brooks thrusts in again, still going slowly, and my body accepts him. The stretch is still there, but it's more a foreign sensation than pain now. He adds more pressure with his fingers, and I can't help the moan slipping out of me. A few more small thrusts, and Brooks is fully seated inside me.

"Fuck," he mutters as he drops his forehead to my shoulder. I feel him trembling—he's holding back. "You're fucking perfect."

I start to squirm, the feeling of fullness creating a need for friction, for action, for anything. "Move. Please move."

As though waiting for my go-ahead, Brooks starts to plunge in and out of me. At first he's unhurried with his movements, but his pace steadily picks up until I'm panting against his mouth, my nails digging into his sweaty back, just holding on. The sounds of our bodies moving together and my filthy moans echo around the room. "Oh, oh my God."

"You're making me feel amazing, baby," he says. "Hold on." That's all the warning I get before he rolls us so I'm now straddling him, his cock still inside me. Just like earlier tonight, I'm caught off guard.

A sliver of panic rises up inside me, as I realize just how inexperienced I am with this. I have a general idea of what to do, but what are the best practices? Should I try to bounce? How exactly does one roll their hips when they're being impaled by an anaconda?

Thankfully, I'm pulled out of my short internal spiral by Brooks' large hands landing on my hips and guiding me through a grinding motion. His hold is firm, but gentle, and a little voice in my head wishes he'd grip tighter, leave bruises for me to find tomorrow.

"Yeah, make yourself feel good. Ride me," he grunts. With his encouragement, I find a rhythm, and soon pleasure unfurls low in my belly. I feel like I'm holding on for dear life, like I might float away if I let go. His hands on me the only thing still keeping me grounded.

I grasp the headboard just behind Brooks' head, my knuckles quickly turning white. Is this what it's supposed to feel like? This pull, this connection. We're as close as two people can get and still my heart beats out for *more, more, more.*

"God*damn,* I feel like I was made for this pussy, Freckles. What the fuck are you doing to me?" he says as he thrusts up into me, fingers digging into my hips, lips on one of my nipples. He hits a spot inside me sending a deep, pleasurable ache all the way down to my toes. I can't find words, just a groan, propelled from somewhere in my chest.

"Oh my God, Brooks. Yes, yes. Brooks." I'm so close, so so close.

I turn my head, and my eyes catch on a long mirror in the corner of the room. I hadn't noticed it before, but now I can't tear my eyes away. The angle is perfect, even with the low light of the single lamp, I can see everything we're doing. Brooks' corded arms holding me in place. His legs, sprinkled with just the right amount of hair and a couple of thigh tattoos—the sight of which makes my core clench around his cock—tensing with each thrust. My own body moving in a way I've never witnessed before, curls wild and skin flushed from my décolletage all the way up to my cheeks.

"Fuck yes, Freckles. Look at yourself. You're fucking stunning riding my cock." I catch Brooks' eyes in the mirror and hold. It's another two swirls of my hips, and I'm coming again. My pussy pulsing around his cock, my breath stuttering in the onslaught.

Brooks follows close behind, and I'm treated to the full volume of his release, unlike earlier. I let go of the headboard and lay myself over him as he wraps his arms around me, planting small kisses on any parts of me he can reach. We lie like that until our breathing calms, his cum dripping out of me as his cock softens inside of me.

Hayes would be so disappointed I didn't use a condom after all the bananas he desecrated to teach me safe sex.

The thought brings me back online, and I extricate myself and hurry to the bathroom down the hall without a word. I pee and wipe up, surprised to not see any blood. I guess I lost my hymen a few dildos ago.

After washing my hands, I look in the mirror. I look the same. Well, I look thoroughly debauched and sated, but the same. Not sure what I was expecting really.

I don't feel the same though. I feel like I might be falling for the amazing man I left in the other room. I also feel like I will never get enough of him, what he can do to me, what I can do to him. There are so many things I want to try, and the images of all we can get up to have me clenching my thighs together.

What's the average refractory period for a guy? I'm not sure I ever learned that in nursing school.

I make my way back to Brooks' bedroom and find him sitting at the edge of the bed, still naked but cleaned up. He looks up at me, slight worry written all over his face.

"You okay?" he asks quietly, a slight rasp in his voice. "I didn't hurt you, did I?" I hesitate for just a moment, wondering if he knows I was a virgin, wondering if he's upset. "I know I'm bigger than... most, and I'd hate myself if I ever hurt you."

His sweet tone melts my heart. He's so different from what I've heard about him, and I can't imagine how people ever describe him as an asshole. I rush over to him, molding my mouth to his.

"No, you didn't hurt me, Killer," I say when I come up for air, skimming my hands over his short hair. "But I do have a question," I start, finding his gaze before continuing, "when will you be ready for round two?"

His chuckle is wicked as he grasps my hips, and we both tumble to the rumpled sheets once again.

CHAPTER TWENTY-ONE

Three times. Margot Mason—the woman I thought I'd only get to be with in my dreams—let me fuck her three times. The last eighteen hours feel like I'm living someone else's life. There's no way someone as perfect as her wants to be with me, but as I open my eyes, I see she's right beside me in bed. In *my* bed.

Our legs are still tangled up from last night, and she's tracing her fingers along the intricate lines of ink covering my skin.

"Morning, baby," I say, and her eyes jolt to my face, her smile so bright it could light up the room on its own.

"Morning." Her voice is soft, still sleepy sounding, but she looks content simply lying in bed with me. I push the thought away, trying not to get too attached to the ideas plaguing my mind.

"How're you feeling?" *Stupid fucking question. Why would I ask that?*

Her brows furrow for just a moment before she says, "I've never felt better. You?"

I pull my eyes away from her, and my brain latches onto her words, playing them over and over. Surely, they aren't true. There's no way being with me is the best she's ever felt. I don't argue though, attempting to not ruin the moment for once in my life.

Before I can consider an answer to her question, she hooks a finger under my jaw, tilting my face to hers. "You okay?"

I nod my head, biting the inside of my cheek as I do. "Yeah, Freckles, I'm good." The flash of hurt in her eyes at my lie twists my stomach with guilt. I'm just in my head. She doesn't need to know all the shit going on in there. She doesn't push the subject and instead looks down at my arms again, her fingers going back to tracing the tattoos.

"Did they hurt?" she asks as goosebumps litter my flesh at her light touch.

I gaze down to the ink she's questioning. "Some of them but not as much as you'd think."

"No?"

"Nah. It's a good kind of pain. Steady, uncomfortable enough to distract you but not painful enough to have any lasting effects," I reply, trying to make sense of something that's nonsensical until you try it for yourself. As she reaches my fingers, I thread my hand through hers, stopping her in her tracks. "Have you ever thought of getting one?

She immediately blushes, and I'm reminded how much I love the shade of pink coating her skin. Even more so today after watching it spread from her chest to her face as she lost herself on my cock last night. My fingers itch to try and recreate the exact hue, and once again, I'm shocked by the need to create when I'm around her or thinking about her.

"Umm... maybe."

I narrow my eyes at her, and she laughs again. *Fuck*. I wish she'd quit laughing so I could stop whatever is happening to me.

"I do want one. I just… it's so permanent, and I don't know how I feel about it. Plus the pain. I won't lie, I'm scared." Her nose scrunches as she says the last words like she's embarrassed to say them out loud.

"What would you get?" I ask as I play with her fingers.

"It's stupid."

"Baby, nothing about art is stupid. And no art could look stupid on you. I promise. Now, tell me, please." I sound like I'm begging. The tone isn't something I'm used to, but I feel like she could pull it out of me daily without even trying.

"Okay… well," she starts, rolling onto her back so she isn't looking at me. Our fingers are still intertwined, delicately sitting on her stomach. Seeing her from this angle reminds me she wore my shirt to bed. I don't know what it is about seeing her in my clothes, but it does it for me. The evidence pushing against the confines of my boxer briefs.

"My mom died when I was two from pancreatic cancer." My entire body stiffens at her words. I had no idea. I never asked her or Hayes because it wasn't my business. "It's okay," she reassures me as if I'm the one who needs comforting right now. "Really. It was a long time ago, and I don't even remember her."

I know she means for it to make me feel better, but it doesn't. I start playing with her fingers again, letting her know she can keep going.

"I found her sketchbook when I was twelve. I asked Hayes about it, and he told me she was always drawing. She took the sketchbook everywhere she went."

A weight plants itself on my shoulders as I listen to her. Plenty of people draw or doodle. It shouldn't catch me by surprise or make me think it's anything but a coincidence.

"Inside were all sorts of drawings, but in the corners of many of the pages was a little clam with a pearl inside. When I asked Hayes about it, he teared up and said it was for me. Apparently, since Margot means 'pearl' in French, she called me her little pearl. I had no idea."

I watch in helplessness as a tear falls down the side of her face. On instinct, I unthread my hand from hers and reach up to wipe the tear away. She turns her face so my hand is cupping her cheek. "I'm sorry you didn't get to know her, Freckles."

She nods her head but doesn't speak. Then she pulls my palm to her lips and plants a kiss in the center. Without another word, I pull away, turning over to open the bedside drawer. "What are you—" she starts as I turn back with a fine tip sharpie in my hand.

"Can I...?" I ask with my hand outstretched for her arm. She places her hand in my hold, and I readjust so I'm lying over her. I need the perfect angle to get the design right.

"Brooks, what're you doing?"

"I'm giving you your first tattoo."

She doesn't say any more as we lie in silence. I let the quiet calm me as I draw a tiny clam shell on the inside of her right arm, in the middle of her bicep. It's a sharpie, so I can't do any shading or tiny details, but I try to make it as tattoo-like as possible. I add in a couple of tiny four-point stars around the pearl sitting inside the clam like it's shimmering.

"I didn't know you could draw," she says as she eyes the design.

I huff out a sardonic laugh. "Uh, yeah, it's something I used to do a lot. I actually want to be a tattoo artist like your brother. Even asked him for a job the other day."

"You did?" she asks, her voice sounding entirely too optimistic.

"Yeah, didn't work out though."

After a few more minutes, I'm happy with the "tattoo" and blow on it to dry it quickly. I watch in rapture as goosebumps break out on her skin where my breath hits.

As I pull away, she tilts her head to look at the little clam now adorning her arm like it was meant to be there all along. Tears prick at her eyes, and I silently beg them not to fall.

"Brooks..." Her voice is breathy, barely audible. "It's so perfect, thank you." She turns her gaze to me and gives me zero warning before she's jumping up and crawling into my lap. She slams her lips onto mine, her tongue immediately seeking access. I try not to shudder as she grinds herself on my now fully erect cock.

Sliding my hands down her back, I grip her ass so I'm holding both cheeks. I squeeze, digging my fingers into her skin and relishing the way her body moves quicker from the contact. She glides her hands up my chest until they're cupping both sides of my face.

Pulling away, I try to catch my breath. "Damn, woman, you're insatiable."

She smirks, letting out a huff of a laugh before placing a kiss on the corner of my lips. "Are you complaining?" she asks but starts kissing all over my face before I can answer.

"Definitely not. But," I say, bringing my hands to her sides to pull her away again. "I have to piss. And I need to step outside for a second." She immediately pouts, looking down at my lap then back at me. "Then," I continue, "I think we should continue this in the shower."

Her face lights up again as she crawls off my lap. I get up from the bed, stretching my hands over my head. I lean down and grab my cigarettes from the drawer, pulling one out and placing it behind my ear. Margot's face scrunches up from the sight, but she doesn't comment on the nasty habit.

As she walks around the bed and passes by me, I spank her ass lightly, making her jump. She looks over her shoulder, her face morphed into shock. "Get the water warm for us, baby."

I'm standing on the warped deck in my parents' backyard, leaning on the questionable railing, smoking a cigarette, and staring at the text Cary sent me last night. I'm not sure I was convinced he'd actually come back. I'm happy for Thea though. I just hope he doesn't fuck it up again. I feel like a hypocrite at the thought, knowing I have a woman waiting on me just inside the sliding door whose heart I'll surely break.

"Fuck." I stub out the smoke on the railing just beside me. My fingers finally move to type out the text I should have sent to Cary last night.

12/21 9:03 a.m.

Me: Thanks, man. Sure thing, glad to hear you're back.

Delivered

I don't waste any more time with my thoughts as I walk back inside to find Margot. She's standing in the bathroom, fully naked, and staring at the sharpie tattoo I drew on her arm. I step up behind her and place my arms around her middle as we gaze at each other in the mirror.

"Come on." I take her hand and pull her toward the shower. Opening the door for her, I lead her in, then shed my boxer briefs to join her. The water is just right, and seeing the way it clings to Margot's skin has me hard again.

Safe to say Margot has surprised the fuck out of me. She always seemed so innocent, I never expected this. Never expected her to not only keep up with me but demand even more. I pull her over to me, pushing her up against the wall of the shower as the low pressure water hits our legs. My hard cock presses into her stomach as I lean my body into hers. Running my hands up her sides to her chest, I cup her tits in my hands, kneading them as I run my tongue along the seam of her mouth.

Just as I go to pinch her nipple, she grabs onto my arms, turning us so I'm pressed against the cold tile now. "Damn, Freckles," that's all I manage before she's dropping to her knees in front of me. For a man who feels like I always get the shit end of the stick, I'm reveling at the sight before me.

She runs her hand up my shaft, sliding her finger through the slit at my tip, gathering the pre-cum there. I bite my lip in wonder as she brings the finger to her mouth and sucks it clean. "Fuck, baby, you're so fucking hot."

She smiles then wraps her mouth around me, making me question my reality as she does. I still can't get over what's happening. This still feels like a dream. One I hope I never wake up from.

As she glides her tongue along the ridges of my cock, her teeth graze the top. Full body shudders take over as I try my best not to come in her mouth at the feeling. "Goddamnit, Margot, what're you doing to me?" My voice comes out husky as she laps at my tip, her hand following the motion all the way from my base.

Looking down at her, I watch as she squirms. "Are you wet for me, baby?" She bobs her head on my dick, answering my question without words. "Play with yourself while you suck me off." The demand is just as much for me as it is for her. Watching Margot do dirty things is heaven on Earth.

With another swipe of her tongue, my release builds. "Yes, baby. I'm so close." The world stops around me as she pops off of me, a cold chill running through me as she does. "Wha—"

"I want..." she starts but stops herself, keeping her eyes on the ground.

"What do you want, Margot? I'll give you anything right now." I laugh, knowing it's the fucking truth.

"I want to hear you beg."

Oh.

She looks sheepish like she's surprised even herself with her request. I'm starting to think this is a side of herself she's been too scared to voice before me. And normally, I wouldn't let a woman control me in bed. Shit, I'd never beg for a woman's touch, let alone the permission to come. But for Margot? For Margot, I think I'd do just about anything. Begging being just the tip of the iceberg. The thought scares the fuck out of me but not enough to stop.

"You want me to beg, baby?" She nods her head as she looks up at me through her lashes. "Wrap those beautiful lips back around me then."

She bites her lip for a moment then pulls me back into her heavenly mouth. I bring my hand down to her head, wrapping her curls around my fist as she takes me deeper than before. "Yes, baby. Deeper, please, fuck." She holds me there, choking on my cock, tears falling from the corners of her eyes as she does. "Fuck, fuck, fuck, Margot." I pull her off by her hair, and drool falls from the corners of her lips. She brings a hand to wipe it away, but I grab it before she can. "Leave it."

I push her head toward me again, her mouth opening instinctually. "Do it again, so I can come. Please, baby, I need it." My words spur her on, and her hand shoots down to her pussy again. I run my fingers along her scalp, letting my nails dig in a bit as I do. I can tell she likes it by the way her movements stutter.

"I'm close again, baby. Let me have it this time, *please.*" I'm not even begging because she asked. It just feels right. In a way I've never experienced. In a way that's fucking terrifying.

She starts going faster, everything feeling sloppier in the best way possible. "Can you come with me, baby?" I ask the question knowing she's got to be close as well. The movements of her hand are becoming jerkier with every second.

I hold her head in place as her throat swallows around my cock, I'm on the precipice, and I might die if she stops before I'm falling over the edge. Orgasm denial has never been my kink, but I can admit her stealing my last one is making this one feel essential to keep on breathing. I know she's open to me coming down her throat based on last night, but I want to paint her in my cum. I want to watch as it glides down her tits and perky nipples. I want to see her covered in me.

"Fuuuuck. I need... I'm gonna... please," I can't get my words out, and I know I'm not making any sense. This is what she does to me. "I need to... fuck," I try again. "On you, baby, please, can I?" I have no idea if she's even listening to me, let alone understanding whatever the hell just came out of my mouth. But at the last second, when I know I'm about to explode, she pulls off of me and looks up expectantly. "Thank fuck."

I close my eyes allowing my release to wash through me. The water is still splashing around us as ropes of my cum land on her beautiful skin. Only when I feel like I'm almost finished do I peel my eyes open to look at the masterpiece in front of me.

No painting, drawing, or sketch can come close to the beauty of Margot Mason painted in my cum. It's an image I wish I could recreate on a sketchpad, but know I could never do it justice.

Chapter Twenty-Two

B y the time the water ran cold, we were finally cleaning off and using the shower for its intended purpose. I left Margot in the bathroom to deal with her hair that I thoroughly fucked up. I'd brought her a brush from my parents' bathroom so she could attempt to tame it, but if I'm being honest, I like seeing it wild. I tried not to think too much as I walked through their room. For the first time, it felt somber and not like I was picking at a gaping wound.

My eyes catch on the microwave clock as I walk into the kitchen. It's a little past ten in the morning. We didn't fall asleep until past two. I should be dragging and tired as fuck, but I feel more energized than ever.

Opening the refrigerator, I grab the carton of eggs, some shredded cheese, milk, and bacon. It'll be the second time I've made her breakfast, and I'm not even mad about it. Confused, sure, but not mad.

By the time I'm adding the cheese to the scrambled eggs, Margot is walking down the stairs in yesterday's clothes. I swear to God, every time I see her, she takes my goddamn breath away.

"You're making me breakfast again, Killer?"

I grin at the nickname. The word itself sounds so wrong yet so right coming from her mouth. "Mhmm, consider it my thank you for making my birthday great." I don't mean anything negative by it, but I watch as her face drops. "Hey, what's wrong?" I ask, leaving the eggs in the pan to walk toward her.

Her light green eyes look up into mine as she says, "I hate that your birthdays weren't always special."

I wrap her up in a hug. This woman is too perfect for this world. "I just needed one," I say, expecting it to be enough, but as I pull away to tend to the eggs, I see her face is still twisted up.

I plate the food, hoping to move away from the topic. My trauma isn't exactly breakfast conversation, nor do I feel like I need to go into it. She walks over to the table as I set the plate down. I pour a glass of sweet tea and hand it to her, grabbing a bottled water for myself.

"Hopefully everything is okay. I know most people have coffee in the mornings, but I hate the taste, so I don't have any here."

Her mouth drops open in shock. "You... hate coffee?"

Laughing, I nod my head. "Yeah, growing up at the diner, the smell was everywhere. It got to a point where it started to make me nauseous. So I could never bring myself to try it as an adult. It's weird, I know," I say, waiting for her to poke fun at me like most do. But she doesn't because Margot's not most people.

"That makes sense. I love it, but only if there's just as much cream and sugar as there is coffee." I can't help the laugh, and she side-eyes me from across the table. "Don't make fun!" she says, pointing her fork at me. Her pouting only makes me laugh more.

I put my hands up in surrender in front of me. "Okay, okay, I'm sorry. It just doesn't surprise me. No wonder you taste so fucking sweet, all you drink is pure sugar." My favorite color flushes across her cheeks again, and I smile smugly.

"So," she starts, clearly needing to veer away from the topic of how her cum tasted on my tongue. I'm getting a semi just thinking about it. "Did you, Brooks Grant, clean for me?"

Her question stops my fork halfway to my mouth. It's not even the partially full name that gets me, it's the fact she noticed. "It's actually *Hugh* Brooks Grant, if you're wanting to pull the full name card," I reply instead of answering her.

"Wait—really?" The adorable shock on her face was worth sharing my horrid first name.

"Really."

"Your legal name is Hugh Grant?" she asks in disbelief.

"Unfortunately."

"And your brother's name is Cary Grant."

"Correct."

Her head falls back as laughter fills the kitchen. It's contagious, so before I know it, I'm joining in.

"I don't know if I think your parents were clever or cruel," she says, her laughter dying down.

"Oh, cruel, for sure. They thought it was so fucking funny to name us after famous actors. At least I got to go by Brooks. Cary tried to go by his middle name too, but it never stuck," I say with a chuckle.

Margot takes another bite of her food then looks back over at me. "I know what you did there. And it's okay, you don't have to answer."

I use it as my out and continue eating my breakfast. Once we're both done, I grab our plates and put them both in the sink. As I turn around, I notice she's looking around at the cabinets. "What?"

"Oh," she turns to me, "I was just imagining how those knobs you bought will look in here. Did you decide on a paint color?"

I shake my head as I say, "Sure didn't." The silence settles around us for a few seconds before I add, "Which color would you choose?"

"What?"

"If it were up to you, what would you go with?"

There's a sparkle in her eye as she thinks about her answer. "I think I'd choose a sage green." She looks down at the island, inspecting it. "What about the counters?"

I huff a laugh. "What about them?"

Running her finger along the edge of the current counter-tops, she brings her gaze back up to me. "What's your plan for them?" I shrug. And this time, I don't have to ask what she'd do with them, she tells me on her own. "I think white or cream granite would look nice. Or maybe marble? Do people still put marble in kitchens? And I'd leave the island a natural wood color so it accents the green."

She could talk all day about kitchen cabinets and coun-ters—shit—she could add in appliances, and I'd be happy to listen.

They're good ideas. Way better than what I came up with. "I'll keep that in mind."

"Sorry, I'm sure you have your own plan for it all."

"Nah, I really don't."

She smiles and walks toward me to wrap her arms around my neck. "Well, I'll keep telling you mine then."

I bend down to kiss her lips. "I appreciate that, Freckles. You ready to go? I assume you have work today."

She nods as she says, "I do. My shift starts at one."

I look over at the clock again, it's almost eleven, and the drive back to her place is a little over twenty minutes. "Let's get going then. Lydia will have my balls if I interfere with your work."

"Ew!" she says as she slaps my arm.

I'm waiting outside for Margot when my phone dings with a notification.

12/21 11:16 a.m.

Cary: How's tomorrow? And will we see you at Louie's on Christmas Eve?

12/21 11:16 a.m.

Me: That'll work. And I don't see why not.

Read 11:17 a.m.

Just as I hit send, the front door opens. I'd forgotten all about the Christmas Eve tradition. With everything going on, it's been the last thing on my mind. Without thinking, I open my mouth and say, "What're you doing Christmas Eve?"

What the fuck? Why does this shit keep happening?

"Oh. Umm... I don't think I have plans, why?" She's right beside me now. Looking up at me with those beautiful green eyes.

I run my hand over my head, trying to push down the nerves. "Uhh, there's this thing on Christmas Eve at Louie's called the Jingle Mingle. I figured you could maybe come hang out with us all."

Her eyes light up, and my heart starts to race. "You asking me on a second date, baby?"

Okay. So I've called her baby. It keeps slipping out. But somehow her saying it to me just about takes me out. Fuck. I need to hear it again. "What if I am?" I smirk, trying to hide the tremor in my voice brought on by a simple fucking word.

"Then..." she starts, wrapping her hand in mine, "I'd say I'll see you then. I work until eight though, so I probably can't get there until around nine."

We walk toward the garage where the truck is, our hands still intertwined. "No problem. It usually lasts until midnight."

We only get a few steps before she's pulling on my hand, stopping me from going any further. I turn around, a puzzled look on my face as I try to assess the issue.

"Could we maybe..." she bites on her lip as she speaks, clearly trying to bring me to my goddamn knees, "take the motorcycle instead?" she finishes.

A huge smile breaks out on my face. "I knew you fucking loved it."

She laughs as she pulls me in the direction of my bike off to the side of the driveway. I hand over her helmet, then grab my own. I watch as she pulls it on, making sure the strap is secure beneath her chin. If having her on my bike is going to be a regular thing, I'll have to get her one that fits just right.

Once I'm satisfied and I have my own secured, I throw my leg over the seat. She climbs on behind me, wrapping her arms around my waist. I reach back and pull her even closer so her chest is flush against my back. I love the feel of her wrapped up behind me.

Twenty minutes later, I'm pulling into her driveway. I park the bike and turn off the ignition, the dread of being alone again creeping in. As she peels herself off of me, it feels like stripping myself of something vital. I hate the feeling almost as much as I hate the idea of leaving her. It's fucking confusing.

"Brooks?"

"What?"

"Did you hear what I said?" She has a concerned look on her face. That's fair. I just zoned out and missed whatever she was saying.

"Uh," I grimace with a huff of a laugh, "No... sorry, what?"

Her brows furrow, letting me know my answer didn't ease whatever worry is etched all over her face. "I said thank you for the ride. And well... everything." That perfect blush comes racing up her neck again. Will it ever get old? "And umm..." she continues, looking nervous now, "I think—I think I want to try. Try this—us, I mean. If you... still want to."

My eyebrows shoot up in shock. That was somehow the last thing I expected her to say. "Really? You sure? I thought you were looking for something more serious?" I ask, not sure why I even bring it up. I... think I want to be serious with her. Maybe.

"I think you might be worth the risk." Before I can respond, she's pushing up on her tiptoes and placing a small kiss on my lips. "Bye, Brooks."

I'm still standing there, shell-shocked, as she walks away. I watch her open her door, the sound of all seven—or however many there are—locks sliding into place.

I think you might be worth the risk.

The words were said as a compliment. She meant it in a good way. A great way. She decided I'm worth the risk. But hearing those words—hearing her say those words, in that order, it only causes me to spiral. My thoughts of potential failure are rampant. A cold sweat rushes over my skin as all the ways I can fuck up race through my mind. I get back on my bike, not bothering with latching my helmet as I drive away from the spot where she cut me open without even trying.

What happens when she finds out I'm not worth the risk, not even close? What happens when she regrets the decision she just made? Will she remember this moment as vividly as I do?

CHAPTER TWENTY-THREE

I'm sweeping up the mess I made when I hear the swinging door open behind me. "Shit, Thea, you can take it out of my paycheck, oka—" I cut myself off when I see it's Cary walking in. "Oh, it's just you."

He chuckles before saying, "Yeah, just me. You smashing bottles now?"

"No, asshole. It slipped out of my hand when I was restocking the bar," I reply as I look down at the shattered glass and bourbon spilt all over the tasting room floor. Surprisingly, Cary grabs the dustpan and walks toward me with it. "Thanks."

He looks up from the ground as he holds it out for me to sweep the glass into. "No problem. And I won't tell Thea. It's just one bottle, not the end of the world."

I try not to let his solidarity get to me. I'd pick Thea over him most days, so I wouldn't blame him for doing the same. But he's right, it's just one bottle. Although, It feels symbolic somehow, like the rest of my life right now. Everything feels like it's slipping through my fingers, just waiting to hit the ground and break into a million pieces. "Appreciate it," I grunt.

We clean the rest of the spill in silence. Once we pick up all the glass, Cary asks, "Where's the mop?"

I point my thumb over my shoulder. "In the closet in the back, you'll see it."

He walks away, leaving me with my own thoughts for a moment. I'm still mentally comparing my life to the disaster in front of me.

As he rolls the mop bucket out, he asks, "How have you been?"

I huff a laugh. "Same shit, different day." It's the same thing I used to tell him when he'd call once every other month for the last eight years he was living in Seattle.

"Let's not do that anymore, okay? I'm back for good. I'd like to figure our shit out so we can have a better relationship."

I'm stunned by Carrington Grant wanting to do something other than shove feelings into a box and hide that shit in a corner. He's never been one to talk about... well, anything. He's the type of guy who barely wants to hash out an argument; he'd rather move on and pretend it never happened. It's where we never saw eye to eye, especially when it came to our parents. He never lashed out at them, except for the one instance when my dad crossed a line and said some shit about Thea. Even I was pissed about it. It was only the one time though, but for Cary that was all it took for him to cut ties with Mom and Dad.

Before, he'd let it roll off his back while I sat in my room wondering if we witnessed the same thing, felt the same disappointment from our father. Neither of us wanted what he wanted for us. Neither of us wanted to work at the family restaurant. Cary wanted to be a chef; same industry, sure, but he said time and time again his dreams were bigger than the diner.

Feeling has always been one of my issues and felt like one of my biggest downfalls. While Cary seemed to never feel anything at all, I felt everything—deeply. Sometimes it was so overwhelming I thought it might actually kill me.

I realize I haven't answered his question, and he's staring at me like I have two heads. "Yeah, sure. Uh, I've been fine. Just working on the house."

He starts to mop up the bourbon, and I shove my hands into my pockets, for once feeling like I'm the one who doesn't want to talk. "I can't wait to see what you do to the place. It definitely needs some upgrades."

A noncommittal hum falls from my mouth as he rolls the mop bucket back. I walk over to the bar, grabbing a bottle of RED and two lowball glasses. As I'm pouring, Cary walks back into the tasting room.

He takes a seat at the bar as I place both our drinks then the bottle in front of him. "So, you want to answer for real this time?" he asks as I walk around to sit beside him.

"Is 'not really' an acceptable answer?" I'm half-kidding. I'm not sure Cary is the person I should talk to about my internal issues with dating Margot, what to do with the house, my whole fucking life. He may have—by some miracle—gotten Thea to take him back, but he still lost her—twice.

"Why not?" he pries.

"So, no, then? Cool. Look, I just have some shit going on. I don't need to have a therapy session about it." The second the words come out of my mouth, I want to stuff them back in. Cary has been in therapy for years now. It's nothing to be ashamed of. Shit, I wish I had the balls to go myself, maybe a shrink could fix me. But it sounds like I meant it as a low blow. "I didn't—" I start, but he cuts me off before I can attempt an apology.

"Right. It's fine. We can talk about something else." He downs the rest of his glass, reaching for the bottle to pour another. I follow suit, feeling like I'll need three more to get through this.

I take the out he gives me though, using it to deflect from any conversation regarding my life. "So you and Thea are back full force?"

He stares into his glass, taking a moment before answering. "No thanks to you, but yeah." He laughs a little, so I'm not sure if he's actually pissed or just being a dick.

"Uh, yeah. Sorry about that, I guess. You kind of had it coming though."

He puts his elbows on the bartop, intertwining his fingers. "I deserved it, you aren't wrong. I fucked up with Iris. I should have ended it with her a long time ago. And I feel like a piece of shit for it. But selfishly, I know I would have done that and more for another shot with Thea. I'm so thankful she took me back. I plan to focus on her and not the mistakes I made along the way."

I want to say, *"How? How do you do that? How do you focus on the good and not all the ways you've fucked up and will continue to fuck up?"* But I don't because I'm sure the answer is therapy. "Don't fuck it up again," is what comes out instead.

His laugh is a full belly one this time, and I feel it in my soul; it almost brings a smile to my face. Despite everything, I do like seeing him happy. I've always wanted the best for my little brother. I never wished ill will on him, I just never shied away from calling him out on his shit either.

"Yeah, I won't. I can promise you that," he responds, his laughter still dying off. We sit in silence for a bit then he says, "So Lydia's nurse, huh?"

"For fuck's sake, can you suddenly not take no for an answer?"

He throws his hands up in surrender. "Look, Thea told me there may be something going on. She asked me to talk to you about it."

And now I'm pissed. "Why would you need to fucking talk to me about it?"

His face turns to one of pity, like I'm a child who doesn't understand something simple. "Brooks..." He stares, waiting on who the fuck knows what. "She's just concerned," he finishes.

I pop my knuckles on instinct, feeling the flames inside me rising. There's no dousing them once they get to the surface. "Concerned about what, Cary?"

His face twists like my question hurts him somehow. "Don't make me say it."

"Oh," I grit out, "I think you fucking should."

He chugs the rest of his bourbon, slamming the glass down with more force than necessary. "Margot is Lydia's nurse. She's twenty-three years old. And from what Thea tells me, she's a fucking saint, just don't fuck it up. Thea and I don't want to have to clean up that kind of mess."

And just like that, the blaze inside of me pushes right past the surface, overflowing like a volcano. Even the revelation of her age isn't enough to distract me from my anger. "You have to be fucking kidding me. You, of all people, are lecturing me on making messes of women? This is a joke, right?"

I'm pushing up from my stool, throwing it off to the side. It clamors to the ground, and Cary's gaze shoots down to it with a this-is-exactly-what-I-was-talking-about expression on his face.

"It's not a joke. Margot isn't the kind of girl you should be messing around with."

I'm seething now, but in the midst of everything, I realize something. "Oh my God, is this why you invited me out for a drink? This is why we're here? Not because you missed me or wanted to wish me a happy birthday in person but because you needed to talk to me about where I'm putting my dick?"

He pushes up from his stool, calmer than I did. "That's not what I said, Brooks."

"You didn't have to, it's written all over your face," I retort. I fist my hands to keep from doing something I might regret.

"Brooks, you took a civil conversation and turned it on its head. When will you grow up?"

At this point, there might be literal smoke coming out of my ears. I haven't been this pissed since the altercation with Colton at that dive bar. "I've been grown up, *little* brother, you just missed it because you were too fucking busy in Seattle pretending none of us existed."

He doesn't waste another second on me, turning on his heel to leave. He clearly needs the last word though, so he shouts over his shoulder, "I thought you'd changed. Apparently, I was wrong."

I don't respond. I'm too pissed off, nothing but vitriol will come out. And those words cut deep, deeper than anything else he said because it's what I've been telling myself for days now. As the swinging door flaps back and forth, I'm left to stew in my own shit once again.

He'd come here to discuss my relationship with Margot. He'd intended on getting me to stop seeing her because she's too good for me. He didn't say those words, but he might as well have with the way his face twisted up about it.

I know she's too good for me. I know I'm not worth her time. I know I'll never change. I just never expected someone else to bring it to light. It's been my own dark secret I've held close to my chest, never speaking it out loud. But now, it's out in the open, it's been given life by the one person I thought would be on my side.

Chapter Twenty-Four

"You've folded those sheets three times already."

I snap out of my daze and find Lydia eyeing me. My blush is immediate, so I quickly finish folding the last of the bedding and move on to tidying up her already neat kitchenette.

I can't seem to get my mind to think of anything but my date a few days ago and everything that followed. The connection Brooks and I shared, the gentle way he touched me, the way he looked at me the morning after. I can't imagine a better first time experience. And now, anytime I have an idle minute, my thoughts drift to him, and I have to fight a huge beaming smile... along with the flutters low in my belly at the memory of us moving together.

It doesn't help that we decided to give this a real shot, and I have no one to talk to about it. I'm dying to tell Thea and Ripley, I'm sure they'll get a real kick out of it, but I don't want to say anything to them until I have a chance to speak with Hayes—I can't have him hearing from someone else and killing my boyfriend.

Oh, Brooks is my boyfriend. I wonder if he'd like the sound of that as much as I do.

It's quiet for a bit, just the low sounds of the TV and me shuffling magazines and pens from one spot to another filling the room.

"You know, I think you have a little something there," says Lydia, and when I turn around, she's wearing an expression of faux concern, pointing at the side of her neck. I slap my hand on the spot she's motioning to—the spot Brooks sucked a huge hickey into just two days ago—the spot that must still be showing even though I wore a turtleneck under my scrubs and my hair down.

When I don't come up with an excuse for the mark, she chuckles and says, "Ah, so I guess you finally got your card punched at the Boom Boom Room."

I blink at her a few times as her words register. "Oh my God. Please never string those words together in that order again," I say as the heat in my cheeks reaches a boiling point.

"Would you rather I say you got *deflowered*?" she coos.

"That's it, I'm going to ask for a transfer to the memory care wing," I say, turning as though I intend to leave but laughing at her antics.

"Oh, stop it. Come here and tell me all about it." She motions me over to her usual table by the window. I grab a mug from one of the kitchenette cabinets and fill it using the new teapot I got her for Christmas that she's set out on the table.

"There's not much to tell. He took me out on a date, and it was lovely. Then I spent the night at his house... and that was lovely too," I say, feeling shy.

"Lovely, sure. Not exactly the word I'd use to describe the way your neck looks like it's been mauled by a Hoover," she says with a chuckle as she takes a sip from her cup.

I shoot her a look I hope comes off as withering, but it's completely undermined by my following giggle. "He was great, very sweet and gentle," I say then sigh. "And we decided to try this—us—but ever since I left his place, he's been... distant." I hang my head, finally voicing my concerns out loud. I'm trying hard to hold on to the happiness I felt when he dropped me off, but it's getting more and more difficult when he seems to be pulling away. He's responding to my texts, but barely. I tried calling him yesterday, but he texted back he couldn't speak.

"Distant how?"

"I feel like I'm in high school complaining about a boy not calling me back. It's okay, I'll figure it out. I'm seeing him tonight for the Jingle Mingle, so I'll talk to him then," I say. "He's probably been busy with renovating his parents' house."

Lydia hums thoughtfully. "I'm a little surprised. I'd think he would be more sensitive knowing how important what you shared with him was."

I bite my lip and glance down at my new bracelet, a Christmas present from Lydia. The charms on it catch the overhead lights. "I may not have told him it was my first time... in so many words." I shift my eyes back up to Lydia and find her looking at me with suspicion.

"What words did you use?" she asks.

"Something like, 'take me to bed?'" I say, but it comes out as almost a question. I sink a little into myself, ready for her to tell me it was the wrong way to handle the situation, that my age and immaturity are showing.

After a pause, her face softens, and she says, "Ah, well, that's a very personal decision, and it's entirely up to you what you choose to share with him when it comes to intimacy. But I tend to find relationships have the strongest foundations if everyone involved is open and honest from the start."

"I know. I wanted to tell him, but I couldn't find a way to slip it into the conversation, and then one thing led to another..."

"And you decided to pass go and hitch a ride on the love train," she says, looking thoroughly amused with herself.

"Okay, we have to take away your cable access. Where are you getting these phrases?" I ask. My face is on fire with embarrassment, but at this point I don't know if it's for me or for her.

After a few more minutes of chatting, I wish her a Merry Christmas since I won't be in for a few days and head to the nurses' lounge to change into the clothes I brought for tonight. After much debating this morning, I chose a simple scoop-neck tee and skinny jeans.

I grab my jacket and purse. Looking at the time, I see I have about half an hour before I promised I'd meet Brooks at Louie's. I shoot him a quick text letting him know I'm heading out. A few seconds later, the little "read" appears underneath it, but no reply.

I sigh at the sinking feeling in my gut. I want to stay positive, live in the bubble of happiness I found a few days ago, but it's getting harder and harder. Did he change his mind? Is it too much for him? I know he doesn't do relationships, but he seemed excited. He pursued me. I thought we were on our way to building something special. Brooks let me see a side of himself I don't think many others have. Maybe that's what's scaring him?

I have to pull my big girl pants up and talk with him. I can speculate and spiral about this like a teenager all night, or I can go meet him and talk this out. If he's decided he's not ready, it'll hurt, but I'll understand. We just have to handle this with clarity, like adults.

The door to the lounge swinging open pulls me out of my self-pep talk. Aubrey rushes in holding a small gift bag with a reindeer on it.

"Oh, I'm so glad I caught you before you left," she says, huffing like she just ran here.

"Hey, what's going on?" I ask.

"I keep forgetting to give this to you," she says, smiling and handing the gift bag to me. "I'm your Secret Santa—surprise! I've had it in the back of my car forever now. Merry Christmas!" I take it from her, but my confusion must be evident because her smile slowly fades. "What's wrong?"

"I-I don't know," I stutter. "I thought I got my Secret Santa gift a few weeks ago. There was no name…" I trail off as a pit in my stomach opens. My heart rate picks up as realization hits me. My lungs stutter.

Miss me?

The pounding hot water feels good on my sore back. Spending the last week in the ER, running around with few breaks, has been wreaking havoc on my body. I'm so tired, I can't wait to crawl into bed as soon as I get out of the shower.

I shampoo and condition my hair as I think back on the last few months. Work has been exhausting since Blackwood kicked me off his service, and I've been relegated to all the scutwork and worst shifts. Despite me hoping he could keep it professional between us after he came on to me in his office, Julian requested I be removed from the cardiac program the following day. I tried to speak with him about it, but he was always busy and wouldn't take an appointment with me.

At first I was angry and considered reporting him to the hospital board, but quickly realized it would be my word against his, especially since I mentioned it to my supervisor, and he dismissed me. What's one second-year nurse compared to the prestige and money he brings to the hospital? I decided I'd keep my head down, work hard, and make my way up to one of the other specialized services.

Unfortunately, I'm beginning to think he blackballed me because no department head wants to take me on, so I'm left with whatever shifts need covering, which typically lands me in the ER with the drunks, vomiting kids, and sometimes violent dementia patients.

Sighing, I turn off the water and stand dripping in the shower for a moment. Maybe it's time to look for another hospital or private practice. I pull the shower curtain back and grab a towel, wiping my face and squeezing water from my hair.

As I wrap the towel around my body, I look up at the mirror above the sink and freeze. My blood runs cold, and if my body could move, I would scream, but the sound seems to have lodged itself in my throat.

Written in the fog created by the steam of my shower is "Miss me?" As I stare, unable to get my body to move, a droplet slowly runs down from the "M," and my eyes track the movement. I feel like I'm floating outside of my body. This isn't happening to me. I'm watching it happen to someone else.

Suddenly, I realize someone wrote this while I was showering. That someone might still be in my apartment. My breath quickens, and my vision goes hazy. I left my phone in my bedroom, anything could be waiting for me outside of this bathroom.

I quietly open the door and peer through the crack, seeing nothing and no one in the hallway. As silently as possible, I open the door more and slip out, still only in my towel. I peer through the doorway to my living room and kitchen—both appearing empty as well. With a steadying breath, I continue down the hall to my bedroom, quickly grabbing an umbrella from the hook by the front door. Not sure what I'll be able to do with it, but it's better than going in there empty-handed.

My bedroom door is ajar, and I wait before going in, listening for any movement. Hearing nothing, I gently press my palm to the door, and it swings open. My bedroom is small, there are no hiding places aside from my closet.

Feeling brave or maybe just a little crazy, I stomp over to the closet and tear the door open. Only my clothes and shoes greet me. I heave out a huge lungful of air and swipe my hand down my face, my hand coming away wet. I didn't even realize I have tears streaming down my face.

Miss me?

I thought this was over. I haven't heard from him in over two months. The strange notes and presents stopped. I thought he moved on. But he was here. He was in my apartment with me. He somehow bypassed my locked door and entered my space. Panic grips me. What if he comes back? I don't even know who he is, not really.

With my heartbeat in my ears and adrenaline running through my veins, I toss the towel to the ground, pull on the first pair of leggings in my drawer along with an oversized sweater. Then I grab my suitcase from the back of the closet and start tossing in clothes.

I run to the bathroom and grab my toiletries—only the essentials I can't live without. As I'm making my way back to the bedroom, I stop in the hall and look over the art I've collected throughout the years. My heart hurts because I know I can't take it all with me, but I grab the paintings of the fish and hurry back to my bedroom and throw it all into the suitcase. Zipping the luggage closed, I jam my feet into sneakers and grab my phone.

As I'm about to open the front door, I remember my Lucky Penny painting and run to the living room to grab it from above the couch.

Wheeling the suitcase in one hand and the other clutching the oversized painting to my body, I manage to lug everything to my car, hurling them in the backseat.

As I sit in the driver's seat, I finally notice my hands are shaking. I open and close my fingers to try to get control, but it barely helps. I take a few deep breaths, hoping to slow my heart rate. The image of the words on the mirror have imprinted themselves on the back of my eyelids, and they're all I can see when I close my eyes.

Once I calm enough to enter the address into my navigation app, I start the car and pull out of the lot toward Indigo Hill.

Aubrey's voice pulls me from my nightmare of a memory, the reason I left Charleston, the reason I'm here. "Oh, no, that must have been from someone else. I picked your name out of the hat at the beginning of the month. Oh! Maybe you have a secret admirer," she teases.

I force a smile, trying to keep calm, trying to keep my breathing steady. "Maybe," I say on a breath.

Aubrey's looking at me expectantly, so I reach into the bag and pull out a sheer sage colored scarf. I go through the motions of wrapping it around my neck and thanking her. All the while my mind is racing with panic.

My fingers are numb as I fold the scarf back up and stuff it into the bag. I pull myself together just enough to whisper another "Thanks" before darting out the door. My head spins all the way to my car, eyes scanning the near-empty parking lot, shadows forming human shapes in my mind.

This is nothing. It's nothing. There's some misunderstanding. My name must have been in there twice. I have two Secret Santas. It can't *be anything else.*

I keep repeating these words to myself all the way to my car, and again as my hand shakes locking the door when I'm inside. I start the engine and take a few deep breaths before I take off. My anxiety is through the roof, and it's not safe for me to drive like this, but I have to get out of here. I have to get to Brooks—

I freeze with my hand on the shift lever. Brooks. My instinct is leading me straight to Brooks. Not Hayes. My whole life I've seen Hayes as my safe space. Somewhere in the last month, that's shifted, and Brooks has become who I seek out when my world is crumbling.

Not letting the thoughts overtake me, I put the car in drive and peel out of the parking lot.

I need to get to Brooks. It'll all be better when I get to Brooks. He'll know what to do.

By some miracle, I manage to grab a spot in the small lot next to Louie's as someone is leaving. I take a few deep breaths before opening the car door and locking it behind me. My eyes scan the parking lot as I hurry to the front door.

The warmth of the bar envelopes me as soon as I enter. It's been decked out in Christmas decor: baubles and garlands hanging from the ceiling, a small Christmas tree by the jukebox, and all the workers are in Santa hats. Some of the tension eases out of me as I look around at faces I recognize from the time I've spent here with Thea and Ripley as well as from Hayes' shop. I can't fully settle though as my mind keeps repeating, *is he here,* over and over.

The space is packed, every table and booth occupied. There are a lot more people here than the night I spent playing drinking games. I've never been to the Jingle Mingle, never being in the area for it since I've been old enough to get into a bar.

I walk around the perimeter of the crammed dance floor, trying to find Brooks. I'm right on time for when we agreed to meet the other day, but since he hasn't responded to my texts, I'm not sure if he's here yet. Or if he's even coming. My throat tightens at the thought he may be standing me up.

I try to shake off the feeling of the chasm in my stomach opening. I want to give him the benefit of the doubt. Despite what everyone says about him, Brooks has been nothing but dependable and authentic with me. Besides his single word responses—and then utter silence today—he's always been reliable and open.

I'm still making my way through the crowd when I hear, "Margot! Hi!" Turning, I find Thea waving to me furiously while festively dressed in tight red jeans and a green sweater. The arm that's not trying to flag me down is wrapped around Cary's waist, and his is circling her shoulders possessively. Huh, I guess that's a thing now.

"Hi!" she repeats enthusiastically when I get closer.

"Hey, guys. Merry Christmas," I say, trying to lace as much cheer into my voice as I can muster, which unfortunately, isn't much at the moment. Thea's brows scrunch in worry.

"You okay?" she asks.

"Yeah, yeah, I'm fine. Have you seen Brooks? I was supposed to meet him here," I say, my skin starting to crawl. The initial warmth I felt coming in here is now almost stifling, and I'm not sure if it's the heat or the anxiousness roiling inside me, but taking a breath is getting harder to do. I just want to find Brooks, I know I'll feel better when I see him.

Thea and Cary share a look I can't read before turning back to me. "Uh, yeah, he's around here somewhere. But Listen, Margot..." Thea starts, but I don't hear the rest of her sentence because I spot Brooks in a corner booth of the bar. He appears laid back, sitting and talking to some people I don't recognize. Just the sight of him loosens something in my chest. Though I still want to climb out of my skin, the relief flooding me is an almost tangible thing running through my veins.

Without cluing into what she said, I wish Thea a Merry Christmas again and move through the crowd, weaving and dodging.

When I'm a few yards away, I watch as a tall, gorgeous woman climbs in the booth and practically into Brooks' lap. He casually slings his arm around her, and his fingers settle on her hip. She whispers something in his ear, and he flashes her that wicked smirk. Something about it doesn't feel right though; his eyes seem dull, the usual glint of playfulness missing.

There are numerous drinks on the table, and Brooks takes a few gulps of the tumbler in his hand as he watches his friends chatting, nodding every once in a while. I'm frozen to the spot, not able to move toward him or back the way I came. His fingers play with the sliver of skin right above her jeans where her shirt rode up just a little. The same spot he was gripping me just the other night as he thrust into me from underneath.

The woman runs her hand over his chest, dipping her fingers into the neck of his T-shirt, following the lines of his tattoos, similar to what I had done. I feel like I may be sick. I watch as that same hand slides up his chest, his neck, and to his face, turning it in her direction.

My vision goes fuzzy around the edges, all I see clearly is her smile—she's beautiful—right before she leans up and kisses Brooks. Right there in front of the entire bar, like it's nothing. Like they've done it a hundred times before. Like my heart isn't breaking in my chest. The pain of it is almost crippling—acute—like I've been stabbed. I'm afraid to look down as though I might see an actual wound.

My thoughts race, and I'm not sure what to do now. I'm scared to leave, to be alone, but staying here might actually kill me. I'm hurt, so hurt, but I'm also embarrassed. Was what he said to me all lies? Was it all just so he could sleep with me? I feel so stupid; just a stupid lovesick girl with a stupid crush, giving her heart to a sweet-talking bad boy. I'm such a cliché.

I fight the tears threatening to flood my eyes, the tell-tale tingle behind my nose. There's a lump in my throat I can't seem to swallow down, no matter how much I try.

Just as I'm about to turn away, Brooks' eyes land on me. They're glassy from the alcohol, and they widen just a bit, but then his face settles back into a blank mask.

Of their own accord, my feet carry me closer to the booth. After a moment, the gazes of all the people sitting around the table land on me, and their chatter dies down. My eyes don't stray from Brooks. The woman next to him—I distantly recall her name is Tiffany—says with a smile, "Hey! You're Hayes' little sister, right?"

I nod, biting my lip and still looking at Brooks. "What's going on, Brooks?" I ask, trying to keep my voice from betraying the turmoil inside me.

He looks around the table, face still unreadable, before turning to me and slipping into his usual cocky persona. "Not much, just having a nice night out with my friends," he says, pulling Tiffany closer into him.

I feel like I'm in the Twilight Zone. He's acting like he barely knows me, and I'm not sure what I've done. What changed between the amazing night we spent together and now?

"We had plans," I say.

"Aw, Brooks. Baby, I thought we were going to spend Christmas Eve like we did last year," whines Tiffany into his neck, she's clearly drunk or close to it. His eyes don't leave me. "I wore that set you like..." she says too loudly for it not to be meant for my ears.

I can't keep the tears back anymore. I nod, giving the table a watery smile, and turn on my heel, weaving through the maze of people and out the front door.

CHAPTER TWENTY-FIVE

I can't get Cary's words out of my head.

"I thought you'd changed, apparently, I was wrong."

He's right. I haven't changed. And I'd be doing Margot a favor if I disappeared from her life. Which is what I've been working up to for the last two days. I try not to look at her messages, but I always fail. She's a magnetic pull I can't resist. I've tried over and over, it never works.

But this time, I have to try for her. She deserves more. She deserves better. She'll be happier when she finds someone else who can give her what she needs and wants.

I'll miss her though, her pure as fuck heart—and the added bonus of that goddamn mouth of hers. Margot brings me to my knees in ways I never imagined possible.

I'm so in my head, I'm not keeping track of the conversation happening around me at the table. Josh is sitting beside me with his girlfriend pushed up against him like they can't stand to have even the smallest amount of space between them. And Nat and her boyfriend are sitting across from me. Every time my phone lights up in front of me, I turn it over to see if it's Margot. A part of me hopes she stands me up—unlikely since she's the most decent person I know—then I won't have to face her and act like a douche.

"You waiting on someone to text you or something?" Josh asks, looking from me to the phone in my hand.

"What? No. Just checking the time. Mind your fucking business."

"Jesus, what crawled up your ass tonight?" he asks, leaning away from me as if being close may cause him imminent danger.

"I need another drink." I walk over to the bar, waving down Shelley and showing her my empty. She gives me a nod but keeps talking to the man in front of her. Turning around to look out at the crowd in Louie's, I lean my back against the bar as I wait. It was the wrong move because Tiffany walks in at the same moment my phone buzzes.

I quickly look down at the screen and see it's Margot. I'm relieved and deflated all at once. I was really hoping she'd forgotten.

As Tiffany walks my way, I turn back around and say, "Make it a triple, Shell."

Tiffany is a bitch, I knew this, but the second Margot walked in, she proved it tenfold.

I'm also a fucking asshole. But she didn't need to add fuel to the fire. I was sabotaging myself just fine on my own. Apparently she had some fight with her boyfriend—Justin? James? Jordan? Whatever the hell his name is. I guess she felt the need to help fuck up my life too.

I should have told her to go away the second she sat down. I definitely shouldn't have put my arm around her. I let Cary's words get to me. Instead of proving him wrong, I leaned into them. Everyone thinks the worst of me, so what's the point in trying to do better—be better? Cary and Thea don't want me with Margot. Hayes sure as fuck won't want me with Margot. Up until last week, Margot didn't want me with her either. She turned me down multiple times. The only person who didn't treat me like a piece of shit about it was Ripley.

But I was kidding myself thinking I could be a boyfriend to her. I couldn't even last three fucking days.

We were doomed before we even started; I couldn't even wear date-appropriate clothes. And I know she said she was just messing with me, but it was obvious I went overboard with the cheese. Part of me wondered if the blow job was just to save the date from being a complete nightmare.

The moment I see the tears in her eyes, everything comes to a screeching halt.

What the fuck is wrong with me? I caused this. I made this perfect woman cry.

Fuck. I thought she'd get pissed, tell me I'm an asshole and exactly who she thought I was. I never thought she'd cry over me. I never wanted to be someone who made her cry. I'm no better than her deadbeat father. I knew it would fucking hurt, but I didn't realize it would gut me to know I caused it. The image of tears pouring from those beautiful green eyes makes me regret every decision I've made for the last forty-eight hours.

Margot rushes in the opposite direction, and it takes everything in me not to shove Tiffany onto the ground so I can run after her. "Tiffany, move." The command in my voice is enough to make her drop the act and draw back whatever body parts of hers she had draped on me.

She gives me a fake-ass pout before bringing her hand back up to my chest. "Come on, baby—"

"I said get the fuck up, Tiffany." Finally, she peels herself out of the booth with me right behind her. I stand up, and she grabs onto my arm one more time.

"Brooks, wait—" She doesn't get another word out before I'm flinging her off of me. The music stops. Everyone's chatter dies down, all eyes on us and the commotion we're causing. I wish I could say I give a damn, but I really fucking don't.

"No, Tiffany. I didn't want you last Christmas or six months ago or two months ago, and I sure as hell don't want you now. Is that clear enough for you?"

She looks around, noticing all the eyes on us, and tears start streaming down her face as she nods her head in response. It doesn't surprise me that I don't care about her crying, it doesn't affect me the way Margot's tears do.

I try not to think about it too much as I push past the crowd of people. Opening the door, the chilly night air hits me. Margot is walking toward the small parking area next to the building. She's not too far ahead of me, but I hesitate, scrambling for what I'll say when I catch up with her.

"Margot," I shout from across the street. She stops in her tracks but doesn't turn around. "Come on, wait up. It didn't mean anything."

I'm almost to her now when she turns around to look at me. Her eyes are red-rimmed and stained from the tears running down her cheeks. I feel a crippling pang in my chest again at the sight. It's no easier the second time.

"Us or her?" Her voice is quiet, almost reserved.

Her question gives me pause. Why would she think I meant us? "Her, obviously."

"Is it obvious, Brooks?" she shoots back, her voice now laced with venom.

My blood starts boiling again. I came out here to apologize, maybe make things right. I wasn't planning on another fight. "I don't know what you want me to say, it's not like we're exclusive."

"Clearly," she says as she turns back around, once again walking toward her car.

"I fucking warned you, Margot," I call to her back, like saying 'I told you so' will make anything better in this situation. She opens the door to her car and spins in place to look at me again.

"Warned me about what, Brooks?" she asks, her voice breaking on my name and splintering my heart in a way I didn't know was possible. "You didn't warn me I'd have to see other women draped all over you the next time you asked me out. See them kiss you. Why did you even invite me here?"

I fucking hate Tiffany.

"I warned you I wasn't good at this."

There's a sudden flip of a switch, and her sadness turns to bitter anger. Her face is all twisted up, and even in the dark, her cheeks are flaming red. "Stop making excuses! Stop blaming this on everyone but yourself. You knew you invited me here tonight, you even read my text confirming I was on my way. You knew I'd see her hanging on you when I walked in. Y-You know how I feel about you. Why would you hurt me on purpose? Do you get off on being cruel?" She's almost yelling now. Anyone outside of Louie's will get an earful of our conversation.

"Look, I told you not to get attached to me. And now you're acting like some lovesick teenager after her first time."

Her keys drop to the ground. Her face morphs into a kind of fury I've never seen from her before. "Want to know why, Brooks? Because it *was* my first time. And I regret sharing it with you of all people. I don't need another person in my life who still sees me as a child."

I'm shocked into silence. She can't—that can't be true. There's no way. She would have told me. She bends down to grab her keys before getting into her car.

"Fuck you, Brooks," is the last thing I hear before she slams the door and peels out of the parking lot.

I'm still standing in the same spot five minutes after her tail lights disappear around the corner. Still trying to figure out what just happened. I'm going back through all the time we spent together, trying to pinpoint how I didn't see it. She never once implied she was a virgin. She didn't act inexperienced. Nothing about our time together could have prepared me for the bomb she just dropped in my lap.

I stole her virginity, made her think I was an option, then I threw another girl in her face. And for what? Just to prove someone else right?

I know my feelings for Margot are real. I know what we have—or had—is real. I showed her the real me, and once she saw me, she never judged like everyone else has, she embraced it. But I fucked it up. I took a perfect woman, a woman who was willing to take a chance on me, and I fucked her over. I called her a teenager when I'm the one acting like a child because I'm scared. Fuck me.

I'm a monster. A real life, full-blown monster of a man. Someone who shouldn't be around anyone because all I do is make shit worse. At least Margot knows now. At least she's seen the worst and won't look at me with hope I don't deserve anymore.

My heart is racing with anxiety. I can't get the broken look on her face out of my mind. I think it might haunt me for the rest of my life.

I'm not sure how long it is before I'm heading back toward Louie's, back to the scene of the crime. The first person I see is Tiffany, her eyes light up when she notices I'm alone. I turn in the opposite direction, throwing my middle finger her way from over my shoulder. Just as I make it back to the booth to grab my jacket, Ripley sidles up beside me, ignorant to everything that just occurred. I have no idea where he's been all night. I saw him for two seconds then he was gone until now.

"Hey, Brooks. Where's Margie? She still coming?"

I throw a fifty on the table then whip around to him. "Her fucking name is *Margot*. And she left," I say as I push past him. I'm not in the mood to answer his questions. He can get the information from Cary and Thea who saw the whole thing play out.

"Left? I never even saw her."

"Yeah, well, get used to it."

The door is swinging shut behind me when I hear him say, "What the hell does that mean?"

Chapter Twenty-Six

I jolt awake covered in a cold sweat. I tossed and turned all night, nightmares of my past chasing me. It's not a dream though, it's a living nightmare. He found me.

It's Christmas morning, I plan to go see my dad. He may not be sober enough to realize it, but it won't feel like Christmas without seeing him.

Checking my phone, I see there are six messages from Brooks, all sent throughout the night, all asking me to call him, let him explain, and all becoming less coherent as the night wore on. The last one was sent at 4:43 a.m. I turn my phone off without responding after sending a text to Hayes letting him know I'll be by for Christmas lunch—our annual tradition.

I take a look in the mirror after washing my face. My eyes are puffy from crying, and the circles beneath them are a dark purple since sleep was hard to come by last night. It was difficult for my mind to settle once I got back home, both because of the lingering threat but also because Brooks' words kept spreading into the deep pockets of my mind. *"I told you not to get attached to me"* and *"you're acting like some lovesick teenager after her first time"* keep floating around me, inescapable.

I've never felt as small as I did in that moment. Our difference in age never seemed like an issue before last night, but now it's clear he only sees me as some young piece of ass. Someone to use. To break.

I feel so utterly stupid for not believing everything I'd heard, everything he told me himself. I should have listened. I guess I didn't want to believe the truth so badly that I only held on to the things I perceived as real. I ignored all the red flags, deluding myself, even when he was waving them directly in my face.

I guess I should be thankful he showed his true colors so soon. He didn't drag it out, string me along for weeks, months. Didn't wait until I was completely head over heels in love with him. Just a little bit. Just enough for the sting of what I saw last night and the things he said to leave a lasting wound on me. Leave my heart tender and bruised, not quite battered and beaten.

At least he had the decency to not leave me in tatters.

Tears well in my eyes again, but I blink them back. I need to get a hold of myself. He's just a guy. So what if he took my trust and threw it back in my face? So what if I shared—unbeknownst to him—something I can never get back? It's a lesson learned, right?

Swallowing down as much of the emotions threatening to overtake me as I can, I blow my nose, pull my hair into a loose bun, and head out to celebrate Christmas.

I pull up to my dad's and sigh at the disrepair of the place as I often do when I come here. I know today's not the day, but Hayes and I have to have a conversation about it. Dad is in no state to take the initiative to get someone out here. It's up to us—well, I guess me. I think Hayes is over the whole situation, he's only willing to invest the bare minimum of his time, money, or mental bandwidth. I don't blame him, twenty years is a long time to take care of someone who refuses to take care of themselves.

Opening the door, my anxiety spikes. Brooks and everything that happened at the bar yesterday was a distraction from my more pressing issue—the reason I was seeking Brooks out in the first place last night, the desperate need I had for him to make me feel safe. I scan the trees around my dad's place. He's secluded here, with no neighbors for miles. I've never thought about it until now, now that every rustle of the wind and change in shadow brings a sense of danger with it.

I had gotten complacent. Months and months of nothing had lulled me into feeling safe. Meeting Brooks, feeling confident from his attention dissipated the usual dark cloud that hung around me. But it's back now and darker than ever.

Miss me?

I hurry from my car to Dad's house. After carefully navigating the crumbling front steps, I make my way inside and lock the door behind me. Just like numerous times before, I find him sleeping it off in his recliner in the living room, the TV playing a Christmas movie quietly. A half empty bottle of vodka stands on the side table next to him, and I can't tell if it's left over from the night before or if he started early this morning. I guess it doesn't make a difference either way.

I pick up a few empty bottles and takeout containers—just like always, it never ends, never changes—but lose steam pretty quickly. Dropping the items in my hands back to the coffee table, I sit on the old sofa in the center of the room. Huffing out a heavy breath, I realize I'm tired. Tired of watching my father drink himself to death day in and day out. Tired of pretending I've got things together so I don't disappoint my brother. Tired of looking over my shoulder all the time.

I feel like I'm keeping it together by sheer force of will and double-sided tape. I don't know how much longer I can do this.

"My heart is heavy today, Daddy," I say, knowing full well he can't hear me in his unconscious state. "I handed my heart over to a man, and he handed it back to me in pieces last night. What was I thinking?" I scoff to myself. "I was pulled in by those stupid blue eyes and the motorcycle and that nose ring. The tattoos..." I trail off on a groan. "Sorry, I'm sure you don't want to hear any of this. I just don't really have anyone else to talk to about it. I definitely can't tell Hayes—especially now—it would end in a bloodbath."

I pause, playing with a loose thread on the couch. "I thought he was one of the good ones, you know? I guess I'm a little naive. Should I be blaming you? Absent parent and all. I don't think it's fair though; it discounts what Hayes did for me. He was a great stand-in for you, I can't even begin to thank him." A tear tracks down my cheek, rolling to the corner of my lips. I taste the salt of it when I open my mouth to continue, "And I'm in trouble, Daddy. He found me, and I don't know how long he's been here.

I'm terrified. I don't want to have to run again. I don't even know where I would go."

I sit in the quiet for a while longer, listening to my father's deep, even breathing and the soft sounds of the TV in the background. I feel better after saying everything out loud for the first time. Not that it helps the situation, but a tiny bit of the tension I carry daily has eased.

Wiping away the tears from my face, I stand, gather up the bottles and containers I dropped earlier, and take them to the kitchen where I spend the next thirty minutes cleaning up.

The Indigo Hill town square is deserted. I would expect nothing less for a small South Carolina town on Christmas Day. It started sleeting on the drive over from Dad's, and now the roads are slick. I've passed only a few cars, and despite my best efforts, my eyes shoot to the driver of each one, looking for anyone who looks like they don't belong.

I park on the empty street right outside of Mark of Mason. The shop is dark, blinds shut to the outside. Hayes has given all the people who work with him a few days off for the holidays as he does every year. They typically pick back up after the new year.

Without the usual faces milling inside the storefronts and on the sidewalks, the center of town feels creepy and ominous. I pull my jacket closer around me to ward off the chill. The wet, icy wind bites at my cheeks as I reach into the backseat to grab Hayes' present, and I pull my parka hood tighter to me. My eyes sweep the gazebo in the center of the square as if I expect to see someone waiting for me.

A shudder runs down my spine, and my skin prickles at the thought of his eyes on me again. I shake it off and make my way to the door between Hayes' tattoo studio and the ice cream shop next to it. After I punch in the code, the door buzzes open, and I hustle up the stairs to Hayes' apartment.

"Merry Christ—" I start as I enter without knocking and then freeze as I stand three feet from a boy who can't be more than fifteen years old. I caught him in the middle of biting off the head of a gingerbread man. His grey eyes, partially hidden by glasses, are wide as they take me in. We stand staring at each other for a beat, then two. The spell is broken when he chokes on the cookie and starts coughing.

"Uh, hi. I'm Margot. Is Hayes here?" I ask when his hacking subsides. He nods and tries to chew quickly to clear his mouth, a few crumbs falling from his lips.

"Yeah," he says, clearing his throat. "He's cooking." I'm still standing in the doorway, unsure of who the kid is when he realizes he's in my way to get to my brother. "Sorry! I'm Sebastian. People call me Sebby. I'm Max's brother. Hayes'... friend?"

Max's kid brother. The reason Max spends his weekends in an illegal fighting ring, trying to win enough cash to help support the two of them. My heart breaks a little as I look over at him. He's sweet looking; almost as tall as Max but gangly, like he hasn't quite grown into his limbs, and still carrying the innocence of boyhood. Another year and he'll be an exact replica of his brother. From what Hayes mentioned, they've had a rough childhood, but it doesn't look like he carries too much of it on his shoulders. He seems relaxed, happy even.

"Margot, is that you?" Hayes calls out from somewhere deeper in the apartment. The space isn't big, just a simple one bedroom, but the entrance is down a hall from the main living space. I move around Sebby and find Hayes in the small kitchen chopping carrots as something cooks on the stove behind him. He's so broad, there's hardly any room for anyone else in the space. The air smells delicious, scents of garlic and roasting chicken waft around me, and I'm transported back to the many Christmases we've spent together with Hayes cooking all day and me stealing bites when he's not looking.

Sebby follows me and hops over the back of the couch, settling in next to Max—arm still in a sling from his shoulder dislocation—who barely acknowledges me with only a nod and a quick "Yo," his eyes on some action movie on the TV.

"Merry Christmas," I say, stepping into Hayes for a hug. He returns it one-handed, the other still holding the knife but at a distance away from my body. "You didn't tell me we'd have company," I add in a whisper.

"Merry Christmas, Booger." He looks behind me, confirming the boys' attention is fixed on the TV. "Sorry, they had nowhere to go. Their uncle is spending a few nights in jail—don't ask. So, I invited them here. We'll have plenty of food." My heart constricts at the thought, remembering plenty of holidays Hayes and I spent just the two of us because Dad was sleeping it off or out drinking somewhere, unaware of the significance of the day.

"No, of course it's fine. The more the merrier. Can I help you with anything?"

"I've got this, but maybe you can set the table? I asked Max, but, well..." He trails off, and I follow where he's looking to the small dining area off to the left. The tablecloth hangs off the sides of the table, askew; the plates are still stacked with the forks and knives on top; a pack of napkins sits next to the dishes, unopened. I smile at how very typical teenager the sight is.

After I sort out the table, I grab a bottle of water from the fridge and sit on a stool on the opposite side of the island from where Hayes is working. He's shoved papers and his open laptop to this end, and my eyes snag on the screen. It's open to a website for a tattoo studio in New York City, City Tats. The page he has up is a profile for one of their artists: Calla Bennett. She's stunning, flaming red hair and a chic goth-rock style. She also looks startlingly familiar.

I'm about to ask Hayes who she is when I catch sight of the papers next to the laptop: town records for renovation and business permits pulled by Calla.

"What's all this?" I ask.

Hayes' eyes flit to me and take in what I'm referring to, and then his eyebrows slant down while his shoulders tense. He starts chopping more aggressively. "Research."

"Who's Calla Bennett?"

"A huge fucking pain in my ass," he grumbles out and turns away to drop the diced vegetables into one of the pans on the stove.

"Hmm," I hum with a small smile. "Well, she's a very pretty pain in the ass."

"Don't start," he says, turning back to me before pausing. When he's quiet and unmoving for a beat, I look over and find him examining me.

"What?"

"Ass? Since when do you swear?" His eyes narrow on me, scrutinizing my face for the first time since I got here. "And why do you look like you spent the night crying? What happened?"

The skin on my face tightens, and I know I've gone pale. I can't tell my brother about Brooks, not that there's much to say. He'd rage and say he told me so. Then he'd probably go find Brooks, and today would become known as the Great Indigo Hill Christmas Massacre.

"Nothing happened," I meek out, unable to come up with anything better on the spot. "And I'm an adult, I'm allowed to swear." I add, trying to infuse some indignation into my voice.

"Who am I fucking up?" He's pretty much growling now.

"Hayes, it's fine. I-I was just... sad yesterday. You know, the holidays." I punctuate my lie with a small shrug, hoping it comes off at least a little convincing.

Hayes deflates a little, but the concern doesn't leave his face. A moment later, he nods. "Yeah, sure," he says, turning back to the stove to stir something.

I let out a silent sigh. No matter my feelings toward Brooks, I don't want to ruin their relationship, especially since Brooks wants to work with him one day.

We spend the next hour chatting about my work and the people around town while I watch Hayes put the finishing touches on the feast he's cooked for us. Once everything is prepared, Max and Sebby turn off the TV and help bring all the dishes to the table where we sit and pass around the food.

"Are there nuts and berries in this salad?" asks Max with a scrunched nose as he eyes the mixed greens topped with pistachios, shaved parmesan, and pomegranate seeds Hayes holds out to him.

"Just eat it," says Hayes exasperatedly, like this isn't the first time they're having this conversation. He's sitting across the table from me, Max on his right.

I'm beginning to think my brother and these boys have been spending a lot of time together. He's told me on several occasions he never wants to have kids of his own. Raising me was more than enough for him. But it appears he can't help but attract wayward young people looking for guidance and in need of help.

"How's the shoulder?" I ask Max, eyeing the sling he's still sporting.

"Getting better," he says in between shoveling forkfuls of food into his mouth. "You did a good job, Doc." My heart clenches at the nickname, the sudden and casual reminder of Brooks a shock to my system.

"Hayes says you're a nurse," says Sebby from my left. "Are you going to help at The Pit now that Becca's not coming around anymore?"

His words catch me off guard, both because he knows about The Pit and also because he seems to know more than I do.

"Who's Becca?" I ask.

"The vet tech who was patching Max up when he got his ass beat," he says with a teasing grin aimed at his brother.

"You little shit," retorts Max. "I definitely beat my fair share."

"Language!" says Hayes, sounding like the dad he doesn't want to be. I smile at the bickering around the table. Though I barely know them, Max and Sebby fit so well with us. These are the simple family moments I always longed for when it was just me and Hayes growing up. This is turning out to be one of the best Christmases I've had.

"Anyway," says Max, rolling his eyes. "Becca broke up with Sean, a guy I fight against sometimes—he's pretty cool. Has a mean left hook."

He continues rambling about the other fighters, and I can barely keep up. The way he talks about The Pit, the fighting, and the people involved, it's clear the whole operation means a lot to him. Despite the violence and inevitability of getting hurt sometimes, he loves the fighting, the discipline of it.

"Anyway," that seems to be a favorite word for Max, "She's not coming around anymore. Are you taking over for her? We need someone with some medical know-how. This guy," he motions to Hayes with his head, "can barely put on a Band-Aid." Hayes huffs at him but continues eating without a word.

"Wait," I say, putting my fork down and turning on my brother. "You don't have a medical professional there when these fights are happening? Hayes, that's so dangerous. Someone could get really hurt, and you're at least thirty minutes from a hospital. That could have serious consequences—things you can't come back from." I put as much emphasis as I can on the last part of my sentence so he understands the gravity of the risk he's taking.

"You want to do it?" he says gruffly in between bites. I'm taken aback by his question. I look around at the three of them, Max looking like he's seconds away from begging me, Sebby's curious eyes on me, and Hayes' resigned face—he's expecting me to say no.

"Okay," is what comes out, surprising us all. "But it can't be willy-nilly. You can't just call and expect me to be there. I have work, and I can try to schedule my shifts, but you have to work with me. And I need a space; I can't just work out of the back of a truck. I'll need supplies, a clean space to work, a table." What am I doing? Am I really agreeing to this?

Seeing these boys, knowing what could happen to them, I can't in good conscience let them keep going with no medical supervision. A vision of Brooks' bruised face flashes through my mind. I know I could be putting my license at stake here, but I also trust my brother.

"You're serious?" asks Hayes, disbelieving. "You're really going to do this? I can get you whatever supplies you need. Just get me a list."

"Where—" I start but then think better of it. "You know what? Don't tell me. I don't want to know how you can get medical supplies. But you have to understand how much trouble I'd get in if the authorities found out. I'd lose my license, probably go to jail." My heart races at the thought of the risk, but I'm not entirely sure if it's only because of anxiety. Layered below the low hum of panic is a small thread of excitement. I'm going to be a part of something with my brother; he trusts me to handle this.

The rest of dinner passes with us listening to Sebby tell us about an online Dungeons and Dragons tournament he's planning with some friends. It sails way over my head, but I love his enthusiasm and how his eyes light up when he gets to explain what D20 and hit points are.

It's not until way later in the evening when I'm hugging Max and Sebby and gathering my things to head out that I remember the messages from Brooks I ignored all day and the empty house that awaits me. I briefly consider telling Hayes about what's potentially waiting for me outside, but the words won't come when he envelops me in a hug at the door.

"Merry Christmas, Booger. I love you," he says quietly in my ear.

"I love you, big brother," I whisper, pulling away. I wrap my jacket around myself, hug the leftovers he packed for me to my chest and head out into the cold.

CHAPTER TWENTY-SEVEN

The sound of sleet wakes me, and I'm immediately reminded of the reason I drank myself to sleep last night. Or this morning, rather. I don't think I actually passed out until after 5 a.m. I'm on the couch with a slew of beer bottles surrounding me on the coffee table, the floor. I regret more than just my choice to get plastered.

Running a hand over my face, I groan at how shitty I feel. Both physically and emotionally. I don't remember much of last night after I ruined the best thing that ever happened to me, but it's the only part worth remembering. I'm not sure I'll ever forget the look on her face the moment I broke us. The moment I broke her.

I fish my phone out from underneath me—grunting at how sore I am—to check the time. It's just past noon. I have multiple missed calls and texts from, well, everyone. Everyone except Margot. The one person I want to talk to.

Before I click on any of the messages, I see one I don't remember sending in my text thread with Margot. Fuck. I am not the drunk texting kind of guy. Or I wasn't until last night apparently. *Fuck me.* I click on the thread to see how terribly I embarrassed myself.

12/25 1:17 a.m.

Me: Fuck, Margot. I'm sorry, I'm such an ass-hole.

Read 8:56 a.m.

12/25 2:35 a.m.

Me: Okay, I getit. I'm not worth your time,

Read 8:56 a.m.

12/25 3:01 a.m.

Me: how cooudl you not tell me ou were a virgin

Read 8:56 a.m.

12/25 4:13 a.m.

Me: I miss you a lready please answer

Read 8:56 a.m.

12/25 4:43 a.m.

Me: I;m a terrible persson and i hate mysekf for what i diid

Read 8:56 a.m.

Okay, so the messages aren't untrue, but fuck. The worst part is she saw them and never responded. I almost wish her read receipts weren't on so I could pretend she hadn't seen them.

I exit out of the thread, sober enough now to know I shouldn't send a follow up. I scroll through the app to see who else messaged me. It seems everyone I know has tried to reach me in the last twelve hours. Sitting up, I reach over to the coffee table and grab my pack of smokes and a lighter. With my cigarette lit, I let it hang from my lips as I open each message, making sure none are important.

12/25 9:06 a.m.

Hayes: Merry Christmas, asshole.

12/25 9:18 a.m.

Thea: Idk what happened last night, but you looked really upset. Can you please come over so I know you're okay? Plus, it's Christmas, meaning you're obligated as part of the family.

12/25 10:24 a.m.

Ripley: You coming to Thea's? Stop being a fucking loser loner. She keeps asking if any of us have heard from you. Answer me so I don't have to let her down again next time she asks.

12/25 10:56 a.m.

Cary: Hey, I'm sorry about the other day. Don't be a stranger, please. Let's do Christmas together. I know it isn't my first without mom and dad, but it is yours. I don't think you should spend it alone.

I definitely deserve to spend it alone. They may not have heard the shit I said to Margot, but I know they all saw her run out of the bar crying. They all watched me prove them right. I'm so fucking tired of proving everyone right. I'm so tired of being a piece of shit with nothing good in life because all I do is sabotage it. The moment I see something going right, I destroy it without a second thought.

I've never been a relationship guy, but it's because I never wanted one. I *wanted* one with Margot. I wanted everything with her, and I still do. The way I acted last night may not have looked like I did, but it's because I'm a fucking idiot. And a coward. I convinced myself it would be easier to pretend I didn't want a relationship with her. I'd burn her before she could burn me. I'd save myself from getting hurt by ending it before she regretted ever giving me a chance. Instead, I hurt us both and fucked everything up.

I look around the living room and the state of it all. It feels like my life—cluttered, trash everywhere, a project in need of fixing. Taking another inhale of the nicotine, I blow out a few smoke rings. What if I'm not fixable? What if I'm doomed to always be the person no one can trust?

Fucking up my relationship with Cary by going off on him the other day was one thing, but he can't completely abandon me. We're bound by blood and the shared trauma our parents blessed us with. Margot doesn't have any reason to keep me around. She'd probably be better off excising me like a tumor. And I've given her zero reasons to stick around.

Snubbing my cigarette in the ashtray on the coffee table, I stand and stretch before grabbing my phone from the couch and walking to the kitchen. I need a fucking beer. The hangover is looming, and the only way to stop it is to keep chugging. Pulling open the fridge, I grab the second to last beer. Pretty sure I had at least seven in there last night, apparently I did more damage than I thought.

Sitting down at the breakfast bar, I flip my phone over in my hand to look at the messages again. Realization hits me, I miss my family. I've been so angry since my parents died, I've pushed them away even more than I had before. I've been angry since long before they died, honestly, but not like this. I'd at least let them in to a certain point before. Recently, I've kept them all at a distance. I've barely spoken to Thea in the last few weeks. All my interactions with Cary have ended in heated words and one of us taking off. Ripley is the only one I've kept in semi-contact with. Even Hayes hasn't seen me as frequently as he used to.

The anxiety of it all is pressing down on me like a boulder. But they all reached out. Every single one of them. Despite what my head is constantly telling me, it makes me wonder if they really do want me around. Maybe they don't see me as the broken shell I think I am.

Running my hand down my face, I contemplate heading to Thea's. Being with them for Christmas might make me feel better. Sitting in my own self-pity isn't exactly doing me any good. I peer over to the left of the stairs where I left the presents I haphazardly wrapped the other day.

I chuckle to myself remembering what I got Ripley. I'm not sure he'll find it funny, but I'm almost certain seeing his twisted up face over it will bring tears of laughter to my eyes. I need that. All joking aside, I need to be around the people I know won't leave me.

With my decision made, I finish off my beer, pick up the remnants of last night, then head into the bathroom to shower.

Christmas music filters from behind the door as I stand in the cold waiting for someone to hear me knocking. "Fuck, someone answer already, it's cold as shit out here," I yell at the door, turning my face away from the freezing rain. I'm lifting my fist to pound on the wood more aggressively this time when it swings open.

"Brooks?" Thea questions, her face twisting in confusion.

"The one and only," I reply back, holding my hand up with the bag stuffed full of gifts, waiting for her to let me in.

"We didn't think you'd show, you didn't answer any of our texts." She folds her arms over her chest, making sure I know she's upset with me. What she doesn't know is I can tell from the tone of her voice, I don't need to see her all pouty and standoffish.

"I'm aware, Thea. Look, can you lecture me inside the house? It's sleeting out here," I say as a shiver runs down my spine. We don't get a ton of winter weather in South Carolina, but when we do, it's usually atrocious. We aren't used to driving in it, and the state barely has the necessities to treat the roads. I chose to bring the truck instead of my bike because of the slick conditions. I may be reckless, but I'm not trying to die on Christmas.

She rolls her eyes, moving off to the side so I can squeeze through, and closes the door behind me. "Thank you, angel," I rasp out with as much charm as I can muster.

"Oh, do not 'angel' me. I'm still upset with you." Despite her words, she leans in to hug me. "Merry Christmas, asshole." The tone in her voice is teasing now, and I squeeze her a little tighter.

As we pull away, I shake off the cold and set my bag down for a second so I can take my jacket off. "Merry Christmas, *angel*. And at this point, who isn't?" I ask, the self-deprecation seeping out through my words.

She looks me right in the eyes and says, "So stop being an asshat, and maybe people will stop being mad at you."

She makes it sound like it's as easy as breathing. Just *stop*. I wish I fucking could. "I'll get right on that."

Before she can get another word in, Ripley yells from the living room, "Is that the loser loner I hear? Did he finally come out of his pity party cave?" Fuck. I cannot wait for him to open this gift now.

The embarrassment in front of everyone will be payback for him being an asshole.

"Anyone ever tell you you're kind of a dick?" I ask as I walk into the room, present bag in hand.

"Once or twice, but I don't hear it nearly as many times as you do," he says with a smirk.

I don't give him the satisfaction of a reply and instead walk toward the kitchen. Cary's got the oven open, pulling out a prime rib roast. The man would live in the kitchen if he could. I should ask him if he likes the upgrades I did in here while he was gone for all those years. The drab cabinets from the 80s got repainted, and I installed a butcher block countertop on her island.

"Hey," I say, "You need any help?"

He turns to look at me, a small smile pulling at his lips as he sets the roast on top of the stove and pulls off his oven mitts. "Nah, it's all almost done. Thanks though. I'm glad you came."

The words are simple, but the meaning behind them is heavy. I'm used to people wishing I didn't show up. Or at least, that's what I tell myself. Maybe I'm the only one who thinks that though. Maybe it's all been in my head all along.

"Yeah, thanks, me too."

Cary walks to the refrigerator and pulls out two beers, passing one to me. I grab it and stare down at it like it's a foreign object. After a moment, I look back up at him and pass it back. "I'm good." Before he can ask or make anything of it, I turn back around for the living room.

Ripley being Ripley—and the biggest fucking pain in my ass—asks me exactly what's on his mind the moment I pass over the threshold into the room. "What happened with Margot? I thought I set you up pretty well with my amazing advice." He's sitting on the couch, a smug look on his face.

"What advice?" Thea cuts in, her puzzled look shooting from me to him, then back to me again. When neither of us answers, she continues, "Pause. You went to Ripley for advice about women, specifically Margot, over me?" We're silent still, and after a few moments, she throws her hands up in the air. "Wow. Okay. And what 'advice' did you give him, Rip?" She makes sure to use air quotes around the word "advice."

"He asked me how to plan a date, so I helped him out. It was no big deal."

"No big dea—" she starts, but Cary walks in and cuts her off.

"Wait, you took Margot on a date?"

Without answering any of them, I walk over to the tree in the corner of the room, crouch down, and start pulling each present out of the bag I brought, placing them next to the others. Their stares burn into my back. I clear my throat before standing up and turning toward them. As I shove my hands in my pockets, I say, "I did, yeah. Doesn't matter though, I fucked it up in less than a week."

Every single one of their faces drop. It's clear they thought I wasn't serious about pursuing Margot—maybe even Ripley to an extent. I don't say anything else, just walk to the couch and fall into it, taking a deep breath as I do.

"Holy shit, you actually like her," Cary says. I look over at him and just nod my head. "I'm sorry, Brooks. I honestly didn't think it was anything serious. I assumed you were just fucking around like usual." He's sitting on the couch next to Thea now, his elbows resting on his knees as the realization hits him that for once, I wanted something out of life. I wanted *someone*.

"It's fine. Clearly wasn't meant to be. Like I said, I fucked it up already, you know, like I always do." I huff a laugh, trying to make light of the situation. I feel like me being here is bringing down the mood.

"Why do you do that?" Thea asks, breaking through my thoughts.

"Do what?"

"Why do you always assume you fuck everything up? When have any of us ever said that? What have you fucked up?"

Her words hit me in the chest. No one has ever called me out point blank. If anyone did, I'd expect it to be Ripley, not Thea. But as I look around the room at them, they're all staring back at me like they've been wanting to ask the same question for years.

"I uh... I don't know. I mean, I fucked up your gala thing. Plus our pre-Thanksgiving dinner and—"

"No," she says.

"No... what?" I ask, not following how 'no' is a response to anything I said.

"The gala wasn't fucked up. It went great. They booked for next year already," she answers, looking me dead in the eye like she wants me to argue with her. She's ready to fight. Fight for me. Ready to battle it out on my behalf, even against my own demons.

"And the dinner wasn't your fault either," Cary starts. "Did you escalate things a bit? Sure. But I got myself into that mess. I'm the one who fucked up, not you."

I look to Ripley, expecting him to jump in next. "Oh, I think you fuck up plenty. Don't think I didn't notice the two bottles of bourbon that went missing after our last tasting. Just glad it turned out you dropped them and not that you're a lowkey alcoholic. I'd hate to have to find another tasting co-host." I only dropped one bottle, he can assume otherwise for now though. He shoots me a smile, but it's quickly wiped off his face as a pillow hits him square in the forehead. "What the fu—"

"That was rude. Apologize!" scolds Thea from her seat on the couch.

Ripley throws the pillow back at her, but Cary catches it before it can hit her. "It was a joke, Jesus!"

I find myself smiling as I watch them bicker back and forth. How I never saw what Ripley was hiding and their true relationship before, I'm honestly not sure.

"Okay, let's eat so we can open presents," Cary says, clapping his hands in front of him as he gets up from his seat. Thea and Ripley follow, shoving each other as they race to the dining room. "I will separate you two if you keep it up," he tells them, sounding like a dad controlling two siblings.

"Sure thing, Care-Bear, whatever you need to do," Ripley quips back as they turn the corner into the dining room. They're too far away now for me to hear his reply, but Thea laughs, the sound filling the whole house.

"Brooks, get in here!" she shouts from the other room. I chuckle and internally kick myself for not coming over sooner, for not knowing this is where I needed to be.

"Ripley, you open yours first this year!" Thea says enthusiastically. Every year, she wants one person to open all their gifts at once while everyone else stares at us. It's actually awkward as fuck, and I kind of hate it. Not that I or anyone can tell her that; she'd bite our heads off.

Ripley reaches for mine first, looking at the tag to see who it's from. "Should probably get this out of the way. I hope it's better than the pack of tube socks you got me last year. I still don't know why you thought I wear those," he complains. I stand by my gifts, they're always practical. Everyone needs socks. So, I got the wrong kind, it's not like he couldn't wear them when he's too lazy to do laundry or something.

"Oh, it's better," I retort, knowing he'll at least get more use out of this gift. I made sure to put it in a box so the shape is concealed. As he unwraps the present, I scooch to the edge of my seat, needing to get as close as possible to see the look on his face. He rips the tape from the side, still mumbling about why I'd get someone socks for Christmas. I'm ignoring him though, solely focused on his face, waiting for the change.

He pulls the box open, his face scrunching up as he says, "What is—oh. Oh my God." His face turns impossibly red, and I cover my mouth to stop the laughter from escaping.

"What is it, Rip?" Thea asks, her mood still high on Christmas spirit.

"Go ahead, Rip, show them what it is." I don't miss a beat. I'm loving how shocked he is. Even his ears are pink at this point.

His eyes find mine as he pulls the present from the box and says, "Brooks got me a donut cock ring," he pauses, shifting his gaze to the other side of the room, "for Christmas."

There's a beat of silence as his words register, then everyone bursts into laughter, even Ripley after the shock wears off. My cheeks hurt from smiling so much, and my abs burn from all the laughter over the last couple hours.

Once he's composed himself enough, he shrugs his shoulders and says, "Hey, it's better than socks."

I shoot a wink in his direction. "I'm sure you can put it to good use."

His face is still vermillion red as he nods his head going, "Uh huh..."

He continues opening the rest of his presents, then Thea makes me go, her eyes shining with holiday cheer and mulled wine. She gets all giddy as I'm unwrapping the one from her. I swear the woman could overdose on serotonin during Christmas, she loves it way too much.

"Hurry up!" she whines.

"If you hadn't taped every inch of this box, I'd be going a lot quicker," I huff as I pull the last bit of tape from the edge, the seam finally releasing. Opening the box, I quickly realize what it is. "Oh, shit. Thea, this is awesome!"

She claps her hands, the excitement pouring off of her. "Try it on!"

I stand up from the couch and pull the black faux leather motorcycle bomber jacket from the box. It's got a gray removable hood giving it a more casual look.

As I'm slipping it on, Thea says, "It's also waterproof! So if it starts to rain while you're riding, it won't seep through."

"I fucking love it. Thanks, Thea." I walk toward her, and she stands. I wrap her in a hug, holding her tightly to me. "Just remember, I'm still an option whenever you decide you're done with Cary-boy but you want to keep it in the fam—" She pulls back and punches me in the arm before I can continue.

"Ouch, who the fuck taught you to punch like that?" I say through a laugh. She flips me off and sits back down beside Cary, scooting in closer than before like I'm an actual threat. "Thank you, Thea, really. I love it. And you."

She beams a smile as she says, "Love you too, loser loner."

My smile fades into a scowl. "That stupid nickname isn't sticking." They all chuckle again at my expense as I finish opening my gifts.

Finally, it's Cary and Thea's turn to open their presents. They reach for mine first, addressed to them both. Cary looks up at me after reading the tag. "You got us a joint gift?"

I shrug my shoulders. "Yeah, you're back together, probably getting married eventually, so you're basically one person. One person means one gift."

Cary just stares at me while Thea pouts beside him. "That's... that's not how gifts or marriage works..." His tone makes it sound like more of a question than a statement. "And we aren't even engaged... yet," he continues. Thea's cheeks pinken as her eyes land on the side of Cary's face.

"Just open the gift."

Thea does the honors, ripping off the paper then peeling open the box I put it in. Without even looking up at me, she deadpans, "You got us a bottle of RED?"

Ripley's head jerks in my direction. "That's where the other missing bottle went?"

Then Cary chimes in, "You not only got us a bottle of our *own* bourbon, but you also stole it from us?"

The three of them are staring me down now. "Whoa, whoa. I did not *steal* it. I left a twenty in the register for it."

They all start yelling at the same time, so I can't make out who's saying what. But I realize I don't care. They can give me all the shit in the world, they're still in my corner at the end of it all. It's something I should have seen before now, something I never should have questioned. I let my self-loathing get in the way.

Hours later when I'm leaving Thea's, hugging them all, and promising I'll come by in the next couple days, I feel a little more whole. I still miss Margot, and I'm still pissed at myself for hurting her. Not sure I'll ever forgive myself for that one, especially if she doesn't forgive me, but at least I have my family. For now, it will have to do.

Chapter Twenty-Eight

"Y**ou're** making this too easy, Grant," Colton taunts. He's gotten in one hit in the three minutes we've been circling each other in the ring. The dude wins one fight against me and thinks he's Mike fucking Tyson.

"Keep running your mouth, Colt. Remember what happened the last time you said some shit you shouldn't have?" That pisses him off, so he charges me. The look on his face makes me chuckle as he throws a punch and misses by a longshot. "Damn, gotta work on that aim, you have to actually get close to me to get the hit in," I chide, hoping I'll hit another nerve.

As I bounce back and forth on my feet, he throws a swing toward me and misses, again. I'm starting to think winning one match actually made him a worse fighter. From what I've heard, he hasn't won another since, against anyone. Doesn't surprise me, he's the type to let shit go to his head.

The one jab he did land split my eyebrow. Blood seeps from the cut, and I swipe at it to keep it from going in my eye. The smell of sweat overpowers my senses as I pull my hand away from my face, clenching my fist in preparation. Colt uses the distraction to make a move, I pivot out of the way but leave my foot out so he trips. His face slams against the ground making a satisfying *smack* sound.

He lets out a deep grunt, slamming his hands down on the ground beside his head and pushing himself up. "That was a cheap shot!" he screams, spit flying from his mouth.

"Oh, don't pretend like you wouldn't have done the same."

His face is crimson with waves of heat coming off of him in the chilly air. One thing about Colton Riley, his temper is unmatched. The dude can go from zero to one-hundred in a heartbeat. The problem is his lack of control when it happens. It's the reason he's not the best in the ring. He lets his emotions control him. The Pit is the only place I don't allow my emotions to take the wheel.

In The Pit, I own the fucking control. I'm strategic, calculated, always thinking about the next move. Colton barely thinks about his current move, his are based off of impulse.

He leans over and spits blood onto the ground, apparently the fall did more than just bruise his fragile ego. He's right, it was a cheap shot, but I'm not above them. Never claimed to be.

"You'll pay for that one," he grits out. His teeth are clenched tight; he might crack a molar. As usual, he's letting his anger fuel him.

"Make a move then." I'm baiting him, urging him to lash out, rain his fury on me, closed fist after closed fist. If he could only land a hit, I want the pain—I want to hurt so I can stop thinking about how I hate myself more and more every day. Hate what I did to Margot. Hate how cruel I was to Tiffany. Hate that I couldn't let myself have something good.

I could have been selfish. I even hate myself for that too. I could have gone against every warning blaring in my mind. I knew all along Margot was too good for me, but I could have ignored it. At least I would have been happier then. I wouldn't feel like an addict going through withdrawal, constantly checking my phone to see if maybe, just maybe, she'd offer another hit by reaching out.

But I wasn't selfish. It's the one decent thing I can say about the whole ordeal. I let her go. Forced her away. I may have hurt her in the process, but I did the hard thing. I'd like to think I'm a better man for it, but I'm not.

Colton barrels toward me again, his arm already twitching at his side. I see the move before he makes it and clock him in the gut where he leasts expects it. As he starts to go down, I uppercut him in the jaw, almost knocking his gritted teeth out of his head. Then, for good measure, I take my fist and go for the knockout. Right in his temple. The same place he scarred me all those years ago.

When I walked away, Colton was out cold. I didn't offer to help—I didn't even give him a second glance. I walked away to the sound of his body colliding with the ground and the wet sound of blood splattering around him.

I'm sitting on a bale of hay on the other side of The Pit, away from the crowd, in the shadows where I doubt anyone can see me.

The last blow I landed definitely fucked up my hand. Wincing, I pull the wrap from the skin, biting the inside of my cheek at the sting. My knuckles are bloodied, bruised, and already swelling, the split open spots stick to the wrap as I pull it away. "Fuck!" I hiss as quietly as possible. I don't need anyone walking over to talk to me or ask me what's wrong. I've kept my distance from everyone at The Pit recently.

Grabbing the water bottle sitting beside me, I pour some over the cuts, cleaning them as best I can. I take a swig from it, swishing and spitting the water out to get the taste of blood out of my mouth before drenching my head with the rest of it. I'll clean my hands up more when I get home. Fuck, my eyebrow too. I'd forgotten about it, but the water mixed with sweat dripping down my face lights the area up with a sharp burn.

I need to piss, then I'll go check in with Hayes, see how much cash I won. As I'm unzipping my pants near the treeline, about to pull out my dick, someone whistles from the crowd followed by, "You can doctor me up any day, baby." I can't place the voice, but I hate the catcalling. It answers my question about how badly I hurt Colton though since someone is here to patch him up.

I have no idea who Hayes called since Becca stopped showing. But I quickly do my business and rezip my pants before heading that way. If I didn't need to pick up my winnings from Hayes before leaving for the night, I wouldn't be going anywhere near Colton. Hayes has been on my ass for disappearing before Christmas though, and being on his bad side isn't on my bingo card.

As I stride past the fighting ring, I hear whispers about the "hot doctor lady." Whoever it is, Hayes has everyone riled up over her. I hope he knows what he's doing. Becca was different. She was claimed. Everyone knew not to touch her or fuck with her.

Voices float out from inside the trailer. I pull the handle and swing the door open, ready to pull Hayes away, touch base, and leave. But my eyes land on the curly-haired woman standing over Colton, her hands touching his face as she examines his injuries. I can't speak. I can't even move. I just stand there watching as she gives him all of her attention. She's *smiling*. I fucking lose it.

"What," I pause, my eyes never leaving the side of her head, "the fuck?" She turns at the sound of my voice, her gaze finding mine. I swear her pupils blow wide as she sees me.

Before she has a chance to say anything, Hayes is pushing me back outside, slamming the door behind him. Fueled by the lingering adrenaline from the fight, my fury floods me. I want to thrash, throw fists at anything in my way.

He puts his hands on my shoulders, the weight of them reeling me back in. I take a deep breath, but I don't release it, not yet. I need to hold it there until my lungs burn, try to calm myself. Hayes yells to Kori, "Go keep an eye on them while I take care of this."

This. Me. While he takes care of me. That's what he means.

I follow Kori with my eyes, watch as she walks toward the trailer, pulls the door open giving me another glimpse of the woman I love inside.

Love? Oh, *fuck*. Fuck, fuck, fuck.

"Calm the fuck down, he's a prick, but I won't let anything happen to Margot. I wanted to talk to you about her anyway."

I bring my focus back to Hayes, the realization I just had is shoved back for me to deal with another time. "Talk to me about Margot?" I grit out.

He releases his hold, his arms falling to his side. "I asked her to help out until I can find some permanent help. She's going to be on-call in case anyone needs medical attention," he says casually, *too* casually. "I need you to keep an eye on her."

I almost lose my shit.

"You fucking what?" I seethe. "You've got to be kidding me. She could lose her license, her fucking career! Why would you involve her in this shit?"

I'm exposing myself, I know I am. I don't even care. I don't give a fuck if Hayes figures it out. I don't care if saying any of this outs me.

His expression turns stony, and he closes the distance between us so our chests are touching. I feel his heavy breaths as he says, "This is none of your business, Grant. If you think I haven't considered the negative impacts this could have on her, you can fuck right off. She's—"

I cut him off. For the first time in our friendship, I don't back down. "That's where you're wrong, *Mason*," I spit. His eyes are trained on mine, bouncing back and forth between them like he's trying to figure out where I'm going with this. "She is my fucking business, and I won't let you or anyone else fuck shit up for her. She deserves better."

It's hypocritical coming from me. And if he knew the things I've done and said where Margot is concerned, I'd be six feet under already. But I've stunned him into silence because he has no idea where any of this is coming from.

I storm off before he puts it all together, rushing toward the trailer. As I pull the door open, Colton's laughing, and Margot's smiling. Again. She turns around this time, and her whole demeanor changes when she sees me. Her eyes go cold, her smile fades into a scowl. Kori slips outside, and I briefly hear her hauling Hayes off before he can charge in.

"Margot—" I start, but she puts her hand up to silence me.

"No. I'm with a patient. A patient whose injuries you caused, apparently. You can sit in the corner until I'm done," she says, her voice stern, cold. It shouldn't make my dick twitch.

Fuck me, I'm so gone for this woman.

"Freck—"

She cuts me off again, "I said no. Sit in the corner—in silence—or get out. Those are your options right now, Brooks."

I inhale a deep breath and slowly back into the corner of the trailer where a lone chair sits. I lower myself onto it and sit in silence, just like she asked as I listen to Colton flirt with her shamelessly.

"My grandfather is actually a resident at Saint Stephen's," he says, wincing as she dabs at the large gash on his head.

"Oh, really?" she asks, then grabs his hand and pulls it up to the gauze she has pressed against the cut. "Hold pressure here for me." I bristle at the contact between them, hating that he's touching her, even if she initiated it.

He does as she says while she sifts through her bag, grabbing a few more items. "Yeah, he's only been there for a few months, but he seems to enjoy it. We were always really close, so I've been trying to visit him as much as I can."

I can see her face soften from my spot in the corner. "He's lucky to have such a thoughtful grandson."

Rolling my eyes, I try not to scoff.

"Thanks," he says, puffing out his chest like a fucking douche. "I'm surprised I haven't seen you around."

She lets out a small laugh, and I clench my fists at my sides. "I don't hang around the nurses' station like most, I'm usually in with the residents. They tend to have all of my attention." It sounds like a line someone would say to brag about themselves, but I know Margot well enough to know it's the truth. Colton, however, sees it as an opportunity to shoot his shot.

"I can tell, you seem like you're extremely dedicated to your patients' care." He puts his hand on her forearm, she stiffens, and I see red. It takes everything in me not to throw him out of this fucking trailer. She's uncomfortable, it's clear as day. He doesn't let it stop him though. "I'll make sure to find you and say hello next time I'm there."

She only nods, an attempt to be polite, I'm sure.

I just sit there, and I fume.

And I wait.

I wait until she's finished patching him up.

I wait until she's removing her gloves and sending him away with instructions on home care.

I wait until she turns to me, looks me dead in the eyes and says, "What do you want?"

"That's a joke, right?"

Her arms cross over her chest, grabbing onto each elbow like she's trying to disappear into herself. Like she'd rather be anywhere else than standing in front of me and dealing with my bullshit.

"No. I have no reason to talk to you. You made it clear where we stand. So, what do you want? Why are you here?" Her words are clipped, but her voice is small, quiet. It's like she's trying to hold it all together, knowing if she gives in to me, it'll all come tumbling down on her.

I rise from the chair, and her eyes trail all the way up to my face until I'm standing a foot above her. She uncrosses her arms, and for a second it looks like she might reach for me as she takes in the cut on my face. But her hand falls to her side, and she continues to stare up at me.

"Don't do this, Margot. Don't get involved in this shit. You have too much to lose."

She scoffs at me then turns around and walks toward the station she has set up. With her back to me, she retorts, her voice stronger than before, "You may think I'm a child who can't make her own decisions, but I'm a grown-ass woman. I know what I'm doing. You can't even talk, you're just as involved. Now, get out."

I don't move. I'm waiting for her to turn around, to look at me, actually see me, talk to me. Anything. But she doesn't. The seconds tick by, and she continues rummaging around with the last of the supplies she has out.

"Just go, Brooks," she finally says, breaking the silence between us.

I don't give her a second look as I storm out the door and slam it behind me, the trailer rattling from the force. Hayes has apparently been waiting and tries to approach me, but Kori holds him off, telling him to leave it for now.

Making my way toward my bike, I avoid the other people milling around. I don't grab my helmet first, I just hop on, start the ignition, and drive off.

Chapter Twenty-Nine

"Fuck, Freckles. *Yes.*" He practically hisses the last word in my ear. "Lift your hips." I do as Brooks asks and am rewarded by the most delicious twist of pleasure deep in my belly. He's reaching a new spot I've never felt before, and I clench around him. His rough hands, adorned with bruises and split knuckles, hold my hips firmly, keeping me exactly where he wants me. His fingertips dig into my soft skin as he continues to piston into me; wet, slapping sounds echoing in my small bedroom.

His lips leave a fevered trail behind as he kisses down my neck to my chest, his tongue finding my nipple. Tingles shoot from the small bud straight to my core, and I grip the sheets to keep myself from bowing off the bed. His stubble prickles my sensitive skin, just adding to the overwhelming tidal wave of sensations he's pouring over my body.

After giving the same treatment to my other nipple, Brooks leans up and continues to thrust but slows his movements into long, languid strokes. His eyes roam over every part of me on display for him. His cobalt gaze cuts to mine as he rasps, "Are you close, baby? Do you want me to beg again?"

It's the sincerity of the question that does me in; a few more deep thrusts and I'm about to come as I moan—

I barrel into consciousness, awoken by my own strangled sound, to find my pussy wet and aching. My eyes flutter open, visions of Brooks' intense gaze and sweat-slicked body dissipate. In my sleepy haze, I realize it was a dream. A great dream, a really great dream. But one that has now left me just on the edge, my belly still coiled tight, ready to unleash.

I groan in frustration. Why does he have to be the center of all my sexual fantasies lately? He might be the hottest man I've ever seen or touched, but can't my imagination get a little more creative? Why can't I have such vivid sex dreams about *Top Gun*'s Miles Teller with that dirty little pornstache? That does a lot of things to me. But no, I close my eyes, and it's always Brooks.

I'm still so angry with him—and if I'm being honest, with myself as well. The audacity of him barging into the trailer last night while I was working on someone and telling me what I can and cannot do. I'm so tired of people treating me like I don't know what's good for me, like I'm a child.

Even through my angry thoughts, I realize one of my hands has found my breast and is gently pinching the nipple. My pussy is pulsing, looking for friction, and I know I won't be able to sleep when I'm this wound up.

With a resigned sigh, I reach over into my nightstand drawer and pull out my favorite clit suction toy. I turn it on, and a soft buzzing sound fills the room. Lying back, I get more comfortable as I pull down my sleep shorts and position it on my throbbing clit. The pleasure is immediate, and I know I won't last long.

Closing my eyes, I search for any sexy image I can muster, but Brooks is front and center. With a small shake of my head, I let my imagination run wild. As the vibrations send tingles all the way to my toes, I picture it's Brooks' mouth working me; his tongue flicking at my little bundle of nerves and making my abs contract as he hits all the right spots.

It doesn't take long, just a minute or two. In my head, he grunts out "Freckles" and "please," and it sends me over the edge. My pussy clenches, and my thighs shake as I ride out wave after wave of my orgasm, crying out Brooks' name into the dark, silent room.

When I finally open my eyes, I feel tears tracking down my temples. With a small sniff, I wipe them away, turn on my side, and try to find sleep again.

I run the thermometer over Mr. Matthews' forehead and frown at the reading. Ninety-nine point six. I make a note of it in his chart on my tablet. I'll have to go find Dr. Shepherd to let her know so we can keep an eye on it.

Mr. Matthews is one of our long-term patients whose dementia has progressed significantly in the years he's been here. It's been heartbreaking to watch him decline and slowly lose function, both mentally and physically, just in the months I've been here. Because of the severity of his disease, we never dismiss even the mildest of fevers as it could be a sign of something more serious.

After taking his blood pressure and recording the results, I tuck the sheets in closer to him and quietly leave the room, letting him rest.

Just as I close Mr. Matthews' door behind me, the receptionist from the nursing home's front desk runs up to me.

"Hey, Margot," she says. "Someone dropped this off for you." She holds out an envelope to me. My name is written on the front in a messy script.

"Thanks," I say as I take it from her hand. She smiles and hurries back to her station. I turn the envelope over expecting more, but it's just my name. It seems innocent enough, though my chest tightens as I slide my finger under the seal and tear it open. My hands shake as I unfold the single piece of lined paper. My stomach bottoms out as soon as I see the first words.

Hi Pretty Girl,

Miss me? Did you really think I wouldn't find you two hours away in your hometown? Oh how I've missed seeing your face everyday. Eight months is much too long.

You'll be happy to know I left her. For you. For us.

I think it's time we give this a real shot.

I'll be seeing you soon,

—)

Bile rises up my throat, and I cover my mouth with one hand, crumpling the letter with the other.

"Oh, Margot, I was looking for you," a voice calls from down the hall. "Margot? Are you okay?" I turn to see Dr. Shepherd. She's making her way over to me, but my world seems to be shifting on its axis.

He found me. He's here. He found me. He found me. The words run through my head on a loop like a news ticker. I lean against the wall. "I think I'm going to be sick," I whisper when the doctor approaches. "I need to go home." My eyes bounce around the otherwise empty hallway, as if I'm expecting to see him rounding the corner at any minute.

"Yeah, you don't look great," she says, reaching out for me. I step to the side, unable to handle anyone touching me right now, and she retracts her hand. "Why don't you head out? I'll make sure we figure out coverage."

"Thanks, yeah," I say absently, already trying to find a way to disappear. Where can I possibly go? I take a few steps down the hall in the direction of the nurses' lounge but turn around. "Oh, Mr. Matthews' temp is up. Can you check on him?"

"Yeah, I'll go examine him now," Dr. Shepherd says with a warm smile. "Take care of yourself, Margot." I nod and practically run the rest of the way to the lounge.

It takes me forever to get my locker open, my hands won't stop shaking, and my breaths are coming in short gasps. I might be having a panic attack, but I don't have time for it right now, so I push it aside the best I can as I grab my things.

I don't say anything to anyone as I rush out the doors of Saint Stephen's and hastily walk to my car. I scan the parking lot, praying he's not waiting for me here knowing the reaction his letter would have on me.

I break all of the speed limits on my way home, keeping an eye on the rearview mirror making sure I'm not being followed. My stomach is in knots, and I can't think clearly. I don't have a plan. I was supposed to be safe here. He wasn't supposed to follow me.

I slam the car into park and run to my door, head on a swivel looking at my neighbors' yards, like he might be hiding behind a bush. The chill bites at my face where tears are streaking down my cheeks. I didn't even notice I'm crying.

After sliding all of the locks on my front door into place, I drop my jacket and purse on the floor, not bothering to hang either. I move throughout my house, checking the windows and pulling down the shades, and confirm the back door is locked as well. Taking the steps two at a time, I run upstairs, locking myself in my bedroom.

I clear my not-dirty-not-clean clothes pile off the chair in the corner of my bedroom and prop it under the door handle before I climb into my bed and pull the covers over my head.

The initial adrenaline of fight-or-flight has left me, and now my body is exhausted but still gripped by panic. Tears keep flowing, and my head is a mess, but all I can do is lie here and try to block the world out.

CHAPTER THIRTY

I haven't had a drink since Christmas. It's been six long days, and I've gone through more packs of cigarettes than I ever have in a week. The decision to quit drinking wasn't even a conscious one. But I knew it needed to happen. My head is already clearer.

I still itch for the burn of liquor. I still crave the buzz and how it puts the world behind a filter. But I'm trying to better myself. I'm trying to prove myself wrong for once. I've seen what alcohol addiction can do to someone; I don't want to wake up one day and realize I've turned into an absentee father who relies on his daughter to care for his drunk ass.

Margot may not realize it, but seeing her dad that day left an impact on me. I haven't been able to shake the image of him on the floor covered in his own vomit. It opened my eyes to how much further I could fall if I stay on the same path. I saw how much it hurt her. I may have hurt her in other ways, and I may never get her back, but I refuse to be a carbon copy of her father.

Those thoughts are to blame for me sitting outside of Keaton Mason's house with a cab full of groceries, a bag from Billy's Hardware, and a truck bed filled with lumber and tools for the stairs. I know it's not my place, but even if she never speaks to me again, I want to lessen the load Margot bears.

And she hasn't spoken to me. Not since she told me to get out of the trailer. She barely looked at me. I've spent every night since then drawing her, in every medium—acrylic, watercolor, pencils, charcoal—anything I could find. I can't get her sad yet fierce face out of my head. If I'm being honest, I don't think I want to.

I open my glove compartment and pull out the original drawing of her I did. The first sketch I'd done in way too many years to count. She brought it all back. She's the spark to my flame.

The pencil lines are slightly smudged from sitting in my pocket for the last two weeks. Tracing the angles of her face with my fingers, I kick myself again for ruining it all. Maybe one day I'll try again. I'll do what needs to be done to grow into the man she deserves, and I'll try again. I'll fight for us, even if she doesn't want to.

After one more longing stare, I put the drawing back in the glove compartment and grab the bags from the passenger seat. I place them on the porch then go back for a second trip. Once the materials are all sitting on the porch, I jump up past the stairs and knock on the door. Ten long seconds of silence pass before I knock again, harder this time.

Just as I'm about to knock for a third time, the door swings open. "What?" Keaton hollers. When he sees it's me, his scowl softens. Smell of day-old beer wafts off him. "What do you want?" He stumbles out of the door a little, peering around the corner. "Is Margot with you?"

I shake my head as I say, "Nope," popping the 'p' dramatically. "Just me this time."

He's looking at all the bags on the porch, confusion evident on his face.

"I hear you have a broken dishwasher, and those steps are a fucking safety hazard." He peers back up at me, not saying a word. "So, you gonna let me in or...?"

It's been two hours. The first thirty minutes were spent stocking the refrigerator and throwing out all the old shit. It was... a lot. It's clear no one has been over in a while. I told Keaton to take a shower, and I'd make him some lunch. He fussed at first, saying he didn't need me to do anything for him. I stared him down until he finally put his hands up and relented.

The shower took longer than I expected. He smelled like the last shower he had was the one I helped him with, so maybe I should be thankful he took his time. I cleaned up a bit while he was gone and had a sandwich ready when he came back out. It was nothing special, but he seemed appreciative regardless.

I'm finishing up with the dishwasher now, checking to make sure it runs properly before calling it done. Keaton has been silently watching me from the dining room table the whole time. Never asking why I'm here or what I'm doing since the first time at the door.

As I shut the dishwasher, feeling accomplished that I fixed it pretty quickly, a throat clears behind me.

I turn around to face him, leaning back on the counter. "Spit it out."

His eyes go wide like he wasn't expecting me to spur him on. "Where is Margot?"

Not the question I thought he'd ask. "Probably at work. It's the middle of a weekday after all."

He shakes his head. "No, I mean why are you here without her? Why isn't she with you?"

I give it a second but stare him right in the eyes when I say, "She doesn't know I'm here." He looks at me, like he's waiting for me to say more. It's unnerving, so much so, I crack. "She hasn't talked to me in almost a week now, and she probably won't anytime soon. I fucked things up with her."

I'm not sure how I expect him to respond. Will he be pissed? Tell me to get the fuck out just like his daughter did? Ask me how I fucked it up?

"So you think coming here and doing shit for me is gonna win her back or something?"

I huff out a laugh. "Not a chance."

"So why're you here, boy?" He pushes his plate away from him and crosses his arms over his chest. His face is stone cold. And I get it, I'm no one to him, but I wonder if that's the face he wears for Margot too.

"To fix all the broken shit in this house," I answer without missing a beat. And I realize how ironic it is. A broken man fixing broken things in another broken man's home, what a joke. Am I more like Keaton Mason than I first thought? Is this a glimpse into my future?

Cutting off my spiraling thoughts, Keaton deadpans, "You still aren't saying why."

The reason I'm here is complicated. It's partly for me, partly for him, but mostly for Margot. I look to the ground, staring at my shoes like they're the most interesting thing in the room as I speak my truth. "My parents died in a car accident seven weeks ago yesterday." I pause to move my gaze to him as I say the next part. "By a drunk driver."

The shame on his face shows in the redness of his cheeks. He wasn't the driver. I'm not sure he's left this house to go farther than the liquor store down the street in years. We know who did it. He's in prison for the next twenty-five years.

"I-I didn't—" he starts, his voice shaking with terror like I'm here to avenge my parents' death.

"I know. But it could have been. Could have been me too. I'm not exactly an innocent man either." I shift my legs so my ankles cross, getting comfortable to douse him with a hard truth. "We didn't have a great relationship. My dad was an asshole. My mom was a pushover. I have... a lot of unresolved feelings where they're concerned. And now they're gone." I can tell from the look of confusion on his face he has no idea where I'm going with this.

"Instead of airing out our shit and making things better, my mom wrote a letter. Not because she knew she was dying an untimely death, but because she knew one day, she'd be gone and I'd wonder why the fuck our relationship was shit. She couldn't say it to my face. Nevertheless, it was good to find out, ya know? To know she didn't see me as the fuck-up I thought she did. But it was also a bullshit thing to do."

I shove my hand in my pocket, finding my dad's knife there. Running my fingers over the cold metal grounds me. "Don't do that to Margot."

His face twists up as he says, "What are you talking about?"

Walking toward the table, I pull out the chair across from him and sit down. Placing my elbows on the table, I lean closer as I say, "Don't wait until you're dead or dying to fix your relationship. She loves you; she wastes her time coming over here and cleaning up your messes, making sure you have food. She shouldn't have to do that. But she does it because she loves you. Be a fucking father and love her back. Stop drinking. Stop wallowing. Stop depending on your twenty-three year old daughter for everything. It's not fair to her, and she deserves better. So *be* better."

His eyes are glassy. Bringing the man to tears wasn't my goal. I just wanted to maybe talk some sense into him, maybe help Margot a little.

"I uh—" He swipes at his eye as a lone tear falls from the corner. "You're right. Margot deserves the world. She's a good girl. Always has been. Too good to have a son of a bitch like me as a father." He trails off, so I take the opportunity to bring up the other Mason.

"I don't know what shit is between you and Hayes, but you need to fix that too. The dude is insufferable, maybe not hating his father would help."

He nods his head, and I don't ask any more questions. Hayes isn't my concern, but I know their relationship being better would benefit Margot as well. I use my feet to push away from the table, just about to stand when he says, "Why do you care?"

Biting the inside of my cheek, I stand and push my chair back in. "Because I think I'm in love with your daughter. Don't worry, she hates me, so it won't work. But I still want her to have everything good in this world. And I know having a better relationship with you would bring some joy back to her life. And maybe you won't listen and you'll make the same mistakes my parents made, but at least I gave it a shot."

I don't wait for him to reply, I don't care what he has to say about it. There's nothing to say. So I grab the glass of water I have sitting on the counter, put my jacket back on, and make my way to the door. "I'll be out here fixing the porch steps if you need me," I say over my shoulder. Then I'm out the door. The bitter cold bites at my exposed skin as I place the glass on the railing and jump off the porch.

Despite the cold air, I'm sweating my balls off. I've built some shit before, I've been renovating parts of my parents' house for the last month, but math was never my strong suit. I've watched five YouTube videos and redone my calculations at least fifteen times. I want to make sure I'm not making this worse than I found it.

Luckily, it's only three steps, and I'm on the last one. I wanted to paint them as well, but I underestimated how hard this would be, so I won't have time today. Maybe I'll come back next week. Or I could leave it to Hayes or Margot. I'll leave the paint in the garage with a note on it or something, just in case.

The good news is they're sturdy as fuck. No one is going to fall through these, which is the point, so I'm calling it a win. Keaton has looked out through the blinds a couple times. I've got music playing, but I feel his eyes on me every time he does it. I'm pretty sure he still doesn't quite understand why I'm here or why I'm doing this. I'm not entirely sure I do either. I just knew I wanted to.

I've got the last boards cut to size, and just as I'm about to take them to the porch, the front door opens. Keaton stands in the doorway, arms crossed over his chest. "I'm gonna quit."

His words shock me. For a second, I wonder if I heard him wrong. "What?"

He takes one of his hands and runs it through his hair then rubs at the back of his neck as he says, "I've been thinking about what you said, and you're right. I think I need to finally put the bottle down and figure my shit out."

Well, this wasn't what I expected. I never for one second thought anything I said would actually make an impact on him.

"You're talking about drinking? Just so we're clear," I clarify, my gaze never leaving his. He nods his head as he takes a deep breath. "Okay. Uh. Have you tried to stop before?"

He pops his knuckles, out of anxiety, I'm sure. "Not seriously. But I am serious this time. I uh... I need some help though."

Setting the boards back down on the ground, I remove my gloves and wipe my hands on my jeans. "Okay."

Keaton walks toward the railing, leaning his elbows on the wood. It's a few more moments before he continues, "I tried to get rid of it, but I can't make myself do it. Can you—fuck. Can you do it for me?" There's an earnestness in his voice. I think he's serious about trying to quit drinking. I'm just still shocked I had anything to do with it.

I clear my throat, trying to push past the lump that's formed from the sheer emotion of the situation. "Yeah. Yeah, Keaton, I can do that."

CHAPTER THIRTY-ONE

Pour Decisions Group Chat

1/1 12:01 a.m.

Thea: Happy New Year, Margot!

1/1 12:03 a.m.

Ripley: MARGIE! Happyyyyy New Year! Mimosas tomorrow? **celebration emojis**

1/1 12:03 a.m.

Hayes: HNY Booger!

1/1 12:06 a.m.

Killer: I know you don't want to hear from me, but Happy New Year, Freckles. Hoping we can talk soon.

1/2 2:46 p.m.

Thea: Hey, my mom said she heard from the other nurses you were sick. Hope you feel better! I'm going to stop by with some soup for you later.

Thea: Also, Happy New Year from my mom **smiley face emoji** **picture of Thea and Lydia in NYE glasses with plastic flutes of a bubbly drink**

1/2 5:13 p.m.

Thea: Hey, I'm here, but you're not answering your door, so I assume you're sleeping. I'm going to leave the food on the porch. Feel better!

Pour Decisions Group Chat

1/3 4:52 p.m.

Ripley: Margie! I have a weird mole. Is that something you can look at?

1/3 4:56 p.m.

Thea: Ripley, leave her alone. I already told you to go see a dermatologist. And the poor girl is sick!

1/3 4:57 p.m.

Ripley: I promise not to use you for your nurse lady skills too much **kissy emoji** and sorry about your sickness.

1/3 4:57 p.m.

Thea: **eye roll emoji** He absolutely will. Don't believe a word out of his lying liar mouth.

1/3 7:26 p.m.

Ripley: You good, Margie?

1/3 8:08 p.m.

Hayes: Dinner Sunday? The boys will be here again.

1/3 8:10 p.m.

Hayes: Also, I got the stuff you wanted set up at the trailer. Installed one of my tattoo tables, hope that works.

1/3 8:14 p.m.

Jan: Hey, are you feeling any better? Do you need someone to cover your other shifts this week? Let me know!

My phone vibrates on the nightstand again. I don't know what day it is at this point. My blackout shades block out most of the sunlight, I can't even be sure of the time of day. Besides a few bathroom breaks and running downstairs to grab some crackers and water—which is about all I can stomach—I've stayed barricaded in my room.

I know this isn't sustainable, but just the thought of going outside, him watching me, causes the panic to rise again. The last time I felt this kind of terror, I ran here. Where could I possibly go now? If he followed me here, he'll follow me anywhere.

Chapter Thirty-Two

"Hey, Brooks, can you run the food to table five? Tiff just got a ten-top," Thea says as she comes around the corner. It's been a busy lunch rush, Saturdays usually are. I've been trying to help out wherever I can since our tastings don't start until this afternoon.

"Yeah, of course." Things have been awkward with Tiffany since Christmas. She's barely spoken to me, and I'm sure she'll be pissed I'm helping her out. Placing the glass I was drying back on the counter, I throw the towel over my shoulder and head for the kitchen. Travis has been gone a little over a week now. I didn't see him much before he left, but I'm glad I got the chance to say goodbye before he took off. We'd seen each other at RED a few times in his last couple of weeks but not much. From what I've heard, he's doing well in Seattle. The staff there is loving him, no surprise.

It's weird having Cary as the head chef here, but it also feels right. And Thea has never been happier which makes me happy.

There've been whispers around town about her and Ripley; people speculating what happened and why she was so quick to leave him. Any time it's been brought up in front of me, Ripley always shrugs and says something about never standing a chance against true love. A couple of times, I've jumped in and told them how I've "been there" to help sell the story, bumping shoulders with him in solidarity. Then there's usually a round of pity glances, and he has to cut them off and tell them he and Thea are still best friends, and he's happy for her—things he shouldn't have to say. But he's not ready to tell the whole town about his sexuality, and I respect that.

Seeing Cary in his element is awesome though. I always knew he loved being in the kitchen, but I never got to witness Chef Cary. The second he puts his apron on, his whole demeanor changes. My reserved brother dissipates, replaced by a very serious take-no-shit kitchen manager. He looks up from the dish he's preparing as I walk up to the window.

I quickly scan the orders for table five. "You grabbing Tiffany's?" Cary asks, most of his attention still focused on the plate in front of him.

"Yeah, she got a ten-top, so Thea asked me to take it. Is it all ready?"

He reaches for a garnish to place on the dish then lifts it up into the window. "It is now." The smirk he's wearing is contagious. I honestly love seeing him so happy.

I reach over and grab a tray to start loading up the orders. Once I feel they're all secure, I walk over to table five with the tray stand in hand.

"I heard you guys were hungry," I say in a teasing tone. As I pass out the food, there's comments all around about how good it all looks.

It's not that Travis wasn't a good chef, but Cary has elevated everything. He's brought a new level of sophistication to the place with his big city experience. We've never gotten as many raving reviews as we have in the last few days.

I make sure the table is set and no one needs anything before I walk back to the kitchen. Tiffany sees me and instead of thanking me for covering her table, she scowls and heads in the opposite direction. I suppose I deserve that. It'll take a while before she forgives me. I just need her to be civil while we're here. The last thing I need is Thea on my ass about upsetting her staff, she already gave me the I-told-you-so lecture about fucking her employees when I got here this morning

Speak of the devil. "So, Brooks, have you heard from Margot?" Thea asks as she walks up beside me. Cary perks up from behind the window at the question.

I take a deep breath, blowing it out dramatically. "No, I told you at Christmas that I fuc—messed things up," I explain, catching myself before getting scolded by Thea for cussing where customers could hear.

Her face scrunches up in confusion. "What? No, I mean because she hasn't been at work. I wondered if you'd heard from her. On New Year's Day, one of the nurses told my mom she was sick, but I went to her house to drop off soup a couple days ago, and she didn't come to the door. Plus, she hasn't answered in our group chat."

The back of my neck prickles with anxiety. "No one has seen or talked to her?"

Thea shakes her head, and it's all I need to lose my shit. I throw the towel down on the counter and turn to walk away.

"Brooks! Where are you going?" Thea shouts.

"To check on her. I'll text you." I don't wait for a response as I push through the door leading to the distillery. I grab my keys and wallet from the back room and sprint to my bike.

I know I'm leaving Thea during a rush, but something is wrong—I can feel it. The second she said Margot didn't answer her door, I got a gnawing feeling in my gut. I'd never forgive myself if something was wrong and I didn't check on her. And if she's fine, I'll take the opportunity to apologize in person since she never responded to my text on New Year's.

As I ride toward Southbury, I ignore every speed limit sign. The sinking feeling in my stomach doesn't give two shits about breaking the law right now. And if a cop sees me, I'll make him follow me to her house in case I need him there, then he can write me a ticket.

The wind bites at my cheeks as I race down the back roads. I'm only a few minutes from her house now, and my mind is going through all the possibilities of what could be wrong. Maybe she's just really sick. That's the most logical thing. But according to Thea, she's been out of work since at least New Year's Eve. Being too sick to check your phone for five days is unlikely. The thought only makes me spiral into the less logical reasons. Like what if she hurt herself somehow and couldn't call for help? What if she was kidnapped? What if her house was broken into and she was hurt? There are too many what ifs that would leave me broken if they turned out to be true. It can't be any of those, it just can't.

As I turn down her street, I see her car in the driveway. I can't decide if it makes me feel better or worse. I park my bike beside the car, lowering the kickstand as I look for anything out of the ordinary around the house. Everything looks normal.

But just as I round the corner, getting a full view of her front door, I notice a bouquet of fresh flowers on her doorstep. Flowers I know I didn't send. So who the fuck did?

The closer I get to her front door, the more pissed off I feel. Has she been seeing someone else this whole time? Or did she just move on insanely quickly? The bouquet is huge, definitely not a cheap one from the grocery store.

I do my best not to look at the card once I'm standing right in front of it, no matter how tempting it is. I may be pissed, but I'm not going to invade her privacy. Bringing my fist up to the door, I knock three times.

While I stand there, waiting for her to answer, I start counting. I'm tempted to knock again already, but I want to wait a reasonable amount of time. After a full sixty seconds, I knock again, louder but only twice this time. Another sixty seconds goes by and nothing.

The panic is setting in, so I knock four times and yell, "Margot, answer the door, or I'm breaking it down." Almost instantly, I hear shuffling from inside, then the frantic hurriedness of unlocking all seven bolts. The door swings open, but the woman who greets me looks nothing like the Margot I know. This girl has deep purple bags under her eyes, her complexion is so pale her freckles stand out more than usual, and her eyes are red-rimmed like she's been crying.

I start to reach for her but then remember the flowers and the possibility of her seeing someone else. For a moment, it's like she's in a trance, but then she comes to and throws herself into my arms. "Fuck, Margot, what—"

"Oh my God, I'm so happy it's you," she says, but her voice sounds weak, almost hoarse.

"You... are?" I'm so confused, I thought she hated me. She hasn't answered my calls or texts in almost two weeks. Why would she be happy to see me? But all she does is nod her head against my shoulder. Her body is warm against me, and her arms are locked around my neck like steel bands. A part of me wants to accept it and move on, but the other part is worried I'm the one being played this time. "Margot... who uh... who are the flowers from? Are you seeing someone?"

Her face pulls away from my shoulder, and I notice she's white as a ghost. "Wha—what are you talking about?"

I lean back so she can look down beside us. Her face twists, but she grabs the card without saying a word. The second she turns it over and sees whatever is written there, her hand flies to her mouth, a sob breaking loose. I bring her back to my chest, caressing the back of her head with my hand. "What's going on, Freckles?"

CHAPTER THIRTY-THREE

I'm not entirely sure the Brooks standing at my door isn't a figment of my imagination. I've spent the last week locked away and barely sleeping. My vision is blurry, and I don't know if it's the exhaustion or if I'm crying again. The instant and overwhelming relief I felt seeing Brooks on the other side of my door is obliterated as soon as I read the card that came with the flowers.

He's so handsome standing there, but his expression is worried as he takes me in. I'm sure I look like a mess, I haven't been able to take care of myself all week. Wrapped in his arms, I feel safe for the first time in what feels like forever. I want to stay like this, I know he won't let anything happen to me if we just stay like this. No matter what happened between us, between him and Tiffany, I know I can count on him to protect me from anything.

"What's going on, Freckles?" he asks softly against my temple. His words drag me back to my current reality, and I stiffen.

Too anxious to look around the yard, I grab Brooks' hand and pull him inside, quickly sliding all the locks into place, holding my breath until I've checked them over and made sure they're holding.

Brooks gently places his hands on my shoulders, and I nearly jump out of my skin, turning around to face him.

He takes a step back, hands up, showing me he means no harm. "Whoa, what's going on, Margot? You're okay. It's just me." I wrap my arms around myself and shiver. I don't know how to control my body, my emotions are frayed, and I'm hanging on by a thread.

"I—I... I need help," I force out. "I'm so scared. Please help me." Tears begin to pour down my face, I'm surprised I have any left. "You have to help." The last of my words end in sobs, and he pulls me into him. I go willingly, letting him envelop me. One of his large hands wraps around my head, stroking my hair, the other is around my waist.

"What happened? I'm here, baby, I'll help. Just tell me what happened, please." His voice is soft, but the worry is evident, and

I sense a tinge of anger in his words as well, but he's restraining himself. I can't get any words out, just heaving sobs. I'm shaking all over and unable to calm down.

After a few minutes of him letting me cry on his shoulder, Brooks says, "Just tell me if someone hurt you. Are you hurt?"

I shake my head, but words won't come. It must be enough for him though because he says, "Up you go," as he hoists me up, one hand under my butt, the other around my back. My legs wrap around his waist, and I bury my head into the crook of his neck. He carries me upstairs pausing just a second in my bedroom, most likely taking in how I've been living—shades drawn, clothes strewn across the floor, food containers littering my bedside table and dresser. I can't imagine what he thinks of me right now.

He keeps moving into the bathroom and tries to deposit me on the vanity. "No, please, don't let go," I say, my fingers grasping his jacket and digging into his back.

"Hey, hey, it's okay. I'm not going anywhere. I just want to turn the water on for you. Can you let me do that?" he soothes.

I loosen my grasp, and Brooks unwinds my arms from his neck. I miss his warmth as soon as he takes a step back, but he keeps his hand on both of mine as he stretches to turn the shower on. It takes a minute for the water to turn hot, and steam starts to billow around us, the humidity of the room increasing by the second.

I'm staring at his hand holding mine when his other one gently tips my chin up so he can see my eyes. Intense concern lines his blue gaze as he searches my face for any hint of what happened. I want to tell him everything, but my teeth are chattering, and I can't form a coherent sentence. His thumb comes up and swipes at the tears I can't control. "Shh, it's okay," he says gently before pressing a small kiss to my forehead. "Let's get you under the water, alright?"

I manage to nod. With slow, measured movements, Brooks releases my hands and pulls my scrub top over my head. I wince as I get a whiff of the shirt. I feel like I should be embarrassed about my state, but all I feel is deep shame. I should be able to take care of myself. It's what I do for a living, but here I sit, completely incapable of even the simplest of tasks. I guess I'm more like my dad than I thought.

Brooks must sense the change in my emotions because he takes my face in his hands and says, "Hey, hey, look at me. I've got you, baby, I promise. Can you stand up? I need to take off your pants."

I slide off the counter, and he kneels to pull my pants to the floor. I hold onto his shoulders for balance as I lift each foot up one at a time so he can remove them fully. I'm left standing in my bra and panties. My skin is prickling with goosebumps even in the warmth of the small, steamy bathroom.

"Alright, you shower. I'll be right out there. I'm not going any-where." Brooks turns and reaches for the door to give me privacy, but I grab onto his arm.

"Please, don't go. Don't leave. I... I need you," I say quickly. I feel desperate for him. His presence might be the only thing keeping everything from imploding.

He looks uncomfortable for a minute, indecision written all over his face, but after a moment, he sighs, nods, and proceeds to remove his jacket. He kicks off his boots and pulls his shirt over his head, that stunning torso on display. His pants follow quickly, and he's left in just his black boxer briefs. I can't help my eyes roaming over every inch of him—broad shoulders, tattoos, hair trailing down to the top of his underwear, coarse and dark. He looks as amazing as I remember from our short time together.

"Do you want to keep your..." he motions to my body, "on?" I shake my head and reach back to unclasp my bra, but I can't get my fingers to comply. Giving up, I turn around with a silent request for him to help.

After a second, gentle fingers grip the band and release the clasp. The bra falls down my arms and to the ground, and then those same fingers catch on the top of my underwear and slowly slide them down my hips until they also reach the floor.

With a soft nudge to my lower back, Brooks leads me into the tub and under the spray of the hot water. It's almost scalding, but the heat feels good, and my tense muscles start to relax. He steps in behind me. I turn around and notice he's still in his boxer briefs—a noticeable bulge straining in the front.

"Sorry," he murmurs, his cheeks blushing a bit. "You're just... I can't help... just ignore it." Witnessing Brooks hesitate and search for words warms my chest.

He still looks sheepish when he leans my head back under the water, running his fingers through the tangled mess, getting my hair saturated. I close my eyes and enjoy the feel of the water and his hands. I keep them closed, hearing only the sound of the water and the occasional snick of a bottle opening or closing as he shampoos and then conditions my hair. I keep my hands on his arms or shoulders, making sure he's there, that this is real.

Once my hair is done, Brooks takes a washcloth, suds it up with my body wash, and runs it over every inch of my body. He's careful to only touch me with the cloth, his hands never wandering from the task. The sweetness of the moment, of his attentiveness, brings new tears to my eyes. I'm thankful I can hide them with the water from the shower.

Once I'm rinsed clean, Brooks turns off the water, steps out, and grabs a towel, which he wraps around me. He wraps another one around his waist over the wet boxer briefs and looks over at me. "Okay?" When I nod, he continues, "Stay in here, dry off. I'm going to grab some clothes for you." I'm about to protest, but he says, "I'll leave the door open, you can watch me." Not waiting for a response, he turns, opens the door wide and steps out.

I watch his back move as he opens and closes the drawers on my dresser, pulling out clean clothes. He's back within seconds and sets the pile he collected on the vanity. "Here you go. Get dressed. I'll change out here. I'm not going to leave your room, promise." He gathers up the clothes he stripped out of earlier and exits the bathroom, leaving the door ajar.

Though I can't see him, I hear him moving around the room. A few heartbeats later, I'm confident he'll stay there, so I drop the towel and start to dress. I almost smile when I pull my favorite pair of knit thigh-highs from the top of the pile of clothes he brought.

I finish getting dressed and brush my teeth. I almost feel normal aside from the overwhelming exhaustion crashing over me. Looking in the mirror, I confirm I look as tired as I feel, but there's a little bit of color to my cheeks. I pick up my detangling comb to try to get rid of the rat's nest my hair has turned into, but just the thought of it drains the rest of my energy.

Soft fingers pull the comb from my hand, and Brooks leads me out of the bathroom. Somehow, in the few minutes it took me to get dressed, he's managed to strip my bed of the sheets and throw them into a laundry basket by the bedroom door along with the clothes that had been on the floor.

He tosses a pillow onto the floor next to the bed and motions for me to sit on it as he sits on the bed behind me. Slowly, methodically he starts on my hair. With great care, he takes small section by small section and brushes each one out with the comb.

"He's—" I croak, then clear my throat. "He's the reason I'm here. The reason I ran away from Charleston." Brooks doesn't say anything, but his hands pause their work for a beat or two. When he continues, so do I, "It started a few months before I left. Just weird things, feeling like I was being watched. I felt like I was going crazy because things kept moving in my apartment. At one point my journal went missing, only to turn up on the passenger's seat of my car one day after work." I take in a few deep breaths. "I told myself I was tired and didn't remember leaving it there. My schedule was crazy at the hospital, the days all ran into each other.

"And then the notes started. I thought someone had confused my car with someone else's, but they got personal, knowing things about me, places I visited, people I'd seen. I finally ran when he broke into my apartment while I was there. I came here to be close to Hayes. And it was good, I felt like I could relax. It's been almost eight months. I thought the distance would keep him away. He can't really leave Charleston, he has a family there, a career, a wife..." I finally trail off, looking down at my hands in my lap.

"Who is he?" Brooks' voice is strained. He puts the comb down and turns me around so I'm kneeling in front of him. His eyes are filled with rage, and every muscle is coiled tight under his T-shirt. His anger doesn't scare me though; I know it's not directed toward me.

"My old boss. He's a big-time surgeon. But it doesn't matter. I tried to report him to my supervisor, but he blew me off. I just didn't think he'd follow me. Why is he here?" I'm not really asking him, it just feels good to finally put voice to all the questions swirling in my mind. I put my head in his lap, wanting to be as close as possible, his warmth offering the comfort I needed all week. Brooks starts running his fingers through my wet hair, grazing his nails lightly against my scalp. We sit like this for a long time, and although the physical tension drains out of me, my mind won't stop churning. "Brooks?"

"Yeah, baby?" he hums.

I pick my head up and meet his eyes, "Can you stay tonight? Can you help me forget? Just for a little?"

CHAPTER THIRTY-FOUR

Margot has a stalker. The truth hit me like a ton of bricks when she'd finally said the words out loud. And even then, she hadn't said it outright, but she'd said enough for me to understand. The reaction to the flowers told me everything I needed to know about her feelings toward the person who left them.

Staying here instead of going after the man who caused all of this was possibly the hardest thing I'd ever done in my life. But I made the decision to stay because I knew being with Margot was more important than being a vigilante. I knew she needed me.

I've never seen anyone this scared, this upset. I've never seen anyone virtually give up on themselves and their life in the way she clearly had. When I walked into her bedroom, it was obvious how she'd spent the last week—alone, terrified, and paralyzed. The realization broke my heart in a way I didn't know was possible. I'm pissed off at myself for not trying harder to get her to talk to me.

Now, with her head in my lap and the silence around us, my mind is spiraling with all the signs I missed.

The locks.

The jumpiness.

The time she asked if I was stalking her with genuine fear in her eyes.

It all adds up now.

It was never about me or random quirks of hers, they were legitimate fears.

I'm trying my best not to let my rage pour out of me the way it wants to. It's simmering just below the surface like an entity all on its own; ribbons of bright red and dark crimson searching for a way out. I want to rip the man to shreds, whoever the fuck he is. Bury him alive and listen to his screams from the surface. I want to end him in ways he'll never come back from so Margot is safe from the trauma he's caused. Keeping a lid on my emotions has never been something I was good at. I've always been more of an act now, think later kind of guy. But I can't do that right now. Not this time.

"Brooks?" Her voice pulls me from my thoughts of fury, pausing the spiral.

"Yeah, baby?" I ask, trying to keep my tone even and calm.

"Can you stay tonight? Can you help me forget? Just for a little?" She's looking up at me now. The light green of her eyes is more haunted than I remember, and it fucking guts me. She looks so tired, like all of the energy's been sucked from her soul after the week she's had.

All I can do is nod. I'm scared to speak because I don't want her to know what's happening inside my head. I don't want her to see the violence sparking to life behind my eyes. I wrap my hand in hers and pull her to her feet so she's standing between my legs.

A drop of water falls from her wet hair to the blazing skin on my arm, sending a shiver down my spine.

I take a deep breath, never taking my eyes off of her, before I say, "I uhh—" Fuck. Clearing my throat, I try again, "I need to know where the sheets are."

She scans my face, her eyes slightly squinted and her nose a little scrunched, and I'm not sure what she's hoping to find. Maybe she expected something less rational, but the truth is, I'm overwhelmed. I haven't drank in ten days, I haven't had a cigarette in two hours, and the woman I'm in love with—who has no idea how I feel—looks like a husk of who she was. I've spent the last week coming to terms with my feelings for Margot, while knowing she'll probably never feel the same. In my thirty-three years, I've never loved a woman in a romantic way, I've never been struck stupid by someone the way I am with her. And now I find out she's in trouble. It's all too much.

Finally, she points to the closet behind her and says, "I have an extra set in there."

I spin her around, setting her down on the edge of the bed and walk to the closet. With linens in hand, I pass one side to her as we silently replace the sheets on the bed, working in tandem.

She grabs the pillows from where I'd left them earlier and throws them toward the headboard then follows them, crawling up the bed. I avert my gaze to the ceiling so I'm not staring at her ass and those fucking thigh-highs. Just the thought of how they hug the silky skin of her thighs has my dick perking up, and I have to bite the inside of my cheek to stop it. I'm an asshole for even having those thoughts right now. She's upset and scared as fuck, and I'm over here getting turned on by the image of her ass and those stockings.

"What's wrong?" Margot asks, pulling me from my self-hatred. She's now sitting at the top of the bed, facing me with her knees pulled up to her chest.

"Nothing," I say, turning around, pulling out my smokes and my phone from my pockets to place them on her dresser, anything to avoid the sexual tension in the room. It's not the time, and I'm trying insanely hard to be respectful. Taking a second to compose myself, I subtly adjust my half-hard cock from the front of my pants before turning back around to her. "You should get some rest," I say, walking toward her, grabbing the comforter and pulling the covers up as I do. She opens her mouth to say something, but I cut her off, "I'm not leaving. I'll be right here."

I reach across the bed, grabbing one of the pillows again and placing it on the floor right beside her head. She says nothing as I sit down, my back against the edge of the mattress, eyes forward so I'm not torturing myself by watching her fall asleep. It's two-thirty in the afternoon, but it's clear she hasn't slept well in quite some time. If me being here will give her enough comfort to finally get some rest, I'll do it.

I listen as she shifts around on the bed, getting comfortable. But then her hand snakes down my shoulder. Goosebumps pepper my skin from the contact. With my right hand, I reach up and thread my fingers through hers, then pull her hand to my lips, and press a soft kiss to the top of it.

She lets out a long sigh but seems to settle in now that we're connected. With my phone over on the dresser, I'm not sure how long it takes for her to fall asleep, but I notice the change in her breathing. The grip on my hand loosens as well. Deciding I should use the time to do some clean up for her around the house, I unlace our fingers and go to stand, but she reaches back out for me.

"Don't leave," she says, her voice groggy.

I turn to face her, watching as she sits up in the bed, prepared to follow me if I do. "What do you need?" I ask, willing to give her just about anything she could ask for. She pushes the covers down her legs and swings them over the side.

"I need you," she says, pulling me back to her so I'm standing between her legs, her fingers trace the hem of my shirt, inching it up my abdomen.

"Margot," I start, shoving my hands deep in my pockets, so I'm not tempted to reach out and touch her. "I don't... I don't think it's a good idea." The confused look on her face forces me to continue, "I'm too pent up. You're too fucking gorgeous. And I'm too—" I cut myself off before I spill my guts to her about my feelings.

While I've spent a week having an epiphany about how I feel for her, she's been trapping herself here, scared sick. Just the thought makes my rage boil again along with nausea knowing she's been going through this alone. "I don't think it's a good idea."

"Please... I need you," she pleads. "I need to feel something—*anything* else. Please." The sound of her begging is only creating a bigger problem for me. And I'm not sure I can resist any longer. She pushes my shirt as far up as she can, waiting for me to do the rest. I take a moment—just one—to make sure she really wants this before pulling my hands from my pockets and tugging the shirt over my head. It drops to the floor, and Margot's eyes graze over my chest, my abs. She leans forward and kisses just to the left of my navel. Her hands fumble on the button of my pants.

Her fingers are trembling, it's the only reason I try once more to resist. "Are you sure?"

She nods her head at the same moment the button she was working on pops free. The sound of the zipper reverberates throughout the silent room.

"Where did your underwear go?" she asks, the tips of her fingers tracing along the trimmed hair right above my bare cock. It sends electric currents through my body, straight to my dick.

"I uhh—" I try not to moan at the feel of her hand as she reaches inside my pants, releasing my cock from the confines. "They were soaked. I had to take them off."

She hums some kind of response I can't make out because my mind is too focused on everything her hands are doing. Within seconds of her touching me, I'm hard as a rock. She moves her hands to push my pants down, and the brief second of clarity allows me to stop her. "Wait, baby, wait. Please." She pauses and looks up at me. The look on her face is full of anxiety. I hurry to explain, if only to wipe the expression away, "I want to take care of you. Can I do that?"

The anxiety turns to relief, then she's biting her lip in—what I hope is—anticipation. "Okay," she says, her voice small and raspy still.

"Scoot back on the bed, and take your shirt off. I want to see those beautiful tits while I taste your pussy." She does as I say, taking off her bra as well. I try not to drool at the sight of her bare. I held it together in the shower, but now that I have permission, I'm not sure I can hold back. Not sure I even want to try. Then she goes to pull off her thigh-highs, but I put my hand on top of hers. "No, those stay on." Her cheeks redden, and my dick gets impossibly harder.

I shuck off my pants, kicking them to the side as I climb on the bed between her legs. She leans back, her head almost hanging off the other side. As much as I want to take my time, I'm not sure I'll be able to. I take a moment to gape at her gorgeous, freckle covered body. She's so goddamn perfect. I'd give anything to spend the rest of my days worshipping at the altar of Margot.

"Brooks, what are you—"

"I'm admiring you, Freckles. Every perfect fucking inch of you. Do you realize how beautiful you are? Do you even know?"

She looks up at me, and as I meet her eyes, I loop my fingers through the band of her thong. The one I picked out for her to wear just an hour ago. I never thought I'd end up taking it off of her too. Slowly, I pull it down her legs, exposing her glistening pussy.

"Fuck, baby, you're so wet for me already." I throw her thong to the side, my mouth already watering at the thought of tasting her. "Tell me you want this," I grit out, needing to hear her say it before I start because once I do, I won't be able to stop.

"I want this, Brooks. I want you." I lie down, and her fingers rake at my scalp. My hair is longer than usual, I've been meaning to buzz it. But since it seems like she'd enjoy pulling on it, I may consider never cutting it again.

Using my fingers, I spread her wide, just to see exactly how wet she is. I lick her all the way up to her clit then suck at it. She's moaning, trembling beneath me, her nails digging even deeper into my scalp.

I lean back up, and she whimpers from the loss of contact. My fingers spread her wide again as I gather her wetness then push it up so I can coat her in it. She's still in her head, her body tense with the stress of the last week. I need to do something quick to shock her out of it before we lose the moment.

"Let's see if we can get you even wetter," I say before I pull away and bring my hand back to her cunt, the sharp sound of the slap cracking in the silence.

Margot yelps, but then it turns into a moan. "Oh my God, Brooks."

"That good, baby?"

"Mhmm," she responds as she sucks her bottom lip back into her mouth, biting down so hard, the skin around it turns white. "Do it again," she demands breathily.

"Fuck, baby," I say as I bring my hand down again, the smacking sound even louder this time. "Seeing how red your cunt gets when I slap it might be my new addiction. It's so fucking gorgeous. I love seeing my mark on you," I tell her as I rub a soothing touch over the blazing skin. My other hand runs up her stomach to cup her breast, squeezing as I lean back in for another taste of her.

Her hands are back in my hair, and the grip tightens as I roll her nipple between my thumb and forefinger. She moans, and I flatten my tongue against her, gathering as much of her sweetness as I can then push a finger deep into her cunt. As I pulse in and out of her, I tell her, "You taste so goddamn good, Freckles. I haven't been able to stop thinking about it since the first time."

Her eyes find mine, and I remember how much she loves to be watched, to be seen. A smirk takes over my face as I pull both my hands away from her, but before she can protest, I slide them up under her ass. She lets out another surprised yelp when I hoist her up so her legs are hanging over my shoulders and my face is buried in her pussy. My eyes still locked on hers.

"Oh, yes—oh my God, yes, Brooks," she screams, only spurring me on more.

I suck at her clit, digging my fingers into her ass as I do. Fuck, I want to fuck her ass too. I know she's never done it, there's no way. My cock twitches at the thought. Maybe I'll be lucky enough one day. Maybe I'll test the waters tonight.

I fuck her with my tongue, and her legs quiver with the on-coming orgasm. Sinking three fingers into her, I thrust a few times. Just before she's about to fall over the edge, I pull away. "Do you want to come on my tongue or my cock, baby?"

She's panting as she says, "Your cock, please. I want your cock."

Without another thought, I reach down and wrap my hand around my dick, slowly pumping it. "Come here," I say, using the three fingers soaked in her to gesture her toward me. The orgasm I ripped away from her has her cheeks flushed.

Once she's sitting right in front of me, I say, "Open." She sticks her tongue out, patiently waiting for whatever I have planned. "Such a good fucking girl. Now, suck," I command, pushing my fingers into her waiting mouth.

She moans around the digits, licking herself off of them. Her nipples harden with arousal. I pull my fingers from her lips and crash my mouth onto hers. I've never yearned to kiss a woman. I've never even cared about kissing. But with Margot, kissing her feels like she's breathing life into me.

Before I lose my nerve, I pull away. "On all fours, ass in the air." Once again, she does so without any hesitation. I pump my dick a few more times, enthralled by the way her body moves, with how perfect it is. Freckles cover every inch of her, leaving no spot bare. Even her ass has a scattering on each cheek. I fucking love them.

I run my fingers over the globe of her ass, flexing my hand on it to get a good grip. "God, baby, I swear I was made to worship every part of you." I spank her lightly, watching as the skin ripples from the force. Leaning down, I take one more taste of her, licking from her clit all the way to her asshole, just to see how she'll react. A visible shiver runs through her, but she doesn't tell me to stop.

My goal is to make her forget, and that's exactly what I plan to do. She may have been a virgin before she met me, but I plan on being her first for everything else she hasn't experienced. She gave me a piece of herself, and I want more. I want everything and anything there is to take. "You ready, baby?"

She squirms on her bed, burying her face in the sheets as she mumbles, "Yes, please."

I slap her ass once more before rubbing the head of my cock at her entrance. "Holy fuck, baby. How are you even wetter now?" I don't wait for an answer before slamming into her. My hands are on her hips to keep her steady so I can thrust in and out. "Goddamnit, you feel so fucking good wrapped around me," I grit out.

She was already close, so I know it won't take long to get her to orgasm. I could come just from looking at her. Wasting no time with my plan, I gather enough saliva in my mouth, letting it fall from my lips, landing right on her asshole where I want it. She's so fucked out, she barely notices. Keeping one hand on her hip, I move the other right above where my dick is thrusting into her.

Gathering the spit, I massage around the tight ring of muscle. The second her pussy tightens around my cock, choking it, I know she's aware of what I'm doing. I slide the tip of my thumb into her hole, and the moment I do, she explodes around me. I keep slamming into her, letting her ride out her orgasm as I sink my finger deeper into her tight hole. Two more thrusts and I'm coming inside of her, filling her to the brim.

Our breathing is erratic, both of us sweating and panting. I lean down and press a line of kisses to her back before pulling out of her. Margot collapses onto the bed, and I fall down next to her.

"Thank you," she says, her voice still breathy.

I don't respond. I'm not sure what to say. *You're welcome for fucking your brains out?* "I'll go grab a washcloth," I say instead, climbing off the bed and walking into the bathroom. Once I'm back, I run it along her legs, gathering the mess from her skin. After throwing it onto the overflowing laundry basket, I crawl back into bed with her. We lie there for what feels like forever before I realize she's fallen asleep.

CHAPTER THIRTY-FIVE

Waking up next to Margot is paradise. I'm not sure I believe Heaven exists, but if it does, this is what it would feel like. Her cherry-lilac scent wafts over me, wrapping around me like a blanket, enveloping me in everything Margot. I never want to leave. I'd gladly lie here for the rest of my life.

Her leg is draped over my hips, but when I open my eyes to confess—well, everything—the look on her face tells me she's pissed. The usual gleam in her eyes is gone, and there's not a hint of excitement in her expression about finding me in her bed this morning. At least she looks rested, not the husk of a human I found yesterday.

"Morning, Freckles," I say in an attempt to make her smile. She doesn't.

"Nope."

Okay. This feels like an alternate reality. If I hadn't woken up in *her* bed, I'd wonder if last night was a dream. My confusion must be evident.

"I'm still mad at you," she says matter-of-factly.

Right. Our fuckfest last night kind of erased the whole she's-pissed-at-me-and-may-never-speak-to-me-again thing from my brain.

"That's fair. I deserve that."

Margot sits up, pulling the sheet up to cover her chest, and the warmth I felt with her cocooned around me dissipates, leaving me feeling empty again. I hate it.

"I was an asshole."

"You were." No beating around the bush with this one then.

"And I'm sorry. So fucking sorry. But you aren't exactly innocent either," I say, not willing to let it go this time.

She crosses her arms over her chest. I'm not sure if her intent is to make her tits more prominent, but that's the result. "Me? You're the one who told me you wanted to try, and then pretty much ghosted me for half a week until I found you with Tiffany. What did *I* do?" she asks, clearly forgetting her own shortcomings in this whole thing.

"Don't play ignorant. You neglected to mention you were a virgin; that was a big fucking deal. I should have known. I would have—I don't know—done things differently. Made it special or some shit. Then I find out you've got a fucking stalker? What the hell were you thinking not telling me? You want everyone to treat you like an adult—well, news flash—running away from an issue isn't exactly adult behavior, Margot. When were you going to ask for help?" I'm being cruel and hypocritical, I know. But being nice and coddling her isn't going to work. She needs someone to call her out on her bullshit, just like I need her to call me out on mine.

"I didn't think I needed help! I left, and I came here. Hayes is here. I never thought he'd follow me," she retorts, her hands flying to her face to cover her eyes. There's a quiet moment before she releases a sob.

"I know, baby, I know," I say as I pull her hands from her face, her tear-streaked cheeks breaking my heart just like last night. "Do you know how fucking scared I was yesterday when I realized what was going on? What you were dealing with alone... I hated myself for not seeing it. The signs were all there. Why didn't you tell me sooner?" I plead, still needing to know why she chose to keep this from me when I could have helped sooner. We could have avoided all of this.

Through a hiccup, she says, "I-I was coming to tell you." My brows furrow in confusion, and she continues, "The night of the Jingle Mingle. That's... that's when I found out for sure he'd found me..." There's just a fraction of a second before her next words are shattering my heart. "But then I saw you with Tiffany. And you—you let her... she kissed you..." Her voice trails off as she looks away, her expression pure dejection, her words sounding smaller and quieter like she lost her nerve halfway through the sentence.

I push the bedding off of me, turning my body and sitting cross legged so I can face her. Pulling her arms away from her body, I lace my fingers through hers. "I know. I... Fuck. I panicked. Everything was so good, and I got all in my head about it," I say as I gently squeeze her hands. "I thought if I pushed you away and messed this up, maybe it would save me from getting hurt when you inevitably come to your senses and leave me."

Her face scrunches up in confusion. "Leave you?"

I pull my gaze down to our intertwined hands, drawing my thumb back to trace the lines of her palm. Clearing my throat, I start again, "You have the ability to wreck me, Margot. And I know, I know it sounds like a cop out. You don't have to believe me, but I've never felt like this before. I've never been consumed by another person the way I am with you."

I pause, still never meeting her eyes. I keep mine trained on the intricate lines of her palm. I feel her staring at me though. Taking another deep breath, I continue, "I know there's a chance you won't forgive me. Honestly, you probably shouldn't." Her body tenses at my words. "I just mean, it won't be the last time I fuck up. I'm far from perfect, but what I did was really shitty. So I wouldn't blame you."

"Brooks—"

I finally look up, cutting her off before she can say much else, "Let me get this out, Freckles, then you can break my heart, okay? I just need to say this."

She nods her head, tears lining her eyes. God, I hope they don't fall. I'd do anything to never see her cry again. I look back down at our hands, I won't be able to get this out if I see one of those tears cascade down her cheek.

"I uhh… I don't feel very deserving of much. And I'm fucking terrified to want something and be let down. I'm terrified to want you. My actions are not excusable, but I really do think the fear of losing you scared me so much I figured I'd get it over with before I was too far gone. I'm an idiot for thinking I wasn't *already* too far gone though." I let out a self-deprecating laugh. "God, I'm such a dumbass. I should have told you how I felt before so maybe you wouldn't hate me now. Although, maybe you would have just laughed if I had. I'm sure falling in love with someone like me was never in your five-year plan or whatever."

I open my mouth to say more, but she's already pulling her hands from mine. This is it. This is the part where she tells me she could never love someone like me. No one could.

Her fingers graze my chin, pulling my gaze back to hers. Those same tears holding on for dear life.

"You deserve so much, Brooks. I know you don't see it, but you do. And you are a dumbass." She chuckles, the sound breathing life back into me. "I never planned on breaking your heart. I was all in with you. But I can't be with someone who lashes out by hurting me because of his own hang ups. It's not fair to me..."

Her hand falls back to her lap. I'm left confused at her words. I can't tell if I'm being forgiven or told to fuck off. "I... I know, Margot. I really do. And it—Fuck. It will never happen again. I swear." I don't even know why I'm pleading my case without her asking me to. She's given me no reason to think she wants to hear it.

"I want to believe you, I really do. But you were so cold the night of the party. You acted like you didn't care." Despite her words, there's a spark of hope.

"Baby, I care. I care so much it hurts. And I want you. I want to be with you. I don't care about Tiffany or anyone else. I just want you. And I'll do anything—anything at all to prove it to you. Please, give me another chance, I'm begging you." My voice cracks on the last words, and I watch as a tear falls, finally breaking the dam. "I love you, Margot. I fucking love you. So much. I've known it for weeks now. I was just so fucking scared."

I've never seen her speechless. Her face is blank, no trace of emotion to tell me which direction this will go. A part of me is preparing to take it back, but she finally speaks. "Anything?"

"Anything," I say nodding my head, hoping this means I've convinced her.

"I don't want you to fight anymore."

I jerk back. "Wh-what?" I stutter, trying to understand.

"No more fighting. I can't... I can't be with someone who spends their free time risking their life and hurting others."

"I—Margot, I'm not—riding my motorcycle is more dangerous than The Pit."

She's giving me the kind of stern look a mother would give her son, it's unbreakable. There's no twisting her arm on this, she's serious.

"I don't think you understand what you're asking of me..." I trail off, not wanting to get too upset.

She nods. "I do understand, I really do."

Jumping up from the bed, I grab the sides of my head with both hands, squeezing to ease the fucking turmoil building in my brain. "No, you don't." I'm louder now, not screaming but louder than before. She doesn't get it. Someone perfect like her never could. "You aren't—you're not *broken* like me, Margot. You don't understand this ache in my chest, the unsteadiness I feel constantly, the need for control in just one aspect of my life." Pacing the floor now, I meet her eyes again, fresh tears falling down her beautiful cheeks. "You don't get it. Being in The Pit, being in control in that way, it's the only way I can cope. It's the only way I've *ever* been able to cope. The second the bell rings, everything else goes silent."

She's looking at me like I'm a wild animal she's scared to spook. "Okay…" she says, nodding her head. "Okay. What do you mean everything goes silent?"

It's not what I expect her to ask. "I mean… the constant voice in my head telling me I'm not good enough. Not deserving. Not amounting to anything. Not someone people can depend on. Literally every fuck up constantly plays on a loop. Every conversation where someone I love tells me how I let them down. And I just… Fuck. It hurts, Margot. It hurts so fucking much. But when I'm in The Pit, when I'm in control of my body with a singular goal in mind, all of it goes quiet." I've never bared myself like this to anyone. I've never talked about my struggles. I've never explained why I am the way I am to anyone. But also… no one has ever asked. No one but Margot. It's always Margot.

She leaps up from the bed, jumping into my arms in such a rush, I almost don't catch her in time. She buries her face in my neck. "You are deserving, Brooks. You deserve to be loved and to feel loved. I wish you would accept that you *are* loved. And not just by me—by Cary and Thea and Ripley and my brother. We all love you. Just… let us."

Did she just… "You love me?"

She leans back in my arms, bringing her hands to my face to cup my cheeks. "I do," she says, the gleam back in her light green eyes. "So we'll find something to replace the fighting, okay? We'll figure something out to give you the same feeling. I promise. Just please, please tell me you won't be reckless anymore. It's my one condition, Brooks."

I don't know which is more terrifying: the idea of losing her for good or the thought of never again having the control I crave. I've already quit drinking for her. She doesn't know, but I did.

The realization hits me square in the chest. If I can give something up without her even asking, why am I questioning if I can give this up for her too? Drawing and sex also clear my mind. It doesn't work as well, but maybe it can be enough.

She's the only person who's ever said I'm worthy of love. There are no 'buts' with it either, no caveats.

"Okay, but you have to quit The Pit too," I say, and she pulls me to her, crashing her lips to mine. My fingers dig into the flesh just below her ass as I press her even closer.

She pulls away but only far enough to lean her forehead against mine, our lips just a breath apart. Nodding, she says, "I will fight for you. I'll *keep* fighting for you. Because you deserve it."

I kiss her again, soft this time, less demanding. "I love you, Freckles."

Wrapping her arms around me, she buries her face back in my neck, holding as tight as possible. "I love you too, Killer. But don't think you're off the hook entirely. I'm still upset. I might be for a while, but I do love you, and I want to be with you."

I pepper her face with kisses, her beautiful laugh filling the tense air around us.

"Okay, okay, okay!" she screams. "Can I go take a shower now? I feel gross." She's wiggling in my arms, attempting to make me put her down.

Walking toward the bathroom, I say, "*We* can go shower, yes. And you're fucking beautiful."

She rolls her eyes at me but kisses my cheek. And for once, I don't question why she'd do that or why she'd want to be with me. My head is silent of negative thoughts, all of them focused on being happy with her.

We kept the shower PG rated.

Okay, maybe PG-13.

Margot wants to go check on her dad; it's been a good bit since she's been over. I didn't tell her I was there on New Years' Eve. She doesn't know her dad vowed to stop drinking; I just hope Keaton didn't fall off the wagon before she gets to see him sober. I should have gone back to check on him, but I got busy. And by busy, I mean I spent all my free time working on the reno of the kitchen in my parents' house when I wasn't at RED. The restaurant has been packed too. People have swarmed since word got out about our hotshot big city chef taking over the kitchen.

It's a little after one when we make it to Keaton's house. She hops off the bike, losing her balance as she does.

"Whoa, I got you," I say as I grab her hand, keeping her from falling. She pulls the helmet off and blows her hair out of her face. Her cheeks are flushed, her freckles bolder than usual.

"Do you... want to come inside with me?" she asks, her eyes shifting around the treeline surrounding the house. I mentally kick myself again for not catching on to the way she's constantly on guard. I look around as well like some psychopath might jump out any moment.

"No, go spend some time with your dad. I'm going to go talk to Hayes. He told me he'd be at The Pit setting up for tonight, so he's not far from here. Gotta tell him I'm in love with his little sister and hope he doesn't break my face for it." I huff out a laugh, not entirely joking. I'm more concerned about him actually killing me and hiding my body in the woods. "But hey," I say, intertwining my fingers with hers, "later, we need to talk, okay? I need to know everything. We need to file a police report. And you'll be staying with me until it's all figured out." She opens her mouth, probably to argue, but I cut her off, "This is *my* one condition, Margot."

She nods her head, her face falling just a bit as she does. It's obvious she'd rather bury her head in the sand and hope it goes away, but he's clearly determined to get her attention, and I can't allow it to escalate to something more dangerous. She won't have to deal with it much longer. I'll make fucking sure of it.

"I also... have to tell him I won't be fighting anymore..." I trail off, but a small smile graces her lips.

"Thank you. For everything." She leans in to kiss me, releasing my hand to cup my cheek as she does.

"No need." She hands me her helmet back, but I stop her. "Keep it until I get back. It's yours anyway."

Her eyes shoot up to me. "Mine?"

I give her a smirk and start the ignition. "You heard me, Freckles." Slamming my visor back down, I take off, leaving her in a plume of dust with a shocked expression on her face.

Today has already been draining. After our morning, I would have preferred to stay in bed the rest of the day, and I would have bribed Margot to do the same. But talking to Hayes is a top priority. He let this go on for too long. He should have told me. She never should have been living on her own after going through this in Charleston. He should have been more diligent about making sure the creep didn't follow her here.

It takes everything in me not to storm the trailer or throw a punch at him with no discussion whatsoever, but I'm trying to be better. For me. For Margot. For everyone. And I know starting a fight with him won't win me any points in the long run.

The drive to The Pit is short, and Hayes is grabbing something from his truck when I pull up.

"Hey," I say, cutting the engine. Hayes gives me an up-nod as he lugs a bag out of the bed of his truck. "We need to talk."

He pauses for a moment, dropping the bag and turning his focus on me. "Sounds serious. Are we breaking up?"

I don't laugh, and I think he realizes at that moment how serious I am. "It's about Margot."

His face goes stone cold. "What about Margot?"

"I should have told you this weeks ago, but I'm in love with her," I blurt out, figuring I should just get it over with. His expression transitions through an array of emotions including confusion and shock before ending on rage. His face turns bright red, and I know he's about to pop off, possibly murder me, so before he can, I add, "And I'm fucking pissed you didn't take care of this stalker situation."

He jerks back like I've swung at him. "What? What stalker situation? What the fuck are you talking about, Grant?"

"The guy from Charleston." There's no recognition on his face, no indication he knows what I'm talking about. "She *did* tell you, right?" My panic rises. I assumed he knew. I assumed she told him why she moved here. She tells him everything. She calls him her best friend. So why is he acting like he has no fucking clue what I'm talking about?

"No," he growls, then his face goes blank for a second before growing impossibly pale.

"What?"

"Fuck! I kept asking why she had so many locks, she brushed me off every time," he recalls, running a hand through his hair. He looks ragged suddenly, like his entire world is falling apart. "And there was a guy—"

"What do you mean? What guy?"

"Just some random dude who came into the shop last week. He asked where the name came from, and I told him it's my last name. He laughed and told me his favorite nurse in Charleston has the last name Mason. I made small talk, something along the lines of it being a small fucking world because my sister used to be a nurse in Charleston. And then… Fuck!" he screams, slamming his fist into the side of his truck.

"Then what, Hayes? What did he say?"

"He asked if her name is Margot."

Chapter Thirty-Six

My knees are actually weak. I feel like one of those Victorian ladies needing to pull out a fan to blow air into my overheated face as I watch Brooks ride off on his motorcycle, the engine rumbling through my chest cavity. I don't think I'll ever get over how sexy the man looks on his bike.

Our conversation this morning helped heal some of the hurt his actions dealt at Christmas. Do I think everything between us is perfect? No, but we'll get there. As long as Brooks doesn't get in his head again, doesn't avoid talking to me, and doesn't push me away, we'll figure it out. It'll take some time to trust he won't turn around and hurt me again, but I'm cautiously optimistic we'll get there because I believe him when he says he loves me. He's sincere about it, he's just also scared, but I'm determined to show him he's worth it. Worth everything.

Though I'm not a violent person, I'm ready to fight anyone who says anything negative about him. Yes, the man has made some questionable decisions, but it's only out of self-preservation. He's learned to be reactive to keep himself safe. I'm determined to show him he's safe with me, safe with his friends, his brother.

With a big sigh and an even bigger grin, I turn to my dad's house, ready to face whatever is behind the front door. Having neglected pretty much everything for the last week, I can only hope Hayes made it out here to take care of Dad.

Since we were on the bike, I didn't ask Brooks to swing by the grocery store before coming here. I'll have to make a list of what I need to get tomorrow after I clean up.

I'm running through my mental to-do list as, out of habit, I tread carefully up the front steps, staying close to the rickety railing just in case today's the day they finally fall apart under my weight.

With my hand inches from the handle of the door, I pause then turn around. Pushing my curls out of my face, I actually look at the front steps. It's not just new boards as a makeshift fix for the rotted ones, it's a whole new structure, like it's been rebuilt entirely.

Huh, I think. *Hayes must have put a foot through the rotting wood if he finally took the time to fix the steps.* I eye the work for a few more moments, impressed by the craftsmanship and pleased my brother finally invested some time into helping around here.

Between waking up next to Brooks and now this, today is turning into a great day—especially after the turmoil of the past week. My tummy is still tight with nerves knowing Julian's out there somewhere, but it's lessened knowing I'll be staying with Brooks. The memory of his arms around me last night and this morning feels like armor. He'd never let anything happen to me.

Still pleasantly buzzing, I enter the house. Expecting to be greeted by the usual stale smell of alcohol and old food, my brow furrows when I find the house smelling strongly of cleaning products—the scent of lemon wood cleaner and bleach most prominent.

The smell isn't the only change. The living room is tidy, clean even. There are no liquor bottles on the coffee table or floor, the curtains are pulled open so the room is bathed in the mid-morning January sun. I place the helmet I'm still holding on the side table and run my hand across the back of the couch, across the neatly folded blanket hanging over the edge.

My confusion grows when I enter the kitchen and find it spotless, minus a couple of dishes in the sink.

Did Hayes hire a cleaner? I can't imagine he did all of this himself. Usually I'm lucky if he throws the trash in the bin. Hayes' resentment of our dad has grown significantly over the last few years. When he bothers to come at all, he typically drops off food, makes sure Dad hasn't aspirated in his sleep, and leaves; so the state of the house is raising more than a few questions.

I snap my head to the door to the kitchen when I hear shuffling coming from down the hall seconds before my dad walks into the room.

"Oh, hi, Margot. I didn't hear you come in," he says.

There's silence for a beat... or sixteen as I take him in. His eyes are clear, a warm coffee brown. He looks like he just climbed out of the shower if his wet hair is any indication. The sweater and jeans he's wearing are clean, not marred by three day-old stains. He looks... sober. Good, even.

Me staring with my mouth agape must make him uncomfortable because he shifts on his feet and looks around the kitchen before clearing his throat. "I, uh—I was going to do some laundry, but..." He trails off, his cheeks turning pink. "Well, I've never used this machine, and I couldn't figure it out. Think you can show me?"

I'm shocked out of my stupor by his words. "Yeah—Yeah, I can show you," I say and follow him down the hall where the laundry machine sits in a closet.

I spend a few minutes showing him the different settings and explaining when to use each one. All the while, my mind is reeling. *What is happening right now? What alternate universe is this?*

Once he's pressed start on the machine and it rumbles to life, we make our way back to the kitchen. Dad goes over to the fridge, cracking it open. "Want anything to drink?"

"No," I say, just a tinge of disappointment seeping into my chest. "Thank you."

When he turns around and shuts the fridge before heading over to the small kitchen table, I notice a bottle of water in his hand. He sits at the table and looks at me. "So, what's going on? How's work going? You're at the old folks' home still, right?"

I'm once again rendered silent by confusion. I can't remember the last time I had a moment with my dad when he was sober, let alone a conversation where he asked me something as mundane as how my job is going.

Not knowing how to stand here and have a conversation with him, I busy myself with opening the fridge and taking inventory of the contents as I answer him, "Yeah, Saint Stephen's, and it's been great so far. The residents are great, and they're flexible with my hours. Just... great."

My eyes scan the milk, bread, and fresh produce, along with a few containers of leftovers which don't look to be more than a day old. My bewilderment grows because this isn't what Hayes typically brings. He usually just throws a few pre-packaged dinners in Dad's freezer and calls it good.

"Listen," Dad starts. "I—"

"What is going on right now?" I cut him off then wince at my rudeness. Unable to voice my question in any other way, I throw a quick look at him before I move over to the sink.

I turn on the water to start on the dishes, but his quiet voice stops me. "Just leave those, I'll run the dishwasher after dinner."

"The dishwasher's broken," I say, turning the faucet off.

"Uh, yeah, it's been—It's fixed," he stutters over his words, like he's nervous. I look over at the machine as if I could see what had been broken before.

"Hayes fixed the dishwasher?" I ask, confused. I've been asking him to take a look at it since I moved back. What finally prompted him to fix it? And the stairs?

"Uh, no. Not, uh, not Hayes." Dad pauses for a few beats before adding, "Your, um, friend. Brooks."

"Brooks? He came by here?" I whirl around to face him. Dad looks sheepish, like he shouldn't be telling me this.

"Yeah, a few days ago. He fixed it. Front steps too. Good kid, handy too," he says with a small smile. My brow furrows. Brooks was here?

"He's hardly a kid," I say, though I have a million questions about what exactly transpired here while I was locked inside my house.

"Yeah, well. You're probably right about that. Definitely wiser than he looks. Had some choice words for me," he says. "Said I wasn't fair to you. Needed to clean my act up. And he's right. I uh... went to one of those meetings you're always leaving flyers for. It was... well, not good, exactly. But it was something. Talked to someone about possibly sponsoring me."

I have no words. Dad seems to have run out of them as well because he's silent for a long moment. The revelations crowding in with us in the small kitchen.

"Leave the dishes, alright?" he finally says, standing up from the chair. "I'm going to go out to the garage and see if I can find a ladder to switch out that lightbulb," he says as he tilts his chin up to the burnt out bulb above me. "Maybe after we can have some lunch or something?"

"Yeah, Daddy," I say quietly with a small nod. "That sounds nice."

I'm left alone in the kitchen, my mind whirring with everything I just learned. Brooks came here to help my dad. Even though I was mad at him. I don't think he did it as a way to get back in my good graces since he didn't tell me about it. My heart squeezes at the thought of Brooks taking care of my dad, something even my own brother can't be bothered to do anymore. Now more than ever, I can't wrap my head around how he doesn't see how *good* he is, how selfless and kind. I wish he'd let other people see this side of him.

And my dad is sober. A few days sober too, if I had to guess. And he left the house for an AA meeting. I feel like I'm in the Twilight Zone, or maybe I'm still asleep in my bed, door barricaded.

After a few minutes of standing around, I'm feeling antsy. I never do nothing here; there's always something to clean, to put away, to throw out. But my dad—or maybe Brooks—has taken care of everything.

With nothing else out of sorts in sight, I step on the pedal for the trash can and see it's three quarters full. I pull out the bag and tie it off before replacing it with a new one. Grabbing the almost full bag, I take it out of the kitchen toward the front door. I can't sit still.

Half way through the living room, I look up and gasp. The bag drops to the floor as I grab my chest where my heart thunders under my palm. My breaths stutter, and a solid lead weight drops to the pit of my stomach.

Julian stands not ten feet in front of me, his back to the front door. He looks wrecked, nothing like the confident, handsome surgical god I knew him as eight months ago. His T-shirt is rumpled like he's slept in it, boots covered in mud. His usually perfect hair is greasy and mussed. There's stubble under the dark circles below his eyes. And his eyes. They look manic, bouncing around the room, over my face and body, not staying on any one spot too long. There's a frenetic energy around him.

"Hi, pretty girl," he murmurs, voice raspy, like he hasn't used it in a while. "It's so nice to have your eyes on me again. *Fuck*, this has been a long time coming."

"J-Julian," I breathe out. "What—What are you doing here?" I'm frozen to the spot. My mind is telling me to run, but my body won't move. My knees feel like they might give out, and I reach out my hand to hold onto the couch for support. My scalp prickles, and tears threaten the backs of my eyes as I watch him shift around, his movements jerky.

"I came for you," he coos in that same rasp. "I had a hard time leaving. Everyone's always wanting something from me. But you—you left. I just wanted to get closer. I figured you came here for your brother; you were always talking about him… But then there's that barback—what is that, why him? Screaming at you in the street like a fucking hillbilly."

I can barely follow his rambling as he jumps from one thought to another. I scramble for something to say, for a way to get him to leave or to let me leave. I'm still not speaking as he reaches behind his back, and when his arm straightens out, I see a gun in his hand.

An involuntary sob bursts out of me, and my entire body shakes, trembling in fear.

"You seem scared," he continues. "No need, I'll take care of you, my pretty girl. He's not going to get you again."

"Julian, you can't—"

"What's going on here?" my dad's quiet voice cuts through my words.

Many things happen all at once. I register my old boss and I are no longer alone. Julian startles and whirls around to face the front door where my dad just walked in, bulb in hand. I open my mouth to scream for him to run, to get out, but my words never come. Or they're lost to the sound of the deafening gunshot, I can't be sure.

It takes a second for all of us to recognize what's happened. There's silence between the three of us—or maybe I just can't hear anything over the blood whooshing in my ears—as we stand frozen in place. But then it all comes rushing back as red blooms on my dad's sweater, right under the palm he's placed against his belly.

Without another thought, I grab the helmet Brooks gave me—*my helmet*—off of the side table next to the couch and swing it at the back of Julian's head. The crack of the plastic against his skull reverberates around the room as he falls to the ground, eyes closed, unmoving.

I don't stop to check on him before I drop my improvised weapon and rush over to my dad, immediately pushing down on his hand to help slow the bleeding from his abdomen.

"Okay. You're going to be okay," I say, surprised my voice sounds calm, in control—so different from just a minute ago. I look around the living room, eyes catching on Julian's motionless body, before deciding there's nothing here to help me. I can't remember where I left my phone; I'm not even sure I brought it with me when Brooks dropped me off. I curse my dad for never keeping his phone charged.

Grabbing a scarf from the coat rack by the door, I move Dad's hand and press it down on the wound. Dad moans with the contact, and I wince, hating to hurt him more than he already is.

"A-are you okay?" he grumbles out between clenched teeth.

"Yes, Daddy, I'm okay. And you'll be okay," I say, swallowing the panic trying to rise up my throat. "Alright, Daddy. We have to get out of here. I'm not sure how long he'll be out. Can you stand up for me? Okay, good," I say as he gets his legs under him with difficulty.

I wrap his arm over my shoulders and grab onto his torso, before placing my hand over his, the one holding the scarf to his stomach. I lead him outside and down the new stairs as quickly as he'll move; I have no options but to get away from here and find a way to stop the bleeding.

Before we're swallowed up by the treeline, I turn back to the house and thankfully don't see Julian following us. What I do see is splatters of my dad's blood trailing down the brand new steps, staining the wood a deep red.

Chapter Thirty-Seven

The moment the words fell from Hayes' lips, my stomach dropped. The sinking feeling I've had since finding out she has a stalker washed over me in full force. I've never seen Hayes' face drain of color the way it did, and I've never seen him look so scared.

"Where is she?" he demands, a slight tremor in his voice like he's barely holding it together.

"I dropped her off at your dad's."

In an instant, Hayes is throwing open the driver's side door and climbing in. I'm barely in the passenger's seat before he's putting the truck in reverse. Gravel kicks up behind us as the wheels spin from the jagged turn he makes out of the makeshift parking lot.

Grabbing onto the oh-shit handle, I glance at him. His stone-cold face looks murderous. "I thought she told you, Hayes. I thought you knew. I would have—"

"Brooks, take a second—one fucking second—and think about what you just said. Do you honestly think I would have taken my eyes off of her even for a moment if I knew? Come the fuck on, you know me better." He shakes his head like he's disgusted by the thought.

From what Margot told me, she thought it was over. She thought leaving Charleston was enough. I assumed Hayes knew but had slacked off for the same reason. And yeah, I was pissed but mostly because I felt so fucking helpless and yelling at him was an outlet. I couldn't yell at Margot. I'd already snapped on her this morning.

I pull my phone from my pocket, scrolling through my recent calls to her name. I need to hear her voice. I need to know she's okay. Even though The Pit is on the same property as Keaton's house and Hayes is cutting through fucking fields to get there faster, it still feels like we're too far away.

Her phone rings and rings and rings. I hold my breath the whole time, silently begging her to pick up.

"Fuck! Drive faster!" I shout, a cold sweat washing over me at the possibility of something being wrong. She's probably fine. My hope is she's bonding with Keaton. She found him sober, and it's been a lot for her, so she hasn't looked at her phone. It's just a big misunderstanding, that's all.

Time fucking crawls as we drive up the long dirt driveway, before Hayes swerves onto the grassy area right in front of Keaton's house, his front door wide open. I jump out of the car before Hayes comes to a complete stop and almost fall from the force of the impact as my feet hit the ground. I stumble back up, racing to the door, Hayes right behind me. He left the truck running, not wasting any time by pulling the keys from the ignition.

Just as I make it to the stairs, my vision lands on the dark red splatters staining the wood. Stopping dead in my tracks, my heart coming to a shrieking halt with my legs, my mind racing with every worst case scenario possible.

No. No. No.

A split second later, I jolt up the steps. Hayes is saying something behind me, but I can't hear him, I can't focus on anything but finding Margot. I don't dwell on the door being left open, instead rushing inside and doing my best not to panic.

And then I see the full picture come together.

The struggle.

The scene of the crime.

The *fucking* crime.

There's blood on the floor, a bag of trash dropped in the middle of the walkway, Margot's helmet on the ground. Hayes is already moving through the house, screaming Margot's and Keaton's names. I can't tear my eyes away from the blood.

What if it's hers? What if I never see her again? What if—

"They're not here," Hayes chokes out as he comes around the corner. "There's no one here. But there's blood leading out the back door as well."

Without saying a word, I jog for the door, getting back to the truck as fast as I can. I don't give a fuck if the truck is Hayes', I jump in the driver's seat. Hayes crashes into the passenger's seat the same way I did before, barely slamming the door shut before I'm taking off.

"Where are we going?" he asks, his voice cracking with the same fear coursing through my veins.

"I don't know."

"What do you mean 'you don't know?'" he demands.

"I mean I don't fucking know! All I know is the woman I love is possibly hurt or running for her life, and I need to find her. So either get out or shut the fuck up!" Spit flies from my mouth as I scream at him. Margot's brother. My friend. A man who could snap me in half if he wanted, and I'm fucking screaming at him.

We drive through the field beside the house. I'm trying to keep my eyes on the treeline surrounding the property, hoping I'll see something. Even if it's just an area that looks disturbed, anything to point me in a direction, I just need *something*.

"There!" Hayes yells, pointing toward the woods. "I saw something!"

It could be an animal rustling between the trees, but it could also be Margot hiding from a madman. With nothing else to go on, no other possibilities, I drive us toward where Hayes pointed, slamming my foot onto the gas pedal.

Throwing the gear into park at the edge of the woods, I jump out of the truck. "Margot!" I scream, running faster than I've ever run before. I can't catch my breath, but I don't fucking care. I have to find her. I *need* to find her.

Branches fly into my face as I barrel through the woods. "Margot!" My voice cracks at the end of her name, my paralyzing fear overtaking me. Hayes is crashing through the foliage behind me, screaming her name with me.

Right as I'm about to shout her name again into the dense forest, I hear her broken voice. "Brooks?"

My head spins in the direction of my name. "Fuck, Margot! Baby, where are you?"

"We're over here," she yells, louder this time.

I push myself, moving even faster than before, and slide to my knees once she's within reach. Keaton is on the ground beside her, they're both covered in blood, but it's obvious he's the one who's hurt. It makes me an asshole, but the relief I feel is unreal. Cupping her cheeks, I pull her face to mine, placing a kiss on the tip of her nose. "Fuck, Freckles, I thought I lost you."

A tear slides down my face, landing on her cheek. "He—he sh-shot my dad, I-I tried to run but h-he can't—he fell," she stutters out, and I know she's trying to keep it together. She's holding pressure to his stomach, her hands over his, but it doesn't seem to be slowing the bleeding down.

"I know, baby, I know. We're going to—" I start, but then I see something out of the corner of my eye. Movement not far from us, deeper in the forest.

Jumping up to my feet, I don't hesitate, I just take off.

I promised myself I'd protect her.

I promised myself I wouldn't let him hurt her again.

I failed her.

Margot wailing my name echoes through the forest, bouncing off the trees, but I don't stop.

I won't fail her a second time.

CHAPTER THIRTY-EIGHT

"**B**rooks!" I scream at the top of my lungs. "Stop! Come back!"

I scream because I can't move, can't follow him. My hands are the only thing keeping my dad from bleeding out. I yell his name a few more times, long after I lose sight of him beyond the trees.

Tears stream down my face, and I swallow down a sob. I've held it together this long, but I don't think I can do it anymore. Not when my father is bleeding out in front of me. Not when Brooks has run off after Julian.

Julian and the gun.

Fuck! Why didn't I think to take it with us before we ran? Or at least hide it.

I bring my attention back to my dad—who lost consciousness a little while ago—and Hayes when he waves in my face.

"Hey, hey, are you okay? Are you sure he didn't hurt you?" asks Hayes, frantic concern lining his face as he looks between me and Dad. "What do you need?"

"He needs a hospital. I... I can't do much. I need something to pack the wound," I say, my eyes catching on the scarf, now soaked in my dad's blood. "I need... help."

"Let's get him in the truck and to the hospital."

I'm shaking my head before he even finishes the sentence. "It's thirty minutes to the nearest hospital, we need an ambulance, they have supplies..." I trail off as my mind whirrs. "The trailer. You said you got what I asked for at the trailer." My eyes meet Hayes', and understanding dawns.

"Yeah," he says, nodding and already in motion to stand. "Yeah. Let's get him in the truck. I'll call 9-1-1 on the way."

I've never been so thankful for my dad's small frame as I am now. Hayes is able to lift him easily in his massive arms. Carefully, with me still applying as much pressure as I can to his belly, we hurry through the woods, dodging branches and bushes to Hayes' truck. He loads Dad in the bed, and I climb in after him.

The ride to The Pit is bumpy. Hayes does his best to not jostle us around, but I silently urge him to go faster since time is not on our side. My dad is unconscious and pale. I feel for a pulse at his neck and find it's faint. He's losing too much blood.

The truck skids to a stop on the grass in front of the trailer, and Hayes hops out. "I called 9-1-1. They're sending an ambulance and cops," he says as he lowers the tailgate.

Motioning for Hayes to hop into the bed of the truck and hold pressure on Dad's stomach, I waste no time running into the trailer. I gather everything I could possibly need from the newly outfitted cabinets: every packet of gauze I can find, antiseptic, a bag of saline with an IV kit, even a suture kit—though I know this is beyond anything I could stitch up. Dad needs surgery, the bullet is still inside him, and with the amount of bleeding, I'm sure it's nicked something important.

Running back outside, I throw everything into the bed of the truck and jump in myself. After opening all the supplies, I move Hayes' hands and the scarf to quickly replace it with gauze. The bleeding seems to be slowing a little.

"Just hold on, Daddy. Please," I whisper and then add louder, "Hold here, Hayes." I push his blood-covered fingers firmly on top of the gauze and busy myself with setting up the saline drip. I'm praying this will be enough to buy him time to get to the operating room.

Just as I'm applying antiseptic to the crook of Dad's elbow for the IV, I hear sirens in the distance, slowly getting louder.

"Thank God," I exhale. Abandoning the IV, I turn to Hayes. He's quiet, brow furrowed, concentrating on his hands where they press into our father's stomach. After checking for a pulse again and finding it even more thready, I gently touch Hayes' shoulder. "Just keep holding. They're going to help him."

He nods, his eyes looking lost. I don't dwell on how seeing my big brother—my rock—so unsure and scared shakes me to my core. He's always in charge of every situation. He always has the answers. But right now, he looks disoriented and unsettled.

The EMS rig pulls up next to Hayes' truck followed closely by two sheriff's cruisers. The sirens cut off right as the paramedics hop out and rush over to us, jump bags in tow.

"What happened?" the female EMT asks, pulling blue gloves out of her bag and assessing my dad, starting vital signs. Her eyes quickly scan over me and Hayes, pausing on the blood on our clothes but determining we're not hurt.

Her partner also gloves up before pulling out a saline bag and prepping it. The woman takes Hayes' place by my dad, and we jump out of the truck bed so the emergency responders have room to work. They're talking quickly to each other, the woman is reading off my dad's vitals, and the man records them. She turns to us and asks again, "What happened?"

Four police officers join us, eyes looking around The Pit. I clear my throat, "My dad—he was shot. About half an hour ago. A man got into his house—just on the other side of these woods—and shot him. I managed to get us away, but he lost consciousness fifteen minutes ago, and I couldn't carry him. My brother," I motion to Hayes, "brought us here in his truck. I've been keeping steady pressure on the wound, but he's lost a lot of blood."

At the mention of the shooting, the police officers spread out, hands on their holsters, one of them talking into his radio relaying the incident, sending more officers to Dad's house.

"I don't think he's there," I say to the officers. "I think he followed us. My boyfriend—Brooks—he ran off after him. Maybe ten minutes ago," I say, my voice wavering.

"Thank you, we're going to find them," says one of the officers. He motions for one of the deputies to stay with us while the other three unholster their weapons and make their way toward the trees.

"Okay, we have to get your dad to the hospital. Please step back," the female EMT says, and I bring my eyes back to what's right in front of me. With my attention on the police officers, I didn't notice the paramedics loading my dad on a gurney.

I grab his hand and pull it to my chest. "Can I come to the hospital with him?"

"You can," says the policeman who stayed with us. "But we'll need to get your statement there."

Just as I open my mouth to respond, a gunshot rings out in the distance, and my world freezes.

There's a flurry of movement as the officers who were at the treeline take off running farther into the woods. The cop next to me barks into his radio and guides us behind the cars.

Hayes' large hands grab my upper arms and shove me to the ground for cover, but I can't feel my body. Blood rushes in my ears, and all I hear is the *whoosh whoosh whoosh* of my heartbeat.

My every thought is focused on only one thing: *Brooks.*

CHAPTER THIRTY-NINE

I take off into the woods, Margot's screaming my name behind me, but I see him. He's heading farther into the forest, fleeing the scene of the crime. I can't let him. I can't allow him to get away, not after everything he's put Margot through and now shooting Keaton.

Tree branches slash against my face as I charge forward. I don't think he knows I'm following him just yet, and I have no idea if he's still armed. There was no gun at the house from what I saw, but my concern was finding Margot.

As another branch hits my cheek, I wonder if this was a bad idea. What if he's got the gun and shoots at me? On the other hand, what if he's unarmed and this is a chance to catch him?

I gain on him, and he must hear me because he turns around, continuing to move away from me, his eyes widening when he realizes he's no longer alone. Just as he moves his arm to point the now very apparent gun at me, his foot catches on a root, and he goes crashing to the ground. His grunt echoes through the forest, and the weapon flies out of his hand.

As he clambers to get it, I jump on top of him. "Absolutely the fuck not," I say through gritted teeth as I pull his arm away from where the gun landed.

"Get off me!" he screams, throwing a punch in my direction. I block his fist, pinning it above his head so I can finally get a real look at him. He has disheveled dark hair with wild, dark eyes to match. He's mildly attractive but overall, just a normal guy. Someone no one would ever think twice about if they saw him walking down the street. And from what Margot has told me, he's a renowned surgeon. Someone people should be able to trust with their lives.

But he shot Keaton. He stalked Margot. Despite his accolades in his career, he's anything but a good person. He should be thrown in prison with no chance of parole for everything he's done.

He's still fighting to get free, his eyes boring into me like he'll murder me on the spot once he gets his hands on the gun. I can't let it happen.

Shifting all my weight so I'm leaning over him, I keep his arms pinned beside him as I quickly survey the forest floor around us, searching for where the firearm landed.

Suddenly, he stops struggling and goes lax under me. "I know who you are," he says, so casually it sounds even more eerie.

"I'm no one."

"Exactly. You're *no one*. I'm someone." He pauses and looks at me, his eyes now seeming empty, the unhinged look from before gone. "I can give Margot everything she wants and needs. Do you think she honestly wants someone like you? Someone who parades other women in front of her? Someone who doesn't have a real job? She deserves better," he grits out as I scan the area around us again, desperately hoping to find the gun. His words bring my attention back to him, which is probably what he was hoping for. "You think you're good enough for her?"

"Oh, fuck off," I say with a laugh. The man is truly delusional.

As I look back up, I finally spot the gun under some foliage. He must realize what I'm about to do because the second I let go of him to go for it, he flips over and scrambles in the same direction, his fingers clawing into the earth for purchase.

We grapple against each other, both reaching, our fingers brushing against the cold metal of the weapon at the same time. The ground below me, wet from the melted snow and sleet, seeps into my clothes, chilling me to my core.

Just as my fingers wrap about the barrel, Julian grabs the handle, pulling it toward us. Using my legs, I try to kick him, leverage him away so I can pull the gun closer and get a better grasp on it. He leans back, missing my foot and gaining some traction.

Dirt goes flying in the air as we fight for the weapon. And just as I think I might have the upper hand, a fist flies toward my gut, and my hold on the gun shifts.

The sound of the gunshot is deafening; I watch as a flock of birds fly off through the trees. My ears ring, and the adrenaline coursing through my body has made me numb. Unsure what I'll find when I look down, I take the risk.

CHAPTER FORTY

I haven't stopped crying for five days. My eyes are so puffy I can barely see. No matter what I do, I can't stop the tears. Even when I feel numb and disconnected from what's happening around me, tears flow.

Looking around my small home, my eyes land on so many people: Cary holding Thea in the corner, Ripley staring blankly at the art on my walls, even Billy from the hardware store is sitting on the sofa, munching on something Cary had delivered from RED. There are a lot more people here than I thought there would be. He never would have believed this many people would show up for him.

Slowly but surely a new wave of sadness and self-blame hits me. I recall everything from my last morning with him. Everything I should have done differently. Everything I should have said. I shouldn't have gone to the house knowing Julian was still out there, I should have told him I loved him one more time.

I should have never come back here.

I had just gotten him back. We should have had more time. It was supposed to be the first day of a fresh start for us.

The what-ifs tumble around in my head, muting the noises around me. I've been moving as though through a fog since the day he died, a fog dense with all of my regrets and grief. I can't seem to pull myself out of it.

Hayes steps in front of me, his eyes glassy too. He hands me a tissue, squeezes my shoulder and walks off. He's barely holding it together. I know he's trying to put on a brave face for me, but I know my brother. He's dying a little inside everyday. He's got his regrets too.

I'm just about ready to shoo everyone out of my house when strong arms wrap around me from behind, immediately followed by the scent of bergamot and leather. I lean back into Brooks' strong chest and let him hold me up for a few moments.

"I've got you, baby," he murmurs into my ear. I don't know what I would do if I didn't have him. He's been picking up my pieces and slowly fitting them back together day and night, holding me through the worst of the heartache of losing my dad. He hasn't left my side, making sure I eat and sleep.

I turn around and wrap my arms around him, enveloping myself in his firm hold. His heart beats steadily under his suit jacket, and I'm once again breathing out a long sigh of relief that he's still here with me.

My mind had gone to the worst possible scenario when the gunshot went off in the woods. I had felt trapped and helpless, hearing the police officers calling to one another among the trees and on their radios.

That afternoon will haunt me forever. Though everything happened quickly, for me time stood still. Even now, I don't know if I waited to hear about Brooks' fate for twenty minutes or two hours. From what he told me, they apprehended an unconscious Julian just a few minutes after he tried to shoot Brooks. Thankfully, my hit to Julian's head had given him a major concussion, and his aim was off, giving Brooks the opportunity to knock him out.

It wasn't until much later, after speaking with the police, that Hayes and I were finally able to get an update on my dad.

He'd been in surgery for over three hours when the doctor came out looking grim.

It wasn't enough. *I* wasn't enough. Whatever I did at the house and at The Pit wasn't enough to save him.

The doctors tried to assure me, even in a perfect situation where he could have gotten to a hospital faster, it's unlikely he would have survived. The bullet had gone through his liver, his cirrhotic liver. Even in a hospital setting the bleeding would have been nearly impossible to stop with the damage the many years of alcohol abuse had done to his body.

Brooks kisses the top of my head and pushes me back a little to look at my face. His large hands hold my cheeks as he asks, "Want me to kick everyone out? Hayes mentioned making dinner."

I sniff and nod. His eyes ping around my face, and he uses his thumbs to wipe at the tears on my cheeks. With a soft kiss to my lips, he steps away.

"Alright, everyone. Thanks so much for coming. Margot and Hayes are so grateful for everyone being here and bringing all the casseroles and shit, but now it's time to get out." This earns him a few quiet chuckles, which cut off quickly when they realize he's not kidding.

After some last condolences and hugs, the house finally clears out, and Brooks and I are left on the sofa. I put my head in his lap, pulling my knees to my chest, and try to clear my head, focusing solely on the way his fingers gently run up and down my arm.

Hayes comes out of the kitchen, trash bag in hand and looks over at me, face grim. "I'm going to take this out, and then I'll make dinner."

"Why don't you just heat up one of the two dozen casseroles people brought today?" I ask.

"I'm going to make cheeseburger macaroni," he says and walks out, not waiting for an answer. He used to make the dish for me often when I was a kid. I think it's the only thing he knew how to make as a sixteen-year-old raising a picky four-year-old, but I've come to associate it with safety and home. Maybe it brings him the same comfort.

Brooks and I sit without speaking for a while, and I track Hayes coming back into the house and into the kitchen. After a few more minutes, I break the silence, "How did you do it?"

"Do what, baby?" Brooks asks, voice soft and rumbly. His hand never stops moving.

"How did you get over it? Your parents, I mean. How did you move on?"

There's a long pause and then an even longer sigh. "I didn't," he finally says. "Not really at least. Time has helped, but I'm definitely not over it. As cliché as it sounds, it does get easier."

I hum in acknowledgement.

"The grief is heavy, and it takes time to figure out how to keep going. But then you notice it gets a tiny bit lighter day after day.

Don't get me wrong, some days the wound feels as fresh as the day it happened, but then it dulls again. As much as I hate to admit it, having Cary here helps. And with you—I don't feel so alone. And you're not alone in this either. I'm going to be here for you, Freckles. I'm going to help share the load so hopefully even the hard days don't seem so overwhelming."

He trails off at the end, and a sweet warmth unfurls in my chest. This man. How does he not see how good he is?

"I love you," I say.

"I love you too, baby," he replies and runs the fingers from his other hand through my hair. The gentle caresses and the sounds of Hayes banging around in the kitchen help soothe the stress I've been holding and empty my mind. It's only a few minutes later before sleep takes me.

Chapter Forty-One

The smell from the kitchen hits my nostrils. I've been so focused on Margot and trying to get her to fall asleep, I didn't pay much attention to Hayes when he mentioned making dinner. I spent the last thirty minutes tracing my fingers down Margot's arms, into her hair, over her cheeks, anything to keep the contact between us.

The last thing I had expected was for Keaton to die. Margot said he was sober when she got there that day. He'd looked like her dad again. And what a cruel fucking world to take that away from her after giving her the smallest glimpse. I hate it.

I hate how much it reminds me of my own parents' passing.

I hate how much it affects Margot.

I fucking hate seeing her cry. And this was more than just crying; she's been sobbing nonstop. This may be the first time in the last five days she's stopped crying for more than a few minutes. It's killing me slowly to watch her fall apart.

She blames herself, which has only made it harder to watch. The first forty-eight hours, she played the 'what if' game over and over.

What if she'd told someone about Julian sooner?

What if she'd never gone to her dad's that day?

What if she'd reported Julian back in Charleston?

What if? What if? What if?

None of it is helpful. Things happened the way they were going to happen. But the sentiment is lost when you're the one those things happen to. I know how unfair it feels. I know how debilitating it is to lose a parent. I may not have broken down the same way about mine as Margot has, but it fucked me up. I'm still fucked up.

Hayes walks in from Margot's kitchen, and I tense up. We never got to talk about my relationship with her. It was clouded by more important things. But now her head is in my lap, and I haven't stopped touching her since we got here. He's unreadable; I can't tell if he's willing to be cool about it or if he's two seconds away from murdering me.

Sitting down on the chair across from the sofa, he leans back into the recliner then gestures toward us as he says, "I think you have some explaining to do."

His voice is low, an obvious attempt to not wake his sister. The same sister he warned me to stay away from. The sister he's so protective over, he wouldn't tell anyone her actual name for years.

Oh yeah, I'm fucked.

Despite my actual terror of the man sitting in front of me, my hand never stops rubbing soothingly over Margot's arm. I listen to her slow breathing for a moment, making sure she's still sleeping before I plead for my life.

"I—uh, fuck. Would you believe me if I said I didn't know she was your sister when we met?"

His eyes narrow at me, but in true Hayes fashion, he doesn't *say* anything, he just continues to glare until I continue on.

"Back in November, she cleaned me up after a fight at The Pit. The day Colton got his first hit on me and split my cheek." He nods his head letting me know he knows the day I'm referring to. I was so pissed. Then so fucking late for the Gala. I'd asked Hayes to make sure I was the first fight of the afternoon because the Gala was happening just a few hours later, never expecting to have my ass handed to me.

"The second Thea saw me, she lost her goddamn mind, called Margot in as a favor. I had no idea she was your sister, dude. I swear it. I only knew her as Lydia's nurse."

He stares me down, but I don't break this time, I need him to say something.

"And then what?" he asks, his eyes never leaving me. I'm not sure he's so much as blinked in the last five minutes.

"Then you sent me to her house to fix her fucking pipes." I pause, realizing a very important detail. "So really... if you think about it, this is all *your* fault. I can't even be blamed."

I laugh. He does not. So I clear my throat and continue before he decides to rip my head off in response. "I'd love to tell you I swept her off her feet after that, made her fall madly in love with me and shit, but it would be a damn lie. She made me work for it. Then I fucked it up. We'd gotten in a huge fight, and it wasn't until the day before your dad—" Fuck. "I mean, we'd just gotten back together. And I was coming to talk to you about it that day. I'd tried before and chickened out."

His brows rise at the confession, the look on his face leaning more toward amused than murderous. Basically a fucking smile in my book when it comes to Hayes. "Yeah, I'm a coward. Believe me, I know. No need to give me whatever look that is," I say as I gesture to his face.

The silence settles between us, but after a few moments, we both start speaking at the same time.

"Do you—" Hayes starts.

"I'm in love with her," I say with all the bravado I can muster. I don't want him to think for one second I'm not serious about her, about us. I keep going before he can say anything else and I lose whatever confidence I've found. "And I know, Hayes, I know I'm no good for her. I know she deserves better than me and anything I can give her, but I've never loved someone the way I love her. She's... fuck. She's everything to me. And I swear, I'll do everything I can to keep her happy."

My hands have gone clammy, but they still caress her arm. Hayes watches as my fingers dance over her skin, maybe noticing how content she looks in my arms, I hope at least. Then his eyes shoot back up to mine.

"You know what will happen if you hurt her."

"I sure the fuck do. I don't plan on it though. I almost lost her once, it won't happen again," I assure him, leaving out the details about *how* I almost lost her. "She'll have to leave me to get rid of me this time, and she very well could when she realizes she can do way better. But I'll never regret having the opportunity to love her and be loved by her."

He leans forward, his elbows on his knees, his hands interlocked as he stares at the two of us. "Despite everything, she looks happy. I have to assume you have something to do with that."

A nervous laugh falls from my lips. "For once in my life, I'm not cocky enough to think I'm the cause, but I sure as hell hope so."

"She's special," he says with so much conviction in his voice.

"I know." And I do. She's my light in a world of darkness. She's the bright swatch of color in my palette of dull grays. She's everything I don't deserve and everything I crave.

I clear my throat before dropping the next bomb. "I uh... I promised her I'd stop fighting."

He doesn't look the least bit surprised. But then he says, "Did you mean it?"

I nod my head. "Yeah. I'll just—I'll find another outlet for my shit. But I want her out too. Find someone else. She can't risk losing her license."

He knows I'm right. It doesn't even need a response. I think he only asked her out of desperation to begin with, but I won't watch her throw her career away for it.

He nods his head as he says, "Might not matter anyway, I'm laying low for a while just in case the cops got suspicious. They couldn't have seen anything, but a random trailer full of medical supplies in the middle of a field isn't normal."

Fuck. I hadn't thought of The Pit being at risk. It's a smart move though, waiting until things die down before starting fights back up again.

After a long silence, he says, "Were you serious about wanting to tattoo?"

His question catches me off guard and has my heart hammering, I'm not naive enough to grab onto the hope dangling in front of me though. I try my best to not let my emotions show on my face, keeping the stone composure Hayes always wears so well.

"I was—I mean, I am."

"Well, turns out I had a snake in my midst." My eyes widen at his words, not sure where he's going with this. "Archer is that redheaded bitch's brother. Something he neglected to tell me all the times I brought her up."

Oh, shit. He's pissed, but he seems irrationally calm about the revelation.

"He'll be vacating his chair effective immediately. He said his loyalties lie with her."

"Oh," is all I say. Tattoo parlor politics aren't exactly my forte, and I honestly can't read the situation with the lack of expression Hayes is giving me.

"It'll be a trial basis for you. I don't even know if you can draw, let alone tattoo a real person."

My heart is racing so fast, I'm scared it'll wake Margot. I'm so shocked, I just stare at Hayes in disbelief.

"Unless you've changed your mind..." he tacks on after I'm silent for far too long.

"Shit. No. No, I haven't changed my mind. I just—really? You're going to give me a chance?" I ask, my voice cracking embarrassingly on the last word.

"A trial. But yeah. Don't fuck it up."

Fucking *hope*. It's too close now. I have the girl I love in my arms and the career I've dreamed of for years staring me down.

"I won't," I say, knowing full well I can't promise it won't happen.

He nods his head toward Margot. "Wake her up. Dinner will be ready in," he checks his watch, "three minutes." Then he stands and walks toward the kitchen, leaving me reeling at the conversation.

Without much prompting, Margot starts to stir. I lean down and press a kiss to her temple as her eyes flutter open. "Hey, baby." The small smile gracing her lips at my words cracks my chest wide open. Soon enough reality must crash into her because the smile falls, and her eyes start to dull again.

I pull her up and spin her around so she's facing me. "Hey," I say. "We're gonna be alright, okay? We'll get through it together, one day at a time." She nods at my words, but I know words don't mean shit. "I love you, Freckles," I whisper, still not sure how open I can be with Hayes within earshot.

She wipes at her face then leans in to place a kiss right behind my ear as she whispers back, "I love you too, Killer."

Epilogue

One Month Later

The last month has been a blur. We've been staying at Margot's since the funeral. I let her think it's because I want her to be as comfortable as possible during her mourning, and while partially true, I also want to surprise her with the kitchen remodel at my house.

Selling is no longer an option. Honestly, it probably hasn't been since the moment she walked through the door and started sharing her dream renovations with me. I can no longer see anyone else living here, cooking in this kitchen, getting ready in the bathroom, sleeping in the room we'd fucked in for the first time. All I can see is her. And I hope I'm not disappointing my mom by staying. I know she wanted me to leave, to follow my dreams, but it turns out, they were right here all along.

Margot brightens every room she walks into. Her presence in this house brought it back to life. It's no longer the house my parents lived in or the last house they slept in, it's the house I see myself growing old with Margot in.

So I can't sell it. What I can do is make it her dream home and—hopefully—be graced by one of her smiles that consistently brings me to my knees. I'd started on the kitchen in our time apart after Christmas, but I hadn't gotten super far into the renovation. The last month I've been working on it nonstop. When I'm not at Mark of Mason apprenticing under Hayes or helping at RED, I'm here installing new cabinets or laying new flooring.

If Margot wasn't so busy, I'd wonder how she hasn't noticed. Since Julian got arrested, she's been living life more freely, spending time with friends, visiting RED more often, even hanging out with Hayes more. She and Thea have become annoyingly close. I swear the two are attached at the fucking hip.

I never thought I could love her more, but seeing her blossom into herself now that she isn't looking over her shoulder constantly has done just that. She laughs more, smiles more, she's more alive. She even gives me more shit, I fucking love it.

I look over at the clock on the stove, she should be here any minute. She got off at five, and the drive here takes her about thirty minutes. When I told her to meet me here, she got suspicious. I'm pretty sure she's convinced I'm going to propose to her or some shit. I may be in love, but marriage seems a ways off still.

The thought reminds me of the rings I have stashed in the safe in the closet. My parents' rings. Cary had taken the engagement ring, and I'd taken their wedding bands. I didn't know why at the time, it just felt right in the moment, so I shoved them in my pocket and offered Cary the other one.

One day.

The creak of the front door brings me out of my thoughts. "Brooks?" Margot calls from the front of the house.

"In the kitchen, babe." This is it. This is the moment.

Fuck, I hope she likes it.

As she walks around the corner, she's already talking, "What's going on? Why did you have me—" Her words are cut off by a gasp. "Oh my God!" she exclaims.

My face heats with anxiety. I didn't realize just how much her loving this meant to me until she walked into the room. "What do you think?" I ask as I shift on my feet, my voice sounding smaller than usual as the nerves seep out.

"Baby, this is beautiful!" Her face lights up, exactly how I envisioned it. Her smile only grows as she looks around. "This is... oh my God, Brooks..."

"Your kitchen," I finish for her. "When you first described it, I assumed it was because you had something similar growing up. But then I saw your childhood home and realized it was literally a dream kitchen for you. And I want to make all your dreams come true, Margot. This is just the start of it, I promise there's—" An 'oof' noise escapes me as Margot throws herself into my arms. I barely catch her, having to lean forward before rebalancing myself.

"I even left a spot over there," I say as I turn us to the opposite wall, "for the art you've collected and any you'd like to add. Plus... my own contribution." Her eyes land on the first sketch of her I drew. The one I kept with me in the times I needed her close but couldn't have her. The one that brought back my love for drawing.

"I love it. All of it. Especially your drawing. It'll be my most cherished piece of art." She pauses for a moment, staring into my eyes before continuing, "I love you, Brooks. So much. You are my dream. I don't need anything else. But I love you for giving it to me anyway." Her eyes are already glassy.

"Hey, no crying, we've seen enough of it this month."

"These are happy tears!" she whines.

"Don't care, it breaks my heart every time," I say as I nip at her nose with my teeth. "Can I continue my speech? I practiced it for hours while you were at work."

She doesn't say a word, just nods her head as she bites down on her bottom lip. Distracting as fuck.

"As I was saying, I promise there's more. I want to redo the whole house. You tell me what you want, and I'll make it happen." I pause, looking around at the kitchen and thinking back on how long it took me to do just one room. "It might take… the rest of the year, but I'll make this the home you've always wanted."

I know she's itching to say something, so I sit her down on the counter, caging her in with my arms. "What do you think?" I ask as I scan her face, trying to decipher how she's feeling.

"My home is wherever you are. I don't need any grand gestures, I just need you. But," she says with the biggest smile, "seeing this kitchen does make me giddy and so excited for the rest."

Huffing a laugh, I place a small kiss on her lips before running my hand up her arm and turning it over to see the small clam shell with a pearl inside inked on her skin. She was my first real "client," and Hayes fought us both on it. Margot stood her ground though and told Hayes she wanted her first tattoo to be from me, even if I fucked it up. It'd made me laugh at the time, though I was shitting my pants internally.

I'll never forget the night she asked me to tattoo her. She'd been so nervous, it was fucking adorable.

"It's healing well," I say, changing the subject but loving the fact my art is living on her skin. "When can we give you your next one?"

She pushes me away with her other arm, laughing as she does. "Not so fast, Killer. I told you, I might be a one and done kind of girl." I can't help the smirk plastered on my face, and she rolls her eyes at the sight. "It hurt!" she whines.

"You're such a baby, but I love it. We could do numbing cream next time?" I say with a waggle of my brows.

"Or... this cute little clam could be my one and only," she suggests with a shimmy of her shoulders.

I lean down and press a kiss right above the covered area of the tattoo in the crook of her elbow. "Whatever you say, Freckles. You'll come running back to me eventually." Before she can tell me I'm wrong, I push my hands under her ass and lift her off the counter and into my arms. There's one more thing I need to show her.

"Where are you taking me now?" she asks as she wraps her arms around my neck, peppering kisses to my cheek.

"I have another surprise," I say with a smirk. I'm a little nervous to see how she'll react but I have a feeling she'll love it as much as I will.

"You spoil me."

"You have no fucking idea how much I plan to spoil you. But this is a selfish surprise."

Her eyes widen, and my cock comes alive at the thought of what I have in store for her. As my erection pushes into her ass, her cheeks blush and a small, "Oh," falls from her lips.

I push through the door to my bedroom, switching on the light before placing her on the floor. She's still in her scrubs from work, but she's as gorgeous as always.

"Strip," I start as her eyes find my very erect cock in my sweatpants.

"But I—Brooks, I've been at work all day in these clothes, I need to shower first," she argues. It's cute. She thinks I care. She could be drenched in sweat from the toughest workout of her life, and I'd still want her.

"You can shower after."

Her arms cross over her chest. "Brooks, I'm—"

"Don't care," I say, cutting her off. "I've been waiting all day for this. I don't want to waste any more time."

She keeps her gaze locked on mine for three full seconds before she concedes and pulls her shirt up her torso by the hem—slowly, fucking torturously. The sound of it hitting the floor fills the room.

"Keep going."

"Brooks—"

"Keep. Going," I tell her. My eyes trained on her perky tits sitting perfectly in the sports bra she wears to work. I know exactly why she wanted to shower first. It wasn't because she thinks she's dirty and needs to clean up, it's because she doesn't think she's sexy in her sports bra and regular panties. There's no lace, no thong to bare her beautiful ass to me, but I don't care. She could wear a trashbag, and I'd still think she's the most beautiful woman alive.

She pushes her scrub pants down her legs next, stepping out of them one foot at a time.

"If you don't start going faster, I'll have to do it myself."

She walks toward me, placing her hands on my chest then slowly starts her descent to my cock. "You say it like a threat when it should be a promise." She squeezes my dick, trying to take control. Normally, I'd let her. I've begged for her, realized I enjoy it too. I'd do anything she asks. But not today. Today I have something planned, and I can't let her distract me. I bend down and haul her over my shoulder. She squeaks in surprise as I walk her to the bed, throwing her down on it.

"Open the drawer," I tell her as I look at the bedside table, stepping closer to her. Margot narrows her eyes at me before crawling to it and leaning far enough over to pull it open, showcasing her perfect ass as she does. Without much thought, my hand comes down on her asscheek, the smack ringing in my ears. A small yelp falls from her lips at the contact.

Fuck, I like that.

She shudders as I run my hand over the red splotch blossoming on her skin peeking out from under her panties and pulls the drawer all the way open. Inside lies a pink dildo, the same one she had hiding in her room.

"Wait. Did you—"

"No. Yours is still exactly where you left it. I just... bought you a new one to use here. For us to use. Together."

Her cheeks go impossibly red. She didn't know I'd found her stash of toys. It was an accident, but once I saw them, I couldn't stop imagining her playing with herself or all the possibilities of using them together.

Margot turns to face me, looking up at me through her lashes as I bring my hand to her face. I run my fingers along her jawline then over her lips. She opens instinctively, allowing me to press my thumb into her mouth.

"I want to fuck your ass while I fuck your pussy with the toy," I say, laying my cards on the table. We've dabbled in some assplay but nothing more than a plug or my fingers. I want more. I've told her as much. She's never said no, but I wanted to work up to it. Before she met me, the most she'd done was oral.

With my thumb still in her mouth, she nods and gently bites down on me making my cock grow even harder. Pulling out of her mouth, I watch the line of drool fall from her lips and groan.

"Let's get the rest of these clothes off, then I want you on all fours."

"Yes, sir," she says with a smirk as she pulls off her bra and panties. I pull my shirt over my head and push my sweatpants down until I'm standing in just my boxer briefs. Margot licks her lips before turning around so she's in the position I asked for, looking over her shoulder to watch as I slide my briefs down, letting my cock spring free.

"How excited are you for this?" I ask as I bring my hand to her glistening pussy, running my fingers along her slit before sinking one in. "Oh, fuck, baby, you're soaked already." She moans at the contact, pushing herself back to thrust on my finger. I lean down to kiss her back, before pushing in a second finger. "I'm going to make you come on my cock first while I get you ready for me back here," I say as I spank her ass again with my other hand.

"Oh my God, yes, Brooks. Please," she whines.

Leaning over, I grab the bottle of lube from inside the drawer and pull the dildo out to set it beside me.

"You ready?" She looks over her shoulder again, nodding her head in response. I pull my fingers from her cunt, and she cries out a whimper at the loss. Uncapping the lube, I pour a generous amount onto her crack, watching as it slides toward her tight hole.

God, I can't fucking wait.

I throw the lube down on the bed, brace my hands on each side of her hips, and thrust into her pussy. Our moans are like a harmonized melody ricocheting off the walls around us.

"Fuck, Freckles. I'll never get over how amazing you feel wrapped around me."

She bucks back into me, pushing me deeper as she shoves her face into the comforter mumbling obscenities. She's started cussing more around me, and I can't even pretend it doesn't turn me on. I love corrupting my good girl.

"Say it louder, baby. I can't hear those pretty words you're screaming," I tease her as I push myself to go faster, feeling her clenching around me.

"I—fuck! I hate you!" she screams, making me laugh. "Stop." *Thrust.* "Laughing." *Thrust.* "At me!"

I take the moment to glide my hand over her ass until my finger is circling the tight rim of her asshole. Her sharp intake of breath tells me she'd forgotten the assignment in all her fury. Teasing her about her newfound love for vulgar language is one of my favorite things. Doesn't matter if I'm deep inside her or we're just walking down the sidewalk, I get entirely too much joy out of it.

Gathering the lube I've poured on her, I push my finger in, loving the way she clenches around the invasion. Her moans only get louder as I sink in farther. "You love this, don't you?"

"Uh huh," she groans. "More," she grits out.

I slow down my pace so she doesn't come before I've properly stretched her out then give her what she asked for.

"God, I wish you could see this, baby. You're fucking gorgeous on all fours with your ass in the air and taking two fingers so well." With my opposite hand, I spank the other cheek, giving her a matching red handprint. Her pussy tightens, squeezing my dick so hard, I'm not sure I can keep from blowing my load. I don't want to come before her. Seeing her unravel is my ultimate undoing, and I want to keep it that way.

In preparation for a third finger, I open the two in a scissor-like motion, watching as she stretches effortlessly.

"Do that again," she whines, turning her head to look back at me. Her makeup is running down her freckled face, but she looks as perfect as ever.

I add a third instead while pounding into her faster, thrusting my fingers in and out with the same rhythm as my dick.

"Oh! Shit! Shoot! I'm so—" She's not able to finish before she's flooding my cock with her release. The sight is more erotic than anything I've ever seen before. But I have plans to top it.

Two seconds later, I'm coming inside of her.

"Fuuuuuuck, Margot!"

I pump one more time then pull out, opening my fingers once more before abandoning the task to flip her onto her back.

She's so fucked out, she doesn't even react to being flipped over. I bring my lips to hers, pulling her into a deep kiss. She wraps her legs around my waist as she moans into my mouth, and my dick perks back up in no time. Kissing Margot is heaven on Earth. If all I got to do for the rest of my life was kiss her, it would be more than enough. Luckily, I get to do it all.

I lean back, breaking our kiss to ask, "You ready for round two, baby?"

She pulls her bottom lip into her mouth, biting down on it as she says, "Mhmm." Leaning into her, I press my lips to hers, pulling her lip free with my teeth.

"I'm going to put your legs over my shoulders, okay?" I murmur into her mouth moments before pulling away and grabbing her thighs. One at a time, I place them over my shoulders so I've got easy access to all of her. Her perfect tits bounce with the movement, bringing my attention to them. They've been neglected.

Running my hands down her legs, I make my way to her taut nipples, pinching each one between my finger and thumb. Her face twists in desire. In the last month together, we've learned she likes a little pain with her pleasure.

My cock slides over her pussy, covering it in both of our releases. I don't want it to go to waste though, so I use one hand to push our combined cum back in. With the other, I pour more lube over my dick and her. Stroking myself a few times to spread it, then I line my dick up with her tight ass. Spit falls from my mouth, mixing with the lube before cascading down until it hits her hole, and I push the tip at the entrance just enough for her to feel me.

"How does that feel, baby?" I ask, not wanting to go further until she's comfortable.

"Keep going," she says, bringing her own hands to her breasts, twisting her nipples as I push in deeper. My fingers play with her clit as I thrust in just an inch then pull out. I do this over and over, going a bit deeper each time. She's so wet, our cum is leaking out, running down to my dick making it slide in and out easily.

"I fucking love you," I say as I'm almost all the way seated in her ass. Her mouth opens up to speak but a moan cuts off whatever words she was about to say. I grab the dildo from the bed table and run it through her opening, covering it in her. I don't think we need more lube at this point, she's got us both soaked. "Think you can take us both?" I ask as I nudge the toy at her pussy.

"Yes. You and the toy, Brooks. Both. Please." Hearing the word "please" leave her lips does something to me every fucking time. No fucking clue what kink it is, but I think mine is just Margot. Everything she does turns me on like I've never been turned on before. It's like witchcraft or something.

"Holy shit, baby," I say as I push the toy into her pussy, watching as it disappears. "You're taking it so fucking well. Goddamn, you're the most gorgeous thing I've ever seen."

I lose myself to the feel of her ass squeezing me so tight, I think I could see stars. Margot brings her hand down to push the dildo in and out so I can focus on keeping the same pace. The sound of our bodies slapping together fills the room, matched by the moans and screaming of each other's names.

"I'm so close, baby," I grunt. "Inside or on you?" I ask, knowing I'm about five seconds from coming. Another thing we've learned about Margot, she *loves* to be painted in my cum, and I love to fucking see it.

"Inside me. I want to feel you inside me this time," she answers. And just like that, spurts of cum shoot from my cock, filling her up in a way I never have before. In a way I could become addicted to.

I don't stop though, I keep thrusting in and out, opening my eyes to see her circling her clit with jerky motions with one hand and keeping pace with the dildo with the other. Without thinking, I pull out of her, push the dildo and her fingers aside, and sink to my knees.

Plunging my tongue into her cunt, I get a taste of us both. Her hand grabs onto my head, pushing me farther into her until I can't breathe, and I'd willingly stay here until my last dying breath.

One, two, three thrusts of my tongue, and she's coming all over my face, just the way I like it. I keep lapping her up until she comes down from the high, and her grip loosens.

Pulling away from her, my face still covered in her release, I look up at her and say, "Move in with me."

Her eyes blink open, and a smile takes over her face. "I thought you'd never ask."

Ripley

National Whiskey Convention

3.5 Years Ago

"**O**h my God, thank goodness you're coming back tomorrow. Between Brooks losing the instructions you left for him and then his constant bickering with Hazel and Owen, I've had it up to here," says Thea, the exasperation clear in her voice.

I chuckle, my focus divided between my best friend ranting in my ear and across the street where the line of scantily clad bodies is slowly moving past the bouncer and into the club. My eyes trace the lines of broad shoulders covered in thin T-shirts a size or two too small and trim waists leading to tight jeans and leather pants. My mouth waters at the possibilities.

Fuck, I can't wait to go in.

I don't get to go to gay clubs very often. There aren't any in Indigo Hill, not that I'd be caught dead in one in my hometown, and the closest ones are in Charleston, which still feels too close to home sometimes.

Coming to the National Whiskey Convention in Louisville, Kentucky seems like the best place to let loose. No one knows me here, and after three days of seminars and networking, I need to let off some steam.

I also need a blow job. And maybe to get seven or eight inches into a warm, wet—

A car horn cuts off my train of thought, just in time for me to focus back in on what Thea's saying. "He really makes me want to pull my hair out sometimes. Why can't he just do the things I ask? Or at the very least show up? If he wasn't their son, Brooks would have been fired long ago." She makes another frustrated sound followed by, "I miss you."

"It's only been a few days, and I'll see you tomorrow. Try not to kill him before I get back. You know half the tourists come just to ogle him," I say with a chuckle, my eyes glued to a pint-sized blonde in a suit and tie who joined the end of the line.

Who comes to a club in business attire? He looks out of place standing next to a gaggle of twinks with their nips out in sheer tops and booty shorts. He also looks uncomfortable, eyes darting around and into every car passing by.

"Oh babe, you know they're coming in droves for you too," she says. "Anyway, are you going to that club tonight?"

"Yeah, I'm here already."

"Oh! Well get in there... and then *get in there*." She giggles at her own joke, and I can't help but join her. I love this woman.

"I can't wait to see you tomorrow," I say.

"Bye! Love you!"

I hang up and look both ways before crossing the street. The line is moving faster now, and by the time I join the end, the dork in the suit is nowhere to be found.

"One Kiss" blasts through the speakers as I press my ass against the hard dick of the guy grinding on me. Todd? Tom? Maybe Tony? Really not sure, and I honestly couldn't care less since I won't be seeing him after tonight.

I'm just about ready to ask him to join me in the bathroom so I can get off and get back to my room. I've been dancing for hours now; my shirt is plastered to my chest, and although it's been fun to dance and feel so many hard male bodies all around me without any concern of the wrong people seeing me, no one has really interested me.

But I guess Tucker will do.

I turn around to proposition him and find he's already making out with someone, the hand not holding on to my waist rubbing over the front of another guy's miniscule gold shorts. The Rocky Horror vibes are strong.

I watch them suck face for a bit, it's really hot; they've got some great chemistry. The song changes, and I realize I'm just watching these dudes kiss like a creep, I'm not even dancing anymore, and Trevor has definitely forgotten about me. Can't say I'm disappointed, I may even be a little relieved. He'll have a great night with Mr. Hot Pants. Maybe they'll hit it off and move in together and get married and have kids. Who am I to stand in the way of true love?

I push my glasses up my nose and look around to see if anyone else catches my eye but decide to grab a glass of water before I head out. I guess it's just me and my hand tonight. Maybe I'll get a little wild and crazy and use my left for a change.

It takes a minute to push to the bar, but I manage to squeeze in between a few bodies, shimmying my shoulders to make room for myself. I see I have my work cut out for me in getting the bartender's attention from the other end. Maybe I should take off my shirt and flash some skin like the rowdy group he's filling shot glasses for. I let out a resigned sigh and resolve to just call it a night. My suitcase won't messily stuff and zip itself after all.

As I turn toward the exit, I notice the suited man I saw in line earlier standing just to the right of me.

Oh.

I rake my eyes over him. I wouldn't call him a twink. Just short-ish, probably a good six inches shorter than my six-foot-two. Even through the pretentious suit he's wearing, I can tell he takes care of himself. Fuck, he probably runs and lifts things, and he probably wakes up at the ass crack of dawn to do it too. Why is the thought making my dick chub up?

He's leaning his forearms on the bartop, glass of something neat and brown in a tumbler he keeps fiddling with. He looks like he's been here all night and just as uncomfortable as outside. His overly formal ensemble appears freshly pressed and wrinkle free, not a hair is out of place in his perfect coif. If I had to guess, I'd think he came in here, planted himself at the bar and hasn't moved from the spot.

What a shame. And oh how I want to change that. Mess him up a little. At the very least get him to loosen the fucking tie.

Thankfully, he's not paying me any attention, his gaze caught on something on his other side; he's not witnessing me check him out so blatantly. Like the full-on creep I apparently am tonight, I lean a little toward him and inhale. He smells fucking delicious. Whatever cologne he's wearing is crisp and spicy, sophisticated and serious.

"Hi," I croak out, internally cursing the fucking bartender for not having the decency to see I'm parched and only have one shot at a first impression. I clear my throat and try again, "Hi. What are you drinking?"

He turns to me in the middle of my lame opening line, and I almost lose the second half of my sentence. Holy fuck. His eyes are so blue. Even under the dim club lights, they're almost glowing.

I'd say he's somewhere around my age and checks off every one of the all-American star quarterback fantasies I had in high school: blonde hair, blue eyes, broad shoulders, full, pouty pink lips, and a well defined nose that's perfectly proportional to his face.

His gaze slides up and down my body quickly, and the blank look on his face is replaced by widening eyes, pink cheeks, and a tight mouth.

A shy boy.

He opens his mouth to say something but is interrupted by a loud, "What can I get you?" Of course the fucking bartender's timing couldn't be worse.

But now that I have this pocket-sized Ken's attention, I abandon my plans of going to my hotel alone. "Two of whatever he's having," I say, dipping my chin toward the glass in front of the man I plan to do ungodly things to later.

As the bartender busies himself with pouring us both two fingers of Buffalo Trace neat, the man next to me says, "Hi," and I just about melt at the perfect, smooth-as-velvet voice that matches everything else on him.

"Do you come here often?" *Do you come here often?* Am I fucking serious right now? I mean, I know it's been a while, but I usually have a little bit more game than this. What is wrong with me?

Fortunately for me, my pitiful second opening line earns a small smirk from him. "No, first time. I'm from the west coast. You?"

"Same," I answer and hand over some cash to the bartender who's delivered our drinks. "But I'm from the east coast. I was here for the bourbon conference that just wrapped up. What brings you to Louisville?"

Seriously, at this point I'm a walking cliché of bar talk; someone take me out back and end me, spare this poor man. I throw back the bourbon, enjoying the burn all the way down. His eyes are on my Adam's apple as I swallow, and I see a flash of hunger on his face before it's gone, back to the timid expression he's been sporting.

"I—I'm here for work. Heading back home tomorrow."

"What do you do for work?"

"Uh, I'm in the restaurant business," he says, stammering a bit. I wonder if he was here for the conference too, but I don't push the topic since he seems to want to keep things vague.

I chuckle. He's cute. "Alright, keep your secrets."

"Pussy Is God" by King Princess starts playing on the club speakers. "Wanna dance?" I ask as I erase the two inches of space between us, pulling him to me by that ridiculous, preppy tie. His body is tense, and his gaze is locked on my lips. I can't help running my tongue over them before smirking. His eyes flare and dart up to mine. Fuck, they're gorgeous, such a clear crystal blue, pupils blown. "Better yet, wanna get out of here?"

I wince internally at how trite I sound, but my brain is not functioning properly. There's something about this tiny, bite-sized man that's doing all the things to me right now. I want to peel all his secrets back and see what's underneath.

Mostly I want to peel his pants off and find out if the fucking log I'm feeling on my hip is as big as I think it is.

He nods quickly before downing his drink in a few swallows. "My hotel is right next door."

Ah, I guess he's just as eager as I am.

"Lead the way, West Coast."

He holds the hotel door open for me, and I walk in first. His room is nice, tidy. I've been living out of my suitcase for the last three days, but the cracked closet door shows me he has his clothes neatly hung up. He probably even put some in the dresser beneath the

TV. My intrusive thoughts keep telling me to open them up, pull everything out just to see what he does. I won't, I'm not an animal.

And I really want to get laid.

I turn back to the mysterious blonde and find he's standing at the entry of the room, slowly pulling off the suit jacket. The crisp white shirt he's wearing underneath stretches over his lean muscles as he reaches to drop the neatly folded jacket over the back of a nearby chair.

Without glancing my way, he methodically unbuttons the cuffs of his shirt and rolls the sleeves up his forearms in one of the most erotic displays of masculinity I've ever seen—and I saw the Magic Mike show with Thea in Vegas last year. I think I'm drooling, but I can't find the hand-eye coordination to bring a hand up to wipe it away.

Some switch flipped the minute we stepped out of the club. This is not the same man I met just twenty minutes ago. There's an easy confidence pouring out of him now. The shy, awkward—I'm going to assume—closeted, first-time-in-a-gay-bar vibe is gone. This man knows what he wants, and I'm ready to rip my clothes off and give it to him.

Fuck. He may be small and maybe inexperienced, but by the look on his face I don't think I'm taking the lead here. And I'm so okay with that.

Leaning a shoulder effortlessly against the wall, West loosens that stupid tie before pulling it off and wrapping it tightly around his hand.

When his attention finally shifts to me, the world stops. His azure eyes freeze me in place. He's the hunter, and I'm the deer that's voluntarily painted a very large red bullseye on myself. My dick is hard behind my jeans, aching.

I'm just about to open my stupid, dumb mouth to say something stupid and dumb when he pushes off the wall and takes a few steps toward me.

"On your knees, pretty boy."

Holy. Fuck.

Extras

Interested in reading more? We have two bonus chapters available! Scan the QR codes below to download them!

WICB BONUS	FFY BONUS
Matters of the Heart	*Kiss Here*

To join our reader group and our newsletter for all the inside scoops, scan the code below to be taken to our linktree.

Acknowledgements

Holy moly we made it through book two! It's still wild to think we've written one book, let alone two. Before we start our long list of thanks, we'd like to express how much we appreciate every single person who chooses to pick up one of our books. We put our heart and souls into these stories, we love these characters like they're real people, and we treat them as such. So if you read and loved them too, thank you so much. We know they aren't perfect, we know they can be frustrating, but it's part of the reason why we love them so much.

Peter

Thank you for always being in my corner and keeping me inspired (in all ways haha). Thank you for creating this beautiful space for me to work and keep my ever growing book collection, just took like eight months, but who's counting... ;-). I love you and the boys so much, and I wouldn't be doing any of this without you. MWAH! Thank you for accepting Alise as part of the family now!

HANNAHHHHH!!!

We hope by now, you know how much we love you, but in case you don't, here comes the sap! You've been here since day one. You've heard every idea, every twist, read every version, and you're consistently in our corner. We aren't sure these books would be here without your support, so please always know how much we love and appreciate you. Not just for that but for being our best friend. Our girls' trips and girl dinners will ALWAYS be our favorites! So here's to another book and another year of friendship. WE LOVE YOU!

Hailey Rodger

The way we're so stinking happy this journey brought us you! Thank you so much for always being someone we can come to for advice and support. Thank you for loving our characters and stories and sharing your own with us in return. You're stuck with us now. Ridiculous voice notes from one of us and hockey commentary from the other haha! Dude, how have we both published two books now?! Insane. ilysm!

Monroe Book Club

Thanks for opening yourselves up to all the crazy smut books I recommend and your support throughout the process of writing WICB and now FFY! Hopefully I haven't scandalized you too much and you stick with it haha.

Grayce Rian

We will forever be thankful to have you on this journey with us! Thank you for always lending an ear to listen, giving us advice when we're lost, and laughing over the ridiculous breeding books we send haha! We're so happy to have you as a friend. AND 2026 is the year we meet. It HAS to be!

Alpha Team

Hannah, Emma, Lynzee, Rita, Andrea, and Haley—thank you SO much for all your feedback and support! This story wouldn't be what it is without you. The nurse knowledge half of you brought to the table was such an added bonus. Without Emma, we'd have people scratching their heads about Keaton's stairs haha. And a special thanks to Rita for loving the cheese scene so much she made bookmarks LOL. We adore you all!

Beta Team

Kacey, Heather, Ana, Sara, Joey, Erica, Paige, and Chelsea—your unhinged comments had us constantly laughing! Thank you so much for catching our typos, telling us when things weren't working, and loving

these two so fiercely. We're so thankful to have your support. Thank you for always so enthusiastic for these characters and their stories. We cherish each and every one of you and cannot wait for you to read Ripley's story!

Joey

Thank you so much for all your help with this release. Choosing you to help us manage ARCs took so much off our plate. You're fabulous at what you do, and we hope to one day call you our full-time PA! And thanks for always being up to chat and putting up with us! We appreciate and love you!

Ana

Thank you once again for putting up with us and making beautiful maps and art so this book shines as bright as it should. We will never not be in awe of your talent.

Mel

Once again, you nailed this cover. Thank you so much for bringing our visions to life! You're so good at what you do, so amazingly communicative, and helpful! We appreciate you!

Street Team & ARC Readers

You've truly been the best! Thank you so much for wanting to read this story early! We hope you loved them. We're still small fish, so we appreciate you taking a chance on us. We hope you'll stick around for the rest!

You, the Reader

You're the reason we were able to do this again. We never expected to have readers out of the gate, but you made it happen. We hope you know every time you tag us, recommend us, or DM us, it makes us so happy! We have a lot more to come, so we hope you'll stay with us for it. Ripley's story is next, but we have big plans for after Ripple Effect as well, and we think you'll be just as obsessed with it as we are!

Also by Alise Monroe

RIPPLE EFFECT
When I Come Back
(Thea & Carrington)
OUT NOW

Fighting For You
(Margot & Brooks)
OUT NOW

Ripple Effect #3
(Ripley & [Redacted])
RELEASING EARLY 2026

Ripple Effect #4
(Callaway & Hayes)
RELEASING MID-LATE 2026

RIPPLE EFFECT SPIN-OFF
Unnamed Standalone
(Iris & Travis)
RELEASING TBD

About the Authors

We're romance co-authors living in South Carolina and Connecticut. Two romance obsessed best friends who decided to write together one day and realized it was the best decision ever. We balance each other out with our similarities and differences but are always the other's biggest cheerleader. In our spare time when we aren't with family, we love to read (obviously), drink coffee, and obsess over Canva edits haha. We're just starting this author journey, but we plan to always write emotional, real, raw romance. Flawed characters who are perfectly imperfect will always be front and center.

Stalk Us

Thank you so much for reading Fighting For You! If you enjoyed Brooks and Margot's story, we would love it if you'd leave a review on Amazon and/or Goodreads.

The third book in the Ripple Effect series (Ripley's story) will be releasing sometime in early 2026. As soon as we have an exact date, it'll be all over our socials!

All of the Ripple Effect books can be read as standalones, but we'd love if you'd read them all! We have intentionally put Easter eggs for every book throughout the entire series, but you'll only catch them if you read them in order!

If you want to stay up to date on everything Alise Monroe and Ripple Effect, please STALK US on all socials haha. For even more updates and in the know information, sign up for our newsletter (on our website), we promise not to spam you!

Instagram: @author.alisemonroe
Threads: @author.alisemonroe
TikTok: @authoralisemonroe

Visit our website for bonus content and any event information
alisemonroe.com